THE RELUCTANT SPACEFARER

MICHAEL TEFFT

Dedicated in loving memory to my father, Marvin Tefft, who instilled in me a love of science fiction and music.

CHAPTER ONE

"Bloody Hell," muttered Sir Malcolm Robertson, Knight Commander of the Order of St. Michael and St. George.

He sighed as he looked at the pile of paperwork sitting on his desk and checked his Granda's pocket watch. Despite his lofty title as Director of Airship Logistics at the Peninsular and Oriental Steam Navigation Company, his job involved moving paper. Reports came in, he processed the data, and sent reports out. It was 2:00 PM, and he had only a few hours to clear up the paperwork before he left for a month for his long awaited wedding with his fiance, Joan de St. Leger.

His office reminded him of his office in his last command as captain of the *HMA Daedalus,* although more spacious. Maritime law books and regulations filled the bookcases that lined the walls inter-mingled with several of Malcolm's own books: Newton's *Principia Mathematica,* signed editions of *Radioactivity* and *Radioactive Transformations* written by his friend Ernest Rutherford, and a dog-eared copy of *The Mechanical Engineers Pocket-Book* by William Kent. Behind his ornate walnut desk was an oil painting of an airship floating over the English countryside. Although the painting's airship was owned by the company, every time he looked at it, he became wistful, thinking back to his time as captain. He missed flying and commanding an airship, which he didn't expect when he first took command.. When he missed the Air Service, he looked at the photograph of his fiance Joan and remembered why he agreed to this job - so they could be married and lead a normal life.

He glanced at the paperwork, sighed, and headed to pour more tea when someone knocked on his door.. "Come," he said.

"Excuse me, Sir Malcolm", his assistant Robert Johnson said, standing at the door. "You have visitors."

"I thought I instructed you I wasn't to be disturbed. I have too much paperwork to finish before I can leave today."

"I know, sir. The visitors are Royal Navy personnel.. A group of Royal Marines led by Lieutenant Bowles is here to see you.. He says it's a matter of utmost urgency."

"Have you told them I am unavailable to talk to them?"

"I told them, but the Lieutenant threatened physical force to gain entry to see you."

"I see," Malcolm said, frowning. "Did he say why he needs to meet with me?"

"No, sir. He wouldn't tell me, only that it was a matter of urgency."

"Very well, show him in, please," Malcolm said. He straightened his suit, a habit from his years in the Service..

Lieutenant Bowles entered the room and threw Malcolm a sharp salute. Malcolm recognised the man as assistant to Admiral Beatty, head of His Majesty's Air Service. Malcolm nodded to his assistant, who closed the door on his way out. He returned the salute. "Thank you, Lieutenant, but that's hardly necessary. I haven't been in the Air Service for a year. Please, have a seat," Malcolm said, gesturing to the stuffed, leather upholstered chair in front of his desk. "Can I have my assistant get you anything?"

"No, thank you sir," Bowles replied.

The sudden appearance of Lieutenant Bowles puzzled Malcolm. He sat and again gestured to Bowles to sit. "What's the matter you urgently need to discuss?"

"Sir Malcolm Robertson, the Admiralty has reactivated you as a captain in His Majesty's Air Service and you must report for duty. I am here to escort you," Lieutenant Bowles said as he handed a letter to Malcolm.

"Surely, you're not serious," Malcolm said as he opened the letter.

"Deadly serious," Lieutenant Bowles said.

Malcolm scanned the letter. Admiral Beatty had invoked an obscure clause that allowed the reactivation of retired officers in times of crisis.

"This is preposterous! You march in here, waving these orders, and expect me to jump. I can't just up and leave. I have a job."

"Admiral Beatty has taken care of that matter already. He has communicated to your superiors the need to recall you to active service, and they have terminated your employment." Lieutenant Bowles stood. "Now, if you'll follow me, we'll escort you to the Admiralty."

"I can't leave now. I'm supposed to meet my fiance for dinner and tomorrow, I will leave for Kent for my wedding!"

"I'm sorry, sir. But my orders were quite explicit. You are to come with me immediately to the Admiralty either by your choice or the Marines will haul you out physically."

"I wish the Admiralty would make up its bloody mind! They couldn't wait to dismiss me last year, but now they want me to return?"

"Regardless, sir, I need to get you to the Admiralty. Will you come willingly, or must I call the Marines?"

Malcolm huffed. "That won't be necessary. May I have a few minutes to gather my things?"

"That is acceptable. I'll wait outside."

"On your way out, can you send in my assistant?"

In moments, his assistant entered. "What's happening, Sir Malcolm? I just received a memorandum that the Admiralty has recalled you to the Air Service and you are no longer employed here."

"Apparently, that's correct. Can you have my personal articles shipped to my flat? I have several books that I would be especially upset to lose," Malcolm said as he emptied his briefcase of papers.

"Absolutely, sir."

"Look at the bright side, Johnson. Maybe you'll end up with a better boss."

"Not bloody likely," muttered Johnson.

Malcolm cast a final glance around the room. Although he was mad at the sudden intrusion in his life by the Air Service, he felt a strange sense of relief that his time at Peninsular and Oriental had ended. He packed the photograph of Joan into his briefcase. "Mr Johnson, please tell Miss de St. Leger at the Savoy that I can't make it to dinner tonight because the Admiralty has summoned me to headquarters. I'll update her as soon as I know more."

"Absolutely, sir."

Malcolm offered his hand to Johnson. "It's been a pleasure working with you, Mr Johnson, and I wish you the best."

"Likewise, Sir Malcolm," Johnson said, shaking his hand.

"Time to face the firing squad," Malcolm said, causing Johnson to gasp. "Figuratively speaking," Malcolm added as he opened the door and joined Lieutenant Bowles and the squad of Marines.

CHAPTER TWO

*M*alcolm took one last look around the offices as he followed Lieutenant Bowles out to a waiting car. Lieutenant Bowles opened the door to the back and Malcolm slid into the large bench seat, followed by Lieutenant Bowles and one of the Marines. Malcolm was dismayed as the Marine locked the door on his side of the car.. As the Marine leaned back over, he brushed his hand over his sidearm; a silent warning to Malcolm to not attempt to escape. Malcolm nodded, then looked out the window as the car turned onto Leadenhall Street towards the Admiralty..

As the car rolled past St. Paul's Cathedral, Malcolm scarcely noticed its grandeur. He wondered why the Admiralty wanted him back after banishing him.. As he watched the car navigating through the tight streets, he remembered a similar trip two weeks prior. He took a cab along this very route, although the destination was not the Admiralty, but the Diogenes Club at the corner of St. James' St. and Pall Mall. After paying the cabbie, he spotted Mycroft Holmes outside a building's entrance.. Mycroft was tall and heavyset, dressed in the unofficial uniform of a businessman in the City; a dark suit with a vest, an overcoat, and a bowler. He immediately noticed Malcolm and nodded. Malcolm walked to Mycroft and offered his hand. "Mycroft, thank you for the invitation, although I am rather surprised. I never took you as a member of any kind of gentleman's club."

"Thank you, Sir Malcolm," Mycroft said as he shook Malcolm's hand. "The Diogenes Club is a very special club most suited to my temperament. I must request that you do not speak a word until I speak to you. We limit speaking to only one location in the club, and it is a cardinal sin to disturb the other club members. Can you do that?"

Malcolm nodded to make the point.

"Very good," Mycroft said. "Follow me." He opened the oaken door, intricately carved with the figure of Diogenes holding a lantern, and ushered Malcolm into the foyer. Malcolm had never entered a gentleman's club, but the foyer was exactly how he imagined. Warm walnut panelling covered the walls and a black-and-white chequered marble floor led immediately to a large desk with an equally large man watching them intently. Mycroft nodded to the man and handed him a slip of paper. The man nodded after he read it and Mycroft continued down the hall. He stopped momentarily to jerk his head for Malcolm to join him. After nodding to the receptionist, Malcolm hurried to catch Mycroft, who had already entered a room. Malcolm followed into a room that may have functioned as a library, with bookshelves covering three walls.. Windows covered the fourth wall, allowing for an unobstructed view of the Mall. The room smelled of paper, leather, and a faint hint of tobacco. Several stuffed leather upholstered chairs graced the room. Next to each chair was a small table containing the current editions of the London papers. Mycroft moved to the corner and settled himself into a chair. He gestured Malcolm to take a seat next to him. Malcolm sat in the proffered chair, but sat ramrod straight. Within moments, a butler arrived with two drinks; a sherry for Mycroft and a whisky for Malcolm.

Mycroft nodded at the butler and took a sip of his sherry before speaking. "You may talk, Malcolm. And for goodness' sakes, relax. You are in the Stranger's Room, the only room where we allow conversation."

While glancing around the room, Malcolm sipped his preferred single malt, Auchentoshan.

"Are we the only people in this club who can converse?" Malcolm asked incredulously.

"Members of this club require little conversation. We prefer a place where we can sit in comfortable chairs, read the paper, smoke a cigar or pipe, without listening to idle chitchat." He opened the humidor on the table next to him. "Would you care for one?"

"No, thank you. I never acquired the taste for them, but, by all means, don't let me stop you."

"Thank you," Mycroft said as he took out a cigar cutter from his pocket. Mycroft perused the stock of cigars before selecting one, cutting off the end, and lighting the cigar.

Malcolm sipped his whisky as he watched Mycroft enjoy his cigar. An increasingly awkward silence lasted for nearly two minutes before Malcolm said, "I suppose at some point this evening, you'll tell me why you invited me here."

"You never change, Malcolm. You always get straight to the point. Can't I invite you for a drink before your upcoming nuptials?"

"Yes, but it's unlike you. The last time I saw you act sociably was aboard the Daedalus when I threatened to make you walk the plank."

Mycroft smiled. "You know me too well, Malcolm. Since we are talking about your nuptials, is everything ready?"

"Yes, in three weeks, I'll be a married man."

"Congratulations," Mycroft offered. "Although I give them begrudgingly, as because of you, my best field agent is now doing a desk job. Speaking of desk jobs, how are things at Peninsular and Occidental?"

"Fine." Malcolm took another sip of his whisky, avoiding Mycroft's gaze.

"That hardly sounds like a ringing endorsement."

"It's fine. The paperwork is… prodigious. I thought the paperwork for the Air Service was mountainous, but it's nothing compared to Peninsular and Occidental."

Mycroft puffed his cigar and regarded Malcolm. "Is it not what you expected?"

"I wouldn't say that. I didn't expect it to match the excitement of the Air Service. But I'm content because I see Joan almost every night."

"But not happy?"

"I'm happy with the choice of made."

"Don't you mean compromise?"

"What do you mean?" Malcolm asked.

"I hardly think keeping you behind a desk is the best use of your talents. Malcolm, you waste your talents shuffling papers behind a desk. You are a captain."

"I was a captain until you engineered the blackmail that forced me to resign so that I could do your bidding," Malcolm replied. He gulped his whisky to prevent his anger from spilling out.

"Touché."

"Why the sudden concern about my employment?"

Mycroft took another puff on his cigar. "I'm asking you to reconsider and accept the job as captain of the first British spaceship."

"Mycroft, this is the third time you've asked me; the answer remains, no. I'm trying to build a life with Joan. Our wedding is in one week's time and I can't go gallivanting around in space! Find someone else!"

"I would if I could," Mycroft said. "I've yet to find anyone with your leadership abilities and technical acumen."

"I know nothing about spaceships, Mycroft."

"That's the point, Malcolm. No one does. We..." Mycroft paused for a moment. "Britain needs you, Malcolm. I can't think of anyone better suited for the job."

"Surely there's some young up and comer wanting to prove his worth that can learn the new technology."

"That's the trouble; we have an ambitious young engineer who learned the technology. What we don't have is someone with technical knowledge and command experience. Men with command experience don't know how to build a ship. Engineering ability does not always translate to leadership. I need a man with both talents. I've interviewed every captain in the Air Service and you are the only person with both skills." Mycroft paused and stared at

Malcolm. "Are you absolutely certain that you will not accept the job?"

"Let me be crystal clear, Mycroft. I will not accept the job. Over the course of fifteen years, I devoted myself to King and country, and scorn, ridicule, and blackmail were my reward. You engineered it all so that you could coerce me into a mission that nearly killed me. I'm sorry, Mycroft, but I've done my bit for king and country. I want something for me. Marrying Joan is my top priority right now. And frankly, I think I've earned it." Malcolm took another large gulp of whisky to calm himself.

Mycroft puffed on his cigar for several moments. "You are right, Malcolm. You deserve something in your life. I am sorry that I contributed to your disillusionment in service to the country."

"Thank you, Mycroft," Malcolm sipped his whisky. "Will we see you at the wedding? I don't recall if we've received your RSVP."

"You'll see me next weekend," Mycroft said. Malcolm noticed a tone of regret in his voice, but decided not to pursue the issue.

Mycroft raised his glass to Malcolm. "Here's to you and Joan. I wish you the best in the days to come. Cheers!"

"Cheers," Malcolm said as he clinked his glass to Mycroft. "I'm really sorry that I can't help you. The job sounds fascinating, but I'm too old for this adventure business. It's time for me to settle down."

"Nonsense, Malcolm. You are uniquely qualified for this job, and I don't believe for a moment that you're made for pushing papers." Malcolm protested, but Mycroft raised his hand. "However, you've made your position crystal clear and I will not press you anymore."

Malcolm sipped his whisky before taking out his pocket watch. "Bloody Hell," he said. "I hate to break this up, but I'm due to meet Joan for dinner in five minutes. I'm already late." Malcolm rose to leave and offered his hand to Mycroft. "Thank you for the drink, Mycroft. Again, I'm sorry I can't help you. I mean that."

Mycroft rose and shook Malcolm's hand. "You're welcome, Malcolm. I am sorry, too."

Malcolm waited for a beat and said. "I'll see you in another week."

Mycroft settled back into his chair. "Yes, you will."

Malcolm downed the rest of his whisky and hurried out, leaving Mycroft to finish his cigar.

The car slowed down and Malcolm realised they had arrived at the Admiralty.

Could that be the reason? Malcolm thought. *Are they forcing me to take the job?*

CHAPTER THREE

$\mathcal{M}$alcolm remembered his last trip to the Admiralty, where they forced him to resign because of allegations of fraternising with Joan, who is now his fiance. He clenched his fist. He took a deep breath to quell his anger, but it wasn't working. When the car stopped, the Marine jumped out and came to Malcolm's side. After unlocking the door, he opened it for Malcolm, keeping a watchful eye. Lieutenant Bowles flanked Malcolm soon after he got out. Malcolm looked up at the impressive building, taking one more deep breath before they entered the Admiralty.

After winding their way through a maze of corridors, they followed a grand staircase to a foyer at the top of the building. Seated on an art nouveau sofa was his fiancé, Joan, with two Royal Marines guarding the door. Lieutenant Bowles said, "Please wait here until the rest of the participants arrive." Malcolm nodded and took a seat next to Joan. He knew from her rigid posture that Joan was angry. When Bowles excused himself, Malcolm whispered, "I'm surprised to see you here."

"As am I," she said, her words enunciated with a sharp staccato. "I was enjoying afternoon tea when a squad of Royal Marines came to bring me here. And you?"

"I was at work when Lieutenant Bowles showed up and told me the Admiralty had reactivated me to the Air Service and brought me here."

"Is this your doing?" she said, turning and glaring at him.

"Absolutely not! I don't know why the Admiralty has dragged us here," he said, gesturing around the room.

"Is this about Mycroft's previous offer? Did you accept and not tell me?"

"No!" Malcolm said, louder than intended. One of the Marines guarding the door turned his head and Malcolm nodded. He lowered his voice. "I haven't spoken to Mycroft since we met; I assume it's related to the meeting, but I would accept nothing without talking to you first."

"I see," Joan said, clipping each word.

Malcolm stayed quiet, knowing she wouldn't listen. After waiting an eternity of five minutes, Malcolm saw Mycroft Holmes and his friend Charles Saxon coming up the grand staircase, escorted by Lieutenant Bowles. When they approach, Malcolm stood to speak, but before he could say anything, Lieutenant Bowles cut him off. "If you would all please follow me. All your questions will be answered momentarily."

Lieutenant Bowles ushered them into a salon with several couches, comfortable chairs, and an ornate desk. Seated at the desk was First Sea Lord Prince Louis of Battenberg. Before Malcolm could say a word, Lieutenant Bowles threw a sharp salute and said, "Your Serene Highness, Sir Malcolm Robertson, Miss Joan de St. Leger, Mycroft Holmes, and Charles Saxon, as you requested." Prince Louis saluted the lieutenant and set his steely gave on Malcolm. Malcolm was unsure whether to bow or salute. He opted for the latter.

"Thank you, Lieutenant, that will be all."

"Very good, Your Highness." Lieutenant Bowles saluted the Sea Lord and left the room.

"Please, take a seat." Prince Louis gestured to the chairs in front of them. Malcolm sat in a chair next to Joan.

Before Malcolm could reply, the First Sea Lord cleared his throat to get their attention. "Sir Malcolm, the nation, nay, the world, is grateful for your service. I know you have many questions and I will answer all in due time. May I offer you a drink?"

"Yes, thank you, Your Serene Highness," Joan said, jumping in quickly. Malcolm was thankful, as Joan knew the correct etiquette for every situation.

Malcolm met the First Sea Lord's gaze for the first time. The First Sea Lord's uniform was still crisp, with creases sharp enough to cut paper. Although Malcolm knew the Prince must be nearly sixty, the only hint of his age was the infrequent strands of grey in his impeccably trimmed beard and large moustache.

The Prince rang a small bell on his desk and within seconds, another lieutenant brought a tray with glasses of whisky, vodka, gin, and two snifters of brandy. The lieutenant served Malcolm the whisky, Joan the vodka, Saxon the gin, and Mycroft and the Prince the brandy. When he finished, he left quickly. The Prince took a sip of his brandy. "Please, drink."

Malcolm took a large sip to steady his nerves. On the way here, he seethed with anger at his reactivation. But now, he was having a drink with the First Sea Lord, the highest ranking naval officer of the British Empire. Malcolm sat up straight, falling back on his naval conditioning when appearing before a superior. He felt self-conscious, as he knew his haircut and beard were not military standard. Malcolm felt the familiar warmth of the whisky and took another sip to calm his nerves.

"Let us begin." The Prince handed a packet of documents to Malcolm and then to Charles. "Sir Malcolm, Mr Saxon, here are your orders now that we have reinstated you as captain and commander in the Royal Space Service." He handed another packet to Joan. "I assigned you to the Royal Fleet Auxiliary as a probationary lieutenant until you finish your Royal Navy Initial Training."

"Excuse me, Your Highness, the Royal Space Service?" asked Malcolm. Joan and Charles both shot him mortified looks, but Malcolm focused his attention on the Prince.

"Yes, Sir Malcolm, the Royal Space Service," Prince Louis said. "A brand new branch of the Royal Navy run in conjunction with the Secret Service. Sir Malcolm, you will take command of the very first spaceship. Mr Saxon will be your Second In Command, and Miss de St. Leger will be Communications Officer."

"With all due respect, Your Highness, I've turned down this offer four times; the last time, only two weeks ago." Malcolm angrily threw the packet back on the desk. "Is this your doing, Mycroft? You refuse to accept my answer?"

"Enough, Sir Malcolm," the Prince said.

"Your Highness, it is fine," Mycroft said. "Sir Malcolm's anger towards me is justified. You're right, I couldn't take no for an answer. I wanted this to be your decision, but you forced my hand."

"What is so bloody important that you had to coerce me back into service?"

"For the last three years, the Secret Service and the Air Service have studied the Martian spaceship you retrieved from Tunguska. We had some success at unlocking its technological secrets such that we began construction of a spaceship of our own at a secret base under Boreray in the St. Kilda archipelago. The plan was to use the spaceship to return the Martian Crown Prince and his crew back to Mars. However, that plan has now gone awry."

"How so?" Malcolm asked.

"The Martian Crown Prince C'thwan T'plua is dying. He has contracted a Martian disease that, while treatable on Mars, is beyond the ability of our medicine to treat. We can slow the disease's progression by placing him back in hibernation, but that only delays the inevitable."

"The problem is," Prince Louis interrupted, "that the ship is nowhere near ready. The construction is being led by Chief Engineer Commander Peter O'Hallarhan. He is the foremost expert on Martian technology."

"Why are you so far behind schedule?" Malcolm asked. "If he's as brilliant as you say, you don't need me."

Prince Louis took a sip of brandy. "The problem is, he's only interested in the Martian technology and won't focus on more mundane matters, such as completing the rest of the ship. We don't have a captain in the Air Service with the technical knowledge to complete the construction or the ability to understand the new technology. You are the only Chief Engineer promoted to captain. You have a proven track record of getting the impossible done in a short amount of time. And, to be blunt, you have a certain stubbornness and... directness that can get our Chief Engineer to finish the project."

"Has anyone asked the Martian Crown Prince to explain the technology?" Malcolm asked.

"Of course," Mycroft said. "We have thoroughly debriefed the Martian Crown Prince and the Chancellor. They provided a basic understanding of the technology involved and it has been valuable as a starting point. Unfortunately, the gap between the basic understanding of their technology and the understanding needed to build a working spaceship is vast. Think of your past assignments. While all captains have a basic idea of how their ship works, how many could repair the ship, let alone construct one from scratch?"

Malcolm remembered his past assignments and his frustrations with his commanding officers' lack of knowledge about the capabilities of their ship. The anecdote of three blind men describing an elephant came to mind; with only limited knowledge and perspective, it would be nearly impossible to see the entirety of what would need to be done. And he would have to depend on heavily on the young engineer who did as he pleased.

"Malcolm, I can't impress upon you how important it is to get the Crown Prince back to Mars," Mycroft continued, interrupting Malcolm's thoughts. "The fact he's been able to contact Mars has forestalled one invasion. If the Crown Prince dies on Earth, it could precipitate an invasion that makes the incident at Horsell Common look like a cloud of gnats at a picnic. I hate to ask this of you. I already asked too much of you when I recruited you to join the Secret Service.."

"Recruited?" Malcolm sputtered. "More like blackmailed."

"Mere semantics," Mycroft said, waving his hands. "Once again, your country, your King… your world needs you, Malcolm. And that goes likewise for you, Mr Saxon and Miss de St. Leger."

"Sir Malcolm, your mission will be to complete the construction as quickly as possible and lead the return of the Crown Prince to Mars. Mr Saxon, you assemble the crew and assist Sir Malcolm in any way possible. Miss de St. Leger, you will complete officer training, while also using your significant linguistic skills to handle any communications with the Martians."

"When are we to report for duty?" Saxon asked.

"Now. You leave immediately," Prince Louis said.

"Immediately?" thundered Malcolm. "I can't leave now! My parents are currently en route from Scotland and will arrive in hours. Miss de St. Leger and I are to be married in a week."

Prince Louis glared at Malcolm, but Mycroft interceded first. "I sent your parents a telegram last night informing them of your return to duty and postponement of your nuptials." Malcolm spoke, but Mycroft cut him off. "I'm very sorry to do this to you and Miss de St. Leger. We would not take such drastic measures if the situation wasn't so dire."

Prince Louis looked at the trio. "Sir Malcolm, I realise that I've put you in a precarious position where your fiancé will be your subordinate. But let me be crystal clear. I do not want to hear any whispers of fraternisation or favouritism with Miss de St. Leger. Understood?"

"Yes, Your Serene Highness," Malcolm answered.

"Very good. Let me reiterate the importance of this mission. The continued existence of humanity rests upon your ability to bring the Crown Prince back to Mars. England and the world, expects every man and woman," acknowledging Joan, "to do his or her duty. My staff tells me that the three of you are our best hope. I hope I am not misplacing my trust."

"No, Your Highness. We will do our utmost," Joan said.

"I expect no less. The three of you may leave. See Lieutenant Bowles on your way out and he will attend to your needs."

Malcolm and Saxon stood up and threw a sharp salute; Joan mimicked their salute, and the trio turned and left.

"That's not what I expected, Mycroft," Prince Louis said as they left.

"Really, Your Highness? I thought it went much better than I expected."

CHAPTER FOUR

*A*s soon as they exited the Sea Lord's office, Lieutenant Bowles was waiting for them. He handed a large packet of papers to Malcolm and Saxon. "This packet contains the information you will need to carry out your duties. Miss de St. Leger, here is the required reading for the officer training and your orders," Lieutenant Bowles said as he handed her several enormous books along with a packet containing her orders. "If you will follow me, we'll see about getting you out of these civilian clothes and requisition you uniforms. Once you are ready, we will transport you to the Hendon Aerodrome, where transportation to your ultimate destination is waiting. Now, if you will follow me, we will go to the Quartermaster's."

In a scant hour, Malcolm and Saxon were back in uniform for the first time in three years. It was both familiar and, after such a long time, somewhat foreign. Finding a uniform for Joan was more difficult. In the end, they created her uniform using dresses from Queen Alexandra's Royal Navy Nursing Service with the addition of a men's uniform jacket and a midshipmen's' cap. Through this, the three remained silent, save for answering questions. When they received a week's worth of uniforms, Lieutenant Bowles escorted them back out.

"If you would like, I can retrieve any items that you may wish to have with you and have them shipped to your assignment."

Malcolm said, "I would very much like to retrieve my footlocker from my flat." Malcolm turned over his flat key and the key to the footlocker. Saxon asked for the same. Joan said, "please send my undergarments, as wearing these all the time will be intolerable." Malcolm couldn't help but notice Lieutenant Bowles blushing.

As soon as they pulled away from the Admiralty, Malcolm exhaled, as if he'd been holding his breath the whole time they were at the Admiralty. "I told you I had nothing to do with this predicament. Bloody hell, I can't believe the lengths that Mycroft will go to get his way! I think he enjoys playing with people's lives."

Joan put her hand on Malcolm's arm. "I'm sorry I doubted you, Malcolm. I was worried that you were tired of the tedium of your job and looking for an escape."

"We've been through this many times. I would have stayed at the job so we could begin a life together. But now, Mycroft has taken that away from us. What about our wedding?"

Joan smiled. "It will happen. We just have to wait a little longer." She paused for a moment. "Maybe this is a good thing." She put her hand up to forestall Malcolm's objection. "We both are not happy sitting at a desk. Now, we can live the lives we both want, but together." She looked at the books that she received at the Admiralty. "Although I daresay I will spend most of my time studying."

Malcolm chuckled. He looked at Saxon, who had been silent this whole time. "What about you, Charles? How do you feel about this turn of events?"

"Mycroft had warned me some time ago that this might happen. I still find myself taken aback by the whole thing. I'm also concerned about my peculiar situation." Charles was a homosexual and would face court martial and prison if the Royal Navy learned his secret.

"Charles," Joan said, putting a hand on his knee, "I don't think you have to worry. Because the Royal Navy needs you so badly, they will do nothing to jeopardise the success of the mission."

"But what about when this mission is over?" Charles said, raising an eyebrow.

"I like to think that the Royal Navy would consider your substantial service."

"Charles," Malcolm interrupted, "have no fear. They'll have to throw me in the brig if they try to take you away, because I will not let that happen."

"Thank you, Malcolm, Joan," Saxon said. He looked at Malcolm and cocked his head. "I'm rather surprised, Malcolm. You're taking this better than I thought you would."

"Don't let my demeanour fool you. I am angry. More angry than I have been in my life. But, as Joan reminded me, we still get to be together and truthfully, we will both be doing things we love. Except for our erstwhile new lieutenant who will study military law, tactics, discipline, and history."

"You know, Malcolm, this means that Joan will be your subordinate. I'm afraid you won't be able to fraternise with her. And Joan, you'll have to take orders from Malcolm without hesitation or questioning. Do think you can do that?" he said with a smirk.

"I suppose I shall have to just close my eyes and think of England," she said.

They laughed, and all took to watching the scenery as they travelled north. Before they realised, they had already left the City proper and were on their way through Hampstead. They continued on to Brent Cross and Colindale. As they approached the Aerodrome, Malcolm noticed an airship and nudged Joan. In the field was a small airship whose skin was a patchwork of burgundy, mustard, royal blue, white, silver, and black. Malcolm had recognised it at once as the *RAS Uhuru*, the airship that had taken them to the other side of the world and back.

As the car pulled closer, Malcolm saw Colfax Mingo, the captain of the *RAS Uhuru*, leaning against the entryway to the ship. To Malcolm's surprise, Colfax wore the duty uniform of the Royal Fleet Auxiliary - a fitted navy blue jacket, pants, boots, and a beret. As the car came to a stop, Colfax walked to the car, opened the door, and threw a very sharp salute. Malcolm and Saxon returned the salute, and Joan, once again, attempted to imitate them. Malcolm noted the rank on the sleeve of Colfax's uniform.

"Lieutenant Commander Mingo, it's a pleasure to see you again. Although rather unexpected to see you in uniform."

Colfax laughed. "No one is more surprised than me. Mr Buskins, please see to the luggage and then inform Mr Jeffries that we will lift off as soon as we stowed your gear." A young midshipman ran down the gangway and hustled back with the first load of luggage.

"You have a crew now?" Malcolm asked. "It appears much has changed since we last saw each other."

"That it has," Colfax said. "Right after we returned, they dragged me to the Admiralty and, using some obscure clause, they returned me to duty in the Royal Navy Auxiliary so that I could fly personnel and supplies to Boreray. The ship is still mine, as they don't want military airships spotted in the area. They gave me a crew," he said, nodding at the midshipman who hustled by with another load of luggage, "the greenest crew imaginable. It took two trips before they stopped heaving. But the *Uhuru* has never been in better shape. I've upgraded the engines, and she's considerably faster. How did you end up back in uniform?" Colfax asked before hastily adding, "sir."

"I was at work when a squad of Royal Marines threatened to drag me out of the building. They took us to the Admiralty, and here we are."

"Come, let's get you settled. We can talk more once we're in the air." Colfax led the way up the gangplank.

Malcolm stopped and said, "Permission to come aboard?"

Colfax stopped, turned around, and grinned. "Permission granted."

Malcolm went to take Joan's arm out of habit and realised that since she was now a subordinate, he shouldn't touch her. Instead, he gestured she should follow Colfax. Charles followed and arched an eyebrow as he went walked up the gangplank; Malcolm shot him a dirty look.

CHAPTER FIVE

*T*rue to his word, Colfax had the *Uhuru* in the sky within minutes. Malcolm peered out his cabin's porthole and watched the lights of London twinkling like stars. He never tired of watching the world expand in front of him as an airship ascended. He realised just how much he had missed this. Dressed in his Royal Space Service uniform, a captain once again, he felt at home. When he felt the airship level, he joined the others in the galley.

As he entered the galley, Joan was studying a primer on military law. He smiled as he remembered struggling through that text more years ago than he cared to admit. Saxon was studying his orders and Malcolm realised he hadn't read his orders yet. He returned in a minute with his orders and sat down in the chair next to Joan.

"Lord, how do you read this without falling asleep?" she said.

Malcolm smiled at her. "It isn't easy, that's for sure. I'm proud of you for tackling this so quickly."

She arched an eyebrow. "It's a challenge, and you know how much I like a challenge."

"Now, you two. You heard the First Sea Lord, no fraternising in the ranks," Charles said.

"You're a killjoy," Joan said.

Malcolm opened his packet and sorted through the extensive stack of documents. It included blueprints, progress reports, the personnel file of Commander Peter O'Hallarhan, and a debriefing summary that Malcolm read first. It confirmed everything that Mycroft and the Sea Lord had told him: the ship construction was behind schedule, despite several attempts to push forward. The number of captains who failed to make significant progress on the project dismayed Malcolm.

Malcolm turned to the Chief Engineer's personnel file. Peter O'Hallarhan joined the Royal Air Service immediately after graduating with honours from the Dublin's Trinity College Engineering program. His initial assignment was airship design, starting as an engineering assistant, rising quickly to become the chief design engineer. His file noted his innovative designs, but also many complaints about his treatment of his subordinates. Based on his technical aptitude, the Admiralty chose him to study the Martian technology and design the spaceship. The file also noted O'Hallarhan worked closely with Ernest Rutherford in reverse engineering the Martian technology. Together, they were successful, although the summary noted Ernest Rutherford abruptly left the project at his own request.

Colfax stuck his head through the entryway. "We should reach our destination by 1600 tomorrow. I'm getting some sleep. Although I can't order most of you to bed, I strongly suggest that you do the same. Good night." He threw a salute, which Malcolm and Saxon returned. By the time Joan realised she needed to return the salute, Colfax had disappeared.

"You need to work on your salute, Lieutenant de St. Leger," Malcolm said.

"How do you do it so quickly?" she asked.

"It's muscle memory," said Saxon. "The first thing we learn in training is the salute and if we failed to do it correctly... let's just say, after a few times, you learned."

Malcolm gathered his papers and returned them to the packet. "We'll work on that salute tomorrow." He turned to Saxon and Joan and saluted them slowly, for Joan's benefit. "Good night, Commander.

Lieutenant." Saxon likewise saluted slowly, and Joan mimicked his movements with more success.

Malcolm pondered how much had changed as he lay in bed. When he woke up this morning, he was a director at a transportation company, leaving for a month's holiday to marry and honeymoon with Joan. Twelve hours later, he was a captain in the Royal Space Service aboard an airship again. Although he wanted to be mad about the interruption to build a life with Joan, he realised he was relieved to return to a familiar environment. Although this could be the hardest assignment of his career, he felt content.

When Malcolm awoke the next morning, he felt rested for the first time since leaving the Air Service. He dressed in his uniform, realising how much he missed this morning ritual. When he was shipshape, he went to the galley for breakfast. The smell of a large pot of tea, toast, jars of marmalade, and a heaping plate of bacon brought a smile to his face. Saxon was already eating, and Malcolm sat down beside him.

Saxon ignored Malcolm's presence as he continued to eat his breakfast. "Not use to military hours?"

"It's not that; I don't have an alarm clock. I fear it will be hard on our new lieutenant; she's not used to rising with the sun."

"I'll pretend I don't know how you know the sleeping habits of our new lieutenant," Saxon said with a smile. "Now that you've reviewed your orders, what do you think?"

Malcolm sipped his tea. "I think we will have our work cut out for us."

"Tell me what you know about this Chief Engineer."

"He appears to be brilliant, but has driven off four commanding officers assigned to this project. Likewise, he also angered the Engineering crews assigned to work for him."

"Sounds like you will have your hands full," Saxon said

"What about you? What are your orders?"

"I must requisition a crew for the ship. I do not know what positions we'll need, let alone who I'll get to staff it. And I'm to write the Military Law and Code of Conduct for the Royal Space Service. I almost envy your task over mine." Saxon said.

"At least you can correct certain grievances you may have with the Air Service regulations as they stand."

Saxon nodded, grasping Malcolm's meaning. "Yes, it will be an opportunity to address some grievances I have."

Malcolm watched as Joan arrived in the galley and fixed her breakfast. "You'll have to make allowances for women serving as well."

"A Herculean task, to say the least," Saxon murmured.

Joan brought her plate and mug and joined them at the table. "Good morning, Malcolm, Charles."

"Excuse me, Lieutenant. You are an officer in the Royal Navy Auxiliary; you will address us as Sir or by rank," Saxon said.

"But Charles," Joan began.

"Lieutenant, you are going to be one of the first women officers in the regular Royal Naval Auxiliaries. Everyone will judge you by your ability to comply with regulations and deportment. Everyone will hold you to a higher standard than your male counterparts, solely because of your sex. It isn't fair, but it is a fact of life."

"Yes… sir."

"Very good, Lieutenant." Charles' expression softened. "I want to prepare you for the challenges you will face. I have great confidence you will meet those challenges and become a first-rate officer."

"Thank you, Commander," she said.

"Now, with your leave, Captain, I'll let you two talk," Saxon said. Malcolm nodded his agreement. "Good morning, Captain, Lieutenant," Saxon said as he left the galley.

Before Joan could speak, Malcolm said, "He's right. You must be twice as good to receive half the respect. And you'll need to learn discipline, I'm afraid."

Joan bit her lip as if in thought. "Permission to speak freely, Captain?"

Malcolm smiled, "Permission granted."

Joan sighed. "Malcolm, I don't know if I can do it. There's so much to learn. For starters, I don't understand why everything is so regulated."

"In a crisis, the commander needs to know how everyone will

respond. The discipline instilled during training makes it an automatic response. Remember the preparation for our mission in Austria? We drilled repeatedly until we knew exactly what we needed to complete the mission. Repeated practice becomes an automatic response. It's the same in the Service; Commander Saxon and I fell back into our familiar roles because it is ingrained behaviour."

"I understand, but… God, it's so infuriating!"

"It can be. Commander Saxon is correct to suggest that you practise before reporting for training."

"When we get to Boreray, will you oversee my training, Captain? Personally?" She raised a provocative eyebrow.

"No, that would not be advisable and I'm afraid I'll have my hands full with my own assignment."

"I'm disappointed… sir."

"You are a devil, Lieutenant," Malcolm said, trying hard to fight the urge to kiss her. "I'll leave you to your mess."

"Yes, sir," she said. She furrowed her brow. "Am I supposed to salute now?"

"No, that won't be necessary. Good day, Lieutenant."

Malcolm walked to the cockpit and found Colfax piloting the ship. Malcolm knocked on the door frame. "Mind if I join you?"

"Not at all, Captain. Please, have a seat." Colfax pointed to the co-pilot seat and Malcolm squeezed into position. He scanned the horizons for a minute to identify their current course.

"Are we nearing Scotland?" Malcolm asked.

"You have a keen eye, Captain. We'll pass near Glasgow within the hour before we turn towards Boreray."

"Excellent," Malcolm said. "Could you let me know when we approach Glasgow? I want to show Joan, I mean Lieutenant de St Leger, my hometown."

Colfax's deep laugh echoed in the cockpit. "It must be difficult remembering to refer to her by rank."

"For both of us. It won't be easy for the lieutenant. She has to follow my orders without question. We will definitely be in uncharted territory."

They laughed. Malcolm sat and watched quietly as the *Uhuru* floated above the Midlands, making its way closer to Scotland. Reluctantly, Malcolm tore himself away from the cockpit and returned to the galley to study his orders. The midshipmen had cleared the food, leaving only a pot of tea. Malcolm smiled and, after getting a cup of tea for himself, settled in to study his orders.

Malcolm laid out the ship's blueprints, taking up the entire galley table. The ship was as big as the *HMA Daedalus*, his last command. Since the ship did not need a dedicated space for balloons, the interior space was larger. Unlike an airship, the engineering section comprised the back third of the ship. He couldn't understand the notations describing the equipment housed in various areas, but he understood the ship's general organisation. He read the status reports, comparing them to the blueprints to understand the status of the project. The Engineering section was complete, but the ship resembled a skeleton. Malcolm found no mention of the hull's construction. Without a hull, it wouldn't be a ship.

Malcolm lost himself in his analysis when a voice started him. "Sir, you asked to be informed when we were nearing Glasgow" Malcolm looked up from his papers and struggled to remember the name of the midshipman standing in front of him.

"Thank you, Mr Buskins. Could you ask Lieutenant de St. Leger to join me in the cockpit?"

"Very good, sir." Malcolm stowed the blueprints and went to the cockpit.

Joan was waiting for him. "You asked to see me, Mal - sir?"

"Yes, Lieutenant. We're nearing my hometown and I wanted you to see it."

"Are you sure that it won't break military discipline? That seems to be a personal discussion."

"I prefer to see it as an opportunity to know your commander."

"There are other ways I'd like to know you," she said, winking.

Malcolm stifled a laugh before knocking. "Come," Colfax said.

Malcolm opened the door. "Lieutenant, please take the co-pilot's seat. That should provide a better view."

Joan sat down as Malcolm moved behind her. To their right, Malcolm saw the city of Glasgow and the River Clyde cutting through it. Smoke from industrial furnaces obscured the city, but Malcolm still identified crucial landmarks. Malcolm found the shipyard where his father had worked. If he hadn't joined the Royal Navy, he might be working there now. Shuddering at the thought, he followed the River Clyde towards the centre of the cockpit window and saw where the river widened. Working his way back, he found Kilmacolm, his hometown.

Malcolm leaned in over Joan's shoulder and pointed to the River Clyde. "Lieutenant, do you see where the river widens there?" He smelled her perfume and struggled to resist the urge to kiss her. She nodded. "Follow my finger back. That insignificant speck is Kilmacolm."

"It's so small that I would not have noticed if you hadn't shown me."

"Aye, it's a tiny town."

She turned and looked at Malcolm. "Thank you for sharing with me... sir." She paused for a moment before continuing. "Does it make you homesick... sir?"

"A bit. I wish I could talk to my ma and da. They must think me mad; cancelling our wedding with no notice for a new assignment. It's frustrating; I can nearly see their house, but I'm no closer than I was in London."

Malcolm stared out the window, watching as Kilmacolm slid out of view. "Mr Mingo, how long until we reach Boreray?"

"Another five hours, sir," Colfax said.

"Very good. Thank you, Mr Mingo. We'll leave you to your duties and thank you for allowing our intrusion."

Colfax smiled. "My pleasure, sir."

After Malcolm and Joan left the cockpit, he asked, "How is the studying going?"

"Slowly. The books are dry reading."

Malcolm chuckled. "That they are." She turned to leave, but

Malcolm touched her arm. "I didn't know that Mycroft would rope you into this."

"Neither did I," she said.

"This is not what I wanted. We should be in Kent, preparing for our wedding, not reporting to duty on a remote island in the North Atlantic."

"I know. We will be together, but we won't spend any time together. It's like seeing your hometown; you could see it, but still separated from it." She lowered her voice. "We'll get through this. If it won't break military discipline, I love you, Malcolm."

"I love you too, Joan," he whispered. Malcolm yearned to hold her hand or kiss her, but instead, he took a deep breath. "I should return to my preparations before landing; I believe you should do the same. Thank you, Lieutenant."

"It was my pleasure, Captain," she said with a wink.

He returned to his cabin and wrestled with his approach to his new assignment. The technological challenges of the project were equal to the personnel challenges, both prodigious. The spaceship's design called out components such as gravity beam drive and electrokinetic thrusters; it may as well have been Greek. Realising that he didn't currently have the knowledge to tackle the technical issues, Malcolm studied the reports of the previous captains to determine where they failed. Malcolm quickly found that the captains failed to grasp the technological issues, deferring to O'Hallarhan's expertise, inevitably causing the project to stall, as O'Hallarhan had free rein to do as he pleased. Malcolm realised in order to keep his Chief Engineer focused on the right tasks, he would need to issue explicit orders to the Chief Engineer. He also realised that he would need to increase the morale of the Engineering crew to complete construction. Slowly, he developed his plan when he assumed command.

True to Colfax's word, five hours later, the airship began its descent as it approached Boreray; a spit of rock alone in the middle of the ocean. Malcolm understood why the Royal Navy and Secret Service picked it as the site of its secret construction base; Malcolm saw nothing but water in any direction. From his cabin, Malcolm was content to watch the airship's descent, but became alarmed as the ship continued to descend until it was barely above the ocean. He watched uneasily as the ocean waves came perilously close to hitting the small airship.

He bolted from his cabin and knocked on the cockpit door. "I don't mean to tell you how to pilot your airship, but aren't you a little low?"

"Not at all, Captain. We're making our approach to the hangar."

"Hanger? What hanger?"

"There," Colfax pointed.

Straight ahead, Malcolm saw a large cave opened to the sea. He swallowed. "That's the hangar?"

"Aye, sir. That's the hangar."

CHAPTER SIX

alcolm watched as Colfax expertly manoeuvred the small airship towards the cave. "Don't worry, Captain. I've done this many times. We're in luck today; the prevailing winds are with us."

"If you say so," Malcolm said. He gripped the doorframe until his knuckles were white. He watched in horror and admiration as Colfax approached the cave. Waves crashed against the cave, threatening to hit the airship. Colfax remained calm while Malcolm watched with growing apprehension as darkness swallowed the airship.

Malcolm saw a series of lights as he adjusted to the cave's darkness. He watched as Colfax followed the lights, guiding the ship through a long passage. Malcolm held his breath until the airship emerged into a gigantic cavern ablaze with light. Ahead, Malcolm saw the spaceship. It looked like the remains of a gigantic animal; a colossal skeleton with no flesh or internal organs.

Colfax expertly steered the airship to the left of the spaceship. As Colfax cut the engines and the airship glided forward, the ground crew grabbed the airship's landing lines. They latched the lines to winches, pulling the airship to the landing platform. As the airship stopped, Malcolm looked at his pocket watch, 1600 right on the nose.

"My compliments, Mr Mingo. It was a flawless landing. And right on time."

"Thank you, sir. Can you let the other passengers know we've landed?"

"My pleasure, Lieutenant Commander." After informing Saxon and Joan of their arrival, Malcolm returned to his cabin to freshen up. He knew his haircut wasn't strictly military, but it would have to do. Malcolm gathered his formal orders and joined the others at the door to the airship.

As the crewmen lowered the gangplank, Malcolm instantly recognised Admiral Beatty, head of the Air Service, and nudged Saxon, who nodded in acknowledgement. Malcolm led Saxon and Joan down the gangplank, stopping before the admiral. He threw his smartest salute and said, "Captain Malcolm Robertson, Commander Charles Saxon, and Lieutenant Joan de St. Leger reporting for duty, sir."

The admiral returned the salute and offered his hand to Malcolm. "It's good to see you in uniform again, Captain. And you too, Commander." He turned to Joan, "Welcome to the Royal Space Service Auxiliary, Lieutenant."

"I didn't realise you would be here, sir," Malcolm said

"I'm here to assist in the transition. Allow me to introduce Commodore Vincent Dexter, commander of this base." Commodore Dexter nodded to Malcolm. Commodore Dexter appeared twenty years older than Malcolm. The commodore's hair was steel grey. He had flinty eyes framed with dark, bushy eyebrows, the stereotype of a wizened sailor.

"Commodore Dexter and I want to discuss your orders. You will meet the members of your command at the assembly at four bells."

"I believe I speak for the group when I say we are eager to start," Malcolm said.

"Very good. This way, please." The admiral and Commodore Dexter led the way. Joan tugged on Malcolm's sleeve and held him back.

"What's four bells?" she whispered.

"It describes the time of the watch. That translates to 1800 hours," he said. "It will make sense, I promise."

"I hope so," she said, as they hurried to rejoin the group.

"May I ask a question?" Malcolm offered.

Admiral Beatty turned to Malcolm. "Yes, Captain, what is it?"

"There aren't sides on the ship. Shouldn't the ship have a hull?"

"One would think so," Beatty said. "Talk to Chief Engineer O'Hallarhan. My understanding is they can't weld the spaceship's exterior to the frame. He abandoned the hull to focus on the engines."

"Without a ship, we can't fly, regardless of the engines."

"I agree. That's why you are here."

Malcolm stopped to take in the base. The enormous cave was lit with a number of powerful electric lights providing the necessary illumination to work. Three gigantic gantries loomed over the work area, littered with large stacks of crates and racks containing steel beams and sheet metal. Several large fuel tanks dominated one wall, located well away from the welding stations. A cacophony of work echoed throughout the cave. Malcolm heard hammering, drilling, and riveting, but without rhyme or reason. The air was a mix of sea water, diesel fuel, and hot metal. They walked past the skeleton of the spaceship, entering a steel door in the cave wall. The admiral led them to a meeting room at the end of a hall. Despite the austerity of the base, the room contained a long mahogany table with eight overstuffed leather chairs and a tea cart laden with tea and biscuits. As they sat down, a midshipman served tea. A commander entered and sat next to Commodore Dexter.

"I've asked my aide, Commander Edward Murray, to join us," Commodore Dexter said. "Miss de St. Leger, you are now a cadet. Commander Murray will oversee your training. You will complete the ten-week training in five weeks in order to receive your rank as lieutenant."

"Are you up to the challenge?" asked Commander Murray.

"Yes, sir," Joan replied.

Admiral Beatty smiled before turning to Malcolm. "Do you have any questions?"

"I have many," Malcolm said. "How has Commander O'Hallarhan run off so many commanding officers? It would seem that he is the problem."

"He has friends in high places," said Admiral Beatty. "Second Sea Lord Jellicoe is his greatest champion. From the start, O'Hallarhan convinced Jellicoe that he was indispensable. Fourth Sea Lord Lambert also sided with O'Hallarhan, hoping to gain the new spaceship. Third Sea Lord Wright is adamant the entire project is a waste of resources. They forced the First Sea Lord to replace the captains and not O'Hallarhan."

"Permission to speak freely, sir?"

Beatty sighed. "I'm sure I'm going to regret this, but permission is granted."

"To complete the mission, I need the widest latitude to deal with Commander O'Hallarhan, as it affects the construction of the ship. For all matters relating to this base, I defer to you, Commodore."

"It's about bloody time," muttered Commodore Dexter. "He's run roughshod over my people and the threats of the brig are all that keep them working."

"You have my support, but the Sea Lords may overrule me," Beatty said. "What do you intend to do?"

"I intend to remind the Commander that no one is indispensable. If necessary, I'll learn this damn technology myself."

"Whatever you do, be careful, Malcolm. O'Hallarhan has powerful friends. They could end your career."

"The Admiralty already forced me out once. What's another time?" Malcolm said.

Beatty looked down. "I'm sorry about that, Malcolm. The Admiralty's decision to force you and Commander Saxon out of the service was inexcusable. I don't intend to let that happen again. I will impress upon the Admiralty the success of this endeavour can't depend on one person. Get this ship completed, within regulations."

"Thank you, sir," Malcolm said. "I will do my best."

"That's all I can ask."

"One more question, sir. When do I meet Commander O'Hallarhan?"

"He was supposed to attend this meeting. I'll send someone for him."

"That won't be necessary, sir," Malcolm smiled.

"I'm not sure I like that look, Captain. What do you have in mind?"

"You'll see, sir."

"That's what I'm afraid of." Beatty turned. "Commander Saxon, do you have any questions?"

"No, sir, I believe my task, though daunting, is straightforward," Saxon said. "As I understand it, I'm literally writing the book that we would figuratively throw at someone."

"Yes, that's correct," Beatty said with a bemused laugh. "Not my choice of phrasing, but an accurate assessment. You also need to assemble and train the crew. Cadet de St. Ledger, you will also reacquaint yourself with the Martian language and provide any needed translation, as you are the only person to master the Martian language."

"Yes, sir, that's correct," she said.

"If there are no more questions, a crewman will show you to your rooms. Someone will fetch you for the assembly."

"Sir, I have two more questions. Will Commander O'Hallarhan attend the assembly?"

Beatty scowled. "Yes, all personnel received orders to attend."

"Very good," Malcolm said. "Sir, do you plan to attend the assembly?" Malcolm asked.

"Yes." Beatty paused. "Why?"

"And you, Commodore?"

"Yes," Dexter said, smiling.

"Very good," Malcolm said.

"Do I want to know?" Beatty asked.

"Probably not," Malcolm said.

Beatty shook his head. "Dismissed."

Malcolm, Saxon, and Joan saluted the admiral and commodore and left the office.

Malcolm's quarters were not as Spartan as he had expected. They were like his quarters aboard the *Daedalus*; a large, canopied four-poster bed, two large overstuffed leather chairs, a small desk, a small bar, two closets, and a private washroom with shower. Malcolm checked the bar and found Auchentoshan, his favourite whisky. He used the time to unpack his luggage and settle into the room.

Just before four bells, a seaman escorted Malcolm to the main platform. Malcolm scanned the crowd, identifying the crew by rank and insignia. Quickly, he spotted the enlisted Engineering seamen and their chief petty officer, a tough-looking man nearly Malcolm's age.

He turned his attention to the officers. He saw the Admiral, the Commodore, and a handful of lieutenants. Malcolm saw Joan. Her lieutenant rank was now replaced by a black edged white square, the rank of a cadet. Malcolm noted the only commanders present were Charles and Commander Murray.

The boatswain's whistle cut through the noise, bringing everyone to attention. "At ease," Admiral Beatty said. Malcolm watched as the assembly moved to parade rest.

Beatty began, "Please join me in greeting our newest arrivals, Captain Malcolm Robertson, Knight Commander of the Order of St. Michael and St. George, and Commander Charles Saxon. They will command our construction project. You will extend the utmost support to Captain Robertson and Commander Saxon. It is vital that we complete this project." Beatty turned to Malcolm. "Would you like to address the crew?"

"Yes, sir, I would. But first, where is Commander Peter O'Hallarhan?"

Admiral Beatty looked around. "Where is Commander O'Hallarhan?"

One of the seaman piped up, "He's working on the ship's engines, sir."

"Will a couple of Marines volunteer to escort Commander O'Hallarhan to the assembly?" Malcolm asked. Two burly Marines stepped forward. Malcolm nodded, and they left for the ship. An indistinct murmur ran through the assembly.

"Malcolm, what are you playing at?" Admiral Beatty whispered.

"I'm setting the tone for my command," Malcolm whispered. "The crew thinks I'll be gone in a few months, just like my predecessors. I don't intend for that to happen."

"Be careful, Malcolm," Beatty said.

"I will. The Admiralty kicked me out of the service once; I have nothing to lose."

"So you say," Beatty said. The murmuring from the crew continued until the Marines returned with Commander Peter O'Hallarhan a few minutes later. A hush fell over the crowd as the Marines led O'Hallarhan to Malcolm. O'Hallarhan's youthful appearance shocked Malcolm. O'Hallarhan looked like a recent college graduate, but Malcolm knew otherwise. His dark hair was barely military standard, and he was in his engineering coveralls.

The Marines escorted the commander to Malcolm. O'Hallarhan glared at Malcolm for a moment before asking, "Why was I interrupted? Who are you?"

"I am Captain Malcolm Robertson, your commanding officer. I expect a salute and for you to address me as befitting my rank."

O'Hallarhan glared at Malcolm before throwing a salute with a precision that underlined his contempt. "Yes, sir," he sneered.

Malcolm returned the salute. "Tell me, Commander O'Hallarhan, why weren't you at the assembly?"

"I was working on the engines, sir," O'Hallarhan hissed.

"Were you ordered to attend this assembly?"

"Yes, but..."

"But, nothing," Malcolm said. "Commander O'Hallarhan, you disobeyed a direct order from a superior officer."

"But.."

"Silence, Commander," Malcolm thundered. He turned to Commodore Dexter. "I believe you mentioned there is a brig?"

"Yes, Captain, we have a brig," Dexter said with a smile.

"Very good." Malcolm turned to the Marines. "Escort Commander O'Hallarhan to the brig."

"You can't do that. I'm..." O'Hallarhan interjected.

Malcolm cut off O'Hallarhan. "I can and I am. Take him away." O'Hallarhan glared at Malcolm. The assembly watched in silence as the Marines marched O'Hallarhan away.

"I hope I have made it abundantly clear that no person is indispensable," Malcolm began. "Not even me. We will fail if we don't work together. That means following orders and doing your job to the best of your ability. If you can't abide by these orders, I suggest you apply for a transfer because tomorrow morning, I will expect your best work. Thank you all."

Malcolm stepped back. Admiral Beatty glared at him; Commodore Dexter had a bemused smile. "Assembly dismissed."

"I hope you know what you're doing, Malcolm," Admiral Beatty whispered.

"*So do I*," thought Malcolm.

CHAPTER SEVEN

alcolm watched the assembly disperse. Malcolm's display caused animated whispering among the men. Saxon joined him as the men returned to their jobs. "I think you made quite the impression, Malcolm."

"That was my intent. After O'Hallarhan cools off, I will bring him back into the fold. And if not, I'll figure this out," Malcolm gestured at the half built ship, "on my own."

"Don't look at me. I'm useless with technology," Saxon said.

Two midshipmen presented themselves, throwing sharp salutes. "Captain Robertson, I'm Midshipman Lennox; I'm your assistant. This is Midshipman Henderson. He is Commander Saxon's assistant. We will escort you to dinner with the other officers. Please follow us, sirs," he said. They were young; they must have barely left the academy. Lennox stood three inches shorter than Malcolm, but was solidly built. Malcolm recognised a well-disguised burr in Lennox's voice. Henderson towered over Malcolm and Saxon but was thin as a beanpole.

As they walked, Malcolm asked, "Is this your first assignment, Mr Lennox?"

"Yes, sir," Lennox said. "I have been here a year."

"What do you think of your assignment?" Malcolm asked.

"It's fine, sir. I wanted to serve on an airship, but I have no complaints," Lennox said.

"What about you, Mr Henderson?"

"This is also my first assignment," Henderson said. Malcolm noted Henderson's refined accent; Malcolm assumed his family had purchased his commission. "I've been here three months. It's a little overwhelming."

"I'm sure," Malcolm chuckled. "Dare I ask about the food?"

The midshipmen hesitated. Malcolm interjected, "I see. Typical service fare."

"Our remote location means we don't receive regular supplies, so they have to last," Lennox said.

"Let me guess; lots of potatoes, root vegetables, and meat as tough as boot leather."

"That's an accurate assessment, sir. We rarely get meat, but have fish instead."

"Haven't you missed the cuisine of the Service, Commander Saxon?"

"Can't say that I have, Captain Robertson."

They arrived at the Officer's Mess. A large oak table with several stuffed leather chairs sat in the centre of the room. To one side was a well-stocked mahogany bar. Several of the officers were already seated, while several midshipmen scurried around the room, serving the officers. A midshipman handed a glass of whisky to Malcolm and a gimlet to Saxon. Malcolm turned to Saxon. "They know what we drink. That's a good sign."

"If you say so," Saxon said.

Malcolm noticed Lennox and Henderson leaving. "Gentlemen, where are you going?"

"This is for officers only. We're not allowed to eat here."

"Nonsense. We need you available at all times. Including meals. You can stay by my authority. Go get something to drink. That's an order."

"Yes, sir," they said in unison.

The two midshipmen hurried to the bar and when they returned, Malcolm asked, "Mr Lennox, will you introduce me to the officers?" The midshipmen led Malcolm and Saxon to a group of officers congregated near the bar.

"Captain Robertson and Commander Saxon, this is Lieutenant Commander Charles Clarke, head of the construction detail." Malcolm deduced Clarke was near his age; his hair starting to grey. "This is Lieutenant Gareth Hughes, head of logistics and supplies." Hughes' receding hairline gave him an older appearance. "And this is Captain Hamish Macdonald of the Royal Marines, in charge of base security." Macdonald looked like a Royal Marine; short hair, a lumpy nose indicating multiple past breaks, and a scar on his cheek.

Malcolm shook their hands. "Gentlemen, it's a pleasure to meet you. I look forward to working with you."

Captain Macdonald spoke first. "You made quite an impression today, Captain Robertson."

"How so?"

"I find it refreshing to see the return of discipline, sir."

"How so?"

"Permission to speak freely, sir?"

"Permission granted," Malcolm said.

"This base has two sets of rules, one for O'Hallarhan and one for everyone else. I was glad he got his comeuppance."

"Everyone will follow the same rules under my command; follow orders and perform your duties as best you can. No one is indispensable, not even me," Malcolm said. "But, I repeat myself. Let's eat. I want to learn more about my officers."

The group left the bar and took places at the table; Malcolm ordered chairs placed for Midshipmen Lennox and Henderson between him and Saxon. Dinner was served; a rack of lamb with mint sauce, peas, and potatoes. As Malcolm started to eat, he looked at each of the officers at the table. They must have repeated this ritual many times before, and he sensed their sense of skepticism. "The midshipmen warned me about the food, but this is rather good," Malcolm said, in an attempt to generate conversation.

"Lamb is only meat we get and infrequently at that," said Lieutenant Hughes. "Sheep live on the island, so we occasionally send out hunting parties. We live on fish; locally caught pollock, haddock, and cod."

"I'd give my eye-tooth for a piece of beef," said Lieutenant Commander Clarke, poking at his meal with little enthusiasm.

"I'm working on it." Hughes said.

"I know," Clarke said. "Captain Robertson, if there's anything you need, Lieutenant Hughes is your man."

"That's good to know," Malcolm said. "When did you arrive here?"

"Last year," Clarke said.

"You're in Engineering, correct?" Clarke nodded. "How do you get along with O'Hallarhan?"

"I get along fine with O'Hallarhan."

"How do you manage that?" Malcolm asked.

"I leave him alone. I focus on my specialty, ship construction. Not that it has helped."

"Why not?"

"It's this damnable alloy we're using for the ship's hull. It's a Martian design and we can't weld it to the frame. That's one reason we're behind schedule - that and O'Hallarhan won't assign personnel. He wants them to do his bidding."

"Mr Clarke, see me tomorrow and bring the chief petty officer in charge of construction. With our combined knowledge, we should solve the problem."

"Yes, sir," Clarke said, trying his hardest to contain a smile. Malcolm noted that the other officers now looked at him with a skeptical interest.

"How about you, Lieutenant Hughes? How long have you been here?"

"It's been two long years, sir. I can't wait to see the sun again, sir."

"You don't get outside?"

"No, sir," Hughes said. "Commodore Dexter has standing orders that no one can go topside without his approval. Although we're isolated, the occasional fishing vessel comes by and they shouldn't see people on this God forsaken rock." Malcolm thought he detected a hint of a Welsh accent as Hughes spoke.

"How about you, Captain Macdonald?"

"My detachment escorted our guests to the island six months ago. Our primary assignment is securing our guests. My men have done nothing interesting except break up the occasional fight. Until today," he said with a smile.

"Is that the extent of your assignment?" Malcolm asked.

"No, sir. My men will provide ship security when it's finished. Can I speak freely?"

"Absolutely," Malcolm said.

Macdonald took a sip of his ale before continuing. "How will you build this ship when no one else has succeeded?"

Malcolm smiled. "I'm an engineer by training. I know ships and their construction. My last assignment was abroad an airship. That knowledge should apply to spaceship construction. Although I know nothing about this ship, I intend to play an active role in its construction. That includes understanding its technology. At the risk of bragging, my talent is figuring things out. I'm too stubborn to let a problem best me."

"Captain Robertson had a reputation as a miracle worker and unconventional thinker, both as an engineer and a captain," Saxon offered. Malcolm noticed that some of the wariness he felt from the group had diminished.

"What about you, Commander Saxon? What is your role here?" Clarke offered.

"I am writing the regulations for the Space Service and assembling and training the crew."

"Are you an engineer?"

"Good heavens, no," Saxon laughed. "I'm useless in technical matters. But Captain Robertson and I served together for many years; I owe my assignment to our relationship."

"I notice you brought a woman cadet. What's a woman doing in the Service?" asked Captain Macdonald.

Malcolm hesitated, but Saxon interjected before he could speak.

"Cadet de St. Ledger is a linguist and speaks Martian. After her commission, she will handle all communication with the Martians."

"Women don't belong in the Service." Macdonald said, shaking his head.

Malcolm took a breath, but before he could speak, Saxon repeated. "She is the only person who speaks Martian."

"A woman on a ship? I fear for her safety," Macdonald said.

"I wouldn't worry about Cadet de St. Ledger," Saxon said. "She can defend herself."

"She might defend herself against sailors," MacDonald boasted. "But she couldn't defend herself against my men. They are fighters. What chance would she have?"

"I wouldn't dismiss the cadet's capabilities. I learned never to underestimate her."

"How do you know her?"

"She was a member of the expedition that discovered the Martian spaceship," Saxon added. "She was instrumental in the success of that mission."

"If you say so," Macdonald said.

"Does the commodore eat with you?" Malcolm offered, steering the conversation away from Joan.

"He usually does; he's stuck entertaining the admiral," Clarke said.

"How is he?"

"Tolerable for a flag officer," Hughes offered. "Dexter has no patience with O'Hallarhan, but he's 'highly encouraged' to give O'Hallarhan the widest latitude. He's a good man in an impossible position. The Admiralty won't replace him because of his seniority. They replaced your predecessors instead." Hughes paused before continuing. "Are you worried the Admiralty will replace you?"

"No," Malcolm said. "I left the Air Service once; An obscure clause in my commission reactivated me and they assigned me here, an island in the middle of nowhere; what more can they do?"

The men laughed with various degrees of unease.

A nervous midshipman poked his head into the mess. "Captain Robertson, Admiral Beatty wants to see you. Immediately, sir."

All eyes looked at Malcolm. "No rest for the wicked. Good evening, gentlemen."

"You should come too, Commander Saxon," the midshipman added.

Saxon turned to Malcolm. "What trouble have you created for me now?"

"We'll find out." Malcolm said. "Gentleman," he said as he nodded to his officers and followed the midshipman out.

As they followed the midshipman, Saxon leaned close to Malcolm and whispered, "That didn't take long."

"What didn't take very long?"

"For the Admiralty to learn about the Assembly and contact Admiral Beatty."

"You're right," Malcolm agreed. "How did they find out? "

"Someone is supplying the Admiralty information directly."

"A spy?"

"Not a spy, but someone whose interests don't align with our mission," Saxon said.

CHAPTER EIGHT

The midshipmen ushered Malcolm and Saxon into the Commodore's office. The walnut panelling and book-shelves made the room feel dark, despite the ornate sconces on the walls and the overhead fixture. Commodore Dexter sat behind the large walnut desk while Admiral Beatty paced behind him while Commander Murray sat at a matching secretary desk to the right of the commodore. To Malcolm's surprise, Joan sat in front of the commodore.

"Please, sit down.," Commodore Dexter said. He dismissed the midshipman, but when Joan rose, Dexter put up his hand. "No, Cadet, please stay. This involves you as well."

Beatty held up a telegram and handed it to Malcolm. "Damn it, Malcolm! You're here a few hours and the Admiralty wants to know why you incarcerated O'Hallarhan."

Malcolm read the telegram before turning his gaze to Beatty. "Did he or did he not disobey orders? As his commanding officer, am I not responsible for my crew's discipline?"

"Yes, of course. However, the Admiralty questions your command ability and wants you dismissed."

"Fine, let them dismiss me. I didn't want to be here in the first place." Malcolm rose and started for the door.

"Sit down, Malcolm. And that's an order. You won't get off that easy."

Malcolm returned to his chair. "Sir, permission to speak freely?"

"Permission granted," Beatty sighed.

"You know we need to restore discipline. The other officers are not happy that one set of rules applies to O'Hallarhan, and another set to everyone else. To build the ship, I need everyone playing on the same pitch. And that starts by setting expectations immediately. Also, Commander Saxon pointed out that we must have an Admiralty spy here. It's only been a few hours since I arrived. How could the news reach the Admiralty so quickly?"

"True, I didn't consider that," Beatty said. "Any suggestions on dealing with our spy?"

Joan cleared her throat. "Yes, Cadet?" Beatty said as he glared at her.

"Permission to speak, sir?"

"Granted."

"I have some experience in dealing with spies, sir," Joan began. "First, we must determine who can contact the Admiralty so quickly. Once we've narrowed down the suspect list, we let slip specific information guaranteed to elicit an Admiralty response to each suspect. When the Admiralty reacts, we will know the spy's identity."

"Very good, Cadet. Thank you." Beatty took a deep breath before turning to Malcolm. "Look, I agree; We must restore discipline. I have the First Sea Lord's ear. You also have the support of Mycroft Holmes. Since this project is a joint venture between the Admiralty and the Secret Service, their support should temper the other admirals' outrage."

"Why is the Admiralty so eager to protect O'Hallarhan?" Malcolm asked.

"Politics. Second Sea Lord Jellicoe sees this project as an opportunity to become First Sea Lord and is using O'Hallarhan to hedge his bets. If he supports O'Hallarhan and the project fails, he can blame the First Sea Lord for assigning incompetent officers to supervise. If it succeeds, he takes credit for supporting the project from the start."

"Is there anyone at the Admiralty who wants the project to fail?" Saxon offered.

"It's no secret Third Sea Lord Wright opposes the project. He only sees the expense and refuses to consider the consequences if we don't return the Crown Prince."

"Speaking of the Crown Prince, how is his condition?" Malcolm asked.

"He's stable, for now," Beatty said. "His condition has showed some improvement since arriving here. Apparently, London's air exacerbated his condition."

"What are our next steps?" Malcolm asked.

"Commander Murray will provide you a list of anyone who has access to the radio room."

Commodore Dexter interjected. "No offense, Admiral, but I don't relish having a spy reporting our every move to the Admiralty. And I've never enjoyed being told how to run my base from someone five hundred miles away. What do I do when you can't countermand the Admiralty's orders?"

"May I suggest, Commodore, that you suddenly have technical difficulties with the radio?" Malcolm said.

Dexter smiled. "I like the way you think, Robertson. Now that you mention it, I believe we've had issues with the radio. And we're far too busy constructing the ship to divert resources to address the problem."

"You realise you won't be able to pull that trick with me," said Beatty.

"I rarely have to, sir, because your orders make sense," Dexter said. "It's been a long day and someone," he said, addressing Joan, "has an early morning. Commander Murray, please escort the cadet to her quarters."

"If it's all the same, sir, I would be happy to escort Cadet de St.

Leger to her quarters," Malcolm said. "If someone tells me where they are."

Admiral Beatty interjected, "Yes, Captain, please make sure she gets to her quarters without incident."

"Yes, sir."

"Without incident."

"Yes, sir. Cadet, do you know the way to your quarters?"

"Yes, M — sir," she said, catching herself.

"Very good. Good evening, sirs," Malcolm said and threw a salute. Malcolm, Joan, and Saxon exited the office.

"I'll make myself scarce," Saxon said. "I imagine you would like a few minutes alone to talk. Good night, Captain. Cadet," he said, turning and heading towards his quarters.

"Lead on, Cadet," Malcolm said. As they started walking, he asked, "How are you doing?"

"It's overwhelming… sir," she said. "I believe that Commander Murray will be a taskmaster."

"I'm glad. It will be important that your training is beyond reproach." Malcolm said. He relayed his conversation with Captain Macdonald. "It's highly likely he will take a personal interest in your combat training sessions."

"Thank you for the warning," Joan said. Malcolm looked at Joan, wanting to hold her hand or give her his arm at the least. Instead, he walked with his hands locked behind his back, keeping him from succumbing to the temptation.

"Here are my quarters, sir. Thank you for escorting me here," she said. She looked around and leaned in close to whisper, "I wish you could join me."

"So do I. More than anything. But we can't; there's too much at stake." Malcolm looked at Joan, wanting more than anything to take her into his arms.

"Pity." Clearing her throat, she said, "Thank you, Captain, for the escort. I hope we can talk again soon."

"I do too," Malcolm said. "Perhaps I might assist in your studying?."

"I'd like that very much, sir." She threw him a proper salute. "Good night, sir."

Malcolm returned the salute with a smile.

"Good night, Cadet."

CHAPTER NINE

$\mathcal{A}$fter he returned to his quarters, Malcolm tried working his way through the myriad of reports, but the words swam on the page. He changed for bed and fell asleep within seconds.

The shrill piping of "Call To Hands" jolted him awake. *"I did not miss THAT,"* he thought as he roused himself. Happy that his rank allowed him a private washroom, he showered and prepared for the morning. As he dressed, he reminded himself to see the barber to get a military standard haircut.

A seaman directed him to the Officer's mess. He poured a cup of tea and ate his eggs, beans, and toast. Malcolm rarely ate a large breakfast. For the last six months, he subsisted on a roll bought from a local bakery. He left the Officer's mess and found a seaman who directed him to his office.

He found Midshipman Lennox at his desk. He jumped to attention when Malcolm entered. Malcolm saluted and said, "As you were." Lennox handed Malcolm a file and returned to his chair. Malcolm took it, asking, "What's this?"

"The day's agenda, sir," Lennox said. "Originally, Commander O'Hallarhan was scheduled to give you a tour of the ship, but I've asked Lieutenant Commander Clarke to substitute for the commander's... absence. I remember you asked to meet with Lieutenant Commander Clarke to discuss the welding issue and I've added time after the tour for the discussion with him and his chief petty officer. Which brings you to lunch. I moved the usual morning briefing to after lunch so you would have time with Lieutenant Commander Clarke. I wasn't sure what else you needed, so I left the afternoon free, sir."

"Thank you, Mr Lennox. Excellent work." Malcolm pulled out his pocket watch and checked the time. "I seem to have a few minutes before our tour. May I ask, is there a barber on base? I'm in drastic need of a military haircut."

"Yes, sir. I can make an appointment for you. When would you like it?"

"Any possibility of squeezing it in before lunch?"

"I believe that will work."

"Thank you, Mr Lennox. Please get me before the inspection tour while I get acquainted with my office."

"Very good, sir."

Malcolm entered the simply furnished office containing a large oak desk, a small round table with four chairs to the right of the desk. The room was beige, and the overhead light did not make it feel inviting. Despite the drab decor, he couldn't help but feel a thrill of returning to service; something he hadn't felt in a long time. On his desk, he found a stack of reports already demanding his attention. *Paperwork springs eternal in the Service*, he thought. He was halfway through the stack when Lennox gathered him for the ship's inspection.

Lennox led Malcolm to the construction area. Lieutenant Commander Clarke and a grizzled petty officer were waiting. They both saluted when Malcolm drew near, and he quickly returned the salute.

"Captain Robertson, this is Mr Entwhistle, Chief Petty Officer of the construction crew."

"Chief, it's a pleasure to meet you," Malcolm offered his hand to the petty officer.

"Thank you, sir." Entwhistle shook Malcolm's hand tentatively.

"So Mr Clarke, Mr Entwhistle, show me this ship, such as it is."

Clarke rolled out the blueprints and explained the state of the ship. Clarke pointed to the ship's centre. "That is the bridge. Navigation is at the front, engineering and communications are on either side."

"How will we steer the ship?" Malcolm asked.

"With the Martian computators. The helmsman enters coordinates, and the computator sends instructions to the engines."

"I see." Malcolm grunted. "What happens if the computator fails?"

"The computator itself has multiple redundant units and there is an auxiliary navigational control panel in the engineering section."

"Speaking of engineering, how will the ship fly?"

"I don't know the details myself," Clarke said. "The main reactor creates a large amount of electrical energy that runs the gravity beam drive and electrokinetic thrusters."

"The what?" asked Malcolm.

"Gravity beam drive and electrokinetic thrusters. I honestly don't understand how they work, but they provide the thrust that radically reduces travel time. To understand how they work, you should talk to Commander O'Hallarhan."

"You said a reactor powered this ship. What kind of reactor?"

"It's called a fusion reactor; it generates energy by fusing two atoms together. The process generates large amounts of heat that's converted into electrical energy by the steam turbines."

"At least I understand that much," Malcolm said.

"I agree; I feel the same way. The technology is so far advanced, it may as well be magic," Clarke said.

"Does anyone understand how this works?"

"O'Hallarhan and Ernest Rutherford know the most, but I think even they don't completely understand it."

The trio continued past the bridge. "On each deck of the ship, there's a five-foot crawl space below the flooring to route the plumbing, if you will. You can see we have laid the main power cables, as well as the actual plumbing. The water heated by the reactor runs the steam turbines and heats the ship. Any waste water returns for purification and is used by the steam turbines. In addition, we ran communication lines for both voice and data."

"Data?" Malcolm said.

"Yes. The Martian computators use a signalling process to pass data between each unit. It's transmitted electrically, similar to how Morse code is transmitted via telegraph."

Malcolm stared at the outside of the ship. "You told me last night that you are having trouble welding the hull to the ship?"

"Yes, it's this damnable metal we're using for the hull. I've been welding for twenty years, and the damn stuff won't stick to anything…. sir," Mr Entwhistle said.

"What is this metal?" Malcolm asked.

Entwhistle pulled out a large metal sheet from a nearby storage bin and handed it to Malcolm. It was light for its size and was barely more than an inch thick. Malcolm studied it before returning it to Entwhistle.

"It's some kind of aluminum alloy," Entwhistle said. "But whatever metals they've added prevents the usual methods of joining aluminum to a steel frame. We've tried bimetallic inserts, coating the steel with aluminum, coating the steel and the alloy with silver, but we can't weld a clean connection."

"Who knows the alloy's composition?" Malcolm asked.

"That would be His Holiness… I mean Commander O'Hallarhan… sir," Entwhistle said.

"His Holiness?" Malcolm asked, raising his eyebrow.

"Permission to speak freely, sir?" Entwhistle asked.

"Permission granted," Malcolm said.

"O'Hallarhan thinks he's God's gift to engineering. I've met some arrogant engineers in my time, but he takes the cake. He acts like his shit doesn't stink."

"Mr Entwhistle, language!" Clarke snapped.

"It's fine, Mr Clarke. When I was in the Engine Room, I used language like that… and worse."

"You were an engineer? You actually know something about ships?" Entwhistle asked.

"I do," Malcolm said.

"Let me ask you, were you the type of engineer that give orders, but never dirtied his hands?"

"No, I was the kind that often got reprimanded for grease under my fingernails or on my uniform. Sometimes the only way to get a job done is by doing it yourself."

Entwhistle gave Malcolm an appraising stare. "Do you have any suggestions?"

"Not yet. For now, let's continue the tour."

Entwhistle nodded. They continued walking through the skeleton of the ship, pointing out its features; crew quarters, the mess, sick bay. They eventually reached the only part of the ship that looked near to completion. One wall held a stack of components in cabinets and to Malcolm's trained eye, they were all wired together. Malcolm quickly identified the steam turbine and saw that it fed the stack of components. Malcolm followed one set of lines to the reactor; a large metal torus that filled the room. Lines fanned out in every direction from the turbine. Several lines led to gigantic cones at the rear of the engine room.

"I'll tell you the little I know, sir," Clarke said. "The torus in the centre will contain a smaller torus within, completely wrapped in copper coils. When we provide power to the reactor, the coils create a magnetic field that helps contain the energy generated by the fusion. The outer torus heats the water that feeds the steam turbine. That, in turn, generates the electricity that powers the electro kinetic thrusters, those cones at the rear, and the capacitor bank," he said, pointing to the wall of cabinets. "The power from the turbine charges the capacitor bank, which creates a pulse that's fed into the gravity beam generator," Clarke said, as he pointed to a large cylinder mounted on the floor.

"Other than steam turbine and capacitor, I didn't understand a thing you just told me," Malcolm said.

"That makes two of us, sir," Clarke said. "I'm only repeating what I've heard from Mr O'Hallarhan, sir."

"Mr Clarke, in you estimation, what do we need to finish the ship?"

"Completing the hull is the priority; to do that, we need to weld the alloy to the ship's frame. If we can't do that, we won't be going anywhere. Once the outsides are built, we can finish the interior. Most of the infrastructure is in place; it's simply a case of making it useful."

"What about you, Mr Entwhistle? What do you think?"

Entwhistle appeared startled that Malcolm addressed him. "Yes, sir. I agree with Mr Clarke; we're not much of a ship if we don't have a hull."

"I agree. Do we have someplace where we can try things out?" Malcolm asked.

"Aye, sir," Entwhistle said. "We have a workroom where we fabricate most of the equipment. We have any tool we might need."

"Excellent. We'll meet at two bells and tackle the problem."

"Is there anything else, sir?" Clarke asked.

"No, thank you, Mr Clarke. Wait, actually there is. Can you direct me to the brig?"

"The brig?" Clarke asked before he realising Malcolm's intent. "Follow me, sir."

Clarke led him back into the offices, down several hallways before they descended a set of stairs. At the foot of the stairs, a Marine stood guard. Upon seeing the two officers, he saluted.

"Very good, soldier," Malcolm said, returning the salute. He turned to Clarke. "I'll see you this afternoon." Clark saluted and returned to the ship. Malcolm turned to the guard. "I'm here to see Commander O'Hallarhan."

"Yes, sir," the Marine said. He unlocked the door behind him and led Malcolm into another hallway, filled with evenly spaced steel doors with openings at eye level. They walked to the third door, which the Marine opened.

O'Hallarhan lay on a cot bolted to the wall. His youth again struck Malcolm. He looked at Malcolm before turning his head and staring at the ceiling.

"Shall we have a discussion or would you rather stay here a while longer?" Malcolm asked.

O'Hallarhan sighed. He sat up and glared at Malcolm. "What is it you want to discuss, sir?" he spat.

"Let me remind you that your current bunking arrangement directly resulted from your attitude. I admire your dedication to duty. I, myself, often ran late while performing my engineering duties. But I never deliberately disobeyed an order, or shown outright contempt to a superior officer."

O'Hallarhan was surprised. "You were an engineer?"

"Yes. Let me introduce myself. I'm Captain Malcolm Robertson, former captain of the *HMA Daedalus* and her former Chief Engineer." Malcolm offered his hand and, after a pause, O'Hallarhan shook it.

"That's a start. Tell me about yourself," Malcolm said.

"I suspect you've read my file. I attended Trinity College in Dublin on a scholarship. When I finished, I joined the Royal Navy. I started in ship design as an apprentice and worked my way up. The Admiralty selected me to lead the design and engineering of the first spaceship."

"Very impressive. Let me ask, how much practical experience have you had? Welding, fabrication, that sort of thing?"

"I've done my share," O'Hallarhan replied. Malcolm knew he was evading the question and that his engineering knowledge had little practical backing.

"I see," Malcolm said. "I understand that you're the expert on the Martian technology."

"Yes."

"Excellent. I look forward to learning how it works."

"You want to learn? Why?" O'Hallarhan asked. Malcolm smiled; he'd piqued O'Hallarhan's interest.

"I think a captain has to know his ship's capabilities. The captain needs to understand just how far he can push the ship. I've worked for too many captains with only a cursory knowledge of their ship. I never intend to be that captain."

"Aren't you too old to learn?" O'Hallarhan asked before quickly adding, "sir."

Malcolm smiled. "How old do you think I am?"

O'Hallarhan said, "I don't know, fifty-five?"

"Really?" Malcolm said. "I'm thirty eight. Not quite ready to collect my pension."

"I beg your pardon, sir. Your hair makes you look older."

"Yes, I have gone white prematurely," Malcolm said, acknowledging the souvenir from his encounter with an alien god. He paused. "Have you eaten yet?"

"I had some porridge this morning."

"Very good. You are released from the brig. Get a shower and join me for lunch in uniform."

"Are you sure, sir?" O'Hallarhan hesitated.

"Sharing a meal is the best way to learn about a person. When Commander Saxon and I first took command of the *Daedalus*, our meal time discussions helped us form our working relationship."

"I'm not much of a conversationalist," O'Hallarhan said.

"I'm not either," Malcolm said.

"In fact, I have a penchant for making people angry," O'Hallarhan said.

"All the more reason to join me and enjoy a meal together. Knowing the facts and being correct isn't enough if you anger people. It took me many years to learn that lesson." Malcolm smiled. "I'm still not always very successful; I, too, have a talent for angering people."

O'Hallarhan smiled for the first time. "You're certainly not what I expected, sir."

"I hear that often," Malcolm said.

CHAPTER TEN

After releasing O'Hallarhan, Malcolm went to the barber for a military standard haircut. He asked the barber to shave off his beard. After O'Hallarhan's comment about his presumed age, Malcolm decided he didn't want to look like Father Christmas. Feeling much more like a naval officer, he returned to his office, settled into his chair, and read reports when O'Hallarhan entered.

"Beg pardon, sir. I thought it best if I arrived early, sir," O'Hallarhan said after throwing a proper salute. He wore a proper duty uniform and his hair, although still not regulation, was slicked back and out of his face.

"Excellent, Mr O'Hallarhan. Have a seat; I'm reviewing these reports. I'll finish momentarily."

"I don't know how you do it, sir," O'Hallarhan said. "Paperwork drives me crazy. I think we spend more time creating paperwork than actually doing the work."

"It certainly seems that way. And it's taken me a long time to understand its importance. Each officer reports information from his staff. As you move up the chain of command, the information volume increases. It's vital that I know exactly what's happening. I evaluate the information and forward the relevant information to my commanding officer. That officer forwards the relevant information to his superior. And so it continues until it reaches the First Sea Lord." Malcolm closed the file. "That being said, I vehemently hate the paperwork, but I view it as a necessary evil."

O'Hallarhan smiled again. "If you say so, sir. I'd rather do something than write about it."

Malcolm smiled. He saw a young Malcolm in O'Hallarhan. O'Hallarhan had the same youthful arrogance, disregard for conventions, and the certainty of his opinions that Malcolm exhibited as a young ensign. It took him several hard lessons to change his ways, and he still struggled. He still retained a singular talent for angering his superior officers for offences both real and imagined.

O'Hallarhan noticed Malcolm staring. "What is it, sir?"

The comment brought Malcolm out of his thoughts. "Nothing. I was just thinking. Shall we go for lunch? You'll have to lead the way. I'm still learning my way around here."

"Yes, sir," O'Hallarhan said. As they walked, O'Hallarhan asked, "What do you think of your new command?"

"It's certainly interesting," Malcolm said.

When they arrived at the mess, several officers were already eating. Everyone looked up from their meals in astonishment that Malcolm entered with O'Hallarhan.

"As you were," Malcolm said. He whispered to O'Hallarhan, "You would think they saw a ghost."

"It's me," O'Hallarhan said. "I usually eat in my office or on the ship."

"We both need to eat here. You need to know everyone of these officers so they can help you do your job. Breaking bread with your fellow officers is an excellent way to build connections. Without Lieutenant Hughes, you wouldn't have the necessary supplies to complete your work; without Lieutenant Commander Clarke, there's no one to direct the work teams."

"What about Captain Macdonald?" O'Hallarhan said, nodding to the marine.

Malcolm thought for a moment. "When I figure it out, I'll let you know." O'Hallarhan smiled.

They sat at an empty table. The midshipmen arrived with their meals; baked fish with lemon and swedes. Malcolm ate his lunch, but noticed O'Hallarhan wrinkling his nose. "Something wrong with your meal?"

"Not really, sir. It's. just… we have this… often."

"Ah. I'll see what we can do to introduce variety into our meals."

"Good luck with that, sir. Every captain has tried without success."

"Where are you from?" Malcolm asked.

"Dunbur; it's a small village thirty miles south of Dublin. Actually, I grew up in the Wicklow Head Lighthouse; my da was the keeper."

"That's fascinating," Malcolm said.

"Not really," O'Hallarhan said. "It was bloody lonely. Unless I went to Mass or went to school, I only saw my parents. That's how I became an engineer. I helped my da keep the lighthouse in working order. I can't tell you how many times I polished the mirrors."

"It still sounds exciting."

"I assure you it wasn't. I don't know how I would survive if it weren't for books."

"Did you have any friends?"

"Not really," O'Hallarhan said. "I lived miles from the nearest village and there weren't any children nearby. I've always been an outsider; at school; at university; even, here."

"You don't have to remain an outsider. Trust me; I know how it feels to be an outsider. Being a Scot serving with British officers is an isolating experience."

"Try being Irish," O'Hallarhan said.

"Aye, it must be even worse," Malcolm agreed. "Do you have any family?"

"Aye, my mum and da still live in the lighthouse; I have a younger sister who is married and has three children. They live near Dublin."

O'Hallarhan turned his attention to his meal for several minutes before realising that the conversation had stopped. "What about you, sir?"

Malcolm smiled. His silence had drawn out O'Hallarhan. Malcolm relayed the abbreviated version of his biography; helping in his Granda's tinker shop as a young boy, going to university, joining the Royal Navy when his father couldn't work because of a crippling accident at the shipyard, and a quick synopsis of the ships and airships on which he served. Malcolm noted he kept O'Hallarhan's attention through the story.

"Permission to speak freely, sir," O'Hallarhan asked

"Permission granted," Malcolm said.

"Pardon me for saying, but you're unlike any officer, let alone captain, I've ever met," O'Hallarhan said. "No disrespect intended, sir."

Malcolm laughed. "None taken. I've been told that many times in my career." Malcolm sipped his tea. "Is that a good thing?"

"I don't know. It remains to be seen," O'Hallarhan said.

They finished their meal in silence. When they finished, Malcolm said, "I'm meeting Lieutenant Commander Clarke and Chief Petty Officer Entwhistle at two bells to discuss the hull problem."

"The hull problem?"

"Yes, the problem is our ship's hull is unfinished because they can't weld the alloy to the steel frame. I need your expertise to solve this problem."

"The engines need my undivided attention, sir," O'Hallarhan said.

"No, we need to finish the hull; without a ship, it won't matter how well the engines work."

"But, sir…"

"No, buts Commander. That is an order. We need your expertise in the hull alloy. We've wasted enough time struggling with this problem. This activity is all hands on deck. Until it's solved, continuing any other work is meaningless."

"But, sir," O'Hallarhan interrupted. "Shouldn't I apply my expertise on the Martian technology instead of working on the hull?"

"Ordinarily, I would agree. We have to complete the hull to complete this project. Besides, I understand you know the composition of the hull plating."

O'Hallarhan was silent, but he wouldn't meet Malcolm's gaze.

"What's the real reason that you don't want to join us?" Malcolm offered.

O'Hallarhan continued to avoid Malcolm's gaze. O'Hallarhan paused, considering his response. "I don't know how to weld, I mean, I understand the science, but I have little experience."

Malcolm nodded. O'Hallarhan's admission confirmed Malcolm's theory that O'Hallarhan wouldn't admit to ignorance on any subject. "Understood. I need your knowledge of the alloy and material science to solve the problem."

"Yes, sir." O'Hallarhan said.

"And Commander," Malcolm added.

"Yes?"

"Your secret is safe with me. However, starting tonight, after mess, I will provide you with private instruction in the practical art of welding."

"Is that necessary, sir?"

"Absolutely," Malcolm said. "If you're to be Chief Engineer on my ship, you need to be able to make repairs yourself."

"Isn't that why we have an engineering crew?"

"True. If a disaster incapacitates the crew, who's going to fix the ship?"

O'Hallarhan offered no response. "Commander," Malcolm continued, "in my experience, there are two types of engineers; engineers who learn by doing and engineers who learn from theory. I'm in the first group, you're in the second. I've found that the best engineers straddle both groups. It's a balance that I've striven to achieve throughout my career."

O'Hallarhan nodded, but offered no response. He still wouldn't meet Malcolm's gaze.

"Commander, I need to understand the Martian technology. Please develop a plan to teach me as soon as possible. I'm particularly interested in understanding how the reactor, the gravity beam drive, and electrokinetic thrusters work. Did I get that right?"

"Yes, sir." O'Hallarhan met Malcolm's gaze.

Malcolm stood up. "I'm going back to my office to deal with more paperwork. I'll meet you in the fabrication area?"

"Yes, sir," O'Hallarhan said, as he turned to leave.

"And Commander," Malcolm said.

"Yes?"

"Wear your engineering coveralls," Malcolm said.

CHAPTER ELEVEN

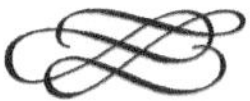

*J*ust before two bells, Malcolm returned to his quarters, changed into his engineering coveralls, and stopped at his office. "Mr Lennox, could you direct me to the fabrication area?"

Lennox jumped. "Blimey, sir, I didn't recognise you. I'm not used to a captain in work clothes."

"This may become a familiar sight, I'm afraid," Malcolm said. "Until we finish the ship, it's an all hands on deck effort, including me. Do you have engineering skills?"

"Sorry, sir, I'm useless with mechanical things. Filing and organising are my skills."

"And very useful skills they are. Who knows, Mr Lennox? We may see you in engineering coveralls yet."

"If you say so, sir."

"Would you direct me to the fabrication area?"

"Yes, sir," Lennox said. He led Malcolm to large double doors behind the construction area. Malcolm entered engineering heaven. Malcolm saw giant saws, welding stations, pneumatic hammers, forges, drill presses, grinding wheels, and racks of every tool imaginable. Everything an engineer needed to build tools or a spaceship.

65

Malcolm smiled; he felt like a kid in a candy store. Chief Entwhistle and Lieutenant Commander Clarke were patiently waiting at a welding station. They had locked a steel beam in a vise at a welding station and placed a large sheet of the alloy on the bench.

"I'd never thought I'd see a captain dressed in engineering coveralls," Entwistle said.

"Mr Entwhistle, that is enough," Clarke said sharply.

"It is fine, Mr Clarke," Malcolm said. "While I found coveralls, can you provide welding glasses and gloves?"

"Aye, sir," Entwhistle said. In moments, he handed Malcolm goggles and gloves. "Shall we start?"

"Just a moment. Commander O'Hallarhan will join us shortly."

"That's supposed to help, sir?" Entwhistle said.

Before Clarke interjected, Malcolm said, "Yes, Mr Entwhistle. I realise he's difficult, but we need his expertise with the alloy."

"If you say so, sir," Entwhistle said. "Here comes His Holiness now."

O'Hallarhan strode into the room, wearing his engineering coveralls. He carried his welding gloves and Malcolm noticed his hands free from the callouses and scars which marked Malcolm's hands.

"Thank you for joining us, Commander," Malcolm said. "We need to attach the metal sheet to the beam. Refresh my memory; what approaches have you tried?"

"We've tried bimetallic inserts, coating the steel with aluminum, coating the steel and the alloy with silver," Mr Clarke said. "We've tried forge welding, carbon arc welding, and oxyacetalyne welding. The metal would not stay together."

"I'm not surprised," O'Hallarhan interjected. "The alloy's melting point is much higher than steel. Without the proper heat, the alloy can't fuse with the steel. Even if it did, it would produce an intermetallic compound between the two metals, creating a weak point."

"We know that, *sir*," Entwhistle spat. "Do you have any… practical suggestions, sir?"

"Give me a minute," O'Hallarhan said. He stared at the metal and

Malcolm could see the wheels turning. "Have you tried using any of the Martian weapons? They might generate the heat necessary."

"Excellent idea; where can we find them?" Malcolm said.

"Locked up in the armoury, sir," Clarke said. "We don't have clearance to use them."

"I'll handle that," Malcolm said. "Commander O'Hallarhan, would you join me? You know what we might need."

"Yes, sir," O'Hallarhan said.

Malcolm and O'Hallarhan trudged to the Armoury, only for the Royal Marine on duty to refuse access without Captain Macdonald's direct orders. Sighing, Malcolm dispatched a passing ensign to bring Captain Macdonald to the Armoury.

"Why do you need Martian weapons?" Macdonald asked.

"We hope to use their technology to weld our ship together."

"You realise they destroy their targets," Macdonald said.

"Yes, I know," Malcolm said.

"Very well," Macdonald sighed. "Sign out anything you take. We keep these under the strictest control. The only reason I'm allowing it is because you are the commanding officer. It's on your head if anything goes missing."

"Understood, Captain," Malcolm said. "Thank you." The Royal Marine unlocked the door and moved aside. Malcolm and O'Hallarhan entered the room. An array of dozens of Martian weapons hung on the wall. Malcolm remembered his first time in the Martian spaceship, three years ago. The weapons filled him with the same awe and curiosity.

"What do you know about the weapons?"

O'Hallarhan lifted a weapon resembling a rifle. "This uses amplified light. It generates tremendous heat." He pointed to a smaller unit that resembled a handgun. "This generates ultrasonic sound waves whose vibrations destroy mammalian organs." O'Hallarhan pointed to an ominous-looking weapon. "And this generates a pure plasma beam."

"What would be most effective?" Malcolm said.

"I don't know," O'Hallarhan said. "Perhaps we should take all three?"

"I agree," Malcolm said. "No need to summon Captain Macdonald every time we need one. Can we build versions of these if they are suitable as a tool?"

"I created schematics for all the weapons, but I haven't built one."

"No time like the present." Malcolm signed for the weapons, and they hurried back to the fabrication room.

"Blimey," Entwhistle said, as Malcolm and O'Hallarhan laid the weapons on the workbench. "We want to weld them together, not blow them to kingdom come."

"We won't know until we try. How good of a shot are you?"

"I'm an engineer, not a marksman," Clarke said; Entwhistle and O'Hallarhan nodded in agreement.

"I guess that leaves me," Malcolm said. "Let's start with this one," he said, pointing to the rifle. "It uses the amplified light beam, correct? Can we control the beam strength? And also, which end do I point at the target?"

O'Hallarhan pointed to a dial just above the gun. "The dial controls the beam strength. Turning it to the left increases the strength; to the right decreases it. And," turning the rifle, "the rifle is now pointing away from you."

"Thank you, Mr O'Hallarhan, for the important safety tip," Malcolm said. He positioned his goggles. "You should put on your goggles now. I'll countdown from five and fire."

Malcolm pointed the correct end of his rifle at the intersection of the sheet and beam. "Ready? Five, four, three, two, one." The beam illuminated the entire room; even with his heavy welding goggles, the light nearly blinded him. He held the trigger for a second before releasing. When the light faded, Malcolm removed his glasses to examine the metal and frowned. At its lowest setting, it didn't harm the alloy, but cut a perfect hole in the beam.

Malcolm laid down the weapon carefully. "If nothing else, we can use this to make holes. What's next?"

O'Hallarhan pointed to the handgun. "Try this one. I think the plasma beam is too powerful."

"Very good. You said this was ultrasonic; do we need ear plugs?"

"No, sir. The sound emanates in a cone from the end. As long as it's pointed away, you shouldn't suffer any negative effects."

"Alright," Malcolm said. "Everyone stand behind me. Does the dial work the same way?"

"I believe so," O'Hallarhan said. "I haven't tested this weapon as thoroughly as the other two."

"Everyone ready?" Malcolm asked. After seeing a nod from the men, he focused on the target. He pulled the trigger for a second and released it. Malcolm examined the beam and found it attached to the metal. Malcolm applied additional pressure to the joint, and the beam shifted loose.

"Damn," Malcolm said. "I thought that did it."

"Don't be too hasty, Captain. I think you've found something," Entwhistle said. "You had a clean join. I think you didn't give it long enough. See the outline of the beam? It looks like it started to join, but the material hadn't bonded."

"Sir, I'll do metallurgic analysis on the beam and alloy, but I agree with Mr Entwhistle, you may have something here," Clarke said.

"The stopped clock is correct twice a day. Mr Entwhistle and Mr Clarke, analyse my weld. Mr O'Hallarhan, I'd like you to get the schematics for this weapon. In the meantime, I'll return the weapons to the armoury."

Twenty minutes later, Malcolm returned to the fabrication room and O'Hallarhan was waiting with the schematics. Malcolm unrolled them and studied them for several minutes.

"Anything you don't understand, sir?" O'Hallarhan said.

"No, I understand how to build it; I'm determining how it works. The power cell feeds the ultrasonic transducer. Is that a triode, amplifying the power?"

"Yes, sir."

"Right." Malcolm continued tracing the schematics. "Does the output of the transducer pass through several amplifiers to boost the output?"

"Yes, sir."

"I think I understand how this works. The output would flare out in a cone shaped distribution." O'Hallarhan nodded his assent. "Can we design something that produces a more focused beam?"

"Yes, sir," O'Hallarhan said. Malcolm let O'Hallarhan take the lead, and twenty minutes later, they had a design for a welding torch. They designed a large wand that delivered a concentrated beam of ultrasound at the wand's endpoint. A dial on the wand controlled the beam strength.

Clarke and Entwhistle returned as Malcolm and O'Hallarhan finished the design. Clarke handed Malcolm the metallurgical analysis. "Good news, Captain. It was a good weld; you just didn't give it enough time. The microscope analysis showed no intermetallic compounds. We've found our solution, sir."

"Excellent," Malcolm said. "Commander O'Hallarhan designed a prototype for an ultrasonic welder. Can we throw this together?" He passed the design to Clarke.

Clarke studied the schematics before nodding. "Yes, sir, we have everything we need to build this."

"Excellent. Mr Clarke and Mr Entwhistle, please fabricate the prototype. We'll experiment with the best combination of beam strength and time. Let me know when it's ready. I'm interested in the end result. Excellent work everyone. Commander O'Hallarhan, could you escort me to my office?"

"Yes, sir," O'Hallarhan said. He and Malcolm left the fabrication area while Clarke and Entwhistle studied the schematic.

After a minute, Malcolm turned to O'Hallarhan. "Do you know what just happened?"

"We solved the welding problem?"

"Yes, how did we do that?"

"You listened to my idea of using the Martian weapons."

"Had you offered that idea before? I'm sure they asked for your help in solving this problem."

"They did. I didn't think it was important, sir. I thought getting the reactor online was more important."

"What skills are required to become an engineer?"

"Engineering knowledge," O'Hallarhan said without hesitation.

"Yes, you certainly need to know what you're doing. In my experience, the most important skill is focusing on the most critical task. What's our mission? Why are we building this spaceship?"

"To return the Martian Crown Prince to Mars, sir?"

"Exactly. Which activity ensures mission success? Working on the fusion reactors or completing the ship's hull?"

"Completing the hull," O'Hallarhan said softly.

"Correct. You're a brilliant engineer, Commander. Your technical grasp of this technology is astonishing. But you lack the practical experience necessary to become a truly great Chief Engineer."

O'Hallarhan lowered his head. Malcolm continued. "I will make you a promise; if you teach me this Martian technology, I'll help you become the best Chief Engineer in the Space Service."

O'Hallarhan smiled. "I already am; we only have one ship."

"We don't have a ship yet, but God willing, we're on our way."

CHAPTER TWELVE

*A*fter evening Mess, O'Hallarhan arrived at Malcolm's office, dressed in his engineering coveralls. "Is now a good time, sir?"

"It's an excellent time, Mr O'Hallarhan," Malcolm said. He quickly donned his coveralls and grabbed the welding goggles and gloves that he took from the fabrication area. Malcolm was excited. He missed working with his hands.

Malcolm spent the next hour showing O'Hallarhan the key to welding; creating a good welding bead. By the end of the evening, O'Hallarhan was successful, although his welding bead needed improvement.

"I think we should stop for tonight," Malcolm said. "Would you join me in my quarters for a drink?"

O'Hallarhan cocked his head. "Why are you nice to me after you threw me in the brig the first time we met?"

"I wanted to get your attention. The success of this mission depends on the collective efforts of everyone. No one person is more important than anyone else. I wanted to instil it from the beginning. If I ignored the fact you disobeyed a direct order from a superior officer, I'd be a hypocrite for treating you differently from any other crew member. I'm being 'nice' to you because I think you're a brilliant engineer and have the makings of a good officer. You've spent all your time behind a desk and not working with others. In my experience, knowing how to work with others makes a successful officer. I solve problems collaboratively. I can't know everything; I rely on people with greater expertise. I won't lie; I see much of myself in you and I'm trying to spare you experiences I learned the hard way." Malcolm paused. "My offer for a drink was a social offer. It's not an order, just a chance to talk in a less formal structure. I'm going to my quarters. You can join me if you feel inclined, or stay in your quarters. I won't judge you either way." Malcolm picked up his goggles and gloves. "Until next time."

Malcolm stopped by his office to grab a stack of reports before he returning to his quarters. He changed out of his coveralls, poured two fingers of whisky, settled into one of the overstuffed chairs, and perused the reports when he heard a knock on his door. "Enter," Malcolm said.

O'Hallarhan entered, carrying a bottle. "I figured you preferred that hideous Scotch. I brought some real whiskey." O'Hallarhan lifted the bottle of Jameson so Malcolm could see the label.

Malcolm laughed. "I'm sorry, Commander O'Hallarhan, that might be grounds for court martial. Not everyone has the good sense to appreciate whisky, or even spell it correctly. Take a seat." O'Hallarhan poured himself a drink, sat next to Malcolm, and raised his glass in a toast. "Sláinte," he said.

"Sláinte," Malcolm responded, raising his glass. After taking a sip, "Tell me about university."

"I got top marks in all of my classes, even the ones I hated."

"Which were?" Malcolm prompted.

"The required Classics courses. I never saw the point of reading these dusty old books, let alone writing papers about them."

"Younger me would agree with you. But as I've aged, I've realised their value and I wish I'd paid more attention."

"Why?" O'Hallarhan asked.

"The classics illustrate our path through history. I think it's important to know the past as a guide for helping us forward."

"If you say so," O'Hallarhan said.

A knock on the door interrupted Malcolm's reply. "Enter."

Saxon entered the room, but stopped short when he saw O'Hallarhan. "I thought I'd update you over a drink, but I see you have company."

"Please, Charles, join us. Commander Charles Saxon, may I introduce Commander Peter O'Hallarhan?" They traded salutes and Saxon headed to the bar, where he made a gimlet. Malcolm left his chair for Saxon and sat on the edge of his bed.

"So, Charles, how was your day?"

"Tiring and chaotic. I spent the day with Lieutenant Hughes, struggling to understand the requisitioning system. To requisition anything requires a great deal of horse trading, which occurs outside approved channels. Our remote location means we have little to trade. I swear, it's a miracle we have supplies at all." Saxon sipped his drink. "I hope you had a good day."

"What do you think, Commander O'Hallarhan? Did we have a good day?"

"It was a good day, despite a terrible start. Thanks to Captain Robertson, the project may be on track."

"It wasn't just me," Malcolm said. "It was a group effort and you deserve as much credit as I do, Commander."

"Now that you're done congratulating each other on your brilliance, what happened?" Saxon asked.

Malcolm described the potential breakthrough in welding the alloy to the interior's steel beams. "Celebration is premature, but we have a way forward."

"That's good news," Saxon said. "Although it means I need to find a crew. Unless, of course, you would like to help, Captain?"

"No," Malcolm said, smiling. "You are much better suited to that task and I trust your judgement implicitly."

"I thought as much," Saxon said, smiling. "Don't let him fool you, Commander. He's the cruelest captain in the Service. He enjoys watching people suffer."

"I figure if I have to suffer, everyone else should suffer, too," Malcolm said.

"Are you always this informal, Captain?" O'Hallarhan asked. "I'm confused; You arrested me for disobeying orders, but you allow Commander Saxon to disparage your command."

"Commander, you're right. If I follow the letter of the regulations, I could throw Commander Saxon in the brig," Malcolm said. "And who knows? Maybe I will; the night's still young. The difference is that while we are on duty, I expect we observe the protocols regarding rank. These types of social gatherings are off the books."

"If I ranted about my treatment and incarceration, there wouldn't be repercussions?" O'Hallarhan asked.

"I'd let you speak your piece and then you get to hear my opinion stated in, shall we say, a less than diplomatic way. But, no. Short of a fist fight, I wouldn't throw you in the brig or bring up any disciplinary charges."

"But Commander Saxon just insulted you," O'Hallarhan said.

"I've known Commander Saxon a long time, and I know when he's joking. We take liberties in our relationship because we've served together and trust one another. I hope to extend that same trust to you, Commander O'Hallarhan."

O'Hallarhan sat for a minute before finishing his drink. "I better go. The captain might arrest me again if I am late for duty tomorrow." O'Hallarhan said it with a smile, but Malcolm couldn't help but notice an undertone of bitterness.

"Exactly what I was saying," said Saxon, who was smiling.

"Thank you for coming, Commander O'Hallarhan, even if you drink that poor excuse for whisky."

O'Hallarhan smiled as he left.

"What do you think of our Chief Engineer?" Malcolm asked.

"Hard to say. He resents you for his arrest and feels threatened by your success today. He's used to being the expert and you threaten his standing. Tread carefully, Malcolm."

"I'm trying very hard, Charles." Malcolm relayed O'Hallarhan's confession that he had no practical welding experience and Malcolm's efforts to hide that from the Engineering crew.

"I think you're handling the situation correctly. Just be wary; a wounded animal can be dangerous."

"Noted," Malcolm said. After sipping his drink, he asked, "Have you seen Joan today?"

"I saw her running this morning under the not so gentle tutelage of one of the Royal Marine sergeants. Commander Morris had her in classes all day. I imagine she's dead tired." Saxon finished his drink. "You know you can't check in on her."

"Yes, I know," Malcolm said. "Why do you think I've spent my time with the Engineering team? If I'm busy there, I'm not tempted to see her." Malcolm drained his glass. "We should be married, not trapped here, unable to see one another."

"Sometimes, Malcolm, life is a heartless bitch."

CHAPTER THIRTEEN

The next few days settled into a rhythm. Malcolm spent the mornings working with O'Hallarhan, Clarke, and Entwhistle, building the ultrasonic welding wands and experimenting to find the optimum process for welding the alloy. He spent the afternoons processing reports and meeting with the other staff. After dinner, Malcolm continued tutoring O'Hallarhan on the art and science of welding. After a few sessions, O'Hallarhan developed into a decent welder. The evenings ended with a drink with O'Hallarhan and Saxon. The cycle would repeat the next day.

After his first week, the Engineering crew completed a dozen ultrasonic welding guns. Now, the actual work began. Malcolm spent every morning welding with the Engineering crew to speed construction. Even O'Hallarhan used his newfound welding skills, working alongside the crew. After another week, the ship's hull gradually materialised.

After his third week, Malcolm stopped welding and focused on the remaining tasks necessary to finish the ship; the list felt endless. Despite the installation of the plumbing, the electrical wiring, and the data lines, much work remained. Although the equipment sat around the Engine Room, neither the steam turbine nor the reactor worked.

Malcolm continually studied the schematics, but still did not understand how the systems worked. The ships's overall design made no sense to Malcolm. He didn't understand the placement of the bridge in the ship's centre. The more he studied it, the more confused and exasperated he became.

He asked O'Hallarhan to explain. "Why put the bridge here?" Malcolm pointed at the ship's centre. "How will we see to navigate?"

O'Hallarhan sighed in exasperation. "If we use windows for navigation, we need this entire section for windows," he said, pointing at the ship's nose. Malcolm realised O'Hallarhan had this same conversation with every one of his predecessors.

"Yes, just like an airship," Malcolm offered in an attempt to demonstrate that he understood ship design principles.

O'Hallarhan rolled his eyes. "But this is not an airship. On a spaceship, windows are the hull's weakest point; a small piece of debris can break a window. The vacuum of space would suck the oxygen and the crew into space."

"How do we navigate if we can't see?" Malcolm asked.

"The Martian visual sensors relay images to the screen."

"How?"

"The visual sensors are a series of cameras. They turn the visual information into a data stream transmitted to the bridge via data cables. A computator reassembles the data on the screen."

"I still don't understand how the images show up on a screen,"

"The cameras turn the visual image into a collection of dots; encoded data denoting the colour and intensity of the light," O'Hallarhan explained with a tinge of condescension in his voice. "The sensors send the data to the bridge computator, which reads it and recreates it on the screen." O'Hallarhan paused. "You are familiar with computators, aren't you?" O'Hallarhan's tone was condescending, almost to the point of insubordination.

"Yes, of course," Malcolm grumbled. Malcolm had no love for computators. Malcolm completed his required course on computators by proving his slide rule more reliable than a computator. He developed a mathematical function that a slide rule could calculate, but caused two computators at the Royal Naval College to self destruct. He later used the same algorithm to disrupt the German computator network while escaping from Germany. "I don't trust them. Are redundancies built in? I don't relish the thought of flying blind."

"Yes, several visual sensors run along the ship's bow," O'Hallarhan said as he pointed to several symbols on the blueprints. "If you follow the data lines, they connect to two Martian computators feeding the screen display; one on the bridge, one in the engine room's auxiliary control."

"I'm still don't understand the design."

"You're thinking of airships. A spaceship has different design requirements."

"Such as?"

"In an airship, atmospheric pressure balances the ship's internal pressure. There is no pressure to counterbalance the ship's internal pressure in space. The ship's cylindrical shape forces the internal atmosphere to push equally in all directions, distributing the pressure across the hull," O'Hallarhan said, as if it was completely obvious. Malcolm felt his anger rise, but tamped it down.

"Aye, that makes sense," Malcolm said. "I understand that now." Malcolm paused before speaking. "Now that we're making progress on the hull, what are your recommendations for next steps?"

"We need to get the reactor and turbines online as soon as possible. We can't test the other systems until we can generate power."

"What does that entail?"

"We have to complete the torus. The torus creates the magnetic field that contains the super-heated gas, which generates the fusion reaction."

"What do we use as fuel?" Malcolm asked.

"Deuterium. We can extract that from sea water."

"Do we have a way to extract deuterium from sea water?"

"Yes, we have a process. We just need to build the system."

"Alright, something I can handle," Malcolm said. "Tell me what you need, and I'll assign personnel to work on the extraction process."

"First, we'll need to construct the deuterium tanks."

"Alright, we'll do that," Malcolm said. He stared at the blueprints. "Commander O'Hallarhan, I clearly don't know the next steps. Can you write a recommendation for the overall construction of the spaceship?"

"Yes, sir," O'Hallarhan said. "I have that nearly complete. You'll have it later today."

"Thank you," Malcolm said. "I will need your help to understand exactly what you need."

"I'll use small words," O'Hallarhan muttered.

"What was that?"

"Nothing, sir. Happy to oblige."

"That will be all, Commander." O'Hallarhan saluted and left Malcolm's office. Malcolm considered his interactions with O'Hallarhan. Malcolm sensed the simmering resentment from O'Hallarhan and the arrogance noted by his former commanders. Malcolm heard his remark, but ignored it. *Perhaps Charles was correct; he's still holding onto his embarrassment from being thrown in the brig. I'll have to watch him,* he thought.

Malcolm turned his gaze to the stack of papers and sighed before digging into the reports. He worked through the morning, not noticing he hadn't eaten, until his stomach growled. He checked his pocket watch and realised it was nearly 1:00 PM. He went to a deserted Officer's Mess, save for Joan. She frantically scribbled notes from several books scattered around her. Malcolm smiled at the way her nose crinkled when she concentrated and remembered a time on the *Daedalus* when Joan sat drawing him while he worked. He smiled and sighed. His smile faded as he realised they should be married and starting their life as husband and wife. He felt torn. He had settled back into the familiar role of captain and, although the work was daunting, he felt more alive than he had since his forced resignation from the Air Service. But the price of his contentment was separation from Joan. He realised now how heavy that price was.

Malcolm quietly walked to the counter, took a few sandwiches and a large mug of tea. He walked to her table. "Hello, Cadet. May I join you?"

Joan looked up and immediately jumped to her feet and threw a crisp salute, which Malcolm returned. "Yes, sir. I'm on my study break and Commander Murray suggested that the Officer's Mess would be a quiet place to study once everyone finished lunch."

"I'm sure. As you were, Cadet," Malcolm said as he sat across from her. He picked up a book, "The Royal Naval Handbook of Field Training. I remember that was quite the page turner," he said with a smile.

"If you say so."

"How is the training going?" Malcolm said before eating his sandwich. Sardines, yet again. He looked forward to eating something other than fish.

"I believe I'm through the worse. I passed my weapons training on the first day. The physical training has been tough; I've never run so much in my life. I'm learning military law, navigation, and operations. Tomorrow I have my final examination in hand-to-hand combat with Captain Macdonald."

"Really?" Malcolm said, raising an eyebrow. "When is that?"

"Four bells, forenoon," Joan said. Malcolm smiled, noting that she had learned the naval time keeping system.

"I'll clear my schedule. I can't wait to see his face when you drop him."

Joan smiled. Malcolm missed seeing that smile.

"I imagine he won't be thrilled with me if I do that," Joan said.

"It wouldn't hurt him to be taken down a peg."

"But it might break discipline," Joan replied. "His troops might lose respect if he's dropped by a woman."

"True. Take it easy on him, then." Joan stared at Malcolm. "What?"

"I have two weeks left until my commissioning. From what I understand, it's customary for a family member to pin the rank on the new officer. Would you pin on my rank?"

"It would be my honour, Cadet," Malcolm said. He whispered, "That's not the only way I'd like to pin you."

Joan smiled and winked. "Only if I let you."

"True enough." Malcolm finished his lunch and stood to leave. "Stay seated, Cadet. I'll leave you to your studies." He turned to leave, but stopped. "Cadet, if you need any assistance with your studies, I'd be happy to help."

"I know you would, sir," Joan said. "I can manage this." Malcolm turned as she said, "But thank you, sir."

The next day, Malcolm watched the clock so that he wouldn't miss Joan's exam in unarmed combat. Just before four bells, Malcolm walked to the training room. On one side sat racks of weights, neatly arranged. In another part of the room, three punching bags hung from the ceiling. In another corner was a boxing ring. But this morning, the centre of the room had been cleared and a number of padded mats were laid out for the upcoming examination. Joan was already waiting on the mats, dressed in padding, meant to minimise injury during training. Malcolm watched as Captain Macdonald entered wearing his workout clothes, but still carrying his revolver in his holster. When offered a padded shirt, he motioned it away. *He'll regret that tomorrow,* thought Malcolm. Macdonald stretched before taking his place. He looked up and saw Malcolm.

"Good morning, sir," Macdonald said after saluting. "I didn't expect to see you here."

"I thought I'd check on the cadet's progress. I'm a silent observer; pay no attention to me."

"Yes, sir," Macdonald said. "Cadet, are you ready for your final exam?"

"Sir, yes, sir," Joan said. Several of the Marines circled the mat to watch the match.

"Don't expect me to go easy on you, Cadet, just because you're a woman," Macdonald said.

"I expect no less, sir," Joan said.

"Let's begin." Joan walked to the centre of the mat. He pulled his revolver from his holster and pointed it at Joan. "You will disarm me. Begin."

Joan took a deep breath and leapt to action. She dropped under the revolver, swept her leg to trip the captain while grabbing the pistol and wresting it out of his hands. Malcolm had seen her do this many times, and she executed the move to perfection. Macdonald rose with a grim look on his face. He walked over to a Marine who handed him a knife.

"Cadet, disarm me." He stepped forward and slashed at Joan. She ducked under the slash, grabbed his arm, and twisted it behind his back. She brought up her knee and pulled his arm down. The force of the impact caused the knife to drop from his hands.

"Alright, Cadet, you can release me," he said. She let go of his arm and Macdonald quickly turned and kicked her legs out from under her. Malcolm felt his temperature rise, but he bit his lip, knowing he couldn't intervene.

"Don't lie around, Cadet. Get up."

Joan's eyes burned with fire, but she simply said, "Yes, sir."

"Let's assess your skill in hand-to-hand fighting." Macdonald entered a boxer's stance. "Come at me."

Joan put up her hands and advanced slowly. When she came within his striking distance, Macdonald threw a punch at her. She ducked down to a low squat and jumped up, wrapping her legs around his neck, and used the momentum to pull him down. She increased the pressure until he pounded the mat three times, the signal to disengage.

One of the Marines leaned to one of his friends. "I wouldn't mind getting taken down like that. I'd like to be trapped between those legs." Malcolm shot him a withering look, and the Marine quieted immediately.

"A most unorthodox tactic," Macdonald said as he rose. "Continue."

The sparring continued. Joan used her speed and agility to counteract Macdonald's size and strength. After each round, Malcolm saw Macdonald getting increasingly frustrated. The Marines in the crowd started muttering among themselves. Malcolm coughed and caught Joan's attention. He looked over at Macdonald, and Joan's gaze followed. She looked back at Malcolm and nodded slightly.

"Cadet, are you paying attention?" Macdonald bellowed. "Continue."

"Yes, sir," she said, taking a deep breath. She moved into attack

Macdonald, but pulled up short as she ducked under Macdonald's punch. His fist contacted her jaw, and she went down. He smiled and his men cheered.

"I think she's had enough," Macdonald said with a laugh. "You did well for a woman,"

Joan sat up, wiping away blood from her split lip. "Did I pass, sir?" she said. She kept her voice flat and respectful, but Malcolm saw her anger.

"You passed. Report to Dr Boyce and have him examine that cut. Dismissed, Cadet."

"Yes, sir," she said as she saluted him. Malcolm waited for Macdonald to rejoin his men before he went to Joan, picking up a towel and handing it to her.

"Excellent job, Cadet," he said.

"For a woman?"

"For anyone," Malcolm said. When Macdonald and his Marines left, Malcolm lowered his voice. "Thank you for throwing the last match. You were making Macdonald look like a fool in front of his men."

"He was," she spat.

"Aye, that's true, but he can't appear weak before his men. Thank you."

"My jaw certainly doesn't feel any gratitude," she said, rubbing in gingerly. "Thank you for your concern, Captain," she emphasised. "I'll be fine."

"All the same, Cadet, please have the doctor examine you in sick bay."

"Yes, sir," she said and threw him a salute. Malcolm noted the hint of a smile and returned the salute.

CHAPTER FOURTEEN

As promised, Commander O'Hallarhan arrived at Malcolm's office with his assessment detailing the next steps to complete the spaceship. Malcolm skimmed through it as O'Hallarhan condescendingly summarised the report.

"The first step will be extracting deuterium from the sea water. We distil the sea water and pump it into this tower at room temperature. We pump in hydrogen sulphide gas, which attracts the deuterium. The system pumps the gas into a hot tower where we add unfiltered water and the deuterium returns to the water. We pump it back into the original tower and repeat the process until we have a sufficient concentration of deuterium in the water."

"I see," said Malcolm, who didn't fully understand the chemistry involved, but it made sense. "How do we separate the deuterium from the water?"

"Simple electrolysis," O'Hallarhan said. "The electrical current separates the deuterium from the oxygen in the same way we separate hydrogen and oxygen."

"Won't that be a little dangerous?"

"This whole endeavour is dangerous, sir. If the fusion reaction occurs and we can't control it, it will destroy this entire island."

"I see," Malcolm said. "Alright, what's next?"

"We should finish the magnetic torus. We can test it if the base generators provide enough power."

"We won't really know if the one thing that regulates the reaction is working until we try it?"

"Aye, sir."

Malcolm rubbed his temples. He didn't understand the technology, and it made him uneasy. He sympathised with his previous commanding officers when he explained the engineering principles that they simply did not understand. "How is the hull coming along?"

"I'd say we've completed twenty percent, sir."

"When should we start on the deuterium extraction?"

"Soon, sir, although I recommend we complete the hull section around Engineering. It would minimise the damage if something went wrong."

"I agree. Have the construction crew complete the hull around the Engineering section. Meanwhile, I'll get the materials we'll need to complete the deuterium extraction."

"I've laid that all out in Appendix C, sir."

Malcolm leafed through the report. "So you have. Excellent work, Commander."

"Thank you, sir," O'Hallarhan said.

When O'Hallarhan left, Malcolm sent for Saxon so they could review the requisition list. As Saxon read through the list, Malcolm relayed his conversation with O'Hallarhan. Saxon's brow darkened as Malcolm recounted the various dangerous scenarios left in the ship's construction.

"Do you believe you can get the supplies?"

"I'm not sure; I don't know what half the items are. However, Lieutenant Hughes is quite talented at requisitioning. Although you should talk to the Commodore. His rank might provide our request extra urgency."

"I'll do that today. How are things going otherwise?"

"As well as we could expect. I've gone through the personnel files and I believe I will have the potential crew list by next week. I'm starting with a rather large pool."

"Why?"

"This is an extremely dangerous mission. We're travelling into the vacuum of space using technology we don't understand on a ship that's basically powered by a controlled explosion. What could go wrong?" Saxon quipped.

"Point taken. Any candidates within the current staff?"

"I think we will have interest. But Lieutenant Hughes has told me he has no interest."

"Really?" Malcolm said, arching an eyebrow.

"His first assignment was this cave; he wants to see the world."

"I certainly understand. I wouldn't want to be stuck on this rock at his age. Speaking of personnel, did you know Joan passed her hand-to-hand combat exam?"

"No. Did you see it?"

"I did," Malcolm said. He described the bout and Joan's decision to throw the last round.

"A wise move. You don't want to anger a Marine Captain before you're a lieutenant. But she won't thank you for your suggestion."

"I know. She will make me pay, I'm sure."

"I'm certain," Saxon said. "Speaking of stormy relationships, how are you getting along with O'Hallarhan?"

"Well enough. I believe you're correct that he still holds a simmering resentment."

"How so?"

"Little things he mutters and doesn't think I hear. And his tone can be condescending."

"You aren't the only one who gets that treatment."

"Agreed. I'm watching him closely," Malcolm said. "And speaking of watching, are we any closer to finding the Admiralty's informant?"

"No, I haven't tackled that matter. I've been struggling with every-thing else. Should I pursue that?"

"Not right now. We're making progress and we have had no more Admiralty interference. Let's not poke that wasp's nest until needed."

"Very good. I actually didn't need another task right now," Saxon said.

When Saxon left, Malcolm asked Midshipman Lennox to arrange a meeting with Commodore Dexter, who suggested a dinner meeting in his private mess. Malcolm drafted the schedule for the construction's next phases until dinner.

Malcolm checked his uniform before knocking on the door of the Commodore's private mess. "Enter," he heard.

"Captain Robertson, reporting as ordered, sir," Malcolm said as he threw a salute.

"At ease, Captain. We haven't talked in person since you first arrived. You certainly have thrown yourself into your assignment."

"Thank you, sir," Malcolm said, although he couldn't tell if the Commodore meant it as a statement or a question.

"Please, sit," Commodore Dexter said.

Within moments, a midshipman brought Malcolm a glass of whisky. "Thank you."

"I never knew a Scot who didn't prefer whisky. I don't like it, but I've been told it's good."

"That it is," Malcolm said. He didn't dare tell the Commodore that it tasted like a watered down blend compared to the Auchentoshan back at his quarters. But, as his mother always said, beggars can't be choosers.

"Tell me, how is the construction going?"

"I believe we're making progress, sir." Malcolm summarised the current accomplishments and the plans for the immediate future.

"It seems we have the right man for the job," Commodore Dexter said, sipping his wine. "You have made more progress than all of your predecessors combined."

"Thank you, sir."

"How is your relationship with Commander O'Hallarhan?"

"I believe we have a good working relationship. On the whole, I trust his judgement and he's given me no reason to think differently."

"Excellent. I worried that after your initial actions, that O'Hallarhan might hold hard feelings."

"I can't speak for Commander O'Hallarhan, but I have no hard feelings."

"Excellent," Dexter said.

They sat silently before Malcolm got the nerve to ask, "How is Cadet de St. Leger's training going?"

Dexter smiled. "Commander Murray tells me she's doing admirably, especially for a woman. I understand she acquitted herself well in her hand-to-hand combat exam with Captain Macdonald, but you already know that."

"Yes, sir," Malcolm said. He felt the heat rushing to his cheeks. "I encountered the Cadet in Officer's Mess during her study break yesterday and she mentioned her exam was today."

"It's a small base, and I know everything that happens. And I mean everything," Dexter said. Although Dexter smiled, Malcolm understood the implicit threat. The midshipman arrived with their dinner. Malcolm was surprised when the midshipman brought roast beef, Yorkshire pudding, mashed potatoes, and green beans.

"One of the few perks I have as Commodore," Dexter said. "And having an enterprising lieutenant keen to impress his superior officer. Please, go ahead."

Malcolm's mouth watered at the sight of beef. O'Hallarhan had been correct; meals were mostly fish, or the rare piece of lamb. Although Malcolm had nothing against fish, he couldn't care less if he ever ate fish again.

"Have you made progress in unmasking the Admiralty's informant?" Dexter asked.

"No, sir. Commander Saxon and I have been busy getting things back on track, and since we've seen no additional interference, it hasn't been our top priority. Why? Should we look into it?"

"No, Captain, I agree with your priorities. We must finish the ship and prepare to leave as soon as possible."

"How is the Martian Crown Prince?" Malcolm asked.

"Still holding his own. His condition has not improved, but it hasn't deteriorated."

"I hope that buys us time. I fear it will be months before we have a ship that we can test, let alone fly."

"It's a daunting task, but I'm sure you will rise to the occasion."

"Thank you, sir."

Several minutes passed as the men ate their meal in silence. After eating a diet almost entirely of fish since he arrived at the base, nothing tasted as good as the roast beef. After the midshipman cleared their dishes, he brought out glasses of port with bowls filled with trifle. Malcolm wished it was more whisky because he never liked port, but drank it anyway. He had no trouble eating the trifle.

As they sipped their port, Commodore Dexter regarded Malcolm. "How are you finding your return to service?"

"Fine, sir. It's very easy to fall back into the routine. To be honest, I've missed it."

Commodore Dexter chuckled. "I wish I still had your love for the Service. Truthfully, I'm considering retirement. I had hoped that I would serve at the Admiralty at this point instead of this rock. I still may get my chance, but I fear that time is not on my side." He sipped his port. "What about you, Captain? What are your career ambitions?"

"To be honest, sir, I haven't thought about it. As you know, I've only just returned."

"Surely you have career aspirations?"

"Truthfully, I never thought I'd even become a captain. My first love is engineering, and I thought that if I was extremely lucky, I might serve as a Captain of Engineering. When I assumed command of the *Daedalus*, I was lost. But I learn by doing and I feel I grew into the role. Now, I don't see myself doing anything else but commanding a ship. Although I thought my next command would be an airship, not a spaceship." Malcolm sipped his port. "Commodore, many in the Admiralty don't think I should serve as captain, let alone aspire to a higher rank."

"Captain, let me speak plainly," Dexter said. "I want to leave this assignment and return to England. I have not seen my wife in nearly two years. I need a successor who can finish the job. As you might have guessed, the Admiralty uses this base to conduct research and development on many new ships, be they naval, air, or space. I'd like you to be my successor and run this base. It seems like a position well suited to your talents. I'm also very impressed with your command skills. The project is progressing well under your leadership. I know that your suggestion allowed Captain Macdonald to save face. As I said, it's a tiny base and nothing escapes my notice. I believe you are the most qualified candidate I've seen." He sipped his port. "What do you think, Captain?"

"I'm a little taken aback, sir," Malcolm said. "This is a tremendous opportunity and I'm honoured that you would extend such an offer. Do you think it would even be possible, given my detractors in the Admiralty?"

"I believe it can happen. This mission is crucial to the security of His Majesty's government. Dare I say, even the world's security?"

"I need to ponder my decision, sir," Malcolm said. "There are... other considerations."

"Yes, Cadet de St. Leger. You were to be married this past month, correct?"

"Yes, sir."

"Think about this offer. Meanwhile, I'll broach the matter with Admiral Beatty. To be blunt, I'm doing this for purely selfish reasons, but I see no reason that you shouldn't benefit."

"Thank you, sir. I will consider this offer seriously." Malcolm paused. "Do I have your permission to talk to Cadet de St. Leger? My decision impacts her as much as it impacts me."

"I understand. As long as you just talk, I have no issues," Dexter said. "Anything else you need, Captain?"

"Yes, sir. I'd like your help to lend weight to our request for additional supplies. Commander Saxon has a list of items we need to continue the next phase."

"Absolutely," Dexter said. "Please have him provide the list to Commander Murray, and I will use whatever influence I have to expedite the supplies. However, you might see a Commodore's rank is not as weighty as it might appear. Anything else you need?"

"Not at the moment, sir."

"Very good. Think about my offer, Captain. Shall we meet in another two weeks? After Cadet de St. Leger's commissioning?"

"Yes, sir. Thank you once again. I'm deeply honoured and I will consider this carefully."

"Very good. If that's all, I'll bid you a good evening."

Malcolm returned, his mind swimming at the genuine possibility that he could become a Commodore. He would need to consider how he would brooch this subject with Joan.

CHAPTER FIFTEEN

onstruction progressed around the ship's Engineering section and within a week, the construction crew completed the Engineering outer hull. Malcolm reasoned if a disaster occurred during deuterium processing, it would minimise the damage to the ship. O'Hallarhan balked at Malcolm's recommendation, but Malcolm overrode his objections and the crew reinforced the wall containing the Engineering bulkhead with the alloy.

Throughout the week, his discussion with Commodore Dexter kept interrupting his thoughts. When Malcolm inspected the ship, he imagined himself running the entire base. During his meetings with the Commodore, he imagined himself sitting at the Commodore's desk. Malcolm used work to avoid his difficult discussion with Joan. As the week ended, he knew he could procrastinate no longer and scheduled a meeting with Joan to discuss the Commodore's offer. While he looked forward to seeing Joan, he simultaneously dreaded the conversation.

On the afternoon of his meeting with Joan, Malcolm found it impossible to focus on anything other than his discussion with Joan. He was pacing behind his desk when Midshipman Lennox knocked on his door and escorted Joan inside. She threw a crisp salute, which

Malcolm returned. "Thank you, Mr Lennox, that will be all. Cadet, please take a seat." She sat at proper military attention, showing Malcolm how well she had acclimated to military life. Even dressed in her unflattering uniform, Malcolm found her intoxicating, which only increased his anxiety and dread.

"What can I do for you, sir?" Joan said.

"I need to discuss a personal matter with you, Joan. We can dispense with the formalities."

Joan let out a breath and relaxed into her chair. "Malcolm, it's such a relief to dispense with the rigid military protocol, even momentarily."

Malcolm smiled. "I know it's been gruelling, especially given the time frame. But from all reports, you are performing admirably."

"Thank you, Malcolm. What do you want to discuss?"

"I don't know how to begin." He relayed his conversation with Commodore Dexter. Joan listened intently and when he finished, she leaned back, crossed her arms, and scowled.

She stared at him intently for several moments. "What did you tell him?"

"I told him we needed to talk before I could give him my decision. That's why we're meeting; we need to make this decision together."

"Is it something you want?"

"I don't know, maybe?" Malcolm said. "I never thought I could become a Commodore. This opportunity may not happen again. I'd be foolish to turn it down, but I have strong reservations about accepting it."

"Such as?"

"Our life together. If I accept the Commodore's offer, it means I'll rarely leave the base. If we thought it was difficult to meet between our duties in the Secret Service and the Air Service, I fear this would be a thousand times worse."

"I see," she said with no emotion.

"Joan, I love you and I want to marry you, truly. I don't know what to do. This affects both of our lives; we need to make this decision together."

"Malcolm, this is an impossible situation. If I tell you to accept, we may never get married. If I tell you no, I fear that you'll resent losing the opportunity."

"I know," he whispered. "I have the same predicament; if I accepted without telling you, you would hate me. Likewise, if I turned it down without telling you, you would be mad that I gave up the opportunity."

She looked at him before sighing in exasperation. "You're right. This isn't easy for either of us. When does the Commodore want your answer?"

"He wants my decision immediately after your commissioning."

"I see. Are you expecting a decision right now?"

"No. You need time before we make our decision."

"Malcolm, I can barely cope with completing my training, and now we have to make a life-changing decision. I don't know how I'll be able to consider anything."

"I'm sorry. The timing is awful. I never sought this; it just happened."

"I know," she said. She smiled. "You always seem to attract attention."

Malcolm laughed. "Must be my charming personality," he said, causing Joan to laugh. He rose and moved next to her, gently taking her hand. "I love you, Joan. If I decline this opportunity, but I have you, I will be content."

She squeezed his hand and leaned against him. "I know. But what about those days when I'm difficult and we quarrel? I don't want you looking at me and seeing lost opportunities."

"You? Difficult?" Malcolm smiled.

She lightly punched his ribs. "You know, you're not the easiest person to get along with, either."

"I'm well aware." Silence fell between them as they leaned into one another.

Malcolm wanted nothing more than to sit here, holding Joan's hand, but he forced himself away. "I've kept you long enough. We wouldn't want rumours spreading that I'm fraternising with our cadet."

"I wish we could fraternise. I really miss our fraternisations," she said in that husky voice that drove him crazy.

"As do I," Malcolm said. They stared into each other's eyes. "That's all, Cadet. I look forward to your commissioning next week."

"I do, too, Captain," she said. "I can't wait to be pinned," she said with a wink. She stood, threw a smart salute, and left his office.

Malcolm returned to his desk and stared at the pile of reports, willing himself to work, but found he couldn't concentrate. His thoughts were consumed by Joan and his decision. Until now, he easily compartmentalised his feelings for Joan from his daily work, but this decision made it impossible. Malcolm forced himself back to work, but struggled to complete anything. That night at the Officer's Mess, Saxon approached Malcolm and asked, "What's wrong, Captain? You look miserable."

"I can't talk about it here. Come to my quarters after dinner," Malcolm said in a low voice.

After dinner, the two returned to Malcolm's quarters and, after fixing their drinks, Saxon said, "What's bothering you, Malcolm?"

"I shouldn't tell you, but I need your word that this stays between us."

"You know me, Malcolm. I'm an expert secret keeper."

Malcolm nodded and recounted his conversations with the Commodore and Joan. Saxon listened and when Malcolm finished, Saxon sat, lost in thought, before he said, "Don't worry about it, Malcolm. I think I can make this decision simpler."

"How?" Malcolm said.

"At the moment, I can't say. You say the Commodore wants your answer after Joan's commissioning?"

"Yes."

"That gives me enough time. Malcolm, don't worry, I've got this."

"How?"

"That's my secret."

CHAPTER SIXTEEN

Although still troubled, Malcolm took Saxon at his word and threw himself back into his work. He wished he could tell Joan that Saxon thought he had a solution to their dilemma, but he didn't know what Saxon was thinking.

The week flew by and it was time for Joan's commissioning ceremony. Malcolm put on his dress uniform, complete with his medals: the Air Service Cross, Conspicuous Gallantry Cross, the Victoria Cross, and the medal designating him as a Knight Commander of the Order of St. Michael and St. George. He inspected his uniform and left for the ceremony in the assembly area.

The entire base turned out in their dress uniforms; it looked like a proper military base instead of a construction site. Malcolm saw looks of disbelief on several of the officers' faces when they saw his decorations. He saluted the Commodore and took his place next to him.

Commodore Dexter leaned to him and whispered, "Do you have an answer for me?"

"Not yet," Malcolm said. "I promise you an answer by tomorrow." He was terrified. With everything going on and Saxon's promise, he hadn't given it any additional thought. And now he just promised the Commodore an answer by tomorrow.

"I look forward to it," Dexter said. "You must be very proud of her."

"I am," Malcolm said.

The boatswain signalled all to attention. At the far end of the assembly area, Joan stood at attention, dressed in her dress uniform; it was nearly identical to Malcolm's; a navy blue double-breasted coat, a long navy blue skirt, and an officer's cap. She carried a sword on her hip and a rifle over her shoulder. She stood at perfect attention. Despite the masculine nature of her outfit, Malcolm thought she'd never looked lovelier.

The boatswain gave the signal, and Joan marched quietly to the reviewing area. When she reached the assembly area, she turned crisply and stood at attention. Commodore Dexter addressed the crowd. "Today, I have the distinct honour of welcoming Joan de St. Leger to the Royal Fleet Auxiliary, earning the rank of Lieutenant." He pulled Joan's commission from his binder and read aloud. "By the Commissioners for Executing the Office of Lord High Admiral of the United Kingdom. To Joan de St. Leger hereby appointed a Lieutenant in His Majesty's Fleet. By Virtue of the Power of Authority to us given by His Majesty's Letters Patent under the Great Seal, we do hereby constitute and appoint you a Lieutenant in His Majesty's Fleet. Charging and Commanding you in that rank or in any higher rank to which you may be promoted to observe and execute the King's Regulations and Admiralty Instructions for the Government of His Majesty's Naval Service and all such Orders and Instructions as you shall from time to time receive from Us or from your Superior Officers for His Majesty's Service. And likewise, Charging and Commanding all Officers and Men subordinate to you according to the said Regulations Instructions or Orders to behave themselves with all due respect and obedience to you, their Superior Officer. Given under our hands and the Seal of the Office of Admiralty. By Command with Seniority of Prince Louis, First Sea Lord."

"Captain Sir Malcolm Robertson, please present the Lieutenant with her rank." Dexter handed Malcolm the shoulder boards, showing the rank of lieutenant. Malcolm stepped forward and pinned the shoulder boards to her shoulders and threw his crispest salute. "Congratulations, Lieutenant."

"Thank you, sir," Joan said as she returned the salute.

"Three cheers for the newest lieutenant in the Royal Fleet Auxiliary," Commodore Dexter said. A meagre cheer rose from the ranks; the majority of the crew did not approve of a woman officer.

"Please join me in a reception for our new lieutenant in the mess hall. Assembly dismissed," Commodore Dexter announced.

A small group of officers offered their congratulations to the newly minted lieutenant, preventing Malcolm from approaching Joan. When the crowd thinned, Malcolm made his way to Joan. "Congratulations, Lieutenant."

"Thank you, sir," she said.

"May I have the honour of escorting you to the reception?"

"I would be honoured, sir," she said.

Saxon came over and threw a sharp salute. "Congratulations, Lieutenant."

"Thank you, sir," she replied.

"When the reception winds down, perhaps we can meet in the Captain's office? I have a surprise for both of you," Saxon said with a bemused smile.

Joan looked at Malcolm. He threw his hand up in defeat. "Don't look at me. I have no idea what his surprise is."

"Good things come to those who wait," said Saxon.

The reception was a modest affair, a poorly decorated cake, biscuits, and punch. The officers made their obligatory appearance and, one by one, they left the reception until only Saxon, Malcolm and Joan remained.

"I think it's the time for my surprise. I'll meet you in the Captain's office momentarily." Saxon left, and Malcolm and Joan stared after him in confusion.

"I wonder what he is up to," Joan said.

"Damned if I know," Malcolm said. "Shall we go?"

As Malcolm and Joan walked to his office, it was all he could do to prevent himself from taking her hand. But remembering the

Commodore's warning about the size of the base, he kept at least an arm's distance between himself and Joan.

They waited in the office for several minutes before Saxon returned with a huge stack of papers wrapped in a bow. Three quarters of the way through the stack, he had placed a piece of ribbon.

"What is this?" Joan asked.

"My present to you both," Saxon said. "Malcolm told me about the Commodore's offer and the distress it was causing both of you. I believe I have a solution. As you know, they tasked me with developing the regulations for His Majesty's Space Service. Not a task I particularly enjoyed until now. If you will, please look at the section I marked with a ribbon.

Malcolm and Joan untied the bundle and carefully set the stack of papers on Malcolm's desk. As they read through the section Saxon had noted, they both smiled.

"Since I had to write the regulations, I decided that the best way to remove the burden of the decision was to allow married personnel to serve together. So in Book Thirty One, Section Three, Paragraphs Fourteen and Fifteen, I laid out the framework for that to occur. There may be some question about one spouse reporting to another. Since our lieutenant is a member of the Royal Fleet Auxiliary and only attached to this command, I think we can get around it. Besides, there are hundreds of years of precedent allowing the wives of ship captains to join the captain. The Admiralty outlawed that long ago, but since the wife in question is also an officer, I think this will work."

"Oh, Charles, I could kiss you! Thank you!" Joan said.

"That won't be necessary. I just don't want to see Malcolm moping around here anymore. That's thanks enough for me."

"Thank you, Charles," Malcolm said, shaking Saxon's hand. Malcolm turned to Joan. "What do you think? Should I take the Commodore's offer?"

"I don't see why not. I'm sure that given your new rank, you can keep me here. Although, I will miss London. And the food."

"Welcome to the Service," Saxon said. "Poor food is the lot of a sailor. I will distract the Midshipman so that you have a moment alone."

When Saxon shut the door, Joan flew into Malcolm's arm and gave him a kiss for the first time in weeks. Malcolm returned the kiss, but pulled away before it became too inflammatory.

Malcolm looked into Joan's eyes. "Are you sure about this?"

"I think so; I'm willing to give this adventure a try, since I know I can be part of it."

"Let's go tell Commodore Dexter about our decision."

They left Malcolm's office and went to see the Commodore. After several minutes, they were let in.

"I'm surprised to see you both here. What can I do for you?"

"I… we have made our decision," Malcolm began. "I will accept the position as Commodore on one condition."

"Which is?" Dexter asked.

"That the Admiralty approves the regulations that Commander Saxon has drafted for the Space Service, particularly Book Thirty One, Section Three, Paragraphs Fourteen and Fifteen, which allow married personnel to serve together."

Dexter chuckled. "That's a rather ingenious approach to the problem. That never occurred to me. I can't promise anything, but I will do everything in my power to see that they approve the section as written."

"Thank you, Commodore," Malcolm said.

"Lieutenant de St. Leger, may I have a minute with Captain Robertson?"

"Yes, sir," she said.

When Joan left, Dexter looked at Malcolm. "If they grant you the rank of Commodore, there is something you should know. I was the mole for the Admiralty."

Malcolm was stunned. After a moment, he asked, "You, sir?"

"Yes. I was desperate to leave this posting. By favouring the other elements of the Admiralty, I thought I might find a posting of my own choosing. To be honest, I was not confident that you could pull this project back together. I've watched experienced captains fail at this assignment and, truth be told, I didn't think that you would succeed. But imagine my surprise when, within a week, construction began on the hull and you seemed to get Commander O'Hallarhan focused on the tasks at hand. That is no mean feat. I realised I was no longer the best officer for this posting and that you would do a better job. And, since I can't wait for the day I'm off of this rock, it seemed logical to pursue this option."

Dexter continued, "I'll wire Admiral Beatty tonight and suggest you replace me as base commander with the promotion to Commodore. I'll also talk to my other Admiralty contacts and suggest that your command of a base in the middle of nowhere will keep you out of sight. The price of that convenience will be your promotion. I think I'll be able to make both cases effectively."

"I'm at a loss for words, sir," Malcolm said.

"Although I'd like to pretend I have altruistic intentions, I'm tired of this assignment. I think this base needs your energy and drive, and I'm happy to leave it in your hands."

"I'm honoured, sir."

"Very good, Captain. If there is nothing else, we should return to our duties."

CHAPTER SEVENTEEN

*N*ow that Joan was part of his group of officers, Malcolm was happy to see her on a more regular basis, but it made it that much harder to maintain military discipline. Every time he looked at her, he still felt the despair that they couldn't be together. Joan's first assignment was a course in radio operations, given her future position as Communications Officer. This involved learning a great deal of theory and practical application. Part of that practical application involved going topside and inspecting the antenna for any damage and making necessary repairs.

Within a month, the supplies arrived to complete the work on the Engineering section. In the meantime, the crew had made significant progress on the hull and the Malcolm could see the ship taking shape. Malcolm spent his mornings working with the engineering crew, beginning the work to set up the deuterium processing station and the deuterium tanks while O'Hallarhan took a smaller crew and directed work on the magnetic torus. Besides making sure that the torus had exact dimensions and curves, they also had to work with strong magnetic materials such as samarium cobalt. The material was devilishly difficult to work with and the team had to develop a whole new set of non metallic tools after one of the construction team nearly had his hand ripped off when he approached the material with a wrench.

Work settled into a regular pace and Malcolm could see measurable progress. As the work continued, Commodore Dexter met regularly with Malcolm, both to receive updates and to talk to Malcolm about the logistics of running the base. One day, three months after Malcolm's acceptance of the offer to become base commander, Dexter summoned him to his office.

"I have good news for us both," Dexter said. He handed Malcolm a packet. "These are your new orders, confirming you as the commander of this base, with a promotion to the rank of Commodore. And these," he said, brandishing his own order packet, "are my orders, assigning me to Admiral Beatty's office in the Admiralty. Congratulations, Commodore."

"I don't know what to say, but thank you," Malcolm said, staring at his orders in disbelief.

"I leave in two weeks, so I have to tear you away from construction to work out the transition details."

"Two weeks? That doesn't give us much time," Malcolm said.

"That's why I've been tutoring you in base logistics for the past three months. All that's left is to work out the transition details."

"Will I need to find a new captain for the ship?"

"No," Dexter said. "Those orders remain the same. You will take command of the new spaceship and ensure that the Crown Prince returns to Mars. You may, at your discretion, advance someone to captain, but that isn't necessary. The Admiralty felt that having a high-ranking officer leading the mission might impress the Martians."

"How difficult was the decision to promote me?"

"Admiral Beatty was onboard from the very beginning. While many in the Admiralty initially opposed it, once I explained you would be out of sight, they rankled less at the thought of making you a Commodore. Frankly, the Admiralty approved it within two weeks, but as you know, the bureaucracy grinds slowly in the Admiralty."

"I don't know if I should feel honoured or insulted," Malcolm said.

"Probably a little of both," Dexter said. "Congratulations, Commodore." Dexter extended his hand, which Malcolm shook.

"Thank you, sir."

The two weeks flew by quickly, with Malcolm spending large swaths of his time with the Commodore. Malcolm spent very little time overseeing the construction, turning that responsibility back to Commander O'Hallarhan. The only times he saw Joan were doing his routine staff meetings and occasionally, they shared a meal in the Officer's Mess, both too tired to talk much.

Once again, the base assembled, this time for Malcolm's promotion and his assumption of command of the base. Wearing his dress uniform for the second time in almost four months, Malcolm stood at attention in front of everyone.

"By order of the Admiralty and the First Sea Lord, Sir Malcolm Robertson is hereby promoted to the rank of Commodore." In a reversal of the last ceremony, Commodore Dexter handed Malcolm's new shoulder boards to Joan, who removed his captain rank and replaced it with his new rank of Commodore. She threw a smart salute and Malcolm couldn't help but notice her attempt to suppress a smile.

Dexter took a position next to Malcolm and addressed the assembly. "I've had the privilege of being your commander for the last two years. While I won't miss this rock, I will miss all of you. Gentleman... and lady," he said, acknowledging Joan, "you are the backbone of the Service. I ask that you continue to provide Commodore Robertson with the same support that you provided me. We have a very important and historic mission at hand. I know that every one of you will do everything in your power to make it a success. And now, by order of the Admiralty and the First Sea Lord, Commodore Vincent Dexter is hereby ordered to assignment at the Admiralty in London immediately. Commodore Sir Malcolm Robertson is hereby given command of the Boreray base, effective immediately. Commodore Robertson, I am ready to be relieved."

"I relieve you, sir," Malcolm said as the two Commodores exchanged salutes.

Malcolm addressed the assembly. "I have little to say except I hope to live up to the example of Commodore Dexter and I know that together, we will make this mission a success. Assembly dismissed."

The reception at the Officer's Mess following the assembly was a more raucous affair than Joan's commissioning. Commodore Dexter had arranged for a large stock of ale and rum to be shipped to the base, and the libations ran freely. Malcolm found drink after drink placed in his hand and decided that he couldn't insult anyone. The reception continued well into the evening, becoming a blur.

Malcolm awoke the next morning to the sounds of "Call to Hands" penetrating his skull like a drill. His head pounded as he stumbled to his washroom to make himself presentable for his first actual day of command. As he made his way gingerly to the Officer's Mess, he remembered as Commodore, he had his own private mess and was thankful that he wouldn't have to talk to anyone. He continued on to his private mess. The midshipman offered to bring him eggs, toast and beans; Malcolm settled for several pieces of dry toast. He filled a large mug of tea and made his way to his new office.

Commander Murray jumped to attention. "Good morning, sir!" he said as he saluted.

Malcolm returned the salute. "It is morning. I'm not sure how good it is."

"Yes, sir. Shall we go over the day's schedule?"

"If we must," Malcolm grumbled.

"Pardon, sir?"

"Yes, of course." Malcolm entered his new office and, much to his surprise, everything from his old office was here and arranged in nearly the same place.

"I moved your office after the reception. I hope you don't mind, sir."

"No, thank you, Commander. This was quite unexpected. Speaking of the reception, did I make a total arse of myself last night?"

"Permission to speak freely, sir?"

"Yes," Malcolm said with some trepidation.

"I wouldn't say you made a total arse of yourself, but you led the men in the singing of several of the bawdier sea shanties. The men took it in good fun, sir."

"Well, thank heavens for small favours. Alright, Commander. What is today's schedule?"

Commander Murray relayed the schedule, which included a meeting of the base staff, inspections, and a visit to the Crown Prince of the Martian Empire.

"I beg your pardon?" Malcolm asked. "Did you say a visit with the Martian Crown Prince?"

"Yes. He often met with Commodore Dexter for updates on the construction of the ship. When he heard you were taking command of the base, he was most intent on having a meeting." Commander Murray paused. "Have you met the Martian Crown Prince before?"

"Yes, I had the honour last year," Malcolm said. "Why do you ask?"

"How shall I say this," Murray said. "Some find the Crown Prince's appearance to be offputting."

"That's one way to describe it," Malcolm muttered.

"What was that, sir?"

"Nothing, I was just agreeing with you."

"It is important that we maintain good relations with the Crown Prince, and I just wanted to make sure his appearance would not shock you."

"I'm long past that stage, Commander Murray. Is there anything else?"

"Yes, Commander O'Hallarhan asked to see you this morning, if your schedule permitted."

"Does it?" Malcolm asked.

"Yes, sir. I believe we have an opening between the staff meeting and the inspections."

"Very good. Please inform him I look forward to our meeting."

"Very good. Anything else, sir?"

"Yes, could you find me some aspirin?"

CHAPTER EIGHTEEN

After a couple of aspirins and several mugs of tea, Malcolm's head finally stopped throbbing to where he could think. Malcolm looked at the stack of paper on his desk and realised that it was even larger than his previous stack. He stopped to consider that he hadn't delegated his paperwork and also inherited the Commodore's. Malcolm decided that the upcoming staff meeting would be a perfect opportunity to rectify the situation.

The staff meeting was subdued, as several officers sported the same headache that plagued Malcolm. Commanders Saxon and Murray graciously accepted the assignment of preparing additional reports, but he knew that neither was happy with the additional responsibility. When the meeting was over, Malcolm caught O'Hallarhan's attention. "Commander Murray said you wanted to see me. Please follow me to my office."

Malcolm returned to the Commodore's office with O'Hallarhan, and when they settled into their chairs, Malcolm asked, "What can I do for you, Commander?"

"I wish to submit my name for consideration for the Captain of the new spaceship."

"I see; I didn't know that you had any interest in commanding a vessel. Commanding a ship is an enormous responsibility; what are your qualifications?"

"I know more about this ship than anyone else," O'Hallarhan said. Although Malcolm was sure he was correct, modesty was obviously not one of O'Hallarhan's virtues.

"I see," Malcolm said. His head throbbed again, although he wasn't sure if it was the aftereffects of the previous night or this fresh crisis unfolding before him. "That is a significant consideration, but what are your command qualifications?"

"I have been in command of the Engineering crew since I arrived here, sir. As you can see, we're making significant progress."

"While that's true, Commander, I should note that much of that progress has occurred since I arrived. If I remember your file correctly, you haven't served on a vessel since you were a midshipman at the Academy, correct?" O'Hallarhan nodded. "Likewise, I believe several of your previous commanding officers did not have a high opinion of your command capabilities."

"Permission to speak freely, sir?"

"Permission granted," Malcolm said.

"They were fools who didn't understand basic engineering principles, let alone the intricacies of the Martian technology. You understand the complexities of this project and can appreciate the challenges I face."

He knew O'Hallarhan was not fit to be a captain, but he couldn't risk alienating the junior engineer on whom he was completely dependent. "Given that the technology used for the ship is unproven, your technical knowledge would be an asset. If I consider you for captain, would you be content to serve as my second in command on the spaceship?"

"I don't understand, sir," O'Hallarhan stammered.

"My orders regarding the spaceship remain unchanged. The Admiralty wants me to command the spaceship that escorts the Crown Prince back to Mars. They feel that having a high-ranking officer would be a show of good faith to the Martians."

"I hadn't considered that," O'Hallarhan said. Malcolm noticed

O'Hallarhan had slumped slightly at the news that he wouldn't have command of the ship, but have to play second in command.

"I will think about your request earnestly, Commander."

"That's all I ask, sir," O'Hallarhan said.

Eager to change the subject, Malcolm asked, "What is the status of the ship's construction?"

"Everything is on track. We completed the deuterium tanks and we're nearly finished with the deuterium processing station. I estimate that it will take an additional week until it's working."

"Excellent. Carry on the good work, Commander. Is there anything else?"

"No, sir. Thank you for your time."

"One moment, Commander; I'm wondering if you could do me a favour."

"Yes, sir, what is it?"

"I believe that it's time for me to understand the Martian technology. Would you spend an hour every evening tutoring me?"

"Yes Commodore. It would be my pleasure. When should we start? Tonight?"

"Not tonight. I believe I will retire early after the celebration last night. I'm not a young cadet anymore."

"As you say, sir," O'Hallarhan said. "What about tomorrow night after mess?"

"That should work nicely. Thank you, Commander."

After O'Hallarhan left, Malcolm poked his head out of his office. "Commander Murray, could you schedule time with Commander Saxon today?"

"We could do it after your meeting with the Martian Crown Prince."

"Thank you. That will do nicely."

The base inspection took much longer than Commander Murray had planned. To the Commander's consternation, Malcolm asked questions at each point, trying to learn more about the base and its personnel. As the inspection continued, Malcolm fell further and further behind of Commander Murray's schedule, causing the commander great exasperation. Eventually, Commander Murray pushed Malcolm to a run to arrive for his meeting with the Martian Crown Prince on time.

Two Royal Marines guarded a heavy steel door with a wheel. As they approached, one marine turned the door handle, and it opened effortlessly, given its size and weight. They entered a small chamber with doors on both sides, lit by a red lightbulb. The marine closed the door and air blew over them.

"The air bathes us in filtered air to…," Murray began.

"To reduce the bacteria or microbes we would bring in," Malcolm finished.

"Very good, sir," Murray said. After thirty seconds, the red light turned off and a green light turned on. Murray turned the wheel on the other door and said, "Mind your step as you cross the threshold. The gravity…"

"The gravity has been readjusted to replicate Martian gravity?" Malcolm offered.

"Yes, sir," Murray said. Malcolm thought he looked crestfallen, disappointed that he couldn't impress his new commanding officer with his knowledge. Malcolm stepped through the doorway and felt the difference in gravity. As he walked into the room, Malcolm concentrated on controlling his steps so that he didn't float. The room looked very similar to the Martian Crown Prince residence at the Secret Service Headquarters; mahogany panelled walls with large, overstuffed leather chairs, although bookcases full of books lined three of the walls. Malcolm realised that was exactly why the Crown Prince's quarters at the Secret Service and the quarters here looked like the Diogenes Club; Mycroft recreated the place where he felt most comfortable, believing that the Crown Prince would feel the same sense of comfort. Bisecting the room was a glass wall, and sitting in a chair on the other side was a Martian that Malcolm assumed was the Crown Prince. The Crown Prince was in a plum coloured hooded robe. Even in the shadows of the hood, Malcolm saw the Martian's tentacles swaying around his mouth. Next to him stood another Martian, dressed in a burgundy robe. He had pulled back his hood and Malcolm could clearly see its octoploid head; dark luminous eyes, a beak, and nearly a dozen tentacles swaying around its mouth.

"Commodore Malcolm Robertson, may I introduce His Highness, the Crown Prince of the Martian Empire, C'thwan T'plua, and his Chancellor, M'qua Cth'rn?" Murray said.

"Your Highness, it is a great honour to meet you again," Malcolm said as he bowed to the Crown Prince.

"Thank you, Commodore Malcolm Robertson, or should I call you Godkiller? The honour is mine."

"I doubt I killed it," Malcolm said. "I imagine it is sleeping, dreaming of the day it will rise again."

"Alas, that is true," the Crown Prince said. "But you have done a great service for both of our worlds."

"Thank you, Your Highness," Malcolm said, inclining his head. "Chancellor, it is a pleasure to meet you."

"I've heard much about this so-called Godkiller; I was expecting someone more… heroic looking."

"I often get that," Malcolm said, hoping that his sense of humour would span the differences in cultures; given the Chancellor's intent stare, Malcolm was sure that it hadn't.

"Commodore, please tell me in your own words what transpired after our meeting at the Secret Service. Please take a seat," the Crown Prince said, as a tentacle slithered out of the robe and pointed at the seat near the glass wall.

Malcolm relayed the story of discovering that the only artifact of faith capable of hurting the Martian God was the Spear of Destiny, stored in the Treasury of the Austro-Hungarian Empire. He narrated his exploits with Saxon and Joan as they infiltrated a diplomatic mission, stole the Spear and their escape across Europe. He described the long flight to R'lyeh, the home of the Martian God. Malcolm described the scene of the Martian God's risen city, with its strange angles and geometry. He described the convergence of stars and planets, whose focused beam opened the door to the temple. He ended with the confrontation with the Martian God, where Malcolm stabbed the being with the Spear of Destiny before losing consciousness from his own injuries.

"I am relieved to know that you were successful and that you and your companions survived," the Crown Prince said. Malcolm marvelled at the technology that allowed the two of them to communicate. To Malcolm, the words of the Crown Prince came through in perfectly enunciated English. The Chancelor's voice was more gruff, but still perfectly understandable. "I understand you will take me back to Mars personally?"

"Yes, Your Highness. It would be my honour to escort you home." Now that Malcolm was closer to the Crown Prince, he could see that the Crown Prince appeared sick. The Chancellor's tentacles were grey and shiny; those of the Crown Prince had a milky sheen.

"To banish us from your world?" the Chancellor asked.

"No, to return the Crown Prince to his home for his own health. I am at His Highness's disposal," Malcolm said. "I don't wish to hold you against your will or to make you feel we want to be rid of you."

The Chancellor's eyes narrowed, but the Crown Prince interrupted before he could speak. "You must ignore the Chancellor; the Chancellor does not trust humans."

"You do?" Malcolm asked.

"I do not trust the race of humans, but I trust individuals," the Crown Prince said. "I trust Mycroft Holmes, who has kept his word to me, and I trust you."

"Me?" Malcolm said. "Begging your pardon, Your Highness, but this is only the second time we've met. How can you trust me?"

"For the simple reason, you are Godkiller. My race does not give that title lightly. To be named Godkiller means you must be pure of heart and motive. By your actions, you have proven yourself to be trustworthy."

"I don't know what to say other than thank you."

The Crown Prince looked at the Chancellor. "My Chancellor does not share my faith in humans and doesn't care about Earth."

"That is not true, Your Highness. I think Earth is a wonderful planet, if not for the humans," the Chancellor said.

"Why do you say that?" Malcolm asked.

"You use your resources unwisely. You fill your sky with noxious chemicals and let your wastes flow into the sea. Humans take from the earth, and return only toxins. Humans themselves are a disease, infecting the entire planet, slowly draining it of life."

"That is enough, Chancellor," the Crown Prince interjected. "Our race is much older than yours, Commodore. In the days before the Great Schism, my people lived much like your society. When we destroyed our atmosphere and nearly perished as a race, we quickly learned the lesson of living in harmony with the world."

"But Your Highness," the Chancellor interrupted, "the earthlings' stupidity and greed have caused your illness."

"That's not true, Chancellor," the Crown Prince said. "I have a common illness among our people, much like what you call a cold here on Earth. The cure is a special fungus that grows only on Mars; without that, the illness can become deadly."

"How is your condition, Your Highness?"

"I am holding my own," the Crown Prince said.

"The Crown Prince is not," the Chancellor interrupted. "Even an earthling like you can see the Crown Prince's colour is fading. It is only a matter of time before the illness forces the Crown Prince to enter a hibernation tube to slow the disease's progress."

"I am fine, M'qua. It is a trifle."

"It is not a trifle," argued the Chancellor. He turned and addressed Malcolm directly. "The Crown Prince refuses to listen to reason and instead spends what time remains reading books."

"Because I wish to understand Earth more. One learns much from reading the stories and histories of human; your history is not dissimilar to Martian history. The Godkiller saved both our worlds from a horrible fate, Chancellor, whether you wish to believe it. I believe that the futures of our worlds rely on forming a strong partnership and that we can create that partnership only through understanding of both worlds."

"You know my views on that manner, Your Highness," the Chancellor began.

"Yes, I am all too well aware of your views, as you've told me countless times. As Crown Prince, it is my duty to represent the Martian race and forge a relationship with the Earthlings," the Crown Prince said. Malcolm couldn't read Martian body language, but he sensed the Crown Prince was angry with the Chancellor.

The Chancellor bowed his head. "I am sorry, Your Highness. While the off-worlder is here, I won't speak of these matters."

"Careful, M'qua. Consider that we are the off-worlders." The Crown Prince turned to Malcolm. "Forgive the Chancellor. When we first sensed the rising of our God, my father, the Emperor, gave me the responsibility of allying with Earth. As you know, the idea repulsed many of my people, including the Chancellor. To the Chancellor's credit, he accompanied me on this vital mission, but his disdain remains. Tell me, Commodore, how goes the construction of the ship?"

Malcolm gave the Crown Prince the status on the construction of the spaceship. The Crown Prince nodded in agreement at the decisions Malcolm and his team made. "I see why Mycroft brought you here; you have made significant progress in the short time since you have arrived."

"I didn't do it by myself. My team does the hard work."

"That may be true, but a team without a powerful leader accomplishes nothing. Having listened to Commodore Dexter's reports, many failed where you alone have succeeded."

"Thank you, Your Highness."

The Crown Prince sighed, and the Chancellor stepped forward to examine the Crown Prince. "As I feared, this meeting has exhausted the Crown Prince. You will leave now, human; the Crown Prince must rest."

"I fear the Chancellor may be correct; it would be best if I rested. Regrettably, I must take my leave."

"I understand," Malcolm said rising. "It's been a pleasure. Please let me know if you or the Chancellor require anything."

"Perhaps one evening you can join me in a game of chess? Mycroft introduced me to the game and I find it fascinating."

"I'm afraid you will find I am not a skilful player," Malcolm said.

"Neither am I, but I find it a stimulating exercise," the Crown Prince said.

"It would be my pleasure," Malcolm said. "Perhaps tomorrow evening?"

"Yes, that would be excellent. And please bring your mate; I understand she is here."

"My mate? Oh, you mean Joan. We aren't married, Your Highness."

"I must have misunderstood," the Crown Prince said. "Mycroft told me you were to be joined."

"Yes, well, Mycroft pulled us here before we could be married."

"That is unfortunate," the Crown Prince said.

"It is, but there's nothing we can do about it now. I will extend your kind invitation. I'll take my leave now. Good day, Crown Prince; Chancellor." Malcolm nodded to each as he turned to leave. As he left, Malcolm felt the Chancellor's stare and suddenly felt like a fish in a bowl stalked by a hungry cat.

CHAPTER NINETEEN

When Malcolm arrived at his office, he found Commander Saxon waiting in the anteroom, talking with Commander Murray.

"Prompt as usual, Commander," Malcolm said, acknowledging Charles.

"I daren't be late, as I hear the new Commodore is a bastard," Saxon said. Commander Murray gasped audibly and Malcolm laughed.

"Pay no attention to Commander Saxon," he said. "His sense of humour is not always appropriate. Before I forget, Commander Murray, could you have Lieutenant de St. Leger report here at her earliest convenience?"

"Yes, sir," Murray said.

Saxon raised an eyebrow, but before Saxon could speak, Malcolm gestured to his office door. "Come, Commander, before you test your theory about the new commodore."

Saxon surveyed Malcolm's new office as he walked to a seat. "This is nicer than your previous office."

"Thank you. Rank has its privileges," Malcolm said. "Sit, I need your advice." Malcolm relayed his conversation with Commander

O'Hallarhan and his encounter with the Martian Crown Prince and Chancellor.

"You've had an interesting first day," Saxon said.

"Aye, you could say that. Let's talk about O'Hallarhan first. Lord knows, I can't make him captain. The crew would mutiny on the spaceship's maiden voyage!"

"And it certainly wouldn't reflect well on the Commodore either," Saxon said. "All kidding aside; please accept my heartfelt congratulations, Malcolm. Whether the Admiralty actually realises it, I think you will make a great Commodore."

"Thank you, Charles. But O'Hallarhan brings up a good point; we'll have a commodore and at least two commanders. That complicates the chain of command if I'm incapacitated, or worse." Malcolm paused. "Would you consider becoming a captain?"

"Good God, no, Malcolm!" Saxon gasped. After he composed himself, he continued. "I appreciate the offer, but truthfully, I'm can't afford the attention that comes with the rank. The Admiralty would thoroughly vet my record, and you know we would both suffer."

Malcolm nodded. If the Admiralty closely reviewed Saxon's record, they might discover he was a homosexual. Although the Royal Navy's last execution for sodomy occurred over eighty years ago, if convicted, Saxon would receive a harsh prison sentence. Malcolm had kept his best friend's secret and would face court martial if the Admiralty found out he knew Saxon's secret. "I thought that would be your reaction, but I thought I'd offer. It is a pity; you would make a fine captain."

"Thank you for your confidence and consideration." Saxon furrowed his brow. "What about Commander Murray? I've reviewed the base personnel records, and he is imminently qualified."

"That might be a consideration. My only reservation is I must still lead the mission to Mars. If I take Commander Murray with me, it leaves the base with no one who could run it while we gallivant through space. And before you respond, you are going to Mars and you won't stay and run the base."

"See? The new commodore is a bastard." The two men laughed

before Saxon continued. "I suggest leaving the role open. You are under no obligation to replace yourself. I would keep the role open and tell Commander O'Hallarhan you will take his request under consideration and his ongoing conduct will be a factor in your decision. It may help coax more compliance from him."

"That's what I thought. I hoped you would accept and I would have an easy out."

"Sorry. That's why you're a commodore; you get to make the tough decisions."

"Thank you ever so much for your support," Malcolm said. "What about my meeting with the Crown Prince and the Chancellor?"

"The Crown Prince sounds less standoffish than when we first met him. I think it's possible that your exploits may have impressed him, although I can't think why," Saxon said with a smile.

Malcolm shook his head. "The Chancellor barely tolerated my presence."

"That I understand," Saxon said.

"You know, keep needling me and I might turn into that bastard commodore. I believe there are issues with the waste treatment centre that might need your personal supervision." Malcolm kept his tone flat, but could barely suppress a smile.

"Point taken," Saxon said. "Why do you think the Chancellor reacted so negatively?"

"The first reason might be the Crown Prince's condition. I'm not sure if the Chancellor is worried about his career or the Crown Prince. Second, I think he despises humans and thinks we are inferior beings. I believe the Chancelor would wipe humans off the Earth, given the chance."

"That is troubling. Tell me, would he lead the Martian delegation if the Crown Prince became incapacitated?"

"That's an excellent question," Malcolm said. "I will ask the Crown Prince when we play chess tomorrow evening."

"Interesting," Saxon said.

"How so?"

"The way a person plays chess provides insight into how they think. I know from our games that you are mostly logical, but make creative moves. And it matches the way you solve problems; you think through the problem logically, but you make imaginative leaps that create a connection that you follow to its logical conclusion or the next leap."

"I didn't correlate the two. I suppose you're right," Malcolm said. "Since we're dissecting each other's play, your play is very by the book. You have several standard strategies working simultaneously and you decide which one you deploy based on the given situation. But you never reveal your true intent."

"Touché," Saxon said. "Let's hope you impress the Crown Prince with your chess play and it doesn't lead into a cross world diplomatic incident."

"The Crown Prince also invited Joan; what do you think about that?"

"Ah, that explains why you asked Joan here. I think the Crown Prince would like to converse without the translating device. And second, I think he may think it's the correct cultural etiquette."

"I hadn't considered that. It should be an interesting evening."

"Yes, it will," Saxon said. "Better you than me."

"Yes, apparently, rank has its privileges," he said wryly. The two reviewed the ongoing activities at the base for several minutes. When Saxon left, Malcolm sighed before pulling the top report from his paperwork stack. After an interminable hour spent reading reports, Commander Murray knocked on his door.

"Commodore, Lieutenant de St. Leger is here."

"Please, send her in," Malcolm said, setting aside his report.

Joan marched into his office and threw a very sharp salute. "Lieutenant de St. Leger, reporting as ordered, sir."

Malcolm couldn't help but smile. Joan looked every bit the officer, but beneath the military bearing, he still saw the woman he loved. He returned the salute. "At ease, Lieutenant. Please, have a seat."

Joan looked around the office before settling into the overstuffed leather chair in front of Malcolm's desk. "This office is very nice, Commodore."

"Thank you. I asked you here for a personal matter; you can call me Malcolm."

"I wouldn't want to act inappropriately," she said with a wink.

"That's too bad," Malcolm muttered.

"I beg your pardon, Commodore?" she said, looking at him with an arched eyebrow.

"I said, very good."

"What is this personal matter?" she said, raising an eyebrow.

"Yes. The Martian Crown Prince has invited us to his quarters tomorrow night. He and I will play chess, but he specifically invited you."

"I assume that's an order, Commodore?"

"I wouldn't consider it an order, but perhaps a personal favour to the Commodore?"

"I see," she said. She smiled, and it made Malcolm nervous.

"What's it going to cost me?" Malcolm asked.

"We'll see; I haven't decided yet."

Silence fell between them. After a long, uncomfortable pause, Malcolm offered, "What is your current assignment?"

"The Radio room, learning radio transmission theory and operation."

"How is that going?"

"Slowly," she admitted. "You know me; science is not my strong suit. And this isn't simple science either."

"You sound like me; I've asked Commander O'Hallarhan to tutor me in the Martian technology. The science behind it is like nothing I've studied."

"Perhaps we can study together sometime?" she said, arching an eyebrow. "You could help me with my fields and waves, and I could help you... in other ways."

Malcolm felt his face flush. "As enticing as that sounds, I think I must decline."

"Pity," she said. "Anything else?"

"I'll pick you up tomorrow after mess. I think you should remain in uniform, if you don't mind. It will help portray a sense of decorum."

"Me? Not display a sense of decorum?"

"I meant to the rest of the base. If it's the Commodore and the Communications Officer in her role as a translator visiting the Crown Prince, that's one thing. If it's the Commodore and his fiancé visiting the Crown Prince, that's a different story altogether."

"I see," she said with a suspicious smile. "It would be a personal favour, Commodore?"

"Yes, it would, Lieutenant."

"How can I say no?"

"Very good, Lieutenant. Will you meet me here at six bells tomorrow evening?"

"Yes, Commodore," she said. "It would be my pleasure."

Malcolm swore she especially emphasised the word *'pleasure'*. "Very good, Lieutenant. That will be all."

"Are you sure?" she said, arching her eyebrow again.

"No, but duty demands otherwise. Dismissed, Lieutenant."

"Damn," she said under her breath. She stood up and threw a salute. "I will be here promptly. Should I wear my dress uniform?"

"Very good question, Lieutenant. Normally, attending a social engagement with a visiting noble would dictate full dress; I believe the dress uniform would be appropriate."

"Very good, sir." She walked to the door, turned, and blew Malcolm a kiss before leaving.

Malcolm shook his head, knowing tomorrow evening would be trying.

CHAPTER TWENTY

The next day, Malcolm arrived at his office and discovered he had his first radio meeting with Admiral Beatty in twenty minutes. Frantically, Malcolm compiled a status report from the piles of paper stacked on his desk. He thought he had control over the paperwork, but soon realised that Commodore Dexter had left it unattended before his transfer. With Commander Murray's help, he assembled his report just before he was due at the Radio Room.

When he arrived, it surprised him Joan was operating the radio. "Admiralty, please stand by for Commodore Robertson," she said. She gestured for him to take a seat near her. He sat down and picked up his headset. When he was situated, she nodded and flicked the switch, activating his headset. Ear-splitting feedback filled the room before Joan adjusted a dial on the radio. She mouthed the word "Sorry," and nodded for Malcolm to speak.

"Commodore Robertson to Admiralty, do you read me? Over."

Static crackled on the line, but Malcolm could hear, "Read you loud and clear, Commodore. Hold for Admiral Beatty. Over."

"Beatty, here. Before we begin, please accept my personal congratulations on your promotion."

"Thank you, sir."

"Now, what should I know?"

Malcolm updated Beatty on the progress of the ship's construction and overall base status. "Very good," Beatty replied. "I see I chose the right person for this job. Anything else?"

"I had my first meeting with the Martian Crown Prince. He's invited myself and Lieutenant de St. Leger to his quarters tomorrow evening. He and I will play chess; I'm not sure what Lieutenant De St. Leger will do." Malcolm was thankful he had toggled off the switch to talk because Joan kicked his shins. "Ow," he said, rubbing his shins.

"Are you sure that's wise?" the Admiral said. "I don't want any reports of favouritism about the Lieutenant."

"There is no favouritism involved. The Martian Crown Prince invited her and she will attend as the Communications Officer and translator." He moved away before she kicked him again. He glared at Joan and continued. "I have a question about protocol. Since we are entertaining a foreign dignity, I assume we should wear dress uniforms tonight?"

"That sounds appropriate," the admiral said. "This is unprecedented. I don't believe His Highness has invited anyone other than Mycroft Holmes for a social visit."

Lucky me, thought Malcolm. *Let's hope I don't start an interplanetary incident.* "Understood, sir."

"I'm sure you'll do well."

"Thank you, sir."

"I know you understand how important this mission is. Please don't jeopardise it."

"I'll do my best, sir. Anything else?"

"No, that's all. Beatty out."

Malcolm removed the headset and turned to Joan. "No pressure tonight."

She smiled and touched his arm. "You'll perform admirably. Besides, I'll be with you. I think I can prevent you from causing an incident." She smiled, and they looked at each other before Joan kissed him.

It took all of Malcolm's willpower to tear himself away from the kiss. "As much as I would love to continue, we can't."

"I know," she said, leaning her forehead against his. "It's been so long and I've missed you so very much."

"I've missed you too," he said. They stayed that way for several moments before Joan broke away.

"I look forward to our 'date' tonight," she said.

"It's not a date, but a social obligation with a foreign dignitary."

"A girl can dream, can't she?"

Malcolm smiled. "I better get back to my office." He reached down and gave her hand a squeeze. "I'll expect you at my office immediately after dinner."

"Yes, sir," she said.

Malcolm took a deep breath and left the radio office. On the way back, he remembered he had scheduled his tutoring session with O'Hallarhan tonight. He walked back to the construction site where he found O'Hallarhan working with his crew on the torus. As he approached, he heard O'Hallarhan berating a worker. This only confirmed Malcolm's initial suspicions of O'Hallarhan's suitability as captain, and he filed this interaction away for later.

"Commander O'Hallarhan, can I have a word with you?" Malcolm asked.

O'Hallarhan dropped his tools and joined Malcolm. "What is it, sir?"

"I apparently have a state dinner tonight, and I can't start our tutoring session."

"State dinner? Is the Prime Minister coming here?" O'Hallarhan asked.

"No, I'm meeting with the Martian Crown Prince. I apologise for cancelling on such short notice."

"That's fine, sir. Any chance I could join you?"

Malcolm admired the engineer's drive, despite his tactless approach. "Not tonight, Commander. I believe it's primarily a social event. We will play chess."

"Ah," O'Hallarhan deadpanned.

"There will be more chances to meet the Crown Prince."

"Thank you, sir," O'Hallarhan said. "Anything else, sir?"

"How are things going?" Malcolm asked.

"Going well, sir. The deuterium processing station and tanks are ready. We're nearing completion on the torus. I estimate within the next week, we can begin the reactor's final assembly and determine if we built it successfully, or if we blow up the base."

"Blow up the base? Isn't that an overstatement?" Malcolm asked.

"I'm afraid not, sir. If we can't control the reaction, we will create a massive explosion capable of destroying this island."

"Then we must make sure everything works exactly as planned."

"Yes, sir," O'Hallarhan said with confidence. Malcolm, knowing the myriad ways machines could fail, wished he shared his engineer's confidence.

"I will see you tomorrow night to begin the tutoring sessions," Malcolm said.

"About that, sir… permission to speak freely?"

"Permission granted," Malcolm said, inwardly bracing himself for what would come next.

"Now that you're a commodore, is that necessary? If I were the captain, you wouldn't have the added burden of learning this complex technology. You could focus on the diplomatic portion of our mission and I could take care of the technical issues."

"That may be true. But as the commanding officer, I must understand how the ship operates. If something happens to you, we need someone who understands the ship."

"Begging your pardon, sir," O'Hallarhan began, "shouldn't we look for someone younger? By your own admission, it's been four years since you were a Chief Engineer. And that was on an airship. I mean no offence, but the difference between the technology of this ship and an airship is like the difference between calculus and simple addition."

"I see," Malcolm said. He felt his blood boiling, but struggled to tamp down his inclination to yell. "Perhaps it's better we stop the tutoring sessions before they start."

"Thank you, sir," O'Hallarhan said. "I'm sure running the base must fill every waking moment; you don't need additional responsibilities."

"As you say, Mr O'Hallarhan," Malcolm said, his voice straining to project calm. "I'll leave you to it." Malcolm turned and stomped back to his office. On the way through the anteroom, Commander Murray tried to get his attention, but Malcolm hurried past and slammed his door shut, leaving a very perplexed Commander Murray on the other side.

Damn that miserable brat, Malcolm thought. *How dare he think that I'm too old to learn?* Malcolm slammed his fist on his desk.

Commander Murray knocked on the door before opening it tentatively. "Are you alright, Commodore?"

"I'm fine!" Malcolm bellowed. He caught himself and said, "My apologies, Commander Murray. I shouldn't have yelled at you." Suddenly, Malcolm had a thought. "Commander Murray, were you here when Commander O'Hallarhan arrived at the base?"

"Yes, sir."

"When he arrived, did he know anything about the Martian technology?"

"I don't believe so, sir. He and Professor Rutherford spent many weeks analysing the rocket ship. Professor Rutherford worked out the theoretical side, while Commander O'Hallarhan worked on the design."

"Really?" Malcolm said. He smiled. "Commander Murray, could you schedule a time when I can meet with Mr Holmes at the Secret Service?"

"When would you like to meet?"

"At his earliest convenience," Malcolm said.

"Anything else, Commodore?"

"No, thank you, Commander. You've been very helpful."

Within an hour, Commander Murray had secured a meeting with Mycroft Holmes just before mess, allowing him time to get ready for the evening with the Martian Crown Prince. Malcolm spent the day working through paperwork until Commander Murray reminded him it was time for his call with Mycroft.

Malcolm returned to the Radio Room, happy to find Joan still at the controls. "Peninsular and Oriental, please stand by for Mister R." Malcolm looked at Joan quizzically.

She flicked a switch and whispered, "We're talking to the Secret Service. We can't very well announce it, can we?"

Malcolm nodded, feeling like an idiot for the second time that day. He took his place next to Joan and, before donning the headset, he asked, "How should I refer to him?"

"Mr H will do." She flicked the switch and nodded.

"Mr H, this is Mr R. Do you read me?"

"Mr R, I read you," Mycroft Holmes said. "Before we start, may I offer my congratulations on your promotion?"

"Thank you."

"This isn't a social call. What can I do for you?"

"I need the services of the Cambridge professor with whom you contracted earlier."

"Really? Why is that? I thought the project was proceeding smoothly."

"It is," Malcolm said. "I, however, don't understand anything about the underpinnings of the project. And… my assistant is not very interested in helping me gain that knowledge."

"I see. From what I've deduced about your assistant, he covets knowledge and likes having all the answers. I imagine your arrival, and subsequent success with the project, threatens his self importance."

"That's why I thought the professor might help. He could arrive under the guise of conducting basic training for the crew while I engage in more in-depth training with him. I believe it will not threaten my assistant and spread the knowledge amongst the crew." His mission to Russia had taught him the importance of not relying on just one person.

"I will do what I can. The professor is very busy and may not be available for months."

"Understood. Although we're making progress, we're still a long way off from getting this project off the ground. Oh, before I forget,

Miss L and I will visit our out-of-town friend tonight. Our friend suggested he and I play chess."

"Really?" Mycroft said. "How interesting." The line fell silent for several seconds. "Please extend my best wishes to our friend."

"I will."

"Anything else?"

"Nothing from my end," Malcolm said.

"Then our call is over. Thank you, Mr R."

"Thank you, Mr H."

Joan cut the channel as Malcolm handed his headphones to Joan. "What do you think?"

Joan smiled. "Officially, I heard nothing. But, I believe Mycroft will send you the professor. Is it Ernest Rutherford by any chance?"

"Yes," Malcolm said.

"I think he agrees you need to understand the technology while also letting O'Hallarhan think he's the only one who understands."

"Yes, O'Hallarhan has increasingly become a problem. Today, he implied that I was too old to learn the Martian technology."

"Is that true?" Joan asked.

"No," Malcolm thundered. "I might not be as intelligent as O'Hallarhan or pick it up as easily, but I can learn anything, because I refuse to quit until I understand it."

"Sorry," Joan said. "I believe you, Malcolm... I mean, sir."

"This technology scares the hell out of me. O'Hallarhan says we could destroy the entire island when we turn on the reactor. While O'Hallarhan is brilliant, I'm not risking my life, and everyone else's, solely on his judgement. I'll learn this technology, even if it means sleeping with the books under my pillow, so I get it through osmosis."

"I know you will," Joan whispered. "Permission to speak freely?"

"Haven't you already?" Malcolm said with a laugh.

"I have faith in you. When you tackle a problem, you are single-minded. I know with Ernest's help, you'll grasp this technology."

"Thank you, Lieutenant," Malcolm said. "Thank you. It means a great deal." He stood up, "I'm leaving now for Mess and then I'll change for our date this evening."

"I look forward to it," Joan said. "Although I can't say I'm enthralled with my dress."

Malcolm whispered, "You would look exquisite, even if you were wearing a burlap sack."

"Flatterer," Joan said with a smile.

Malcolm took a deep breath before leaving. "Thank you, Lieutenant. Will you meet me at my office after mess?"

"That would be fine, sir," Joan said, winking.

"Very good," Malcolm said as he left.

Malcolm went to his mess, unsurprised by the smoked kippers and mashed turnip; food chosen not for its taste, but for its longevity. Eating quickly, he hurried back to his quarters and showered before his evening with the Crown Prince. He looked at the mirror, inspecting his dress uniform. He still couldn't believe that he, a shipyard worker's son, had earned the highest medal for bravery, was a Commodore in the Royal Space Service, and knighted. Seeing himself in his dress uniform with his decorations, he felt proud of his accomplishments.

"But," he thought, *"Can I handle the responsibilities that come with my new rank? I hope I get through this evening without creating an interplanetary incident."*

He took a deep breath, smoothed his uniform one last time, and strode to his office, where he found Joan waiting. She wore the navy blue dress coat over a high-necked white blouse and a long navy blue skirt. She wore her hair in a tight bun swept up under a tricorne. Although she wore very little makeup, Malcolm thought she had never looked lovelier.

"You clean up, well, Lieutenant," Malcolm said, unsuccessfully dodging a dig in the ribs by Joan's elbow.

"Thank you, sir. May I say the same?"

"Let's not keep the Crown Prince waiting," he said. "After you." Malcolm let Joan lead, as it would keep a distance from her and he wouldn't take her arm.

"I don't know where we're going," she said.

"Very well, I'll lead," he said.

"If you insist," she said with a smile.

Malcolm lead the way and soon they approached the Royal Marines guarding the steel entryway to the Crown Prince's quarters. Malcolm nodded, and the Marines opened the large door and, after the air bath, they entered the Crown Prince's quarters. There were two chairs and a chessboard. On Malcolm's side of the glass sat an identical chess board. In the corner, a bottle of wine and a platter containing cheddar, Stilton, and Gloucester cheeses, and water biscuits were arranged on a small table.

Within moments, The Crown Prince and the Chancelor entered their side. The Crown Prince turned off the translation device. He turned towards Joan and spoke Martian. Joan smiled and replied in the Martian language. The Crown Prince nodded and turned on the device so Malcolm could understand the conversation.

"Welcome, Commodore and Joan. Hold, you have a rank now. What is it?"

"I'm a Lieutenant, Your Highness."

"Welcome, Lieutenant. May I introduce my Chancellor and mate, M'qua Cth'rn?"

"It is a pleasure to meet you, Chancellor," Joan said.

"We shall see," the Chancellor said.

"M'qua, please be civil. They are our guests and I would like an evening free from your enmity towards the humans. Say nothing if you can't say anything nice."

"It may be a silent evening," the Chancellor said.

"It would be preferable to hearing you rail against our hosts."

"You mean our captors?" the Chancellor said.

"Enough. Please, Commodore and Lieutenant, help yourselves to refreshments."

"This is a social meeting," Joan said. "You can dispense with ranks. Just call us Malcolm and Joan."

"And you may call us C'thwan and M'qua," the Crown Prince said.

They poured glasses of wine at the table. Malcolm looked over the cheese, picked several slices of cheddar and Gloucester, and several water biscuits. He avoided the Stilton; why anyone would purposely eat mouldy cheese was beyond him. Malcolm settled in the chair near the chessboard. "How does this work?"

"The two boards work together. When you move, the squares on the opposite board light up and show you the path your piece moved. See," the Crown Prince said as he moved a pawn two spaces ahead. On Malcolm's board, a blue light lit up the square under the corresponding pawn and the squares over the pawn's move lit up, transitioning from blue to red, showing the pawn's final destination.

"Good, I will admit I'm not very good at chess notation. Where did you get this board?"

"Mycroft had it made once he taught me how to play. He is a worthy adversary. Have you had the pleasure of playing against him?"

"No, although knowing Mycroft, I'm sure he would beat me handily."

"Shall we begin?" The Crown Prince said. "Since you are my guest, you may play white."

"Thank you, Your… C'thwan," Malcolm said. He studied the board, considering his moves before starting with the Italian Game as his opening strategy. As he started the game, he noticed Joan move her chair closer to the Chancellor, and she began a conversation in Martian.

As Malcolm suspected, the Crown Prince had a very unorthodox approach to chess. Although Malcolm was not an experienced chess player, he had learned several predictable responses from his play with Saxon. The Crown Prince often responded unpredictably to standard gambits, which left Malcolm constantly re-evaluating his strategy.

"Do you mind if we converse or will it distract you from your game?" The Crown Prince asked.

"No, it will hardly damage my game," Malcolm said. He looked up from his board and looked at the Crown Prince. His tentacles still lacked the sheen of the Chancellor's and the way the Crown Prince sat gave Malcolm the feeling the Crown Prince was tired. "Do you need a rest, C'thwan?"

"I am tired, but I need to talk with someone other than M'qua. Three years is a long time to be quarantined with one's mate."

"I didn't realise M'Qua was your mate," Malcolm said.

"Yes. Our joining occurred many years ago." The Crown Prince continued, sensing Malcolm's next question. "Martians don't have biologically assigned genders like humans. We are both what you would consider masculine and feminine. We are defined by how we express ourselves."

"Ah," Malcolm said. "How did you meet?"

"M'Qua's family is one of the great ruling houses. Our families made our match, cementing the union between our two houses."

"Were you consulted about the match?"

"No, as Crown Prince, I must follow the Emperor's orders without question. On the whole, it's been a suitable match. Tell me, how did you and Joan meet?"

"We met because of you," Malcolm said. As they continued playing, Malcolm relayed the story of the mission to Russia, where he first met Joan and the encounter when he realised she was a spy; she pulled a derringer to shoot him, which Malcolm prevented by hitting her with a bedpan.

"Interesting," the Crown Prince said. "Is that a traditional element of your joining?"

"No," Malcolm said. "Very little of our 'joining' is traditional."

"What do your families think of your joining?"

"My parents are supportive, although my mother wishes Joan had more domestic skills."

"Domestic skills?"

"In our culture, it's traditionally expected women do the cooking, cleaning, and management of the household. The vast majority of women do not work outside the home," Malcolm said.

"How do you feel about it?"

"All I care is Joan is happy. If working brings her happiness, I don't care if our home does not comply with society's expectations. We nearly lost one another, so whether she can cook or clean is insignificant."

"What of Joan's family?"

"Joan isn't very close to her family. She told her father, and he's been very accepting. She has not yet spoken to her mother."

"Why not?"

"Her mother wanted her to marry nobility, but Joan wanted her own career. They have not talked for some time."

"Interesting."

Malcolm focused back on the game and suddenly saw his path to victory. He moved his knight into position where the Crown Prince's bishop could take it and waited.

The Crown Prince took the bait and captured Malcolm's knight. Malcolm moved his bishop into position and waited. Malcolm was relieved when the Crown Prince ignored Malcolm's move, focusing instead on pressing the attack.

Malcolm moved his queen into position. "Check and mate."

The Crown Prince studied the board. "You are correct, Malcolm. While you appear to be the model of convention, you are unconventional."

"Thank you, Your... C'thwan," Malcolm said. "Traditions are important and have their place, but one must change and adapt as circumstances warrant."

C'thwan studied Malcolm before saying, "Yes, Mycroft made an excellent choice in choosing you. I, too, feel much like you. I honour my people's traditions, but our worlds are changing. When our god stirred from its slumber, I knew we could not face it alone and we needed the help of good earthlings, like you and Joan. My view was unpopular with many of my people, including M'qua. The less enlightened among my people view Earthlings as barely intelligent apes."

"Does M'qua share your opinion? I noticed he has a deep disdain for humans."

"M'qua has reasons. M'qua's father was part of the so-called invasion at Horsell Common and perished with the rest of the invasion force. The weight of running the family house fell on M'qua. I believe

M'qua resents humans, believing humans caused M'qua's father's death and the premature assumption of that burden."

"When did that occur?"

"Nine and a half cycles; eighteen years in earth time. While the length of our days are nearly identical, our year, or Cycle as we call it, is six hundred eighty-seven of our days, or roughly six hundred and sixty-nine of your earth days."

"I have much to learn about your planet and culture," Malcolm said.

"If you can convince him, M'qua is an excellent resource. M'qua is the traditionalist in our joining and adheres strongly to our culture's customs. My expertise is history and politics."

"Your planet's history must be very fascinating," Malcolm said.

"Alas, I fear it's not different from your history. The Great Schism nearly destroyed us as a race. Although we never evolved into territorial rivalries, we fought bitter wars over ideas. Our history is littered with wars rivalling your history. It's only within the last century we've learned to live peacefully with one another. Now, we settle differences through debate, not weapons."

"Can either of you explain your technology?"

"No, I only have a basic understanding," the Crown Prince said. "My cousin, C'thwan N'pagu, who piloted our ship, was the technology expert. I believe you and C'thwan would get along famously, had C'thwan not perished during the crash."

"C'thwan? The same name as yours?"

"Yes. In our culture, the family name comes before our personal designation. We call each other by family name, unless multiple people of the same family are present. Then we use the full name."

"Fascinating," Malcolm said. "You must find our custom strange."

"In one sense, I do," the Crown Prince said. "However, as I learn more about humans, you are driven by your individual talents and passions. While many have a strong sense of family name and honour, I feel the wishes of the individual often outweigh the wishes of the family. Your people are driven to provide a better life for your progeny. In my society, how you live your life is dependent entirely on your family."

"Before you judge us, consider this," the Crown Prince said. "Our Great Schism nearly decimated our people. Those who survived did so by dividing the roles of our society amongst the various families. It took several generations before enough Martians were born that it would be possible to veer from your role. By then, the practice became engrained in our society."

"No one challenges this system?"

"Yes, frequently. Those who leave their families to pursue a different life become the Nameless."

"That must be difficult," Malcolm said.

"Yes, it is. The Nameless are not welcome in Martian society; they are a society unto themselves. They live away from our cities. I have yet to meet a Martian who hasn't wished to become Nameless at some point in their lives."

"That I can understand. Many times, I've wished I could chuck my obligations and go off and do something else."

"And why haven't you?"

Malcolm laughed. "I don't know. I suppose I have an overdeveloped sense of responsibility. When I joined the Service, I knew I could help provide for my parents, but I felt guilty leaving them."

"Provide for your parents?"

"Yes. My father was a shipbuilder, and an accident at work crushed his leg. Although it healed, he could no longer work. I wanted to work in the shipyards to support my parents, but they wouldn't allow it. They insisted I finish my studies, but I could only continue by joining the Service. And fifteen years later, here I am."

"Commander of this base and a hero who will forge a new relationship between our worlds."

"You are too kind." Malcolm fidgeted. "Would you care for another game?"

"No, I think I am tired. I should retire for the night. I enjoyed our game and conversation very much. I hope we can do it again."

"Thank you, C'thwan," Malcolm said. "It would be my pleasure."

"M'qua," C'thwan said, "I will retire for the night. We should let our guests retire as well."

"As you wish," M'qua said. The Chancellor turned toward Joan. "Thank you for an enjoyable conversation. I enjoyed hearing someone speak our tongue instead of that infernal machine." He turned back toward Malcolm. "You have quite a mate, Commodore. You should cherish and honour Joan. Joan is a very special human."

"Thank you, M'qua," Malcolm said. He thought the Chancellor rankled at the use of his family name. "I cherish her very much. I heartily agree she's a very special person, Chancellor." Malcolm noticed the use of the Chancellor's title relaxed M'qua.

"I do hope we can do this again sometime," Joan said.

"We would look forward to it, wouldn't we, M'qua?" the Crown Prince asked.

"Yes, Crown Prince," M'qua said.

"Let's take our leave and perhaps we can set up such an evening for sometime next week?" Malcolm said.

"Yes," the Crown Prince said. "Good night, Malcolm, Joan," he said. As he turned, M'qua took one of C'thwan's tentacles and walked with the Crown Prince into the shadows of their chamber. After they left the Martian quarters, Malcolm asked, "Would you come back to my office and debrief me on your conversation with the Chancellor?"

"I'd love to be debriefed," Joan said seductively.,

"That's not what I meant and you know it," Malcolm hissed.

"You never let me have any fun."

"Not when you're one of my subordinates and Lord knows how many spies for the Admiralty are just waiting for me to 'fraternise'. They'll use any excuse to run me out of the Service. I just became a Commodore; I'd like to keep that rank for longer than two days."

"I know," she sighed.

They walked silently until they reached Malcolm's office. Commander Murray had gone for the evening, so they truly had time alone. Malcolm poured vodka for Joan and whisky for himself. Joan settled into her chair and sipped her drink. "I think this evening was successful."

"I thought so. I had a pleasant conversation with the Crown Prince, although I wasn't successful with the Chancellor." He relayed his conversation with the Crown Prince, including the story of M'qua's father and his obligation to lead his family's house. "You seemed to connect with the Chancellor."

"It took hard work. I believe the fact I spoke in his native tongue helped win him over. It took all of my charm, but I think I made a connection."

"That's excellent!" Malcolm said. "I can't say I'm surprised. When you turn on the charm, you are quite irresistible."

"Really?" Joan said, arching an eyebrow. "Do you tell your other lieutenants that?"

"Only the ones I'm engaged to," Malcolm said.

"You have more than one fiancé?" she said playfully.

"There is only one," Malcolm said.

"And who's that?"

He took her hand and gently guided her to her feet. "Just you," he said as he leaned in to kiss her.

"I thought you were against fraternisation," she said, looking into his eyes.

"I've made an exception," he said as pulled her close for a long and very overdue kiss.

CHAPTER TWENTY ONE

O'Hallarhan's initial estimate for the reactor was overly optimistic. Given the danger of starting the reactor, Malcolm insisted on a second quality testing round and was glad he did. The testing found leaks in the oxygen line feeding the deuterium processing tank, and imperfections in the torus's wiring. After addressing the problems, they discovered the torus would not maintain a steady magnetic field when charged. Without a stable magnetic field, the reaction could race out of control, causing an explosion that would destroy the island. O'Hallarhan spent weeks trying to solve the problem.

Work continued on the ship while O'Hallarhan puzzled over the problem with the torus. The engineering team spent many days completely sealing the hull plating inside and out, ensuring the ship was airtight. The sealant coloured the ship pitch black. Meanwhile, Charles and Malcolm reviewed the applicants for the ship's crew, and drew up the preliminary crew assignments.

Once a week, Malcolm and Joan kept their weekly meeting with the Crown Prince and Chancellor. On their fifth visit to the Martians, Malcolm noted an obvious deterioration in the Crown Prince's health. As they sat to start their weekly chess match, the Crown

Prince stopped and Malcolm sensed the Crown Prince was in great pain. "Are you alright? I don't know anything about Martian physiology, but you seem to be in pain."

"I'm fine," the Crown Prince said.

"He is not fine," M'qua interrupted. "His condition has worsened of late, but the Crown Prince still insists on keeping up with this meaningless ritual."

"M'qua, this 'ritual', as you say, means much if we are to forge an understanding between our races." Before M'qua could respond, the Crown Prince said, "I don't want to hear yet another one of your diatribes about the human race. Let us enjoy an evening free of your hostility." M'qua stomped back to his living quarters. Joan moved her chair to join Malcolm at the chessboard.

"Perhaps we should suspend our game for tonight. I would rather spend our time in meaningful discussion."

"Absolutely," Malcolm said. "What do you want to discuss?"

"I've been reading the history of your world, and I find it perplexing."

"How so?"

C'thwan started to speak, but stopped. Malcolm felt a wave of pain wash over him and realised that it emanated from the Crown Prince. "Are you alright, Crown Prince? Is there anything I can do for you?"

The Crown Prince was silent for a long moment. "It has passed. However, I am greatly fatigued. Perhaps we should draw this evening to a close?"

As Malcolm and join took their leave, Malcolm realised that the Crown Prince's condition was worsening, and the ship needed to be ready as soon as possible so that the Crown Prince could receive the care that was desperately needed.

After the reactor delay stretched into its fifth week, Malcolm knew he had to intervene. He joined Commander O'Hallarhan in the ship's Engine Room to better understand the issue. Commander O'Hallarhan set up a gaussmeter near the torus and applied power to the torus. "Watch," O'Hallarhan said. "The magnetic field strength keeps fluctuating. I can't determine the cause. I've checked, double checked, and triple checked the torus windings. Everything is sound."

"How is the power quality? You're using the base generator, correct?"

"I've checked that," O'Hallarhan said. "The input voltage and current are steady, with no fluctuations."

Malcolm watched the gaussmeter and observed the magnetic field dip regularly. The pattern reminded Malcolm of something he had seen before in his time as Chief Engineer. "Commander O'Hallarhan, refresh my memory. What is the base generator's operating frequency?"

"It's the standard fifty cycles per second, sir."

"Are the fluctuations occurring at a regular frequency?"

"Yes, but… oh, for Christ's sake," O'Hallarhan sputtered. "This ship sits right above the base generator."

"The generator is interfering with the magnetic field," they said simultaneously.

"I feel like a right git," O'Hallarhan said. "I was sure the problem was the torus itself."

"I understand. I can't tell you how many times I've spent time on problems, looking for elaborate causes when the real reason was something simpler. Do you know how to fix it?" Malcolm asked.

"Yes, sir. We need to stop the generator's magnetic field from interfering with the torus. The generator should be encased in iron, but we don't have that much iron."

"After you determine what you require, see Lieutenant Hughes and he will requisition what you need."

"It may take a while before we can shield the generator, sir. What can we do in the meantime?"

"What do you recommend, Commander?" Malcolm asked.

"We should test the ship for leaks, since the hull is nearly complete."

"How will we do that?" Malcolm asked.

"Since they built the base for ship construction, the water is deep enough to submerge the entire ship. If we don't see bubbles, we can feel confident the ship is airtight. And since we can't do anything with the engines, if it leaks, it won't damage anything."

"Very good, Commander. Proceed at once," Malcolm said.

"Sir, may I ask? How did you solve the problem so quickly? I've been wracking my brain for over the last month."

"I hadn't seen the problem before. Second, you did an excellent job ruling out any other causes. And finally, it was my years of experience. Once I realised the fluctuations were happening at fifty cycles per second, I realised the generator was the interference source. Sometimes, all it takes are fresh eyes. There's no shame in asking for help."

"I see," O'Hallarhan said. He was silent for a moment. "Thank you, sir."

O'Hallarhan was correct; there wasn't enough iron to encase the generator. Mingo's airship couldn't carry the necessary amount of iron, requiring delivery by boat, which wouldn't arrive for another month.

Within the week, the leak test was ready. They attached the ship to a working crane. Malcolm and the entire base watched as the crane strained to lift the ship. Once it was off the ground, the crane slowly rotated and delicately lowered the ship into the water. As they lowered the ship into the water, Malcolm held his breath as the ship slipped beneath the waves. As the water calmed, Malcolm held his breath, waiting to see if any bubbles rose to the surface. After several minutes, there was no sign of air bubbles. Malcolm breathed a sigh of relief and gave the order to raise the ship.. Malcolm smiled as a cheer went up. They were one step closer to completing the ship.

The interior work began after the ship dried. They built the interior walls on steel frames covered with the same alloy used on the hull. Throughout the ship, the crew built doors to seal a section in the event of a hull breach. The doors would isolate that section, preventing additional loss of atmosphere.

Malcolm's attention turned to starting the reactor. Although it would be weeks before the iron arrived, Malcolm considered the disposition of the base staff when they activated the reactor. Finally, he gave the entire base, except for Commander O'Hallarhan and himself, extended leave. He felt he must stay if he was risking O'Hallarhan's life. He ordered Commanders Saxon and Murray to work out the logistics of getting the crew off the island in an orderly fashion, including moving the Martian Crown Prince and Chancellor and keeping them safe from the human crew.

As the crew received the orders describing the extended leave, the crew's morale increased, with one notable exception. One afternoon, Commander Murray knocked on Malcolm's door, "Excuse me, sir, but Lieutenant de St. Leger demands to see you. I told her you were busy, but she said it was urgent and refused to leave until she saw you."

"That's alright, Commander, show her in," Malcolm said.

Joan bolted through the door and started, "What the bloody hell are you doing, Malcolm?"

"Lieutenant, is that how you address a superior officer?" Malcolm asked.

Joan glared at him before throwing a perfunctory salute.

Malcolm returned the salute. "Thank you, Commander Murray. I will deal with the Lieutenant."

"Very well, sir." Murray closed the door quickly.

Malcolm looked at Joan. "What can I do for you, Lieutenant?" he asked with particular emphasis on the word *Lieutenant*.

"My original question stands; what the bloody hell are you doing, Malcolm?"

"You mean, Commodore. What is it I'm doing that has angered you so that you've forgotten your training?"

"This leave. You're sending me away?"

"Yes. I'm sending everyone away except Commander O'Hallarhan and myself. I won't risk the crew's lives on the chance we blow up the entire island by starting the reactor. And that includes you."

"I'm not going." Joan said.

"If I order you to go, you will go, Lieutenant."

"I will not. You'll have to drag me off in chains. A fair number of Royal Marines will come out worse for wear."

"Why are you adamant about defying a superior officer?"

"Permission to speak freely, sir," Joan said; the word *sir* filled with malice.

"As opposed to how you've been speaking to me?" Joan glared at Malcolm. He sighed. "Permission granted."

"Malcolm, I won't let you risk your life without me. I thought I lost you once and I won't go through that again. There won't be a miracle recovery if something goes spectacularly wrong. You will be gone and that would kill me." Malcolm could see tears streaming down her cheeks, but she refused to cry outright.

"Joan, I…"

"Malcolm, I mean it. I couldn't live with myself if you died while I was in London. I love you. I've never said that to anyone else."

"I don't want you to die if something happens to me."

"But that's the problem; if I lose you, I will lose my life," Joan said, sniffing. "Please, Malcolm. Let me stay. If you're worried about appearances, I will stay locked in my quarters. Besides, you need a radio officer to report to headquarters when you are successful."

Malcolm considered Joan's plea. Although he could operate the radio, it was a fair reason for her stay.

"Very well, Lieutenant. Because of your insubordination, I revoke your leave."

"Thank you, Malcolm," she said as she launched herself towards him and kissed him. After a moment, she pulled away. Straightening her uniform and drying her eyes, she said with a smile, "Yes, sir. I understand"

"Very good, Lieutenant," Malcolm said. "Is that all?"

"Yes, sir," she said. She pantomimed to Malcolm to wipe his face to remove the lipstick smeared around his lips. She turned and left his office.

Malcolm later recounted the meeting with Saxon over drinks.

"Is that wise, Malcolm?" Saxon asked.

"What can I do? If I let her stay, it appears I've sent the entire base away for a tryst; if I force her to leave, she'll injure half a dozen Royal Marines before they restrain her."

"All too true," Saxon said. He stared at his drink. "Would it help if I stayed?"

"Charles, I can't ask that of you. Besides, someone needs to pick through the smouldering remains if it goes poorly."

"You always give me the best assignments," Saxon said.

CHAPTER TWENTY TWO

*D*uring the next month, the base population dwindled as personnel departed for leave. The Royal Marines and the Martian Crown Prince and Chancellor left first. Although the Chancellor protested moving the Crown Prince, the Chancellor agreed once Malcolm explained the potential threat.

There was barely anyone left to unload the iron when it arrived. Malcolm helped the engineering construction crew, carrying the iron to the base generator. With the remaining crew, they encased the generator in iron, shielding the torus from the generator's magnetic field. Multiple tests of the magnetic containment field confirmed the shielding prevented interference between the generator and the torus.

Saxon stayed until the end, leaving on the last airship with the Engineering crew. "Godspeed, I hope we'll see each other again. Although if the reactor startup goes spectacularly wrong, it would be quite a dramatic departure from the Service." Saxon offered his hand, but Malcolm pulled him into a hug. After a second, he clapped his hand on Saxon's shoulder, unable to speak the words he wanted to tell Saxon.

"Lieutenant, you have the unenviable task of keeping the commodore in line," Saxon said to Joan.

"Someone has to handle the tough assignments," she said with a smile, but Malcolm saw tears welling in her eyes. Saxon saluted them and boarded the last airship to leave the base.

They watched the airship until they lost sight of the ship. The vast cave, the centre of base activity, was so silent, Malcolm could hear the waves lapping against the dock. He turned to Joan and said, "Shall we find our Chief Engineer?"

"Eager to get it over with?"

"Yes, I'd rather not have this dread hanging over my head any longer than necessary."

Without the usual din of construction, the silence in the cave was eerie; only their footsteps broke the hush. As they entered the ship and walked to the Engine Room, Malcolm noted it finally felt like a ship. For a moment, he felt he was aboard the *Daedalus*, his last command.

Malcolm and O'Hallarhan spent the day hooking up the reactor, working until the evening before Malcolm and O'Hallarhan finished their work. Malcolm decided they would start the reactor in the morning when everyone was fresh and alert. After a cold dinner of sardine sandwiches, everyone turned in early.

But sleep eluded Malcolm as he lay in bed as he repeatedly reviewed the reactor start sequence. But every step started a chain reaction in his mind that ended in disaster. He tossed and turned for hours before he threw on his uniform and went to his office. He thought if he worked on the never-ending pile of paperwork, it would divert him from thoughts of death and destruction.

Joan burst into his office, startling Malcolm. "There you are!" Joan said. "I couldn't sleep, so I went to your quarters. After I got no answer, I started looking for you. How can you do paperwork this late?"

"I'm trying to take my mind off of tomorrow." Malcolm looked at Joan properly. Her hair was mussed, and she had hurriedly put on her uniform. As he rose and went to his bar, he asked, "Can I offer you a drink?"

"Please," Joan emphasised.

Malcolm gave her a glass of vodka and poured himself a large shot of whisky. "Here you go," he said, handing her the glass. He raised his glass, "Cheers!"

"Cheers," she echoed without enthusiasm.

They both drank in silence for several moments. "I've faced many nights before a life and death mission," Joan said, breaking the silence. "I could sleep because I knew I could accept the mission's outcome. But tonight, I'm so worried I can't sleep."

"Worried about what?"

"Worried if something goes wrong tomorrow, we will never have lived our lives together. That scares me more than any mission I've ever faced."

"While I can't say I'm unhappy since I've rejoined the Service, I regret we are more distant than before this whole mess began."

"We don't have to be distant," Joan said.

"Joan, you know we shouldn't…"

"Shh," she said, putting her finger to her lips. "O'Hallarhan is the only other person on the base and he won't bother us." She set her drink down and walked around the desk. "Please, let me stay with you tonight, Malcolm. We might not survive tomorrow, and I don't want to be alone tonight." She leaned in and kissed him.

"Neither do I," Malcolm said, before he returned the kiss.

The next morning, Malcolm was up and showered before Joan was awake. He looked at her, sleeping peacefully, and he knew how lucky he was. He gently touched her and leaned down and gave her a kiss. "Good morning, Sleeping Beauty."

"And you're supposed to be Prince Charming?" she said with a yawn.

"I'm making tea, getting a cold roll, and heading to the ship. You can use the shower here, but don't leave until after eight bells."

"Why so late?" Joan asked.

"Because that's when I told O'Hallarhan to meet me on the ship. If we don't arrive together, he won't think anything of it."

"Ah, good thinking," Joan said. She reached up and held his hand, gently pulling him back to the bed. "Must you leave?"

"Unless you want to make the tea, I'm afraid I must," Malcolm said.

"Good God, no!" she said. "You better go."

Malcolm leaned in and kissed her. "I'll see you after eight bells and act surprised when I pretend to be upset about your tardiness."

"You'll have to punish me later," she said with a smile.

"See you soon," he said, kissing her on her head before he left.

After making the tea, he ate a cold roll and washed it down with tea. He refilled his mug, poured a second, and made his way to the ship. It didn't surprise him O'Hallarhan was already there, going through his checklist.

"I thought you could use this," Malcolm said, offering the second mug of tea.

"You really shouldn't have drinks around the equipment, but God, I could sure use it. Thank you," O'Hallarhan said as he accepted the mug. "This is bloody awful tea," he said after taking a sip.

"I know it's awful, but unless you can do better, this is the best we have until the mess staff returns."

"Wouldn't Lieutenant de St. Leger be a better choice for making the tea?"

"I have it on excellent authority that, no, she wouldn't," Malcolm said. "How are you coming on the pre-ignition checklist?"

"I'm about halfway through. If you could read the remaining items, I'll execute them one by one," O'Hallarhan said, handing a clipboard to Malcolm.

"Excellent," Malcolm said as he noted O'Hallarhan was halfway through the list. The two men started work and were so engrossed they didn't notice Joan enter until she said, "Lieutenant de St. Leger, reporting for duty."

Malcolm took out his Granda's pocket watch. "Lieutenant, I believe you were supposed to report at eight bells? You're twenty-three minutes late."

"Sorry, sir, it won't happen again," she said with a wink. "What can I do, sir?" Joan said.

"You can read this checklist and as the Commander and I perform each task, note its completion and the time. Here, take my watch," Malcolm said, offering his Granda's watch.

"Thank you, sir," she said. She handled the watch gingerly, knowing it meant a great deal to Malcolm.

After they completed the checklist an hour later, Malcolm and O'Hallarhan finished their stone-cold tea. An awkward silence settled, before Joan said, "Where did you get the tea?"

"From the mess," Malcolm said. "I made it."

"Oh, I'll pass then," Joan said.

After a long pause, O'Hallarhan said, "Shall we start?"

"No time like the present," Malcolm said, settling into the deuterium flow station as O'Hallarhan settled into the primary engine station. Malcolm took a moment to familiarise himself with the gauges.

"Lieutenant, you'll monitor the magnetic containment field, that console to your right. Once I turn on the magnetic containment field, monitor the gauge and tell me if it fluctuates at all. I assume since you're a Communications officer, you know how to read the gauge?" O'Hallarhan said.

"Yes, sir," Joan said. Malcolm noted the tone of irritation in her voice that O'Hallarhan ignored.

"Commodore, on my signal, you'll start the deuterium flow. Keep it low - approximately two on your dial. Starting vacuum pumps in the torus," O'Hallarhan said, flipping the switches to engage the vacuum pumps. A rhythmic pulse filled the Engine Room as the pumps worked to purge the torus of air, and within minutes, the pressure gauge showed a complete vacuum.

"Excellent. I've engaged the magnetic containment field. Lieutenant, start monitoring the field for fluctuation." A low hum added its voice to the sound of the pumps maintaining a vacuum.

"Aye, sir," Joan said.

"Commodore, start the deuterium flow."

"Flow started," Malcolm said as he adjusted the dial at his station and watched as the needle on the deuterium flow gauge slowly raised.

O'Hallarhan took a deep breath. "I'm applying the current to heat the plasma. Commodore, I'll ask you to increase the deuterium slowly until my mark. We will know in the next few minutes if we are successful."

O'Hallarhan pushed the ignition button and Malcolm held his breath. Malcolm heard a loud whoosh come from the reactor; he decided to focus on the deuterium flow gauge to distract from thoughts of the alternative.

"Starting plasma heating," O'Hallarhan said. "Commodore, increase the deuterium flow."

Malcolm held his breath as he slowly increased the flow, stopping for a few seconds before O'Hallarhan nodded to increase it again.

"Lieutenant, how's the magnetic containment field?"

"Holding steady, sir."

"Commodore, increase the deuterium flow by twenty per cent."

"Increased by twenty per cent."

"The temperature in the torus indicates that we have converted the deuterium to plasma," O'Hallarhan said. "Commodore, increase the deuterium flow by another ten percent."

"Increased by ten per cent."

"Hold on," O'Hallarhan said. "I'm seeing fluctuations in the torus temperature."

"What do we do?" Malcolm asked.

"I don't know," O'Hallarhan said. "If we can't stabilise the plasma quickly, the reaction will get out of control." Malcolm looked at Joan and saw the fear he felt reflected in her eyes. O'Hallarhan stared at the gauge for several seconds before he said. "Reduce the deuterium flow by ten percent."

Malcolm reduced the flow and held his breath, praying that O'Hallarhan made the right decision. As seconds ticked by, Malcolm's feelings of dread intensified. He looked at Joan and saw the same dread mirrored on her face.

"Temperature is holding steady." They all let out a collective sigh of relief. "Commodore, any reading on the reactor output?"

"Not yet."

"Increase deuterium flow by five per cent."

"Increased by five per cent," Malcolm said, turning the dial.

"We need to dissipate the energy from the reactor soon or we'll melt the reactor. Any reading on the reactor output?"

"Not yet," Malcolm said.

"Damn, what is wrong? The reactor should produce voltage." O'Hallarhan banged his fist on the console.

Malcolm's heart lept to his throat. Even with his incomplete knowledge of the reactor, he reviewed each of the components in his head. *Is it my imagination or is the Engine Room getting hotter?*

"Is the turbine on?" Malcolm asked. "That should be dissipating the heat from the reactor."

"Of course, it… oh," O'Hallarhan said. He flipped the switch, and the turbine began spinning. The engine room filled with sound as the turbine spun up to speed.

"The reactor temperature has stabilised," O'Hallarhan said. Although there was no immediate danger of a reactor meltdown, the trio held their breath, waiting to see if the reactor could generate power.

A few seconds later, Malcolm noted the generator output gauge steadily climbing. "Getting a reading on the reactor output. Bloody hell, is that right? Three thousand megawatts?"

"That's correct, Commodore. We've done it," O'Hallarhan said.

The trio breathed a collective sigh of relief as the thrum of the turbines joined the hum of the containment field and the rhythm of the vacuum pumps. To someone else, it might sound like a cacophony, but to Malcolm's ears, it sounded like a majestic symphony.

They sat in silence for several seconds, listening to the sounds of the first operational fusion reactor before Malcolm asked, "Now what?"

"We'll reduce the deuterium flow and monitor the reactor for several hours. We'll take shifts during the night to ensure the reactor remains stable."

"Congratulations, Commander. You successfully started the first fusion reaction. This is an impressive accomplishment."

"Thank you, sir," O'Hallarhan said.

"Now the actual work begins; we must get this ship space worthy."

CHAPTER TWENTY THREE

$\mathcal{M}$alcolm waited patiently as he watched the *Uhuru* approach the docking area, returning the first crew members to the base. Unsurprisingly, the first person off the ship was Saxon. After saluting, he said, "I see you left the base intact and not a pile of smouldering ruins."

"Sorry I disappointed you," Malcolm said. "There's still plenty of opportunities left to destroy the base."

"I brought a surprise with me that should reduce your chances of blowing us to kingdom come."

"Are you ruining my excellent designs?" a familiar voice said. From behind Saxon stepped Ernest Rutherford, the renowned physicist. The two men first met on Malcolm's first mission as captain aboard the *Daedalus* and, despite Rutherford trying to punch Malcolm during their first meeting, became good friends. "Hello, Malcolm," he said, offering his hand. "Who did you anger to get sent to this godforsaken rock?"

"Hello, Ernest," Malcolm said, shaking his hand. "You know me; I have a way with people."

"Yes, and now you've got me banished here," Ernest said.

"Misery loves company, as they say."

"So they say."

"All kidding aside, I'm very grateful you've come and will teach my crew and their obstinate commander about the Martian technology," Malcolm said.

"I'll do my best," Ernest said. "Honestly, the Martian technology has few underpinnings in our current understanding of space, matter, or energy."

"I wish I knew you were coming. I would have given you my old quarters."

"It's already arranged. I radioed Lieutenant de St Leger and she made sure the room was ready," Saxon said. "And I have another surprise; the Admiralty has approved our crew assignments, and they will arrive shortly."

"I can't believe the Admiralty moved so swiftly." Malcolm asked, "Any other surprises I should know about?"

"None right now," Saxon said.

"Thank you, Charles." Turning to Ernest, Malcolm asked, "Shall I escort you to your quarters?"

"If it's all the same, I'd like to see your spaceship," Ernest replied. "And I understand the reactor is fully functional?"

"Yes, it's been running for the last two weeks with nary a problem."

"Excellent, I can't wait to see it!" Ernest's face suddenly darkened. "O'Hallarhan will be there, won't he?"

"Yes, I can barely drag him away from the ship," Malcolm said. "Why do you ask?"

"We didn't part on good terms when I left the project. If Mycroft hadn't told me you asked for my help, I wouldn't be here."

"I see," Malcolm said. "Commander Saxon, perhaps you would be kind enough to have Commander O'Hallarhan report to Sick Bay for a physical."

"But Commodore, no one is in Sick Bay, as the medical crew won't return until next week."

"We know that, but O'Hallarhan doesn't. By the time he gives up, I will have given Ernest a tour of the ship and escorted him to his quarters."

Saxon nodded, saluted, and left.

"Commodore?" Ernest asked. "I did not know. Congratulations!"

"Thank you," Malcolm said. "I can hardly believe it myself." As they talked, Malcolm watched as a clearly frustrated O'Hallarhan stomped out of the ship and made his way across the cave towards Sick Bay.

"This way, Ernest," Malcolm said, leading Rutherford to the ship. As they drew closer to the ship, Ernest said, "Good God, Malcolm! It really looks like a ship now!"

"Aye," Malcolm said. "We've tested for air leaks and as I mentioned before, the reactor is fully functional. O'Hallarhan has been hooking up several systems single-handedly as Lieutenant de St. Leger and I kept watch over the reactor."

Malcolm led Ernest inside. With the generator powering the ship, the interior was now fully lit, making the ship feel closer to completion. Malcolm gave an abbreviated tour of the bridge before taking Ernest to the Engine Room.

Ernest rushed into the Engine Room and went directly to the torus. He reached towards the torus, but Malcolm yelled, "I'm sure the water in the outer casing is pure steam by now, so I wouldn't touch it if I were you."

"Ah, yes. Good point," Ernest said. He immediately inspected the control panels, monitoring all aspects of the reactor: magnetic field strength, steam temperature, deuterium flow, and power output. "It's true; the reactor really generates that much power! That is truly astonishing! Congratulations, Malcolm!"

"I barely worked on the reactor. Commander O'Hallarhan deserves the credit for its success."

"I see," Ernest said, his expression darkening.

"We hooked up the electro kinetic thrusters and the capacitor bank will supply the pulse to the gravity beam generator."

Ernest smiled. "You don't understand a single word you said."

"Not a word," Malcolm said, smiling. "That's why I asked you here. Commander O'Hallarhan thinks I'm too old to learn this technology, but someone needs to understand it. I won't put all my eggs in one basket."

"Particularly that basket," Ernest muttered. "I'll happily teach you what I know, but I don't understand the physics behind aspects of this technology myself."

"You're a Nobel Prize-winning scientist and you don't understand it? How can I hope to learn it?"

"I can teach you what I know. But our physics simply can't explain certain principles of the Martian technology. We have theories, but unfortunately, our Martian guests aren't physicists or even engineers. The only way you'll learn Martian technology is by using it."

He was happier about this than Rutherford; Malcolm learned best by doing and applying knowledge. "Let's adjourn to my office, where we can catch up. How are Mary and your daughter Eileen?" Malcolm asked as they started to his office.

"Well, I'm sure Mary is cursing me for leaving her in Manchester while I 'gallivant' around the world."

"Aye, gallivanting to an island in the middle of the North Atlantic. I understand why she would be jealous," Malcolm said, smiling.

"How is Joan?" Rutherford inquired. "I understand she's a lieutenant?"

"Yes. When our mutual friend Mycroft reactivated my commission using some obscure regulation, he transferred Joan to the Royal Navy Auxiliary. She completed her officer training and is now a first rate communications officer."

They soon arrived at Malcolm's office, without crossing paths with Commander O'Hallarhan. Malcolm poured whisky for Ernest and himself. "Tell me," Malcolm said, offering Ernest his drink, "what is your problem with Commander O'Hallarhan?"

"He's a pompous, arrogant bastard," Ernest said, before sipping his whisky.

"I know that, but there is more you aren't telling me."

Ernest sighed and sipped his whisky. "As you know, our friend sent me to this godforsaken rock when this project started. He tasked O'Hallarhan and I to understand this Martian technology and design the ship. We spent months reviewing everything in minute detail and we spent hours theorising the physics behind everything. We finished the work after several months and presented the findings to the Admiralty."

Ernest sipped his whisky before continuing. "He asked me to handle the presentation as he said he didn't feel comfortable talking before a large crowd. The presentation was going well until O'Hallarhan pointed out a mathematical error. He corrected my work and presented new conclusions, embarrassing me before the other physics experts. I'm convinced the bastard purposely discredited me so he could take credit for the brilliant new theory." Ernest sipped his whisky before continuing. "I've never been so angry. It took all my restraint to prevent taking a swing at the bastard. I've spent years building my reputation as an expert in physics, and this bastard made me look like a fool." Ernest sipped his drink again. "The problem was, he was right. The mistake in the calculation invalidated all the work and subsequent conclusions."

"Do you think he purposely waited to point out the error?"

"I'm certain! We spent days reviewing our work and double-checking our calculations; he had many opportunities to show me the error. He didn't just 'stumble' upon it during my talk. Bloody hell, I looked at the calculation God knows how many times and I couldn't find it!"

"It's certainly keeping in character," Malcolm said. He told Ernest about the conversation where O'Hallarhan discouraged Malcolm from learning about the Martian technology because of his age.

"How did you take it?" Ernest said.

"Not very well. I came back and pounded my desk, scaring the hell out of my assistant. That's when I contacted Mycroft to get your help. No young whippersnapper tells me I'm too old to learn." They sat silently, sipping their whiskey. "What do we do about our commander? I need his knowledge and skill if this ship ever leaves this cave."

"And that's why you are a Commodore and I'm only a consultant. It's not my job to deal with O'Hallarhan, but it would be better for everyone involved if I spent minimal time with him. I'm liable to punch him as soon as look at him."

"You tried to punch me when we met and look how we get along now?" Malcolm said.

"Who says I still won't punch you?" Ernest replied.

"Punching me won't help us. We desperately need your expertise shared with the crew and you can't teach effectively from the brig."

"But it would make me feel better," Ernest said. Malcolm glared at him before Ernest replied, "I'm kidding!"

"Good, I don't want to throw you in the brig again."

"How do you intend to handle him?"

"I'll leave him be; he spends his waking hours on the ship, and I suspect he sleeps there. While he's occupied with the ship, I'll discretely rotate our engineering crew into your lectures. I recommend you start with the broadest possible introduction so the ship's crew have a basic understanding of the ship's operation and more detailed classes for myself and the Engineering crew. Since we don't want to keep you here any longer than necessary, I'll take over as the instructor when you leave. We get you home and away from O'Hallarhan as quickly as possible, and I receive a thorough understanding of the technology aboard this ship."

"I believe that could work. But I won't leave until you can competently teach the course without me."

"It might take months before I can teach this," Malcolm said.

"That's what I'm afraid of," Ernest said.

CHAPTER TWENTY FOUR

The morning of the first test of the propulsion systems, Malcolm cancelled lectures so that Rutherford could attend. Rutherford was dead-set against it, reluctant to meet with O'Hallarhan, but Malcolm persuaded him to attend. At two bells, Malcolm escorted Rutherford aboard the ship. They went directly to the Engine Room where they found O'Hallarhan double-checking all the connections to the gravity beam generator, the large metallic cone where the large end faced the ship's fore.

"Commander O'Hallarhan, I brought a special visitor for a tour of the ship," Malcolm said.

"Sir, I'm extremely busy, can't it wait?" O'Hallarhan said without looking up from his work.

"No, it can't," Malcolm said, his voice sharp. "I'm afraid I must insist."

O'Hallarhan sighed, "Very well, sir. I..." he stopped when he looked up and saw Rutherford. "Professor Rutherford! What are you doing here? I had no idea you were here. Yes, of course, I would be happy to give you a tour of the ship." Before Rutherford could respond, O'Hallarhan began showing Rutherford around the Engine Room.

O'Hallarhan went on for nearly an hour, describing everything in the Engine Room as if he had personally built every square inch. Rutherford worked hard to appear interested and shot daggers from his eyes at Malcolm every chance he got. Malcolm followed behind as O'Hallarhan led Rutherford through the ship; to the main electronic computators, the bridge, and the auxiliary control room. It was a good refresher for Malcolm; he knew the layout of the ship from studying the blueprints, but seeing the ship nearly completed helped him appreciate its size. "How do you intend to conduct the test, Commander?" Malcolm said.

"I've set up a temporary control station outside of the ship," O'Hallarhan said. "From there, we can apply the voltage to the gravity beam generator. I'll remain in the Engine Room in case something happens and I must disconnect the power."

"Won't the capacitors continue to hold the voltage?" Malcolm inquired.

"Yes, I've built a circuit to discharge the capacitors' voltage from the capacitor bank over the exterior surface of the ship when I disconnect the power. At the voltages we use, it won't cause any damage."

"Are we ready to conduct the test?" Malcolm said.

"Yes, let me take my station in the Engine Room and I'll notify you over the headset."

As Malcolm and Rutherford left the ship, Malcolm leaned over to Rutherford. "You handled that very well."

"The insides of my palms are nearly bleeding from digging my fingernails into my hands so I wouldn't say anything. You owe me, Malcolm."

"I know. What's your price?"

"I'll think about it," Rutherford said.

Within a few minutes, O'Hallarhan signalled he was in place. Malcolm dismissed the crewman at the control station, insisted on running the test himself. "Ready when you are, Commander," Malcolm said into the headset.

"Commodore, you're running the controls?"

"Yes. Shall we begin?" Malcolm said in a tone that prevented additional discussion.

"Very well. Set the voltage to one hundred kilovolts."

Malcolm slid the lever to the one hundred kilovolt mark. "one hundred kilovolts; no noticeable effect."

"I didn't expect it would. I just want to ensure the capacitor bank can take the voltage. Increase the voltage slowly until you reach one thousand kilovolts."

Malcolm slowly increased the voltage, keeping a careful eye on the ship. "At one thousand kilovolts. The ship is rocking in place; like a hot-air balloon that can't quite get off the ground."

"Excellent; I expected that. Set the voltage to one thousand five hundred kilovolts."

Malcolm increased the voltage, and as he did, the large ship rose slowly. "Excellent work, Commander. We have achieved lift. We're approximately 20 feet off the ground."

"Noted. Increase to two thousand kilovolts."

"We should be careful - we don't want to damage the ship before we go anywhere."

"Just increase the voltage to two thousand kilovolts... sir," O'Hallarhan added as an afterthought.

"Very well, but if I feel we are putting the ship in jeopardy, I'm stopping," Malcolm said.

"Very well, sir," O'Hallarhan said.

Malcolm slowly increased the voltage, and the ship rose quickly. At nearly one thousand eight hundred kilovolts, Malcolm stopped. "Commander, the ship is wobbling. The field strength appears to be fluctuating along the ship."

"What? That's impossible," O'Hallarhan said. There was a pause before O'Hallarhan spoke. "Bloody hell! An entire row of capacitors has burned out! Let me see if I can bypass them," O'Hallarhan said. Suddenly, there was an earsplitting snap, and the line went quiet.

"Commander O'Hallarhan, are you there? Commander, report immediately," Malcolm yelled in the handset. He repeated the call several times, but there was no answer. "Damn it, O'Hallarhan, answer!" he yelled.

Malcolm gradually reduced the voltage, and the ship began its descent. Once the ship made a gentle landing, Malcolm quickly cut the rest of the voltage. After yelling to a crewman to get the doctor, Malcolm ran to the Engine Room, finding O'Hallarhan sprawled on the floor.

Malcolm knelt next to O'Hallarhan and assessed his condition; his hands were badly burnt, and he was not breathing. Malcolm began pressing O'Hallarhan's abdomen and releasing it. After nearly a dozen compressions, O'Hallarhan breathed on his own. Malcolm turned his attention to O'Hallarhan's hands. Blisters were already forming. O'Hallarhan stirred.

"Commander! Can you hear me? Do you know where you are?" Malcolm asked.

O'Hallarhan mumbled unintelligibly, but after a moment, he opened his eyes. "Commodore, what happened?"

"I was going to ask you the same thing," Malcolm said. O'Hallarhan tried to sit up, but Malcolm gently pushed him back down. "Don't sit up. You've had a nasty shock and your hands have extremely nasty-looking burns. Dr Boyce will be here shortly. Just relax."

After laying back, O'Hallarhan winced in pain.

"Is it your hands?" Malcolm probed.

"Yes," O'Hallarhan said through gritted teeth.

"What happened?"

"Things were going well when suddenly one row of the capacitor bank burned out. I tried to remove them before the failure could cascade and destroy the whole capacitor bank. As I tried to disconnect the row, my screwdriver slipped, and I contacted the direct voltage from the reactor." Malcolm glanced at the capacitor bank and saw the screwdriver's blade sitting on an ash pile on the Engine Room floor; the wooden handle must have gone up in flames.

"The doctor should be here soon, and he can check you out."

"I'm fine, sir," O'Hallarhan said, again trying to sit up.

"You are anything but fine, Commander," Malcolm said. "When I arrived, you were not breathing and you have severe burns on your hands. You are not going anywhere else but sick bay and you'll remain there until Dr Boyce gives his blessing for you to return to duty. That's an order."

"Yes, sir," O'Hallarhan said glumly. "But what about the ship? How will I get that ready to fly if I'm cooped up in sick bay?"

"Leave that to me. I want you to concentrate on getting better. Rushing you back to duty won't help anyone." As Malcolm finished talking, Dr Boyce entered the Engine Room with two corpsmen.

"Commodore, I didn't expect to find you here," Boyce said. "Do you know what happened?"

"We were testing the ship and Commander O'Hallarhan sustained a severe electrical shock from malfunctioning equipment. When I arrived, he wasn't breathing. I performed chest compressions, and after a dozen compressions, he started breathing. He has pretty nasty burns on his hands."

"Thank you, Commodore. I'll take it from here."

Malcolm stepped back and watched the doctor listen to O'Hallarhan's heart and took his pulse. He reached into his bag and gingerly bandaged O'Hallarhan's hands, causing O'Hallarhan to hiss in pain. He probed around O'Hallarhan's body to check for other injuries. Once he finished his initial examination, he motioned to the corpsmen, and they gently put O'Hallarhan on the stretcher.

"Doctor, I'll be by later today to check on O'Hallarhan's condition." Boyce nodded as the corpsmen bore O'Hallarhan away.

Malcolm assessed the condition of the Engine Room. The acrid smell of burnt capacitors filled the air. He examined the capacitor bank and found O'Hallarhan's assessment correct; the voltage had burnt out nearly an entire row, but O'Hallarhan successfully disconnected the row before it caused any additional issues. Malcolm reached for one of the intact capacitors and stopped himself, remembering it probably still had a fair amount of voltage stored in it. He rummaged around the Engine Room until he found a pair of heavy rubber gloves and a rubber handled screwdriver. He carefully pulled the capacitor from the bank and laid the blade of the screwdriver across the capacitor's two terminals. A large spark of electricity erupted and, in a flash, was gone. Malcolm examined the capacitor, looking for any information. He compared it to capacitors in the row above and below. He furrowed his brow; the capacitor wasn't the same as the capacitors above or below. He sighed, knowing he would need to solve this mystery later. After safely removing and discharging a capacitor from the row above and below the burnt out row, he marked the capacitors with a pen, and put them in his pocket.

When he returned to the control station, Rutherford rushed to him. "How is the Commander? I saw them take him away on a stretcher and I feared the worse."

"He had a pretty nasty shock and wasn't breathing, but he came around. He has nasty burns on his hands. I think he'll be fine eventually, but I leave that up to the surgeon."

"I'm glad. While the man irritates me to no end, I don't wish him actual harm," Rutherford said. "What happened?"

"It was exactly what O'Hallarhan reported. One row of the capacitor bank burned out; O'Hallarhan got shocked while disconnecting the row to prevent a cascade failure."

"Why did it burn out?"

"Look at these capacitors; Numbers one and three came from the row above and the row below, respectively. This capacitor was in the burnt out row. What do you see?"

"Number two is markedly different from the other capacitors." Rutherford paused in thought. "That shouldn't be; the design clearly specified that all the capacitors must be the same."

"I thought as much," Malcolm said.

"What does that mean?" Rutherford said.

"We must examine every single capacitor in the bank, ensure each capacitor is correct and functioning before trying again."

"That doesn't sound fun," Rutherford said.

"No, it doesn't," Malcolm agreed.

CHAPTER TWENTY FIVE

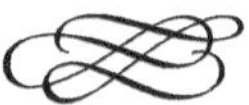

 alcolm ordered the Engineering crew to disconnect the capacitor bank and to report to him when they completed the work. He and Ernest returned to Malcolm's office to find Commander Saxon waiting for them.

"I hear you had a little excitement this morning," Saxon said.

"You could say that," Malcolm replied. Malcolm asked Commander Murray to get tea for the three of them as they settled around Malcolm's table. Malcolm explained what had occurred and the conclusion that he and Rutherford reached.

"And what does that mean?" Saxon asked.

"It means we have to order replacement parts and potentially rebuild the capacitor bank. This will put us way behind schedule."

"And your chief engineer will be out of commission for some time," Saxon added. "That won't help the situation."

"You are just a ray of sunshine, Commander," Malcolm muttered.

"Always doing my best to dampen the mood," Saxon said with a smile; he was happy to note that he had elicited a wan smile from Malcolm.

Malcolm took a deep breath. "Let's think through this. Our Chief Engineer will be unavailable for some indeterminate time. I'm not a doctor, but I'm sure he won't be returning to duty in a few days. How can we keep working without him?"

"How knowledgeable is the rest of the Engineering crew?" Saxon asked.

"My guess is not very. I bet that O'Hallarhan only assigns them the routine work while he focuses on the work he prefers," Malcolm replied. He sipped his tea as he collected his thoughts. "So, how do we replace him?"

"I'm not sure how you can," Rutherford said. "He's the only engineer who understands the design of the ship."

"But," Malcolm interjected, "we have the scientist who helped design the ship, and we have at least one engineer with some familiarity with the Martian technology."

"Who's that?" Saxon said.

"Me," Malcolm said, glaring at Saxon before he could make another comment. Saxon silently put his hands up in surrender.

"While I don't doubt your technical ability, you're a commodore now," Saxon said. "You have a great deal of responsibilities. Not only are you responsible for preparing the ship to travel to Mars, you also have a base to run. I don't believe you can do both jobs simultaneously."

"You're right," Malcolm said, as he smiled.

Saxon's brow darkened. "I'm not sure I like that smile."

"You're absolutely correct, Commander. I can't do both jobs at once, but I have two excellent commanders to whom I can distribute some duties while I'm working on the ship."

"I was afraid you'd say something like that," Saxon muttered.

"Is there anything I can do?" Rutherford asked.

"I need your help with the designs for the rest of the ship."

"But I'm a scientist, not an engineer," Rutherford protested.

"I'm afraid I need you to be both," Malcolm said. "Commander Saxon, could you ask Commander Murray to join us? It will take everyone to figure this out."

When Commander Murray joined them, they spent an hour of discussion and argument before they had a plan. Rutherford and

Malcolm would spend the morning working out design or technical requirements; after noon, Rutherford would resume teaching basic theory while Malcolm worked with the Engineering crew on the assigned tasks for the day. Commander Murray would handle the routine paperwork and administrative issues, while Commander Saxon would deal with personnel issues and logistics. Malcolm would spend the evenings dealing with anything that absolutely required either his attention or authority as a Commodore.

"This is an ambitious schedule," Saxon said. "How long can you maintain that pace?"

"Hopefully, it won't be very long," Malcolm said. "Maybe a couple of weeks?"

That notion disappeared when he went to Sick Bay to check on Commander O'Hallarhan. "Dr Boyce, what is O'Hallarhan's condition?"

"I gave him codeine to help with the pain from his burns. He's sleeping now. Other than his hands, the electrocution didn't appear to cause any other damage. I'm going to keep him in Sick Bay for observation for the next two days."

"When can he return to duty?"

"He can't return to duty until his hands heal. While I can treat the worst of the symptoms, he needs more advanced care than I can provide. I request he receive medical leave and return to London, where he can receive proper treatment."

"Will he ever be able to return to active duty?"

"I believe that with the proper treatment, he should keep full use of his hands and can return to active duty."

"How long will that take?"

"I estimate at least two months."

Malcolm sighed. "Very well. Make the arrangements to transfer him to London as soon as possible. I need him back to duty as soon as he's able. Thank you, Doctor."

As Malcolm reached his office, Commander Murray stopped him. "I received an urgent message from the Martian Chancellor. He wishes to see you immediately." Malcolm turned around and trudged to the Martian's quarters. When Malcolm arrived, the Chancellor was pacing on the other side of the glass.

"Commodore, the moment we've dreaded has arrived. The Crown Prince's health has deteriorated to the point that the Crown Prince has entered a hibernation tube to slow the effects of his condition. That will only delay the inevitable. It's imperative that the Crown Prince returns to Mars as soon as possible."

"I'm very sorry to hear that, Chancellor. How much time do we have before the Crown Prince's condition is untreatable?"

"I do not know. I am no physician. The hibernation chamber slows the metabolism, but I do not know whether the Crown Prince has weeks or months left before his condition is terminal."

"Is there anything else we can do?"

"Get the Crown Prince off this accursed planet."

"I'm doing my best, Chancellor. However, I won't lie. We have hit a… set back."

"What is it?"

Malcolm weighed his words. "During our first test of the engine, our Chief Engineer sustained a serious injury. It is not life threatening, but he is unavailable for the next two months. We have a plan to finish the ship and will execute it in all due haste."

"See that you do," the Chancellor said, returning to the darkness of its chamber.

When Malcolm returned to his office, Lieutenant Commander Clarke was waiting for him to report on the capacitor bank. "Commodore, there are several mismatched capacitors in the capacitor bank. The reason the row failed first was the entire row differed from the design. Initial estimates are that thirty percent of the capacitors need to be replaced."

"This day just keeps getting better," Malcolm mumbled.

"Beg pardon, sir?"

"Nothing. I want you to remove and test every capacitor for damage. Throw out any capacitors that do not match the design specifications. In the meantime, I'll see what I can do about getting the correct capacitors."

"Begging your pardon, sir," Clarke said, fidgeting in place. "I mentioned to Commander O'Hallarhan when we were building the capacitor bank, some capacitors didn't match the design specifications. He told me not to worry about it. I noted it in my report, if you care to check."

Malcolm let out an exasperated sigh. "I believe you Lieutenant Commander."

"How will we finish the ship? There's much work to complete and my team needs direction."

"I'm afraid you're stuck with me directing the work until Commander O'Hallarhan returns to duty in another two months." Malcolm briefed Clarke on the outline of the plan.

Clarke nodded. "I look forward to working for you, Commodore," he said.

Malcolm smiled. "You're too kind, Lieutenant Commander. You may end up regretting those words."

"We'll see," said Clarke. "If I can be so bold, I think I will enjoy working for you more than Commander O'Hallarhan."

"How so?"

"Permission to speak freely?"

"Permission granted," Malcolm said.

Clarke hesitated for a moment, taking a deep breath. "Commander O'Hallarhan is very brilliant, without a doubt. But he also liked to prove that at every chance he could. He provides vague directions and gets angry when we didn't do something to his liking. Then, he lectures us on how we should have done it." Clarke paused. "You don't work that way. You look for the best solution to the problem, whatever the source. You work with us and guide us instead of issuing vague orders and getting upset that we couldn't read your mind."

"Thank you, Lieutenant Commander," Malcolm said. "But I'm afraid you may still get vague orders because I only have a small understanding of the technology."

"Then we'll be in the same boat... or spaceship," Clarke said.

Malcolm chuckled. "Lieutenant Commander, would you attend

my morning design sessions with Professor Rutherford? I'm sure we could use another hand."

Clarke looked puzzled for a moment before replying, "Me, sir? What would I offer? I know very little about this technology."

"Neither do I, but you have years of engineering experience. You know more about the practical construction of the ship than anyone else, including our erstwhile commander. I could use another engineer to keep me honest."

"Thank you, sir. I'm honoured. Yes, I would be happy to join the design effort."

"Excellent," Malcolm said. "Come to my office right after the morning mess. We'll start here and adjourn to the ship as necessary." Malcolm paused for a moment before asking, "Is there anything else, Lieutenant Commander? If not, I don't mean to be rude, but I have an enormous pile of work I must finish before we start tomorrow."

"No, sir," Clarke said. He threw a very sharp salute as he left. He paused at the door to say, "Thank you for this opportunity, sir. I won't let you down."

"I'm counting on it, Lieutenant Commander," Malcolm said. Clarke nodded and left.

Malcolm focused first on getting the correct capacitors to rebuild the bank. After reviewing the design specs, he had his list and asked Commander Murray to send for Lieutenant Hughes.

"Lieutenant, I need you to requisition the following parts as soon as possible. And they must match these specifications exactly. No substitutions."

Lieutenant Hughes looked at the list and furrowed his brow. "Begging pardon, sir, but I ordered these same parts about a year ago."

"Unfortunately, we did not receive what we requested. As a result, Commander O'Hallarhan is now in Sick Bay with nasty burns on his hands."

Lieutenant Hughes sighed. "Permission to speak freely?"

"Granted."

"The problem is Commander Holdsworth at the Quartermaster's office. This isn't the first time we didn't receive what we requested.

It's my belief he thinks that he's doing the Service a favour by spending as little money as possible, even if it means skimping on items."

"I see," Malcolm said. "Shall we have a talk with the Commander?" When they arrived at the radio room, Malcolm was happy to see Joan manning the station.

"Commodore, what can I do for you?" she said.

"Lieutenant, if you would be kind enough to contact Commander Holdsworth at the Quartermaster's office. Lieutenant Hughes can provide you with the information you need."

After several minutes while as she patched the call through, Joan said. "Commander Holdsworth is on the line. Who should I say is calling?"

"Lieutenant Hughes will make the call. Can you put it on speaker so we all can hear?"

"Yes, sir," Joan said. She gave a hand set to Lieutenant Hughes and completed the call.

"Yes, Lieutenant, what can I do for you?" said the voice over the speaker. Malcolm could detect the fake sincerity in the voice.

"Commander Holdsworth, I'm sorry to bother you, but we need the following requisition filled as quickly as possible," Lieutenant Hughes said before reading the requisition request.

"That's quite an order. I'm not sure if we have that many components in stock. I'll send you what I can."

"Begging pardon, sir," Hughes stammered. "The parts have to be exactly what we requested. We've already had a major injury because we didn't get the correct parts."

"You'll get what I give you, Lieutenant. Is that clear?" Holdsworth said.

Malcolm motioned to Hughes to turn over the handset. "Commander Holdsworth, is it?"

"Who is this?"

"This is Commodore Malcolm Robertson, the base commander. Did I understand you are unwilling to fill our requisition exactly as requested?"

"No, sir," Holdsworth stammered. "It's just, we don't have large supplies of components and I often have to scrounge to find comparable components."

"Except you don't," Malcolm said. "We placed a requisition for the same parts over a year ago. And we didn't receive what we requested. As Lieutenant Hughes said, our Chief Engineer is in sick bay because we didn't receive the correct parts."

"But, sir," Holdsworth began.

"But nothing, Commander. Let me ask you, do you like your current assignment? I assume you are at the Admiralty in London?"

"Yes, sir," Holdsworth hesitated.

"Let me be crystal clear, Commander. You will send us exactly what we requested and you will do it with all haste. I will inspect every item we receive to determine if it matches our request. And before you think I won't be able to tell the difference, I've spent fifteen years in Engineering and I will know the difference. If a single item does not match our requisition, I will make it my personal mission to see your next assignment will be to the most godforsaken post in the Royal Navy. Do you understand?"

"Absolutely, sir," Holdsworth said.

"And Commander, in the future, please see you fill future requisitions exactly as requested. Lieutenant Hughes will let me know if we aren't receiving the level of cooperation that I expect. Do I make myself clear?"

"Crystal, sir," Holdsworth said. "I'll get this requisition filled as soon as possible."

"See that you do," Malcolm said. He handed the handset to Joan, and they concluded the call.

"There we go, Lieutenant Hughes. I don't think you'll have any problems. Be judicious about pressuring the commander. I don't really care if you make concessions for base supplies, but with requisitions for the ship, I expect you to hold his feet to the fire."

"Yes, sir," Lieutenant Hughes said.

"That will be all, Lieutenant," Malcolm said. After Lieutenant Hughes left, Joan smiled at Malcolm. "What?"

"I haven't seen you throw your rank around very often. It was interesting to see," she said.

"It's good to know it's useful for something," Malcolm said. Joan gave him a puzzled look. Malcolm relayed the events of the day.

Joan reached her hand to Malcolm's, but stopped. "I'm sorry, Malcolm... I mean, sir."

"Not as sorry as me," Malcolm said. "I would love to stay, but I must finish a large pile of work before I can sleep tonight."

"Promise me you won't work yourself to death," Joan said.

"I don't have that luxury," Malcolm said as he left the radio room.

CHAPTER TWENTY SIX

$\mathcal{M}$orning came too early for Malcolm. After sorting out the supply issue, Malcolm returned to his office to finish paperwork and write his report about the day's activities. While they should have expected a setback in the testing, losing O'Hallarhan put the entire project in jeopardy, especially considering the condition of the Martian Crown Prince. He spent hours trying to assuage any potential fears from the Admiralty, but when he was done, he still expected a stern dressing down from Admiral Beatty. By the time he got to bed, he was dead tired, but had a fitful night dreaming of failed capacitors.

He awoke the next morning in a fog. Once dressed, he wandered to the Officer's Mess Hall, grabbed a large mug of tea, and asked for a pot to be brought to his office. He grabbed some toast and settled into his desk, and reviewed the design specifications for the ship. He took copious notes and prioritised the work that remained. Besides fixing and retesting the propulsion systems, there was the matter of the flight control system for the ship. As O'Hallarhan mentioned, the Martian computators controlled the flight control system. To his relief, O'Hallarhan had created detailed notes of how to interconnect the computators to the various systems of the ship. Malcolm prioritised the interconnections. At present, life support and environmental controls were his priority; with the propulsion systems down for the time being, he focused his effort on understanding the environmental systems. Creating deuterium from the recycled water used to drive the steam turbine produced oxygen as a byproduct. However, the key problem was the control system to adjust the internal ship atmosphere to the correct mix of oxygen; too much oxygen and the slightest spark could blow up the ship; too little and they would all suffocate. Likewise, the steam generated from the steam turbine provided the heat for the environmental systems. Again, careful control was necessary to keep the crew safe from the cold vacuum of space.

Lieutenant Commander Clarke and Rutherford soon joined him, and the three of them spent the morning going over the system and discussing the details of its construction. Rutherford had very practical suggestions that were incorporated into their work. At one point, Malcolm remarked, "Ernest, we may make an engineer out of you yet."

"Good heavens, I hope not. I won't be able to show my face at the Royal Society."

When they finished at noon, Malcolm and Lieutenant Commander Clarke had the work laid out for the Engineering team. Malcolm and Clarke spent the afternoon until evening mess, working with the Engineering team, answering their questions and sometimes having to huddle together to provide answers to their questions.

Malcolm took his dinner to his office and spent several hours working through the operational issues of the base. When they left at eight bells at the end of the dog watch, Malcolm spent another two hours reviewing and signing paperwork before falling into his bed around midnight into a fitful sleep until the piping of "Call to Hands" woke him up and the whole cycle repeated.

As the endless days turned into weeks, and then a full month, they made slow progress. After successfully connecting life support and environmental systems, they moved the propulsion control systems back into the ship. Navigation followed, and the team reached a new obstacle; these systems needed programming, but no one knew where to begin. After searching O'Hallarhan's quarters, they found notes he had made on interfacing one of their computators to the Martian computators. It involved turning the mechanical output of the computator into an electrical signal that the Martian computator stored. From the notes, O'Hallarhan had success in his initial attempts. Malcolm requisitioned five computators and scoured the base for anyone with a computational background. By the end of the month, the mechanical computators arrived. Once the programming began, they found another hurdle. While they could program the Martian computators by using binary codes, the resulting output on the displays was in Martian. Malcolm immediately summoned Joan to the ship.

"How is your written Martian?" he asked

"Not very good. I've seen very few examples of it. Why do you ask?"

"We started programming the controls, but when we tell the computator to output a number or code, we get this." He pointed to the swooping characters on the display.

"That's a problem, isn't it?"

"Unless we teach the entire crew to read Martian, we'll have to reprogram the displays into English. I'm afraid I need to assign you to work with the computator team to work this out."

"Won't you be working on this? I would love the chance to work with you one on one?"

Malcolm sighed. "As much as I'd enjoy that, I can't. First, I'm not a good coder. I can get things done, but I certainly couldn't help code the translation. And two, I have too much work to dedicate time to coding. Even if it meant working with you."

"Mores the pity," she said.

"I know. I'll leave you to it. Go find Lieutenant Collins. I believe he's the sharpest of our coders."

While Malcolm worked on other issues, he was pleased to learn that within three days, Joan and Lieutenant Collins had found ninety percent of the Martian vocabulary in the computators and had provided a translation matrix for the coders to use. Now the coding could begin.

Malcolm's first inclination was to code the Engineering control section himself, but as he studied the existing code, he quickly realised that he needed to work on a less critical system. It had been nearly twenty years since he had coded and even then, it took him multiple tries to get his card deck to process correctly in the computators. By the time he met with Commanders Murray and Saxon, he was exhausted and had an increasingly hard time following the discussion. In their meeting, Malcolm realised he had another problem to solve. When the Martians landed in Horsewell Commons, they died as a result of common Earth diseases. On the ship, there would be no way to prevent close contact. He struggled over this problem while trying to code. Each night, it took him longer to complete his work and when he did finally get to sleep, his dreams involved trying to solve a coding problem he did not know how to solve.

After six weeks of this cycle, Malcolm found himself increasingly short-tempered. The smallest inconvenience or setback made him angry. He found it harder to hide his accent and caught himself slipping back into it frequently. Late one day after returning to his office after an afternoon of coding, he found no trace of Commander Murray and only a note that said Commanders Murray and Saxon could not attend their customary meeting.

"Bloody hell, what are they playing at? How the hell are we supposed to run this damn base?" he muttered. Before he could answer his question, he heard a knock on the office door. "Enter," he yelled.

Joan entered and saluted.

"What do you want?" he snarled.

"And a very good evening to you, Commodore," Joan said. "I am here under orders from Commander Saxon."

"Orders from Saxon?"

"Yes," Joan said. "Commander Saxon is concerned about your ability to keep up this pace and he has ordered me to force you to take the evening off for your wellbeing and the wellbeing of the base."

"I can't do that. I have a base to run. Where is he? He needs to come here and explain himself!"

"Respectfully, Commodore, he will disobey that order. He insists you do not work tonight."

"And what if I do?"

"He anticipated your response, and he said that if you don't take the evening off, he will ask Doctor Boyce to order a medical evaluation of your fitness for duty."

"So, this is a mutiny?" Malcolm said.

"Commodore... Malcolm, please listen," Joan pleaded. "Charles and I are concerned about you. You are running yourself ragged and you can't keep up this pace. He and Commander Murray have taken care of anything urgent, and anything that needs your signature or approval can wait one night. Saxon gave me this," she said, producing a picnic hamper, "and suggested that we have a picnic top side."

"Top side? Only the base commander can authorise that!" he protested.

"And you are the base commander."

"Oh." He paused for a moment. "What will people think if I go topside with you?"

"Nothing. Charles arranged for a special assembly for all hands, except for you and I."

"But.."

"No buts, Malcolm. You can either leave this office with me or report to Sick Bay after I tell Saxon you refused."

Malcolm started to reply, but stopped himself. He crossed his arms. "Very well. I suppose I have no choice. But I don't have to enjoy myself."

"We'll see about that," Joan said.

The corridors were absent of any crew as they left his office. They made their way to the stairway leading to outside and began the long climb to the top. When they reached the top, Joan handed Malcolm the hamper and opened the trap door.

When Malcolm climbed out, he stopped. The sky was a carpet of stars and although there was a crescent moon, Malcolm could see the

Milky Way. They emerged at the highest part of the island and, despite the darkness, he could see the island's rugged landscape that reminded him of the highlands of Scotland.

"Bring the hamper over here," Joan said. "Look lively!"

"Aren't I the commanding officer?" Malcolm said as he lugged the hamper and set it down by Joan's feet.

"Not tonight. Tonight, we're Malcolm and Joan and not the Commodore and Lieutenant." She pulled a large blanket from the hamper and, with Malcolm's help, spread it over an area with the fewest rocks. "Sit," said as she unpacked the hamper.

"Yes, ma'am," Malcolm said as he complied with her order. He watched as she pulled out several packages wrapped in brown paper, a large bottle of Auchentoshan, a bottle of vodka, and two glasses.

"You pour. I'll unwrap the food," she said.

As Malcolm poured a rather large whisky for himself, and an equally large measure of vodka for Joan, he watched as she unwrapped the food. "Tonight, we have a highland feast," she said as she laid out the food. "Scotch eggs, scotch pies filled with haggis, smoked kippers, cold black pudding, Isle of Mull cheddar, and oatcakes. For dessert, we have Scottish macaroons." She pulled plates and utensils from the hamper and set them down. "After you, Malcolm."

"How were you able to get all of this?" Malcolm said, filling his plate with two scotch pies, a scotch egg, four kippers, three slices of black pudding, three slices of cheese, and half a dozen oat cakes.

"I talked to Colfax Mungo last week and arranged for him to get our picnic. He delivered it two days ago, so it's somewhat fresh. Although as I understand it, most of this will keep for days."

Malcolm had to finish his bite of scotch pie before he could speak. "This is wonderful. I can't tell you how much I miss eating something other than fish and root vegetables."

Joan raised her glass. "Slàinte Mhath!"

"Vashe zdorov'ye," Malcolm replied, raising his glass and clinking Joan's.

Malcolm took a sip of his whisky and let out a contented sigh. He enjoyed the smell of the ocean and the tapestry of light overhead. Searching the skies, he found Mars and pointed to it. "There's our destination, Mars."

"Do we have to think about it tonight?" she said.

"No," He took a sip of his whisky and attacked the scotch egg. He loved the crispy outside of the sausage, combined with the softness of the hard-boiled egg inside. "How did you arrange everything without me knowing?"

"It really wasn't difficult, Malcolm. You've been so preoccupied with your work and your schedule, it was very easy."

"When did you hatch this plot to mutiny against me?" he joked.

"About two weeks ago. Charles noticed how ragged you looked and how testy you were becoming to all around you. He and I worked everything out, and it was just a matter of waiting until Colfax brought the picnic."

"Thank you, Joan," Malcolm said as he reached for her hand. "I really needed this."

"You're welcome, Malcolm," she said, squeezing his hand.

"I really must thank Charles."

"Don't worry. I've already taken care of it. I got him a bottle of Tanqueray, a bag of fresh limes, and Battenberg cake."

"What can I do to thank you?"

"Malcolm, you could thank me by slowing down. You can't keep this up. It's not healthy for you or the crew. Would you give this schedule to a subordinate for two straight months? Wouldn't you be concerned about their performance after a few weeks? Malcolm, I hate to break it to you, but you're human, just like the rest of us. You need a rest."

Malcolm sipped his whisky and was quiet for several moments before speaking. "I know you're right, but I don't know if I can slow down."

"What do you mean?"

"First, there's the condition of the Crown Prince. We bought some time by using the hibernation tube, but none of us know how much time we have until the Crown Prince's condition is fatal. I don't need to remind you what the ramifications will be should that occur."

"I understand that, but that can't be the only reason you're pushing yourself to the point of exhaustion."

Malcolm shook his head. "From the moment I joined the Service, I've always been at a disadvantage purely because I'm Scottish. I worked twice as hard as my peers to become Chief Engineer on the *Daedalus*. Also, I know that I'm not always the smartest person in the room. My only advantages are hard work and my stubbornness. I refuse to give up and I'll work myself ragged to fix a problem." He paused and took another sip of whisky. "I'm afraid if I slow down, I'll lose everything I've achieved and I'll have proved all of those people right who said a Scotsman shouldn't be an officer, let alone a Commodore." He paused again before whispering, "I'm afraid I'll lose… me."

Joan pulled him close into a tight embrace. After several moments, she released the embrace and held Malcolm's cheeks in her hands. "Malcolm, listen to me. You are one of the smartest men I know. Mycroft would not pull you into Secret Service missions if he doubted your abilities. I know you never give up on problems and I'm not asking you to do that. All I'm asking is that you just give yourself time to breathe."

"But," Malcolm began.

"Shush," she said as she put her fingers on his lips. "Answer me truthfully. What will the Admiralty say if you finish it on time? Will they praise you for your work?"

"Maybe, but…," Malcolm began.

"Shush! What will they say if things are one week late? Two weeks late? A month late? Would the consequences be better or worse?"

"They'd be disappointed, but I think, given the circumstances, that there would be few consequences."

"Alright then. How are you compared to your original schedule?"

Malcolm did some quick calculations. "I think we're roughly two weeks behind the original schedule."

"Alright. What I'm saying is that you need to give yourself time to relax. If you're bleary headed because you can't sleep, your work will help no one. Please, Malcolm, give yourself some time to relax."

"I hear what you say and I know you're right, but…"

"But, what Malcolm?"

"I don't want to disappoint anyone. I don't want to disappoint… you."

Joan pulled Malcolm's head close until their foreheads were touching. "Malcolm Francis Robertson, you are never a disappointment to me. Exasperating? Yes. Infuriating? Often. Stubborn? Absolutely. But you are never a disappointment. I love you, Malcolm. I don't care if you're a commodore, First Sea Lord, or a crewman shovelling coal in Engineering." To emphasise her point, she gave him a tender kiss.

When she pulled away, Malcolm said, "I don't know what to say."

"Then say nothing. Lie back, cuddle me, and we'll look at the stars together."

Malcolm reluctantly laid back and Joan snuggled next to him, her head resting on his chest. He hugged her close.

"There, isn't that better?" Joan said. She waited several moments before she heard Malcolm snoring.

"Yes, I guess it is," she whispered.

CHAPTER TWENTY SEVEN

After letting Malcolm sleep for an hour, she gently nudged him awake, and they packed up their picnic dinner to return to the base. Before they opened the door, Malcolm pulled Joan close and said, "Thank you. I'm sorry I wasn't an exciting date, falling asleep so quickly."

"It's fine. You obviously needed it," Joan said.

Malcolm leaned in and kissed Joan. After several moments, he pulled himself away and said, "I wish we could just stay up here."

"Me, too, Malcolm. But as you frequently remind me, it would look bad if they caught the Commodore fraternising with the only female lieutenant in the Space Service."

"You're right, but it doesn't mean I like it."

"Me either, but it's our fate for now. When we finish this mission, we can marry and we won't have to worry about such things."

"If we finish the mission," he said.

"When we finish the mission," she said emphatically. She gave Malcolm one last kiss and said, "Time to return to reality." She lifted the trapdoor and descended. Malcolm took one last look at the sky and drew in a breath of the sea scented air and begrudgingly followed Joan.

Malcolm slept better than he had in weeks and felt more prepared to face the day. That feeling quickly left when Commander Murray interrupted the morning work session to inform him he needed to go to the Radio Room to receive an urgent call from Admiral Beattie.

He was happy that Joan was on duty in the Radio Room. He nodded to her as he picked up a handset and slid into a chair next to her. Joan nodded and Malcolm spoke in to the handset, "Commodore Robertson to Admiralty, over."

"Please hold for Admiral Beattie, over," a voice said on the other side. Malcolm pantomimed to Joan to flip the switch to play the conversation on the speaker instead of the handset.

"Malcolm, what the hell is going on up there?" Admiral Beattie exploded.

"I'm sorry, sir. What do you mean? Haven't you received my reports?"

"Yes. I've received reports that the project is falling apart and you're two weeks behind schedule?"

"As I explained, sir, with our Chief Engineer injured, we've had to make accommodations to continue and frankly, we're lucky we're only two weeks behind."

"That's not the message that is making it to the Admiralty. I have the Second and Fourth Sea Lord telling me they feel you are unsuitable and incapable of completing this project, let alone on time."

"And where are they hearing this message, may I ask?"

"Commander O'Hallarhan has been lobbying any admiral he can find to put him in charge of the project. He blamed you for his injuries."

"Blamed me?" The heat rose in Malcolm's cheeks and he had to bite his tongue before he said something he might regret. He took a deep breath and said, "Respectfully, sir, my reports have detailed the exact cause of the accident that injured the Commander. If he needs to blame someone else, he should blame the quartermaster for not delivering the parts he required."

"I know; I read your report," Beattie said. "I believe you, Malcolm, but there are many looking for any excuse to bust you down."

"I know, Admiral. Is there anything I can do to ease the Admiralty's concerns?"

"In a perfect world, I'd order you here to explain, but I don't want to take you away for so long."

"What if we bring the admirals for an inspection so they can see for themselves?"

"Excellent idea," Beattie said.

Joan flipped the switch to the microphone. "Malcolm, ask that he includes Mycroft," Joan said. "He is your advocate and despite his hatred of travel, I think he would do what he can to help."

"He should. He's the one who got me into this bloody mess to begin with!" Joan glared at him and Malcolm raised his hands in surrender. Malcolm nodded at Joan to turn on the microphone. "Admiral, I think it might be helpful if Mycroft Holmes joined the inspection, especially since this is a joint venture between the Secret Service and the Royal Navy."

"I can ask, but I doubt he will come, as he notoriously hates travelling," Beattie said.

"I know, sir," Malcolm said, recalling the voyage to Tunguska to retrieve the Martian ship. "I believe that Lieutenant de St. Leger might convince him of our need."

The line was silent before Beattie said, "Very well, Malcolm, I'll arrange a delegation for an inspection in, shall we say, another month? It will take me most of that time to work out the logistics."

"Thank you, sir. I'll make sure the base is in tip-top shape and I'll redouble our efforts to get this project back on schedule." Malcolm paused for a moment. "Is there any word on when Commander O'Hallarhan will return to duty?"

"The surgeons tell me they will clear him within the next two weeks."

"Excellent. I want him back here as soon as possible."

"Keep your friends close, and your enemies closer?"

"Yes, I suppose. I need him so we can make up for lost time. And it's two fewer weeks for him to spread more... inaccurate information."

"I will do everything I can to get him up there."

"Thank you, sir. Is there anything else you need?"

"No, Malcolm. I like the idea of the inspection. Perhaps you can be at a point where you could provide some kind of demonstration."

"I think that will be possible. We have most of the control systems in place and I think it's only a matter of time before we have the engine system back online. Who knows, we might take the ship out for a brief trip."

"That would assuage the fears of the other admirals. By the way, have you thought about naming the ship? If you intend to take her out, she should have a name."

"I didn't think it was my prerogative to name the ship."

"It isn't, but I would take any suggestions you have to the Admiralty."

Malcolm thought for a moment and then smiled. "I have a suggestion, sir. Since my first command was the *Daedalus*, perhaps we should call her *Icarus*."

Beattie laughed. "After the person who flew too close to the sun? I must admit, it seems very fitting. I'll make it happen."

"Thank you, sir."

"You better get back to work. You have a great deal to do before the inspection."

"Yes, sir."

"God speed, Malcolm."

"Thank you, sir."

Joan closed the call, and Malcolm turned to her. "So much for that relaxation."

CHAPTER TWENTY EIGHT

*M*alcolm gathered the senior officers immediately after the call and they spent several hours pulling together a plan to get the ship and the base ready for inspection. The thought of being ready for a flight in a month's time put the fear of the Admiralty in all of them.

The base buzzed with activity like a hornet's nest as crews worked around the clock to ready the ship and the base for inspection. The Engineering crewmen focused solely on the construction efforts of the ship, while everyone else focused on presenting the base in the best possible light. Malcolm made sure that there was sufficient rest for everyone, including himself.

Within a week, the message came from the Admiralty that they named the new ship *His Majesty's Spaceship Icarus*. And true to Admiral Beattie's word, the following week, Commander O'Hallarhan returned to the base.

Malcolm was supervising the final construction of the bridge when he heard, "Commander O'Hallarhan reporting for duty, sir."

Malcolm turned to find O'Hallarhan dressed in his duty uniform. O'Hallarhan saluted Malcolm, and Malcolm returned the salute.

While Malcolm was glad to have O'Hallarhan back to take over the Engineering duties, he had to swallow his anger at O'Hallarhan's attempt to usurp his position. "Welcome back, Commander. We've made significant progress during your absence."

"How did you manage that, sir?"

"We pressed Professor Rutherford into Engineering work, much against his protests, and Lieutenant Commander Clarke has been extremely helpful in the design and construction work."

"Oh," O'Hallarhan said, clearly taken aback by Malcolm's response.

"Commander, as soon as you stow your gear, change into your engineer work clothes and report back here. I'll bring you up to speed and go over your duties."

"Yes, sir," O'Hallarhan said. He saluted Malcolm and left. Within twenty minutes, O'Hallarhan was back, dressed in his engineering overalls.

"How are your hands?" Malcolm asked.

"Fine, sir. They look awful, but I was fortunate that there was no actual damage."

"Excellent. That means you'll be able to jump into the fray."

"Into the fray?"

"Yes. The Admiralty will be here in two weeks for an inspection, and they expect a demonstration of the ship."

"A demonstration?"

"Yes, it's my intent to take the *Icarus* on its maiden flight to show the Admiralty that we are nearly ready."

"The *Icarus*?"

"Yes, the Admiralty gave the official name to the ship last week."

"Will it be ready?"

"God willing," Malcolm said. "As you can see, the bridge is nearly complete. We have the Martian computators connected, and we now have complete control over the ship from the bridge." Malcolm went to the navigation console and flipped a switch. The large screen came to life and gave them a view of the base. "We have connected the cameras and we now have visual display all around the ship." Malcolm flipped various switches and the display showed the roof of the base, the floor, starboard, port, and aft.

"Impressive," O'Hallarhan said with little enthusiasm.

"Life support and environmental controls are also complete and tomorrow, we try to fire the engines again."

"It seems like I got here too late," O'Hallarhan said.

"Not at all. There is still work to be done. We need to complete ship-wide communications and the crew quarters, and we will have to resolve any problems that arise from our maiden voyage."

O'Hallarhan was silent.

"Shall we go to the Engine Room?" Malcolm asked.

Malcolm led O'Hallarhan back to the Engine Room, but O'Hallarhan hesitated at the door. The Engineering team had already reassembled the capacitor bank and connected it to the reactor. The Engineering console now controlled the function of the electro kinetic thrusters, the gravity beam generator, and the reactor. O'Hallarhan walked over to the capacitor bank and studied it for a moment before he said, "This will have to be redone. This doesn't conform to the design specification."

"I assure you that this design is fine."

"But, sir…"

"But what? It's not done how you would have done it?" O'Hallarhan nodded. "Commander, as Chief Engineer of a ship, you must make do with what you have, given the circumstances. We just have to make her work. We no longer have the luxury of making everything perfect. And, may I remind you that the previous design had no failsafes, resulting in your injury?" O'Hallarhan bowed his head.

"I'm not here to lay blame on you," Malcolm continued. "But we've learned from the problems and have built something, while not the most elegant design, that will get the job done. We don't have the luxury of second guessing all the work; we only have time to make it work. You're not to redo any of the work unless there is a reported issue. Do I make myself clear?"

"Yes, sir," O'Hallarhan said.

"Excellent," Malcolm said. "I do have one problem that I'd like you to solve. Once aboard, the Chancellor will be in close contact with our crew and we need a means to prevent him from catching any Earth diseases. Do you have any ideas?"

O'Hallarhan thought for a moment. "It might be possible to build a small personal force field, similar to what's installed on the ship. We would have to calibrate it to allow oxygen to flow in, but not allow germs to escape.

"Excellent. Please see to it."

The next day, Malcolm and the soon-to-be crew of the *Icarus* gathered to test the engines. This time, Malcolm was on the bridge and sat at the navigator's console to control the lift. Lieutenant Commander Clarke monitored the Engineering console on the bridge to provide updates on the engine status while O'Hallarhan monitored the Engine Room.

Malcolm flipped a switch to activate the ship wide communication. "All hands, are we ready?"

"Engineering ready," O'Hallarhan replied.

"Excellent. I'm engaging the gravity generator beam now." Malcolm slid the lever ever so gently to the lowest level. "Status?" he asked Clarke.

"All systems nominal, sir."

"Excellent," Malcolm said. He slowly slid the lever up and, to his amazement, he saw the view on the display raise. "How is she holding together?"

"All systems are good," Clarke said.

"Excellent." Malcolm inched the level up and the ship gained more altitude. "I'm going to engage the electro kinetic thrusters now." He slid a different knob forward and the ship suddenly lurched forward, nearly causing Malcolm and Clarke to lose their balance. "Sorry about that. It's a little touchy." Malcolm gingerly pushed the lever up, and the ship moved forward ever so slowly. "Reversing thrust now." Malcolm clicked the thrusters to stop and flipped another switch to reverse the thrusters. Learning his lesson, Malcolm eased the lever up and the ship slowly floated back. When Malcolm thought they were close to the ship's original position, he lowered the lever for the gravitational beam ever so slowly. The ship descended until there was a gentle thud; the ship had landed.

"Excellent work, everyone. I believe we have a working ship!"

CHAPTER TWENTY NINE

After a week of continual testing, the flight systems and engines were in working order, and that meant that Rutherford's time at the base had ended. As Malcolm walked Rutherford back to the airship waiting to return him to the rest of the world, he said, "Ernest, I can't thank you enough for your help in the last few months. We could not have done it without you."

"Thank you, Malcolm. I actually enjoyed the practical application of my theoretical knowledge. But if you tell anyone, I will most vehemently deny it."

"Are you sure you don't want to wait for the maiden voyage?"

"No," Rutherford answered immediately. "I'm not one for feats of Derring-Do. I think I'd rather wait until you have worked out any problems before I attempt a trip."

"There's always a place for you here if you get sick of the life of a researcher."

"That's alright. I'm ready to go back to civilization where I can get a proper meal. I don't know how you can eat the same thing day after day. It will be a long time before I can even look at fish again."

Malcolm shook Rutherford's hand, "Good bye, Ernest. And again, thank you."

"I'd say it was my pleasure, and actually, it was. Good luck, Malcolm. And what do they say? I wish you good air?"

"I'm not sure how appropriate that will be for the new ship, but thank you."

The following week, the representatives from the Admiralty arrived with the usual pomp and circumstance. All hands were in their dress uniforms and standing at attention as the gangplank from the *RAS Uhuru* lowered. Malcolm took note as Admiral Beatty led the assembly down the gangplank. Malcolm took careful note of its members; he recognised Admiral Poë, head of the Mediterranean Fleet; Commodore Godfrey Paine, head of the Royal Air Service; and several admirals that Malcolm did not recognise. To Malcolm's surprise, bringing up the rear were all four Sea Lords. First Sea Lord Prince Louis of Battenberg held back from the group, talking to Mycroft Holmes. Malcolm shot a glance to Saxon, who was standing next to him, and Malcolm gestured toward the assembly. Saxon nodded and whispered to Malcolm, "This is going to be an interesting day."

"That it will be," Malcolm whispered.

When the assembly approached Malcolm and the base crew, the bosun gave the signal on his whistle and the crew threw a salute in perfect unison. The First Sea Lord moved to the front of the assembly and returned the salute.

"Welcome to Boreray, Your Serene Highness. At your pleasure, we can begin the inspection," Malcolm said.

"Excellent," Prince Louis said. "Speaking for myself, I would like to freshen up after the flight."

"Very good, Your Serene Highness." Malcolm turned to the crew. "Please reassemble in one hour for inspection. Crew dismissed." He turned to the assembly and said, "If it pleases you, I have refreshments laid out in the Officer's Mess Hall. This way." Malcolm gestured as he lead the assembly.

"Is that the ship?" the First Sea Lord asked, pointing at the *Icarus*.

"Yes, Your Serene Highness," Malcolm said.

"It's not all like I imagined," the First Sea Lord said.

"It's modelled after the design of an airship, but certain design changes were necessary to allow it to operate in space."

"Such as?"

"For example, the cylindrical shape. Since we will operate in the vacuum of space, the cylindrical shape allows the internal pressure to be dispersed over the outside of the ship. If it had a more angular design, the pressure might cause a rupture."

"Ah," the First Sea Lord said.

The trip to Officer's Mess was silent. Malcolm showed the dignitaries into the Officer's Mess Hall and after getting a glass of whisky to steady his nerves and a roast beef sandwich, he found Saxon and whispered, "This is going to be an interesting visit. I have to say, I'm not pleased to see Commodore Paine here. He has no love for me at all."

"Look at the bright side. At least he isn't your commanding officer anymore; you share the same rank."

"Thank heavens for minor miracles. I am astonished that all the Sea Lords turned up for this assembly."

"I'm sure that's Mycroft's doing. If Joan impressed upon him the importance of his presence, I'm sure he intends to use his influence with the First Sea Lord to sway any naysayers from the Admiralty. Like the other Sea Lords, for instance."

"Do you know any of the other Sea Lords?"

"No, only by reputation. I've been out of the service for a while, Malcolm. And even then, I tried to keep away from the notice of admirals."

"Point taken."

Malcolm noticed Mycroft in a corner, observing the rest of the assembly. Malcolm made his way over and said, "Thank you, Mr Holmes, for making this trip. I know it was difficult for you."

"Thank you, Commodore. I would not be here were it not for the imploring of Lieutenant de St. Leger. She can be most insistent."

"You don't have to tell me," Malcolm said, and the two laughed. "I trust the presence of all the Sea Lords is your doing?"

"Yes," Mycroft said, sipping his brandy. "After the lieutenant impressed upon me the need for my presence, I deduced that if you can suitably impress the First Sea Lord and the other Sea Lords, everyone else will fall in line." He sipped his brandy. "I don't envy you this task, Commodore. Half of the assembly wants to see you bust back to Seaman, while many are indifferent. You have a vigorous supporter in Admiral Beattie, and his word carries some weight with the First Sea Lord. I don't exaggerate when I say you must do an excellent job of mollifying the naysayers. Commander O'Hallarhan was most effective in portraying you as inept and the cause of the delay."

"I'm sure."

"Is the ship ready?"

"I think it's as ready as it will ever be for its first flight. I intend to only take a short flight. We haven't sufficiently trained the crew to operate in space. We've been more focused on this damnable inspection, and I don't even have someone trained to pilot the ship. I'm the closest thing we have to a pilot, as I have at least controlled the tests to ensure that the engines and gravitational beam work."

"That doesn't inspire much confidence, Commodore."

"I know. But let me remind you, you got me into this mess. It's only fair that you reap the rewards."

"So you say," Mycroft said as he took another sip of his brandy.

"If you'll excuse me, I should attend to my other guests.

"Good luck, Commodore. I fear you will need it."

"I agree."

Malcolm gritted his teeth and purposely went to Commodore Paine. "Commodore, so good to see you again," he said, offering his hand.

"Hello, Commodore," Paine said through gritted teeth. He gave Malcolm's hand a perfunctory shake. "I don't know how you returned to the Service, let alone get promoted."

Malcolm bit his tongue before replying, "I am rather surprised myself. I was happily living a civilian life, but the First Sea Lord himself recalled me to active duty. As for the promotion, I am most honoured."

"You should be," Paine muttered. "If I had my way…"

"Yes, I know my fate if you have your way," Malcolm said. "All I ask is that you keep an open mind and judge me on my actual performance instead of my perceived character flaws."

Paine snorted and turned away from Malcolm to talk to another admiral.

So much for diplomacy, Malcolm thought.

After the assembly finished the refreshments, Malcolm sent Saxon to assemble the base crew and led the party back to the assembly area. The First Sea Lord led the inspection of the crew, peppering Malcolm with questions which Malcolm answered with ease. Malcolm gave them a tour of the base, showing off the facility. To Malcolm's great relief, the crew's answers to the party's questions seemed to mollify any concerns. At last, he led them to the *Icarus.*

"Sea Lords, Admirals, Commodore, Mr Holmes; I present the *HMS Icarus.* If you'll be so kind as to follow me, I will give you a tour of the ship before we begin the maiden flight."

"I believe you're forgetting something crucial," the First Sea Lord said. Malcolm looked at him quizzically. "We must christen this ship before it takes its maiden voyage."

"Yes, of course, Your Serene Highness," Malcolm said, cursing himself for forgetting the ceremony. He motioned to a crewman and asked him to fetch the bottle of champagne Malcolm had ordered for the occasion. In minutes, the crewman return with the bottle and handed it to Malcolm. He turned to the First Sea Lord and offered the bottle, saying, "We would be most honoured, Your Serene Highness, if you would christen the ship."

The First Sea Lord took the proffered bottle. "In the name of his Royal Highness, King George V, I name this ship *Icarus.* May God bless her and all who fly in her." He smashed the bottle against the front of the ship and a cheer went up among the assembled crew.

"Thank you, Your Serene Highness. If you will follow me, I will give you a tour of the ship and we can begin with the flight."

The tour ended at the bridge, where they had added several chairs to allow the dignitaries to sit. O'Hallarhan was at the Engineering station, Joan was at the Communication station and Saxon sat with the dignitaries. As Malcolm took his position at the Navigation console, the First Sea Lord gave Malcolm a puzzled look.

"Your Serene Highness, I thought that as the commanding officer of this ship, it's only right for me to pilot the ship for its maiden voyage. It is tradition in the Royal Air Service that the commander of the ship takes it out of port."

The First Sea Lord nodded, and Malcolm thought he saw the glimpse of a smile. There were some whispers among the dignitaries, but Malcolm ignored them.

"All hands," Malcolm said through the ship wide radio. "Prepare for departure. Please acknowledge."

When all stations acknowledged they were ready, Malcolm turned to the First Sea Lord, "We await your orders, First Sea Lord."

"Proceed," the First Sea Lord replied.

"Beginning lift off." Malcolm took a deep breath and tried to ignore the slight shake in his hand as he gently nudged the gravity beam generator lever, and the ship slowly lifted off the ground. Malcolm nudged the electro kinetic thrusters, and the ship moved. Using the console, he manoeuvred the ship to face the exit of the cave and the *Icarus* slowly moved down the tunnel. Malcolm's eyes darted between the primary display and the viewscreen as he manoeuvred the large ship through the tunnel. As they rounded the last turn toward the opening of the tunnel, Malcolm realised the ship was perilously close to striking the cavern wall. He abruptly adjusted the course, causing everyone to lurch in their seat, but the ship missed the cave wall. "Sorry," Malcolm muttered. He gently nudged the controls, and the ship was back on course. When they cleared the tunnel. Malcolm increased the strength of the gravity beam, and the ship lifted higher and higher and he let out a sigh of relief. He switched the display so that the party could see that the island was rapidly receding below them.

Malcolm piloted the ship as it slowly circled the island. "Everyone, hold on; I'm going to increase the speed." Malcolm increased the lift so that they were soon travelling above the clouds, and he increased the speed for 2 seconds and then cut the thrusters. He stopped the ship and gradually lowered the ship to the bottom of the clouds so that the most of the ship remained hidden by the clouds, but they could see below them. Malcolm checked the readout on his station. "We are now over Russia at Latitude fifty-eight degrees thirty-three minutes north, Longitude thirty-one degrees sixteen minutes east. According to the map, that puts us over the Russian city of Novgorod."

"Are you saying that in those few seconds, we flew east to Novgorod?" Commodore Paine asked. "Do you seriously want us to believe that?"

"Actually, Commodore, our course was west. We have nearly circled the globe," Malcolm said.

"That's preposterous!" Paine exclaimed.

"I invite you to see for yourself," Malcolm said. He nudged the controls ever so slightly and the ship moved again. "As you can see, we're leaving Russia and approaching Sweden. In a few seconds, we'll be over Norway, and then Scotland. If you care to compare our position to the navigational maps, be my guest," Malcolm said as he gestured to the maps laid out on a table next to his console. "Lieutenant de St. Leger, scan for local radio transmissions and if you pick anything up, please put it on the speaker."

In seconds, a radio conversation was playing over the speakers. "Sirs, we are picking up a conversation between a Russian ship and the port, requesting permission to dock. I can translate the details if needed."

"Thank you, Lieutenant. That won't be necessary. You may turn the transmission off now."

The First Sea Lord was the first to examine the map. After looking between the map and display, he shook his head in amazement. "The commodore is correct. Even now, we are approaching the eastern Scottish coast. Look, there are the Orkney Islands and John o' Groats. Commodore Robertson, I would suggest you slow our speed or we will end up in Canada."

"Yes, sir," Malcolm said, trying to suppress the grin on his face. He decreased the speed until they were flying at a respectable hundred miles an hour and nudged the thrusters to change course back to Boreray.

The First Sea Lord turned to the assembly. "I don't know about you, but I have seen enough. Commodore Robertson and his crew have done an exceptional job. This ship is a technological wonder." Turning to Malcolm, he asked, "How soon will she be ready to fly to Mars?"

"While the ship is ready for more test flights, we are behind in training the crew. For a simple flight like this, we have sufficient crew. However, I don't want to take the ship into space without a fully trained crew. We will need a few more flights before we dare start the trip to Mars."

"Understood. Commodore, you have all the resources of the Navy at your disposal. This mission is the highest priority and you have my full support."

"Pardon me, Your Serene Highness, I would like to add a few words," Mycroft said. The First Sea Lord nodded his ascent. "I have had a hand in this project for over three years now. I have seen many captains come and go, but only Commodore Robertson has brought us to this point. There have been many rough spots in an endeavour such as this, but Commodore Robertson and his staff have been able to weather the storm. He has my full support and the resources of the Secret Service are also at his disposal."

Malcolm turned to the First Sea Lord. "Shall we return to Boreray, or is there anywhere else you would like to go?"

"If you will indulge me, I would like to see my ancestral home of Schloss Heiligenberg," The First Sea Lord said.

"It would be my pleasure," Malcolm said as he looked for the coordinates on his map.

CHAPTER THIRTY

After the flyover of the First Sea Lord's home, Malcolm piloted the ship back to Boreray and executed a perfect approach and landing. "Commander Saxon, will you escort our guests to the conference room? I will join you after we complete the shutdown sequence."

"This way, sirs," Commander Saxon said as he led the assembly off the bridge.

As soon as they were gone, Malcolm turned to Joan. "Lieutenant, please engage the ship-wide communication." Joan activated the channel and nodded to Malcolm. "To the crew of the *Icarus*, I want to give you my personal thanks for a successful maiden flight. While there is still a great deal of work to do, I am proud of what we've all accomplished in such a short time. Tonight, there will be a celebration, but tomorrow we are back at it again. Please execute the shutdown sequence and when complete, I release you from duty for the day."

Malcolm turned to Commander O'Hallarhan and said, "Congratulations, Commander. Your work on this ship contributed to a successful maiden flight."

"Did it, sir?" O'Hallarhan said, arms crossed. "It seems like this flight was all about you... sir."

"No, Commander, this was about the ship and showing her capabilities."

"May I speak to you... alone?" O'Hallarhan said, nodding toward Joan.

"Of course. Lieutenant, if you're done with your duties, you may leave."

"Yes, sir," Joan said. She shutdown the communications station and left.

O'Hallarhan watched her leave and when she was gone, asked, "Permission to speak freely?"

"Permission granted," Malcolm said with a sigh. "What is it you want to say?"

"How dare you?"

"How dare I what?" Malcolm replied.

"Take credit for my design and work!"

"I did no such thing. If you noticed, I explicitly said that the success of this mission was because of the contributions of the entire crew."

"But what about my contributions? It's my design that made this possible!"

"That's very true, Commander," Malcolm said. "And without it, we wouldn't be standing here having this conversation. But let me remind you of the state of this ship when I arrived here. It was barely a skeleton with few prospects of ever seeing it get off the ground, let alone fly to Mars."

"Regardless, I should get the credit for the success of this flight, not you! I stood here on the bridge like a piece of scenery while you took all the credit."

"Is that what you honestly think? Remind me again, Commander, were there any engineering issues that required your attention?"

"No, but..."

"Then you were doing your part. Tell me, would you have been capable of piloting the ship?"

"No. Because of my injury, I never had the chance to learn."

"Are you suggesting that I should have told the First Sea Lord, 'Sorry, we can't fly today because Commander O'Hallarhan hasn't had the chance to learn how to fly the ship?'" O'Hallarhan lowered his head. "This whole demonstration wouldn't have been necessary if you hadn't spent your recuperation time telling the Admiralty that I should be relieved of duty."

"I did no such thing!"

"Don't lie to me, Commander!" Malcolm bellowed. "I'll tolerate a great deal of insubordination, but I will not tolerate lies. Admiral Beattie told me about your activities at the Admiralty. While you were trying to get command of this ship, I was the one working myself to the bone, trying to keep things going."

"Aye, and what a masterful job you did," O'Hallarhan sneered. "I've seen better engineering work from a raw recruit."

"If you could have done a better job, then why didn't you?"

"I was injured! I wasn't here to make sure they did it right."

"Right, or your way? Look, Commander, your injury was a horrible accident and I'm genuinely sorry for it. But even before your injury, how much time did you spend on the hull construction compared to experimenting with the Martian technology? How much actual work did you do ensuring that the crew implemented your design?"

Malcolm took a deep breath. "Commander, the design of this ship is first rate, and I give you full credit for the overall design. But for actually implementing the design, you have proven repeatedly that you are not up to the task. You refuse to use the experience at your disposal and focus on the wrong tasks."

"You mean Clarke? He's an idiot! He knows nothing about the Martian technology!"

"And why is that? Did you ever spend anytime trying to teach him?"

"Why should I? He'd never be able to grasp it."

"That may be true, but he has a great deal of practical experience. We would not have been able to make this flight today without his expertise. You have a great deal to learn about leading men if you ever think you will have a command of your own someday."

"I don't know. It doesn't seem that hard. You do it."

"Yes, I do, and learning how to do that was one of the hardest things I've ever had to do in my life. Do you want to know why I insisted on piloting the ship?"

"To take the credit?"

"No, to ensure that I would take the responsibility for any failure that might occur. This mission is more important than you or I. This ship needs to fly to Mars. If something went wrong, the Admiralty can replace me, but it would spare the people who need to finish the work any repercussions. Tell me, Commander. Would you do what I did if you knew there was a possibility of failure?" Malcolm waited for a reply, but there was none.

"I think that we've both said enough," Malcolm continued. "Return to your quarters and think about what I've said. I do hope you will join the rest of the crew for tonight's celebration."

O'Hallarhan stomped out of the bridge while Malcolm let out a long sigh and put his head down on the Navigation console. He hadn't meant to let his pent up frustration with O'Hallarhan explode. As he contemplated how to deal with the young engineer, the touch of hands on his shoulder jolted him from his thoughts. He turned to see Joan. "You heard all that? Were you eavesdropping?"

"I'm a spy; old habits die hard," she said with a smile. "Are you alright?"

"I suppose. I knew this moment was coming and I've tried hard to head it off. But he's such a.."

"Stubborn, pig-headed engineer?" she finished. "Does that sound like anyone we know?"

Malcolm laughed. "I know. There's so much of the younger me in him. I was ambitious, but all I ever wanted was to be a Chief Engineer. I never sought command of a ship, let alone becoming a commodore."

"Malcolm," she said softly, "you have earned this through your own skills and hard work. You know what it was like to shovel coal in an engine room. Do you think O'Hallarhan has ever done that?"

"Well, he's young enough that most of the ships don't run on coal any more."

"That's not what I mean and you know it," she said, lightly slapping his arm. "You have said it yourself. He never gets his hands dirty. He's always been told how brilliant he is and how he'll go far. You challenge him because not only are you as smart as him, you have the wisdom of experience and know that success doesn't just come from brilliance, it comes from hard work."

Malcolm nodded. "I just don't know what to do about him. I need him to get this ship ready for Mars, but I don't have the time or energy to supervise him on every little thing. And I certainly can't let him play the 'poor, hard done by' card all the time."

"I know. You'll figure it out, Malcolm. You always do." She kissed the top of his head. She offered her hand and said, "Come, Commodore, you have a group of dignitaries to entertain."

"This day just keeps getting better, doesn't it?" Malcolm said.

CHAPTER THIRTY ONE

$\mathcal{A}$s Malcolm left the ship, he was surprised to find the delegation from the Admiralty ready to board the *Uhuru*. On his way, Saxon intercepted him. "The First Sea Lord decided that there was nothing more to talk about, as the demonstration was enough for him to give his unconditional support to you."

"Was there any dissent?"

"There was some grumbling from the usual suspects."

"Paine?"

Saxon nodded. "Whatever did you do to get in that man's bad graces?"

"I don't know. Be Scottish?"

Saxon laughed "Congratulations, Malcolm. You really made an excellent impression on the First Sea Lord. He thinks you are an exceptionally competent commander. I don't know how he ever came to that conclusion," he said with a smile.

"You know, you're not half as funny as you think you are, Commander. Did I hear that the waste treatment plant needed your personal supervision?"

"Point taken," Saxon said. He looked at Malcolm. "What's wrong? You don't seem half as relieved as you should be."

"I had a… discussion with Commander O'Hallarhan after everyone left."

"Oh. Do you want to talk about it?"

As Malcolm summarised their discussion, Saxon frowned. "He is going to become a big problem."

"Going to? I think he has always been a problem. I thought I had made some headway with him, but now, I'm not so sure if it isn't a lost cause."

"Can we afford to keep him?"

"Unfortunately, we can't afford not to keep him. The ship is in sufficient shape to do a short fly about, but it's nowhere near ready to go into space."

"Is there anything I can do?"

"Watch him for me. I'm going to be too busy in the days to come to keep track of his activities. We don't need him sabotaging the mission just to play the hero. Too much is at stake."

"Do you really think he'd do that?"

"In a heartbeat," Malcolm said. "Come on, let's say goodbye to our guests."

Malcolm and Saxon began their goodbyes to the delegation. When he reached the First Sea Lord, the prince shook Malcolm's hand. "What you've done here is nothing sort of miraculous, Commodore. You have my fullest support. This flight disproved any rumours of your incompetence and I will do my part to quash any such talk in the future." He paused for a moment before continuing. "When we first met, I was not sure that Mycroft had made a wise decision to bring you back. I see now it was a foolish decision to have forced you out of the Service in the first place."

"Thank you. Your Serene Highness. I don't know what to say."

"Just get this ship of yours ready for space; that will be thanks enough."

Admiral Beattie pulled Malcolm aside from the rest of the group. "Excellent job, Malcolm. You made quite an impression on the First Sea Lord and many other Admirals. Even Commodore Paine had to admit that the flight was impressive. Mind you, he'd never actually say that to you, but I thought you should know."

"Thank you, sir."

"I look forward to your continued success. If you need anything, please contact me. God speed, Commodore." As Malcolm turned to rejoin the delegation, he caught sight of O'Hallarhan having an animated conversation with Commodore Paine and the second Sea Lord. While he couldn't hear, he saw Paine vigorously shaking his head and putting a stop to the conversation. O'Hallarhan saluted the men and left, shoulders slumped as he stalked back to his quarters.

Saxon came over and whispered to Malcolm, "Our Chief Engineer was making another plea to Paine and Second Sea Lord Jellicoe to place him in command of the ship construction. To my great surprise, Paine told him in no uncertain terms that they made the decision that you were in command and there would be no further discussion about it."

"Commodore Paine? Supporting me?" Malcolm said in surprise.

"Paine knows that doing anything to you now while you have the support of the First Sea Lord would be detrimental to his future."

"That would explain it. It must have killed him to say that."

"You should be so lucky," Saxon quipped.

After the delegation departed, Malcolm invited Saxon and Commander Murray back to his office. After everyone poured their drinks and settled into their chairs, Malcolm said, "I want to thank both of you for everything you've done in the past months that led to today's success. Honestly, this would not have been possible without the two of you. Cheers!," Malcolm said, raising his glass.

After taking a sip, Saxon said, "But..."

"Why do you think I'm going to say 'but'?"

"I know you too well, Malcolm. You always try to talk us up before you give us an impossible task."

"I'm afraid you're right. We now have to not only finish the final construction, but train a crew. I can't very well pilot this thing all by myself."

"From all reports, you did an admirable job, Commodore," Murray said.

"Thank you. Now, where are we with training the crew?"

"I thought we were off duty for the rest of the day," Saxon said with a smile.

"No rest for the wicked, Commander." Murray and Saxon left to retrieve the personnel files, and when they returned, they set to work.

"The crew has completed Professor Rutherford's course on the basic operation of the ship. I don't know how much of that they actually understood, but they have completed it," Saxon said.

"Excellent. I think now we have to train everyone on ship operations," Malcolm said.

"How do you intend to do that?" Saxon asked. "We only have one ship and I don't know about you, but I don't relish the thought of damaging the ship as the crew learns how it works."

"Excellent point," Malcolm said. "Suggestions?"

After a long pause, Commander Murray offered, "We have several computators left over from programming the ship. Could we use them somehow?"

"I see what you're getting at, Commander," Malcolm said. "The computators should react the same way as the ship. If we were to rig up some sort of dummy console based on the Martian design, we could put the crew through drills so that they could understand how the ship would react. Excellent idea, Commander!"

"That's fine, but who is going to build these consoles? Do you have anyone with the engineering skill to make that happen?"

"I believe that this would be a perfect task for Lieutenant Commander Clarke. He was with me as we connected every system on that ship. I daresay he knows more about how everything is connected than Commander O'Hallarhan."

"Can you spare him?" Saxon asked.

"I believe so. Most of the tasks left for the ship are basic carpentry tasks that require minimal supervision; adding lights, finishing crew quarters, that sort of thing," Malcolm said. "Commander Murray, have

Lieutenant Commander Clarke report to me tomorrow morning and we'll start work on building the training consoles."

"Very good, sir," Murray replied.

"Now the question becomes, who runs the training?" Saxon asked. "Do we have enough people who know how everything works in order to run the training?"

"We'll use the crew from today's flight. Lieutenant de St. Leger can train Communications; I daresay that will be the easiest job as there isn't anything special about the communications systems. I can offer my admittedly limited experience in piloting to train the navigators."

"What about Engineering? Who is going to do that?" Saxon asked.

"I suppose I have no choice but to let Commander O'Hallarhan lead the training. However, I would like Lieutenant Commander Clarke to attend as many sessions as possible. If my hunch is correct, most of the Engineering crew will not get much out of O'Hallarhan's lessons, and Clarke can provide remedial training. It's even more important that the Engineering crew know what to do in case of an emergency, as we are almost solely dependent on the technology of the ship."

"Speaking of which, what do we do if the ship sustains damage while in space?" Saxon asked.

"Ever the pessimist, Commander," Malcolm said with a smile.

"It can't be all rainbows and sunshine," Saxon replied.

"We'll have to do some kind of training in little to no gravity," Malcolm said, thinking out loud.

"Do we have any means to ensure survival in space? It's not like you can just climb out on the rigging like on an airship," Saxon said.

"Agreed. We'll need something akin to a deep sea diving suit to provide oxygen and protect the wearer from the cold vacuum of space." Malcolm thought for a moment. "Commander Saxon, am I correct in remembering that you have dive experience?"

Saxon groaned. "Yes."

"Excellent. We'll use your dive experience to simulate the weightlessness of space and working in a dive suit. You will be in charge of the training for external repairs. All hands will be required to take the course, including me."

"Me and my big mouth," Saxon grumbled.

They worked for the next hour, building a training schedule dependent on the completion of the training consoles. When they finished, he released his two assistants and retired to his quarters. He sat in his chair and let out an enormous sigh of relief. He had proved that the ship did indeed work and had the full support of the First Sea Lord. Providing he kept everything on track, there would be no further interference from the Admiralty. For the first time in what seemed like ages, he picked up a technical journal and lost himself in the reading until it was time to attend the celebration of the christening of the *Icarus*. He straightened his uniform, and as he started out of his door, nearly ran into Joan.

"Fancy meeting you here... sir," Joan said with a smile.

"May I escort you to the celebration?" Malcolm asked.

"I would like that very much," Joan said.

Although Malcolm's first instinct was to take her arm, he forced himself to keep his distance. Joan did not help the situation by finding opportunities to move closer as they passed other personnel in the hallway leading to the Mess Hall.

When they arrived, the Mess Hall was already alive with conversation. Malcolm had requisitioned a great deal of ale and rum, knowing that this may be the last chance for his crew to relax for some time. After leading Joan to the Officer's table, he did a circuit of the room, doing his best to talk to all the crew and thanking them for their work. When he thought he had talked to everyone, he started for the Officer's table to get his own food when he saw O'Hallarhan standing in a corner by himself, nursing an ale. Malcolm sighed to himself, took a deep breath, and made his way to his Chief Engineer.

"Commander O'Hallarhan, come join the festivities," Malcolm said as cheerily as possible.

"Is that an order, sir?" O'Hallarhan replied.

"No, merely a suggestion. This may be our last opportunity in some time to celebrate our collective success."

"Don't you mean your success?"

"No, I mean our success," Malcolm said, emphasising the word 'our.' "It's true that without your designs, we would not be here at all. But everyone here in this room," he said, sweeping his hand across the room, "played some part in today's success."

"I'm sorry, but I don't understand how a seaman cleaning the privies played any part in the success of my ship."

"Tell me, Commander. Did you ever worry that you wouldn't be able to use the privy while you worked? Or where your meal would come from? Where the parts you needed came from or how they got to you? The answer is you didn't. Because everyone did their job, you didn't have to worry about such trivial pursuits and could concentrate on your work."

"I supposed that's true," O'Hallarhan said. "But I still don't understand why they get to celebrate my success."

"Because, to put it bluntly, this was not just your success," O'Hallarhan protested, but Malcolm cut him off. "Yes, your design and technical knowledge made this ship possible, but did you tighten every bolt or turn every screw? Weld the hull panels? The construction of any ship is the culmination of the work of everyone. No one person owns all the recognition."

"Easy for you to say. You got all the accolades from the Admiralty."

"And why is that, do you suppose?"

"Because you take credit for everyone else's work?" O'Hallarhan sneered.

"Remind me again, Commander. How long had you been working on this project before I arrived? What did you have to show for all of that work? A skeleton of a ship. We had no engines, no power, nothing. So again, how were we able to get to today's flight?"

O'Hallarhan took a drink of his ale and turned to leave.

"Hold on, Commander. I know you think I'm some sort of glory seeking fraud who's bluffed his way through his career and Lord knows, you're not the first person to think that. I have got to my position through hard work and hard work alone. My first assignment as a midshipman was shovelling coal in the Engine Room. I hated every minute, but looking back, I see the value in that, especially once I had command over other people. Tell me, what was your first assignment?"

"I was assistant to the Captain of the Engineering division at the Admiralty. I prepared blueprints and wrote specifications."

"Have you ever served on a ship before?" Malcolm asked.

"No, after that, I went to the Admiralty and worked in Ship Design."

"And it shows. When you are aboard a ship, your very life can depend on the ability of every member of the crew to execute their job to near perfection. You don't have to like them. Lord knows I certainly didn't. But you have to put aside your feelings and pride for the good of the ship."

O'Hallarhan took another drink and remained silent. "Commander, I don't care if you like me or not. But I need you to be part of this crew. I just got done telling Commanders Saxon and Murray that the Engineering division is the most important division on this ship. Every single person on the *Icarus* will depend on that ship running in perfect order. The number of things that can go wrong is astonishing. The reactor, life support, and environmental controls have to operate perfectly or we all die. That's a great responsibility and as Chief Engineer, that responsibility lies solely on your shoulders. But you can't do it all by yourself. You must have people you trust who can do the job because you simply can't do it all by yourself."

Malcolm waited for a response. "I suppose you're right," O'Hallarhan muttered.

Malcolm studied O'Hallarhan. There was something still bothering him. "Is the real reason that you are upset because we could get the ship off the ground without you?"

O'Hallarhan stared at his drink before mumbling, "Yes."

"That's the problem, Commander. Every one of us could be transferred, injured, or killed, from the lowest ranking seaman to the First Sea Lord. While no one is indispensable, we need every single man… and woman to do their part." Malcolm looked at his empty glass. "Well, perhaps the barkeep is indispensable. Shall we get another?"

O'Hallarhan chuckled. "Is that an order?"

"In this case, I would say yes." Malcolm smiled. Malcolm led O'Hallarhan back to the bar, and they refilled their drinks. "Have you eaten yet?" Malcolm asked.

"No."

"Neither have I, and I'm famished. Come join me at the Officer's table."

"Is that an order?"

"No, a request," Malcolm said.

"Very well," O'Hallarhan acquiesced.

As Malcolm and O'Hallarhan made their way to the Officer's table, he caught the eye of Saxon, who arched an eyebrow. Malcolm nodded slightly, and Saxon returned the nod.

As they took their places at the table, Saxon said, "Congratulations, Commander O'Hallarhan. You must be very proud of the ship."

"Thank you, Commander," O'Hallarhan said.

Malcolm gave a nod of thanks to Saxon and they sat down to enjoy a veritable feast of roast beef, potatoes, and green peas. Malcolm ate until he couldn't take another bite. Most of the crew had long finished their meals and singing had broken out amongst the crew. Soon, the entire hall was singing along, even O'Hallarhan.

One by one, the officers took their leave until only Saxon, Joan, and Malcolm lingered at the Officer's table. "You seemed like you were having a rather intense conversation with our Chief Engineer. How did you get him to join us? Did you hit him over the head?" Saxon joked.

"Why does everyone think I can't be charming and diplomatic?" Malcolm replied. Joan and Saxon gave Malcolm a look, and he threw up his hands in surrender. "Fine, don't answer that question. Our Chief Engineer doesn't feel valued. Thank you, Commander, for giving him a bit of praise. There is hope we can get through to him yet."

"There's always hope. I seem to remember a Chief Engineer who was constantly at odds with his commanding officers and look how he turned out," Saxon said with a smile.

"Why, Commander, that's uncharacteristically optimistic of you," Malcolm said.

"It must be the drink talking," Saxon said. "I'll return to my pessimistic self when I have to train you."

"What kind of training is that?" Joan asked.

"Our Commodore has requested me to train all the crew to repair the ship while in space. To do that, everyone will have to complete dive training."

"Sounds like fun," Joan said.

"We'll see," Saxon replied.

CHAPTER THIRTY TWO

The next morning, Lieutenant Commander Clarke reported as ordered. Malcolm laid out what he wanted done and, as he finished, he added, "Mr Clarke, I would request a favour of you."

"Anything, sir," Clarke said.

"Please spend a great deal of time with Commander O'Hallarhan before you design the consoles. Tell him you'll worry about the construction details, but you need to rely on his expertise. I know you could do this assignment on your own, but Commander O'Hallarhan feels I have ignored his expertise. And I want you to make him feel you couldn't possibly design this without him. You don't have to follow any of his suggestions because I think you know more about how the systems are connected and programmed than anyone on this base. The important thing is the Commander thinks you need him."

"Must I, sir?"

"I know I'm asking a great deal of you, but consider it as a personal favour to me."

"Very well, sir."

"Thank you, Mr Clarke. That will be all."

Over the next few days, Malcolm watched and noticed that Commander O'Hallarhan appeared less surly. Lieutenant

Commander Clarke and his small crew built the training consoles in just three days' time. Malcolm and the other officers spent this time building the training curriculum for their areas of expertise.

As Malcolm addressed the first class of recruits, he was surprised to see Lieutenant Blackburn, who had served as navigator for Malcolm's last mission as captain of the *Daedalus*. "Mr Blackburn, what a pleasure to see you again. Why did I not know you would be joining the crew?"

"Thank you, sir. I'm a last-minute replacement for Lieutenant Anderson. I arrived with the delegation. My former commander delayed my transfer. I'm very excited to serve under you again, sir."

"How are things on the *Daedalus?*"

"Permission to speak freely, sir?"

"Of course," Malcolm said.

"In a word, miserable. Captain Bromley is a tyrant and Commander Davies is a fawning sycophant who will do anything to curry the captain's favour."

"Please, Mr Blackburn, don't hold back and tell me how you really feel," Malcolm joked.

"Sorry, sir. But every word is accurate. Serving on the *Daedalus* under Captain Bromley was nothing like serving under you and Commander Saxon. When I saw the posting under your command, I jumped at the chance to leave. I'm not the only one; most of the crew you knew is now serving somewhere else. I would have been here weeks ago, but the captain kept coming up with excuses to delay my transfer."

"I'm very glad to have you here, Lieutenant. You will need to catch up, but I have every faith in your abilities."

"Thank you, sir."

Malcolm started with the basics of the navigational control systems; demonstrating the controls that controlled the altitude of the ship, direction, and speed. He gathered the trainees around the console and replayed the maiden flight of the *Icarus*. Malcolm surprised himself that he could complete the program without imaginary damage to the ship. One by one, the trainees attempted the program with varying degrees of success; from merely banging into the tunnel walls to destroying the ship by ramming into the tunnel walls at top speed. Malcolm was pleased to see that Lieutenant Blackburn received the best score on his first attempt.

Malcolm was relieved to see an improvement in most of the trainees after four weeks of training. At the end of the training, Malcolm was forced to reassign two of his trainees to a support role, as they failed to complete the program without causing damage to the imaginary ship.

It gratified Malcolm to see similar results across all the divisions. Only six of the trainees failed their training in their operational area of expertise and had to be reassigned in support roles.

A week after they completed the operational training, Malcolm reported to the cove for his extra vehicular training. Saxon was waiting with a smirk on his face.

"Look alive, sailor," he said when Malcolm reached the training area.

"You are enjoying this far too much," Malcolm replied.

"It's the little things that give one pleasure in life," Saxon quipped. "Alright, let's begin. Here is your dive suit." He handed Malcolm the bulky suit with a large brass helmet. "Put that on over your uniform and when you've finished, we'll check the fit and make sure you have a complete seal."

Malcolm struggled for nearly five minutes to get the bulky suit on, as Saxon watched with an amused look on his face.

"How are you fairing?" Saxon asked.

"Fine," Malcolm snarled as he struggled with the suit. The fabric was stiff and unyielding; he felt like a sardine being stuffed into a can. When he finished, he presented himself to Saxon for inspection.

"Sloppy work, sailor," Saxon said as he re-latched the suit in three different places. "Before you put on the helmet, we'll go over your assignment. You will take this wrench and attach this metal beam with a bolt to the platform located just above the bottom of the cove. You can't stand on the floor of the cove as that would defeat the purpose, and I've ensured that even if you do so, you won't be able to reach the platform."

"You realise we won't be bolting anything together in space, don't you?"

"Of course I know that. But if you have the manual dexterity to do that here, you should be able to handle any task outside of the ship." Malcolm couldn't fault Saxon's logic. "This is a timed exercise. You will have five minutes to attach the beam and return to the surface. We will be in constant contact via radio. This line is your tether and also runs the light on your helmet. This line is the communication line, and this is your oxygen line. See that you don't get them tangled or it might be a brief trip. Are you ready?"

"Ready as I'll ever be," Malcolm said. He put the helmet on and carefully closed the latches, making sure the suit had a complete seal.

"Can you hear me?" Saxon asked, his voice coming through the speaker in his helmet.

"Loud and clear," Malcolm replied.

"Excellent. The first thing I want you to do is bend down and stick your head under the water. We need to see that the seal is complete before we drop you down."

Malcolm struggled to walk to the water's edge, the weighted boots making each step a struggle. He forced the unyielding suit to bend as he got to his knees and submerged his head under the water.

Saxon watched for bubbles and, after a few seconds, said, "Very good. You sealed the helmet successfully. When I say go, I want you to fall forward and begin your descent. Your time begins when you enter the water. Make sure you have the wrench and the beam. We strapped the bolt to your suit. Are you ready?"

"Ready as I'll ever be," Malcolm said.

"Go."

Malcolm fell forward. It was an eerie feeling as he floated the forty some feet to the bottom of the cove. The light on Malcolm's helmet only illuminated about ten feet in front of him. He fell for several seconds until he found the object standing above the floor of the cove. Making sure he had the wrench, he made his way to the platform.

As he approached, he suddenly felt dizzy. He tried to find the platform again, but it left his field of vision and he had no sense of where he was. He started breathing faster, but the dizziness persisted.

He started thrashing around, trying to grab for the platform, but it was in vain. The more he struggled, the more disoriented and dizzy he became. Suddenly, he found it very hard to breathe.

"Everything alright, Commodore?" Saxon's voice said in Malcolm's ears.

"No, can't breathe," Malcolm whispered as his vision clouded and his world slowly went black.

CHAPTER THIRTY THREE

When Malcolm awoke, he was looking at the roof of the cave. He sat up, but Saxon pushed him down. "Lie still for a minute, Commodore, and take some time to get your bearings."

Malcolm took several deep breaths before asking, "What happened?"

"I believe you experienced an episode of vertigo. Once you became disoriented, you panicked, and you twisted your oxygen line, cutting off the supply of oxygen. I dived in, untwisted the oxygen line, and brought you to the surface. You gave us quite a scare."

"Thank you, Charles," Malcolm said, forgetting protocol. "Am I alright?"

"I think so, but I will insist that you visit the doctor before returning to duty. That is standard protocol in cases like this."

"I take it I failed my test," Malcolm said.

"You could say that," Saxon said.

"Good, I'll leave the extravehicular work to you."

"And that's my reward for saving your life?" Saxon quipped.

"As you often remind me, no good deed goes unpunished."

"Well, you certainly seem back to your old self, but I do insist that you report to Sick Bay immediately. Is that clear?"

"Yes, sir," Malcolm said as he struggled to sit up. The dizziness was gone, but everything still felt a little fuzzy. He struggled to his feet. The unyielding fabric of the suit made the process difficult. With Saxon's help, he got out of the suit and, without protest, went to Sick Bay for an examination.

Once the doctor examined him and cleared him to resume duty, Malcolm returned to his office and tried to concentrate on paperwork, but he couldn't keep his mind on the task at hand.

An hour later, there was a knock on his door. "Come," Malcolm said.

Saxon entered. "Are you alright, Malcolm?"

"Yes, I'm fine. The doctor cleared me for duty."

"That's not what I mean, and you know it," Saxon said.

"I… I don't know," Malcolm said. "I was scared, Charles. More afraid than I've been in a very long time."

"I understand. A dive gone wrong can be a terrifying experience."

"Has it ever happened to you?"

"Once. During my dive training, we were exploring a scuttled ship off the coast of Portsmouth. As I navigated through the wreck, the deck gave way below me and my foot became stuck. No matter how I tried, I couldn't pull myself free. I started to panic and breathe quickly, using up my oxygen supply. I radioed for help and by the time they pulled me loose, I barely had any oxygen left. Suffocation is a horrible way to die."

"I just couldn't make sense of anything around me; I couldn't tell up from down."

"It happens to the best of us down there. Don't be upset with yourself."

"I'm not. But it really brought home to me how dangerous this mission is."

"Flying in airships wasn't dangerous enough for you? Falling out of the sky is not a pretty fate."

"True," Malcolm said. "But I always felt that I had my fate in my own hands. Even when I climbed the rigging, I trusted the rigging and my harness. I knew everything there was to know about the balloons and the fractional distillers that created the helium. Whether it was actually true, I felt like I had control. With our mission, it seems like there's a million ways we can die and all of them are out of my control. Doesn't that scare you?"

"Yes, it does," Saxon said.

"How do you handle that fear?"

Saxon looked squarely at Malcolm. "I handle it because I have faith in you. Malcolm, you have got us out of more deadly situations than I can count. You are level-headed in a crisis, today's exercise exempted. I have faith that you can meet any challenge head on. After all, didn't the Crown Prince call you 'Godkiller'? I think that justifies my trust."

"I wish I shared your confidence," Malcolm snorted. "Charles, can you do me one favour? Can you record my failure of the test as didn't complete the mission in time? I really don't want this getting back to Joan, who might kill me where your training failed."

Saxon smiled, "Of course, Malcolm. Mostly because after she killed you, I might be next."

"Tell me, how did Joan fare?"

"She completed the task with the second shortest time of anyone so far," Saxon said.

"Of course she did," Malcolm chuckled. "Thank you, Charles. I owe you my life."

"I'm just returning the favour," Saxon said.

Malcolm was crushed to learn that he was one of a handful of the crew that failed the extravehicular training. However, he rationalised it was just as well as a Commodore really had no business travelling outside of a spaceship to affect repairs.

With the crew having a fundamental knowledge of the ship's systems, they spent the next month on training flights. Initially, Malcolm still piloted the ship out of the tunnel before turning the controls over to the navigational officer. After just a week, he allowed Lieutenant Blackburn the honour of taking the ship out by himself and within the following week all the other navigators followed suit, although the Engineering crew grumbled about having to repair the scrapes and dents from the occasional brush against the tunnel walls.

Malcolm was happily surprised when O'Hallarhan reported he had been successful in developing the personal force fields. "They aren't powerful because we simply can't supply enough energy to stop something like a projectile, but they are sufficient to stop us from sickening the Martians." Now that this issue was resolved, Malcolm realised the ship was now ready for its ultimate test: a trip into space itself. The crews spent an additional two weeks of preparation, reviewing all the disastrous scenarios that might occur on such a flight. Malcolm double and tripled checked the scenarios and wracked his brain to think of anything else that might go wrong. For the ship's maiden flight into space, he picked the crew that received the highest scores in their operational areas. The night before the flight, he was working in his office, going over the flight plan, which was relatively straightforward. The *Icarus* would leave Earth, make one orbit around the planet before flying to the moon and back again. With the power of the engines, it would only take them about two hours to fly to the moon. The entire trip would last six hours. As Malcolm read through the flight plan, re-plotting the course to the moon for the fifth time, there was a knock on his door. "Come," he said.

Joan entered. "I saw your light on. Burning the midnight oil? Shouldn't you be sleeping?"

"Yes, I probably should, but I want to make absolutely sure I have memorised our flight plan down to the last detail. Shouldn't you be taking your own advice? I'm going to need my communications officer at her peak performance level."

"I tried, but I couldn't sleep. I figured you would be here, and I thought that seeing you might take my mind off of tomorrow."

"I'm very glad you did. I don't think I can stand to look at this flight plan any longer," Malcolm said as he set the flight plan to the side.

Joan sat in the chair in front of Malcolm's desk. She was uncharacteristically quiet and fidgety, smoothing out her uniform skirt and adjusting her coat.

"What is it?" Malcolm asked.

"I… I'm scared, Malcolm. I've never done anything like this before."

"Come now, I'm sure you've undertaken many missions just as dangerous."

"I have. But that's not it. I'm scared I will freeze up or not know what to do. I'm used to working alone or with a small team. This is totally beyond my experience."

"I know. I feel that way too," Malcolm said.

"You? Malcolm, you've commanded airships and you've been onboard every single training flight we've conducted."

"That's true, but I do not know what will happen when we get into space. We're truly going where no one has gone before. Once we leave the atmosphere, everything is uncharted territory."

"Are you scared?" Joan asked.

"Terrified," Malcolm said.

"How do you get past that fear?"

"I try to think about all the things that can go wrong and I try to work out a solution for all of them. Charles is usually very helpful in finding all the ways any mission could go wrong."

Joan laughed. "How do you do this?"

"Do what?"

"Handle the responsibility that the lives of every single crew member rely on you."

"That's just it," Malcolm began. "I don't. Truthfully, I'm the one that has to trust that the crew can faithfully execute their duties. I can order and yell all I want, but if the crew doesn't perform, there's little I can do about it."

"Doesn't that frighten you?"

"It does. But that's why we train for what we can. When the crew can do things by rote, there's little time for second guessing or hesitation."

"I wish I had your confidence. I'm scared I'm going to freeze or forget what I need to do," Joan said.

"Quick, what's the operating frequency of the base communication?"

"One hundred fifty-six point nine five zero."

"You rattled that off the top of your head without a moment's hesitation. Why? Because we have drilled it into you to the point, you can probably recite it in your sleep. Joan, I truthfully wouldn't risk your life on this flight if I didn't have the confidence that you could handle it. No one knows more about the communications systems of that ship than you. You are up to the task and you're an amazing woman capable of anything you want to do."

"Thank you, Malcolm," she said, smiling. "Tell me, Commodore, do you still have your strict policy of not fraternising with the female crew?" Joan rose from her chair and circled around Malcolm's desk before sitting in his lap. "Do you think you might see fit to relax your policy for tonight?"

"I think you might convince me," he said.

CHAPTER THIRTY FOUR

The next morning, the crew assembled for the last inspection of the ship before its launch. As Malcolm walked through the ship, he could sense their nervousness. He peppered them with questions about their station, which they answered immediately, taking their mind off of what was to come.

When Malcolm completed his circuit, he stopped at his office door. He touched the brass sign next to the door "OFFICE, COMMODORE MALCOLM ROBERTSON, KCMG". Although it had been months now since he attained that rank, it still seemed unreal. He entered his office and sat at his desk. The office was spartan by the usual standards for a ship, but was completely functional. Besides his desk, there was a small table with four chairs, enough to hold a briefing with his senior officers. As he sat there, the implications of this flight hit him. He and his crew would be the first humans to leave the Earth and travel into space. He knew he should have remarks prepared before the launch, but he couldn't find any words that adequately conveyed the gravity of this mission. *Gravity*, he thought. *Now is not the time for puns.*

A knock on his door interrupted his thoughts. "Come," Malcolm said.

Saxon entered. "I thought I might find you here. The crew is ready, just waiting for your pre-launch instructions."

"Thank you, Charles."

Malcolm sat lost in thought, before Saxon asked, "Is everything alright?"

"What? Yes, my mind is reeling at the implications of what we're about to do. I've been so preoccupied with getting to this point, I haven't thought about what this flight actually means. We are going to be the first human beings to leave the Earth. It's astonishing."

"It is," Charles said. "I wish I had some pithy remark to put you at ease, but I don't. This is a huge milestone, not just for us, but for humanity. We're so focused on what we are doing for the British Empire, but this is a step for the entire world. This is bigger than you or I, or even the British Empire. This flight has implications far exceeding our mission to return the Martian Crown Prince to Mars. We will now be able to explore well beyond our world."

"I know. I'm at a loss for what to say to the crew."

"I understand. I'm just glad that I don't have to address the crew."

"Thanks for your support," Malcolm said.

"Are you ready?"

"Ready as I'll ever be," Malcolm said. He rose from his desk, pulled down the hem of his jacket and tried to project a confident image as he strode from his office to the Bridge. The crew was at their stations. Lieutenant Commander Clarke sat at the Engineering monitoring station while Commander O'Hallarhan controlled everything from the Engine Room; Joan at Communications, and Lieutenant Blackburn at Navigation. Malcolm took his place in the captain's chair as Saxon moved to the Environmental monitoring station. Malcolm took a deep breath and turned to Joan. "Lieutenant de St Leger, please open the ship-wide channel."

"Open, sir," she replied.

"Crew of the *Icarus*. Before we begin this flight, I wanted to say a few words, but honestly, I can't think of anything that can adequately convey the importance of what we are about to do today. We will be the first humans in the world to leave this planet. We've long stared at the stars and wondered 'What's out there?' Today is the day that we answer that question. We've worked extremely hard to get to this point and but the success of that work will be determined by our actions today. I have full faith in every one of you and I'm proud to share this moment with each of you. I know today will be the day that history records the exploits of the *Icarus*. Let's make it memorable. Begin pre-flight checks."

"Engineering, all systems nominal," Clarke said.

"Navigation, all systems nominal."

"Environmental Controls, all systems nominal."

"Communications, all systems nominal."

Malcolm nodded. "All hands, prepare for launch. Mr Blackburne, take us out."

The ship rose every so gracefully and floated through the tunnel. Upon clearing the opening, the clouds hung low. He nodded, content that the clouds would provide cover to the ship.

"Mr Blackburne, take us up. Mr Saxon, correct the artificial gravity to compensate for our course. Miss de St. Leger, open a channel to the base."

"Open, sir," she said.

"Boreray base, this is *Icarus*. We have cleared the base and beginning our ascent."

"Acknowledged, *Icarus*."

The ship turned upwards towards the clouds. As the ship pushed through the clouds, Malcolm smiled. Malcolm was never tired of the view of flying over the cloud level. The wide expanse of brilliant blue sky over the blanket of the cottony clouds filled his heart with joy. The *Icarus* continued to climb and, as it did, the brilliant blue sky faded away, replaced by the inky blackness of space.

"Switch to aft view," Malcolm said.

As the display switched, Malcolm caught his breath. Below him was Earth, a blue green circle awash with sprays of white. "My God," Malcolm muttered. "It's more beautiful than I could have imagined." Regaining his composure, Malcolm said, "Mr Blackburne, what is our position?"

"We are five hundred miles above the Earth, sir," Blackburne said, his voice catching as he read the altitude.

"Excellent. Begin our orbit, bearing twenty-four hours right ascension, zero degrees declination."

The ship turned and Malcolm watched as the globe below them rotated, first past Europe and then to Africa. He watched in awe as the continents rotated below them as if he were watching a spinning globe. Soon, Africa disappeared from view as India entered, only to be replaced by Australia. Then nothing but ocean until South America came into view and again replaced by Africa.

"We've completed our orbit, sir," Lieutenant Blackburne added.

"Excellent. Set course to right ascension twenty-three hours, thirty-three minutes, thirty-eight seconds, declination negative nine degrees, eight minutes, forty seconds."

"Course set, sir," Blackburne replied.

"Engineering, are we ready to increase speed?"

"All systems ready."

"Excellent. Mr Blackburne, increase to cruising speed."

"Acknowledged sir,"

Malcolm watched as the world slowly shrank from view. "Display forward view," Malcolm said. The screen became a sea of stars, a tapestry of twinkling white and black. *"Twinkle, twinkle, little star indeed"*, Malcolm thought. "Environmental controls, status."

"All systems functioning normally. Life support and environmental controls are well within normal, artificial gravity holding steady at level one."

"Thank you, Mr Saxon. Miss de St. Leger, contact the base and inform them we're heading out."

"Aye, sir."

"Nothing left to do but to enjoy the ride," Malcolm said.

CHAPTER THIRTY FIVE

Malcolm watched in amazement as the Moon slowly grew in size from the ha'penny sized moon he knew on earth until it filled the entire view screen. Malcolm could not help but gawk at the beauty of the silver white orb.

"Mr Blackburn, what is our position?"

"Five hundred miles above the moon, sir."

"Begin our orbit, twenty-four hours right ascension, zero degrees declination."

"Changing course now, sir," Blackburne replied.

Malcolm watched again in amazement as he watched the Moon run beneath him. He recognised the Aristarchus crater, which he had seen many times through a telescope. He watched as the familiar side of the moon turned and the Moon presented a view never seen by humans before.

"Engineering. Is there any way to record the visuals we're seeing on the display?"

O'Hallarhan's voice came over the speaker, "No, sir. We have no mechanism to record visual data."

"More's the pity," Malcolm said. "Mr O'Hallarhan, put on your thinking cap and see if you can devise a means to record visual data before our next mission. It would be useful if we have a record of what we're seeing, not only to us, but to the scientific community."

"Yes, sir," O'Hallarhan said.

Malcolm tried to memorise as many details as he could to record for posterity. He noted a large, dark crater that looked like a pockmark in the Northern Hemisphere. In fact, craters filled this whole side of the moon, evidence of the Moon's bombardment by meteors. Malcolm watched as the view rotated to the familiar view he had seen many times from Earth.

"One lunar orbit completed, sir."

"Thank you, Mr Blackburne. Set a return course for home, eleven hours, forty-six minutes, forty-seven seconds right ascension, one hundred seventy-eight degrees, fifty-one minutes, twenty seconds declination."

"Aye, sir," Blackburne replied.

As the ship turned away from the Moon and back into space, Malcolm saw something on the screen.

"Full stop, Mr Blackburne."

"Aye, sir."

"What is it, Commodore?" Saxon asked.

"Do you see that?" Malcolm said, pointing at the viewscreen. "It looks like a giant piece of rock."

"Now, I see it," Saxon said. "What of it?"

"Mr Blackburne, take us close to that rock. I want to examine it in more detail." The ship swung around and soon they were within two miles of the space rock.

"Now what?" Saxon asked.

"Engineering, Commander O'Hallarhan. Please report to the bridge."

"Within a few moments, O'Hallarhan entered the bridge. "What is it, Commodore? Is something wrong?"

"No, Commander. I'm curious. Can we use the gravity beam to retrieve an object?"

"It's possible; what do you have in mind?"

"I'd like to retrieve that space rock," Malcolm said, pointing at the screen. "Do you think we can do that?"

"I don't think we'll be able to bring it aboard. It's too big."

"Can we attempt to bring it closer?"

"Aye, sir."

"Can you do that from the Engineering console?"

"Aye, sir." O'Hallarhan all but pushed Commander Clarke aside and began making adjustments. "Ready when you are, sir."

"Excellent, let's bring that space rock closer to us. You may begin."

At first, nothing seemed to happen.

"Mr O'Hallarhan, increase beam strength."

"Aye, sir.," O'Hallarhan replied. As O'Hallarhan increased the beam strength, the rock began floating towards the *Icarus* when suddenly, the rock crushed into dust, followed by an explosion of light. The ship lurched forward, throwing everyone off balance.

"What the hell is happening?" Malcolm barked.

"I don't know," replied O'Hallarhan. "Something is pulling us forward."

"Full reverse, now, Mr Blackburne!" Malcolm bellowed.

On the viewscreen, there was a circle of light surrounding the blackest hole that Malcolm had ever seen. The remains of the space rock circled around the hole like water in a drain before disappearing into the black nothingness. The *Icarus* moved backwards for a short time before coming to a stop.

"Mr Blackburne, I said full reverse!" Malcolm ordered.

"The engines are at full reverse, but we've come to a stop. Something is preventing our motion."

Malcolm looked at the screen as the light around the hole itself seemed to stretch and the circle of light turned into a cylinder, reaching back to the ship.

"Mr O'Hallarhan, turn off the gravity beam. Is there anyway to get us more thrust?"

"No, Commodore. The engines are at maximum output."

"Commodore, the Environmental control monitors are showing

extreme stress on the ship. If we keep this up, there will be a hull rupture," Saxon reported.

"Reduce reverse engine thrust by ten per cent, Mr Blackburne."

"Aye, sir."

The *Icarus* now moved closer to the hole. The cylinder of light shortened, following the *Icarus'* path into the hole.

"Stress on the hull is no longer critical, sir," Saxon added.

"Mr O'Hallarhan, is the gravity beam off?"

"Aye, sir."

"Then why are we moving forward?"

"I don't know, sir," O'Hallarhan said. "Unless we've created a tear in space."

"What do you mean, a tear in space?" Malcolm replied.

"If we created a tear in space, we've created a point where gravity is nearly infinite. It pulls in everything, including light, to a single point in space."

"That doesn't sound very good," Saxon quipped.

"Mr Blackburne, can you change course?" Malcolm ordered.

"I've changed the course, but it's having no effect."

"Are the thrusters working?"

"Aye, sir," O'Hallarhan added. "Thrusters are firing at full power."

"Lieutenant de St. Leger, radio the base that we are in distress," Malcolm said before mumbling to himself, "for all the bloody good it will do." Malcolm looked at the viewscreen, the *Icarus* definitely moving toward the hole. "Mr Blackburne, how far are we from the tear?"

"One and three-quarter miles and decreasing."

"What's our speed?"

"Approximately twenty miles an hour, sir."

"That means we have less than five minutes to come up with a solution."

"Likely less than that, sir," O'Hallarhan added. "Our speed will accelerate the closer we get because of the gravitational attraction."

"Sir, our speed has increased to nearly thirty miles an hour, and we're now one and a quarter mile from the hole," Blackburne reported.

"Hull stress is increasing, Commodore," Saxon added. "What are your orders, Commodore?"

"Damned if I know," Malcolm muttered under his breath.

CHAPTER THIRTY SIX

"What are your orders, Commodore?" Saxon repeated.

"I don't know," Malcolm whispered.

"Mr Blackburne, on my mark, execute full thrust to twenty degrees left of the hole." O'Hallarhan said.

"O'Hallarhan, what are you doing?" Malcolm said.

"Saving the ship. Now, Mr Blackburne!" O'Hallarhan said.

The ship sped toward the hole and as it approached; the hole contracted and winked out of existence.

"Mr O'Hallarhan, what just happened?".

"When we created the tear in space, it became a source of nearly infinite gravity. Reversing the engines only trapped us within the hold of the tear, much like a Chinese finger trap. When we accelerated towards the hole, it released the gravitational hold on the ship. Before we reached the hole, I fired the beam with a reverse polarity and sealed the hole before we were pulled in."

"All stations, damage report."

"Engines are nominal, sir," O'Hallarhan reported.

"Environmental systems are nominal. No reports of hull rupture."

"Communications are nominal, sir. Message to Earth acknowledged by base."

"Lieutenant de St. Leger, radio Earth that we are no longer in distress and are returning home."

"Mr Blackburne, set course for Earth. Commander Saxon, you have the bridge. I'll be in my office," Malcolm said as he left his chair and entered his office.

Malcolm sat at his desk, staring blankly at the walls, replaying the events of the last few minutes repeatedly in his head. A knock on the door interrupted him and Joan entered.

"What are you doing here? You should be at your station!" Malcolm growled.

"Commander Saxon relieved me from my station and ordered me to check on you."

"I'm fine. You've done your job. Now return to your post," Malcolm ordered.

"You are not fine, and I will not leave until you talk to me."

"Do I need to bring you up on charges of insubordination?"

"If it will make you feel better, be my guest. I'm not leaving until you talk to me!" Joan fired back.

They glowered at each other for several seconds before Malcolm relented and said, "Fine. Sit down."

"What is it, Malcolm?"

"I nearly killed every one of us! All because I got cocky and deviated from the flight plan."

"We're still here, aren't we?"

"Not because of anything I did!"

"Malcolm, did you have any idea that using the gravity beam would cause what happened?"

"No," he muttered.

"Did anyone else onboard know what would happen?"

"No."

"Then you learned something about the ship and this technology. That is the point of this mission, is it not?"

"Yes, but..."

"No buts," she interrupted. "Yes, you deviated from the test flight, but if you hadn't done it just now, it seems probable that you would have done it later." Malcolm crossed his arms, refusing to answer. "Am I right?"

"Yes," Malcolm relented.

"Then what's the problem?"

"I was useless just now. No, worse than useless, dangerously incompetent."

"Oh, for crying out loud, stop with the self pity. You are not incompetent, you didn't have the information you needed to make the correct decision. You can't know everything."

"It's my job to know everything," he retorted.

"That's ridiculous. Didn't you say to me just last night that you have to rely on the crew to do their duty and perform under pressure? That's exactly what happened. Are you upset because you couldn't figure out the solution, or are you upset that O'Hallarhan did?"

"Of course... I... I don't know. Perhaps you're right."

"Malcolm, you said it yourself; we have to depend on one another. Everyone has a job to do."

"I just felt so useless. I'm always able to come up with some sort of solution to any problem. This was a problem I couldn't solve."

"I know you pride yourself on your ability to come up with solutions in the heat of the moment. And you're excellent at it. But, Malcolm, you are a human being. You're not perfect."

"I know." Malcolm said. He sighed, realising once again that Joan was right. "Thank you, Joan, for talking sense into me. I need to practise what I preach, as they say."

"Are you settled now?"

"More or less," Malcolm replied. "What did I ever do to deserve you?"

"Lord, if I know," she said with a smile.

"Thank you. Could you please ask Commander O'Hallarhan to join me in my office?"

"Yes, sir," she said with a salute, and left.

Moments later, there was a knock on the door. "Come," Malcolm said.

O'Hallarhan walked in and stood at attention. "Commodore,

before you say anything, I take full responsibility for what just occurred. I made a careless mistake when applying the gravity beam; I forgot the scale was logarithmic and not linear. Instead of increasing the strength by a factor of ten, I actually increased it by a factor of ten billion."

"That explains the tear," Malcolm said. "At ease, Commander. Please have a seat. I asked you here not to discipline you, but to thank you for saving the ship. Your quick thinking saved the lives of every person on this ship. In fact, I intend to recommend you for the Distinguished Service Order for distinguished service under extraordinary conditions."

"I... I don't know what to say. Thank you, sir," O'Hallarhan said. "I thought for sure this was the end of my career."

"There's plenty of blame to go around. I never should have deviated from our flight plan to experiment with untested technology. The fault lies more with me than with you, Commander. I know we have our differences, Commander, but sincerely, please accept my gratitude for your actions today. I can't impress upon you enough that we would not be having this conversation if not for your quick thinking."

"Thank you, sir," O'Hallarhan said.

"Come on, let's get this ship home and when we get there, drinks at the Officer's Club are on me," Malcolm said.

CHAPTER THIRTY SEVEN

"Commodore, we are approaching Earth, approximately seven hundred miles," Blackburne reported.

"Thank you, Lieutenant. Set the course for base and begin your approach. Mr O'Hallarhan, are the gravitational shields ready?"

"Aye, sir. Shields are ready to deploy. "

"Excellent, deploy the shields." There was no visible sign the shields were active until they entered the atmosphere when flame wreathed the ship in flame from the friction of the atmosphere against the speed of the ship.

"What's the status of the Environmental systems?" Malcolm asked.

"All within normal parameters. Hull temperature remains constant," Saxon reported.

"Mr Blackburne, take us home. Miss de St. Leger, contact base to request landing clearance," Malcolm said.

The *Icarus* entered the atmosphere just above the Hudson Bay in Canada. Once they reached cruising altitude, Mr Blackburne turned the ship east and began the slow descent to Boreray Island. With the same deft hand he showed during the launch, he executed a perfect landing.

When the ship settled gently to the ground, cheers erupted from the bridge crew. Malcolm engaged the ship-wide channel. "We are once again Earthbound," Malcolm said. "My heartiest congratulations to the crew and especially to Commander O'Hallarhan for his quick thinking today that saved all of us. As soon as you stow your gear, please join me for a celebration in the Mess Hall. Crew dismissed."

Malcolm watched as the crew left the bridge. Satisfied, he took one more look around his new ship and smiled. He realised just how much he had missed command of a ship and, despite what had happened today, he knew he was in the right place. He left the ship and returned to his office to write the report of the mission, as the Admiralty was quite keen on learning the results.

After he completed his report and dropped it off to the Radio Room to transmit to the Admiralty, he joined the crew in the Mess Hall for the celebration. O'Hallarhan had become the centre of attention, with many crewmen buying him rounds. Malcolm went to the bar and nodded to the midshipman serving, who disappeared under the bar and produced a bottle of Jameson's. Malcolm held up two fingers, and the midshipman poured two generous helpings of the whiskey. He carried the glasses over to O'Hallarhan and offered him the glass. He found a spoon and clinked his glass to get the attention of the room. "Everyone, may I have your attention?" Malcolm shouted. The room gradually fell to a hush. "Today, we achieved something that no person has ever done. Three cheers to the crew of the *Icarus!*"

"Hip, hip hooray; hip hip hooray; hip hip hooray!" the crowd roared as everyone toasted their good fortune.

"But tonight," Malcolm said, waiting to regain their attention, "tonight we celebrate Commander Peter O'Hallarhan, without whom we would not be enjoying this celebration!"

"Hip, hip hooray; hip hip hooray; hip hip hooray," the crowd roared again before erupting into a spontaneous chorus of "For He's A Jolly Good Fellow."

"That's all I have to say for now. Next stop, Mars!"

The crowd erupted in cheers once more and, as it died down, he watched as O'Hallarhan receive many congratulatory thumps on his shoulders. Malcolm smiled. Before he could bring his glass to his lips, a seaman interrupted him, "Begging your pardon, Commodore. You're needed in the Radio Room. The First Sea Lord is on the line."

Malcolm took a quick sip of his whiskey; it was good, but no match for his Auchentoshan. *"No rest, for the wicked,"* Malcolm thought as he followed the seaman back through the crowd to the Radio Room.

He took his seat and waited as Lieutenant Barnes, the base Chief Radio Officer patched the call through to the headset. Malcolm nodded, and the lieutenant left the room.

"I understand congratulations are in order, Commodore," the First Sea Lord said. "Well done!"

"Thank you, Your Serene Highness."

"Can you explain the distress signal you sent?"

"Yes, sir. We were attempting to use the gravitational beam to see if it could pull an object toward the ship. There was a fluctuation in the beam strength which pulverised the rock and created a point of exceptional gravity. It nearly pulled in the ship and surely would have destroyed us if not for the quick thinking of Commander O'Hallarhan. I'll be putting him up for the Distinguished Service Order for his actions. Without him, we would not be having this conversation."

"I see. Was this expected?"

"No, sir. However, we have isolated the cause of the fluctuation and will take measures to ensure that it doesn't happen again."

"Excellent. That's what I hoped to hear. How soon will you be ready to make way for Mars?"

Malcolm did some quick calculations in his head. "We need to inspect the ship and repair any damage that might have occurred. Getting the ship supplied for the Mars trip will be the deciding factor; the sooner we can get the supplies, the sooner we can leave."

"I'll do everything in my power to expedite the delivery."

"Thank you, Your Serene Highness."

"You say Commander O'Hallarhan saved the ship?"

"Yes, Your Serene Highness."

"And you want to award him the Distinguished Service Order?"

"Yes, Your Serene Highness."

"This is the same Commander O'Hallarhan that sought to have you replaced and caused our trip to your base?"

"Yes, Your Serene Highness."

The line went silent for a moment before the First Sea lord said, "I will personally approve the commendation."

"Thank you, Your Serene Highness."

"Congratulations, again, Commodore. I hope you and your crew are celebrating this historic occasion."

"I believe the crew is ahead of me in the celebration, but yes, it is a moment for celebration."

"Excellent work, Commodore. That's all. Get back to the celebration and that's an order!"

"Yes, Your Serene Highness."

The line went silent and Malcolm left the Radio Room and returned to the celebration, which was well under way. Malcolm found a quiet corner to watch, and in a few minutes, Saxon joined him.

"You know, O'Hallarhan is going to be insufferable now," Saxon quipped.

"Let him enjoy his moment of glory. This time, he deserves it," Malcolm said, sipping his whiskey.

The next morning, the base was in a much more subdued mood, recuperating from the previous night's festivities. Malcolm was up early and was at his office before Commander Murray reported for duty. When he arrived, Malcolm asked, "Commander Murray, please schedule a meeting with Chancellor M'qua at his, I mean, their earliest convenience."

Later that morning, Malcolm made the trip to the Martian's quarters. Although Malcolm was five minutes early, the Chancellor was already waiting for him.

"Greetings, Chancellor."

"What is it, Earthling?"

"I bring good news. The *Icarus* took its first flight in space and we are ready to begin the trip to Mars."

"How soon?" M'qua asked.

"I believe in another two weeks; it depends on acquiring the supplies for the trip, but my superiors have given me assurances that delivering the supplies is their highest priority."

"I certainly hope so. I can't wait to leave this prison. Tell me, how do you intend to keep us from contracting any of your hideous Earth maladies?"

"I believe we found a solution. We will provide each crewman with a small force field generator to contain the surrounding atmosphere. The force field will permit gases to flow in, but prevent germs from escaping."

"For your sake, it better work. If we take ill or even die from your Earth maladies, it would trigger a war."

"I understand, Chancellor," Malcolm said. *It will be a long two weeks to Mars if I have to listen to this the whole time,* Malcolm thought.

"What was that, Commodore?"

"Nothing, Chancellor." Malcolm cursed himself; he had forgotten that the Martians had mild telepathic powers. While they couldn't read his mind, they could sense his emotions.

"Is there anything else, Earthling?"

"No, Chancellor. I just wanted to deliver the good news in person."

"It will only be good news when we leave this prison. If there is nothing else, you may take your leave."

"As you say," Malcolm said, keeping his emotions in check. "Good day, Chancellor."

CHAPTER THIRTY EIGHT

The two weeks leading up to the mission to Mars were a whirlwind of activity, interrupted only by the ceremony to present the Distinguished Service Order to Commander O'Hallarhan. The base personnel assembled in their dress uniforms, freshly shaved and ship shape; even Commander O'Hallarhan's hair met military standards. Malcolm addressed the assembly. "It is my honour to award the Distinguished Service Order to Commander Peter O'Hallarhan, who's quick thinking and ingenuity saved the crew of the *Icarus*. Without his quick thinking and expertise, many of us wouldn't be here to celebrate." Malcolm motioned to O'Hallarhan, who stepped forward. Malcolm pinned the ribbon to O'Hallarhan's uniform, first throwing a sharp salute and then shaking his hand. "Thank you, Commander O'Halarhan." Malcolm turned to the assembly. "Please join us for a small celebration in the Mess Hall. I fear that given the work we need to complete before we leave, it will be more modest than befits the circumstances."

Supplies arrived daily, and it became Commander Murray's full-time job to make sure the supplies were unloaded and transferred to the *Icarus*. Commander O'Hallarhan spent every waking moment ensuring that the *Icarus* was in optimal shape for the flight.

Commander Saxon dealt with the assignment of the crew. Adding to the complexity was the need to find isolated quarters for the Chancellor and the Crown Prince's hibernation chamber. This took additional work by the Engineering team to route additional power lines to the quarters. Malcolm did his best to keep the entire operation working as smoothly as possible, solving any problems that his staff couldn't.

The night before the departure for Mars, Malcolm entered the *Icarus* to ensure that everything was in order with the ship. As he entered the bridge, he saw O'Hallarhan sprawled beneath the Communications console. "Commander O'Hallarhan, I'm surprised to see you here. What are you doing?"

"Something I should have done months ago," he muttered. "I was just about to settle in for the evening when I remembered that I still had to install the Martian radio."

"Martian radio?"

"Yes. We salvaged the Martian communications system from the Martian spaceship. It's been operational for some time. I installed the antenna months ago, but I forgot to wire it into the console with everything going on."

"Quite understandable. Do you need a hand?"

"No, well, if you could hand me tools, that would be a great help."

Malcolm took off his uniform jacket and knelt next to the toolbox. "Let me know what you need."

"Thank you, Commodore. Could you hand me the wire strippers?"

"Here you are."

"That's funny. Never in my life would I have thought a Commodore would assist me in wiring a radio."

"No, I suppose not," Malcolm said with a laugh.

O'Hallarhan worked in silence for several minutes; Malcolm couldn't see what he was doing, but he assumed O'Hallarhan was preparing the wires to connect to the console.

"Can I have the soldering iron and solder?"

Malcolm carefully manoeuvred the hot soldering iron, so it didn't burn him or O'Hallarhan, and handed O'Hallarhan the solder.

The smell of the melting solder soon reached Malcolm's nose. "You never forget that smell, do you?"

O'Hallarhan laughed. "No, you don't. After this assignment, I'm not sure if I ever want to smell it again."

Malcolm laughed. After a few minutes, O'Hallarhan said, "I think that does it. Commodore, there's a red switch on the upper left of the console. Can you turn that to the On position?"

Malcolm got up, studied the console for a moment, and flipped the switch. "It's on."

O'Hallarhan listened for a moment and cursed, "Bloody hell, what's the feckin problem?" He paused before he blurted, "Sorry, Commodore."

"Think nothing of it; I've said that and much worse. It's a sign that you're a real sailor now!"

"Turn the switch off and give me a moment." O'Hallarhan thought for a minute. "Bloody hell, I got the polarities reversed. Just a minute." Malcolm smelt the burning solder as O'Hallarhan first undid his work and, moments later, when he reconnected the wires. "Alright, try again."

This time, when Malcolm flipped the switch, the speaker made a pinging sound at regular intervals.

"That's music to my ears," O'Hallarhan said.

"What is it?"

"It's a signal beacon the Martians use when navigating through space. It's used for communication, but it's also used to help them set their course home."

"Can we use it?" Malcolm said.

"I don't see why not," O'Hallarhan said. "It might help us make sure we don't get lost and fly by Mars."

"Excellent, I'll keep that in mind."

O'Hallarhan sat up. "Thank you for the help, Commodore."

"Always happy to help a fellow engineer," Malcolm said, offering O'Hallarhan a hand to help him up.

"Commodore, thank you again for my citation. My parents have never been happy that I joined the Royal Navy, but they were ecstatic when I told them."

"When's the last time you saw your parents?"

"I saw them while I was convalescing from my injury. How about you? Are your parents still alive?"

"Very much, so. I haven't seen them in over a year. I was supposed to pick them up the day after they reactivated me to duty."

"That's tough. When do you think you'll see them again?"

"Some time after this is over," Malcolm said, gesturing around the ship. "Whenever I get leave, I'll probably see them at my wedding."

"Wedding? You're engaged?"

"Yes, to Lieutenant de St. Leger. We were to marry before they assigned us to the Service."

"I did not know!" O'Hallarhan said. "I'm not very good with people, as you might have guessed. It must be hard being her commanding officer."

"You have no idea, Commander," Malcolm said, laughing. "Come on, join me in my office for a nightcap. I still have half a bottle of Jameson's left."

"That sounds like an excellent idea."

The next morning was a whirlwind of activity as Commander Murray supervised the settling of the crews to their quarters. Once Commander Murray settled most of the crew, Captain Macdonald and his troupe of Royal Marines were the honour guard as Chancellor M'qua and the hibernation tube of the Martian Crown Prince, powered by a very large battery, boarded the ship. When Commander Murray received notification that the Crown Prince's hibernation tube was connected to the ship's power, he nodded, and it was finally Malcolm's turn to board the *Icarus*. Malcolm turned to Commander Murray and offered his hand.

"Commander Murray, I can't thank you enough for everything you've done. Your service here has been exemplary. While I hope you stay, if you want any other assignment in the Service, say the word and I'll do what I can to make it happen."

"That's most kind of you, sir. But believe it or not, I like it here. I don't have any attachments and I'm happy serving here."

"I'm glad to hear that. Again, thank you."

"Thank you, sir. Godspeed!"

"Thank you, Commander."

Malcolm briefly inspected both his quarters and his office to ensure that his belongings had made it on board. When he saw everything was in order, he entered the bridge.

"Commodore, on the bridge," Saxon said, and the bridge crew stood at attention.

"As you were," Malcolm said. Malcolm took his seat and nodded to Joan to switch on the ship-wide communications. "All hands, this is Commodore Robertson. They say a journey of a thousand miles begins with a single step. We're going to be travelling a little more than that. Today, we begin the trip to a brand new world. We are now all ambassadors of the Earth, and I expect all of you to represent humanity in the best possible light. If everything goes according to plan, we shall return home in just over a month and a half and we'll have a celebration to end all celebrations. But until then, we must all be vigilant and do our jobs to the best of our ability. I ask nothing more of you than I ask of myself. All hands, prepare for launch and Godspeed!"

CHAPTER THIRTY NINE

$\mathcal{M}$alcolm had come to the realisation that space travel is inherently a very boring pursuit. After they left the Earth and flew past the Moon, there was nothing more to see, just the same twinkling blanket of stars. The *Icarus* gradually reached its final cruising speed. Initially, they couldn't see Mars as its orbit placed it behind the sun, forcing the Icarus to take a curving path around the Sun. Two weeks into their trip was the first time they saw the red dot that was their destination.

Malcolm was in his office reading reports when Saxon knocked and entered. "Anything to report?" Malcolm asked.

"No, same status as yesterday, which is the same as the day before that and the day before that," Saxon said, settling into the chair in front of Malcolm. "Here, I thought this would be a heroic journey when it's just damned boring. I'd be excited to see a space rock or anything."

"Any response on the Martian radio?" Malcolm asked.

"None, Lieutenant de St. Leger has been monitoring the channel and not a single utterance."

"I would have hoped that we would have heard something by now. How much longer until we reach Mars?"

"According to Mr Blackburne, about six more days."

"How is the ship holding up?"

"Everything is fine. All systems are running as they should."

"So same as yesterday, and the day before and the day before that," Malcolm said.

"I'm afraid so."

A knock at the door interrupted them. Lieutenant Blackburne opened the door and said, "Commodore, Lieutenant de St. Leger has picked up a signal on the Martian radio. I think you better come back to the bridge."

Malcolm and Saxon lept from their chairs and hurried to the bridge.

"Lieutenant de St. Leger, report," Malcolm said as he sat in the captain's chair.

"I'm receiving a signal, but it's very weak."

"Put it on speaker," Malcolm said.

A sibilant sound came from the speakers. At first Malcolm mistook it for static, but as he listened closer, there was a kind of rhythm to it that differed from time to time. "What do you make of that, Lieutenant?"

Joan listened intently for a moment. "I think it is Martian. I can only pick out a few words here and there, but I am almost entirely sure that it's Martian."

"Excellent," Malcolm said. "Please send the following message: This is the *HMS Icarus*. We come on a mission of peace to bring the Crown Prince C'thwan T'plua and Chancellor M'qua Cth'rn to Mars. Repeat, we are on a mission of peace to bring the Crown Prince C'thwan T'plua and Chancellor M'qua Cth'rn to Mars. Please acknowledge."

Joan translated the message and waited for a response. Moments later, the sound reappeared. When the sound finished, Joan spoke again and waited for a response. Malcolm looked at her quizzically. "They responded. I think I heard the word 'acknowledged', but I asked them to repeat it slower."

The signal came again. Malcolm watched as Joan's face pinched in concentration. When the sound ceased, Joan nodded. "Commodore, the Martians acknowledged the message. They provided coordinates for us to meet the Martian ship."

"Please tell the Martians that we acknowledge their message and are adjusting our course accordingly."

Joan relayed the message and once she relayed the coordinates to Lieutenant Blackburne, the *Icarus* headed to the rendezvous point. "How long until we get there, Mr Blackburne?"

"At current speed, three days."

"Very good. Mr O'Hallarhan, any way we can get more speed?"

"I'm not sure, Commodore. We're running at eighty-five percent of maximum speed; we haven't tested the ship at higher speeds."

"See if you can increase our speed by another five per cent. I don't know about the rest of you, but I want to get this mission over as soon as possible. Commander Saxon, you have the Bridge; I'm going to deliver the news to our guests. Lieutenant de St. Leger, please join me."

Malcolm and Joan left the bridge and headed to the aft of the ship, to the quarters of the Chancellor and the Crown Prince. When they reached the door, they double checked that their personal force fields were on. Malcolm nodded to the Royal Marines guarding the door and pressed the button to turn on the special intercom that was installed for the Chancellor. "Chancellor M'qua, this is Commodore Robertson and…. his mate Joan." The Royal Marines turned to look at Malcolm, but his withering glance soon made the guards face forward. "We have received a signal from Mars and communicated that we are on a mission of peace to return you and the Crown Prince. I'd like to discuss our next steps."

"Very well, Earthlings, you may enter."

Malcolm opened the door and found the Chancellor sitting next to the hibernation tube of the Crown Prince. Malcolm was pleased to note that they had installed the translation device, making this conversation much easier for him.

"Chancellor M'qua, I bring excellent news. We have contacted your world."

"Tell me, in Martian, what did you say?"

Joan repeated the message. "Very good. What was the reply?" Joan repeated the reply. "Excellent," the Chancellor said. "The coordinates given match the general patrol route of the Crown Prince's flagship. It will be most appropriate that the Crown Prince's ship returns him to Mars. How long until we reach the coordinates?"

"Our best guess is three days, although we're trying to increase our speed to get there as soon as possible."

"May I ask a boon of you, Commodore?"

"Of course, Chancellor," Malcolm said.

"Will you permit me to make a personal call on your communications device? If possible, I would like to do it privately. It has been many years since I have talked to my family and I wish them to know I am returning."

"Absolutely. I'll arrange a time for you to do that tomorrow."

"Thank you, Commodore, you are most kind."

"We'll leave you now, Chancellor. Until tomorrow," Malcolm said.

"Until tomorrow," the Chancellor replied.

As they left the Chancellor's quarters, Joan waited until they were out of earshot of the Royal Marines. "That was very odd," she said.

"How so?"

"Did you notice that when you arrived, he addressed you as 'Earthling', but before we left, he addressed you by your title?"

"Perhaps he was trying to show some respect for letting him send a message."

"Perhaps," Joan said. "I can't put my finger on it, but something doesn't seem quite right."

CHAPTER FORTY

The next day, Malcolm arranged for the crew to leave the bridge for a ten-minute period between shifts so that the Chancellor could send his message. When the Chancellor arrived escorted by the Royal Marines, only Malcolm and Joan remained on the bridge. Given the distance left to travel, Malcolm considered it safe to leave the Navigation console unattended. If they drifted off course, it would add very little time to their trip.

Malcolm showed the Chancellor to the Communication console. "I'll let the Lieutenant, I mean, my mate, show you how to send your message. We'll both wait in my office. When you finish, knock on that door," pointing to his office, "and we'll have you escorted back to your quarters."

"Thank you, Commodore, you are most kind."

Malcolm smiled and entered his office. In a few moments, Joan joined him.

As she sat in her chair, Malcolm said, "I believe this is the first moment we've spent alone since we've boarded this ship."

"I believe you are right," she said.

"What do you think of your first space trip?"

"It's rather boring. I don't know, I expected something more… interesting."

"Me, too. But, I think boring is alright. That means no life-threatening crises."

"Until yesterday, I felt like I had nothing to do."

"I know. Welcome to the monotony of the Service."

"Is it like this when you're at sea?"

"No, this is far more boring. On the sea, the weather is a constant concern. If you get caught by a storm unawares, it can be disastrous. I was fortunate that it never happened to me, but I heard enough stories from the old salts that I knew I didn't want to experience it."

"You call experienced sailors 'old salts'. What will we call experienced space travellers?"

"That's an excellent question. You're the linguist, I'll leave that up to you."

A knock on the door interrupted their conversation. Malcolm opened the door.

"My message is complete. I am ready," the Chancellor said.

"Excellent. Allow me to escort you to your quarters."

"That won't be necessary, Commodore. I've already taken up too much of your valuable time."

"Nonsense, Chancellor. It would be my honour. Come, this way." Malcolm led the Chancellor to the door of the Bridge and opened it for him. He nodded to the Royal Marines who, along with Malcolm, escorted the Chancellor back to his quarters.

"I trust you reached your family?" Malcolm inquired.

"Yes, they were overjoyed to hear from me. After such a long time, they feared me dead."

"I'm very glad that you could talk to your family. On Earth, we find family is very important. I don't know if that holds true for your culture."

"Yes, family is everything," the Chancellor replied. "Family defines who we are and what we can become. It is the beginning and the end. Is that not the way in Earth culture?"

"To an extent. Being born into the right family can set your life on a very specific path. Some people, like myself, make our own path."

"How so?" the Chancellor asked.

"I come from a family of labourers. Yet through my talents and hard work, I am commander of this ship."

"How interesting," the Chancellor said.

"Here we are, Chancellor. When we near the rendezvous point, I would appreciate your presence on the bridge to handle any differences in communication we might have. I want our races to cooperate and I would hate to cause some kind of misunderstanding between our races."

"No, I'm sure that won't happen. But it would be my honour to join you, Commodore. Until then."

"Until then, Chancellor." Malcolm gave a slight bow and returned to supervise the shift change on the Bridge.

Malcolm found Joan waiting for him at the entrance to the Bridge. "What are you doing here, Lieutenant? Aren't you off duty now?"

"I am. Can I speak to you a moment?"

"I have to supervise the shift change, but if you would like to wait in my office, I'll join you as soon as I'm finished."

"Thank you, Commodore," Joan said.

They entered the Bridge, and Joan made a beeline for his office. As the new bridge crew took their stations, Malcolm gave the Bridge crew their orders. After Malcolm briefed everyone, he went to his office and found Joan pacing back and forth.

"Careful, you'll wear a hole in the carpet; it's brand new. I don't want to replace it after our first mission."

"What? Yes, sorry," she said as she sat in the chair in front of Malcolm's desk.

"What is it? You seemed worried."

"It's probably nothing, but while you escorted the Chancellor back to his quarters, I replayed his message."

"Joan, that was supposed to be private."

"I know. But something about this whole thing struck me as odd. Regardless, I translated the message, and I found it confusing."

"How so?"

Joan paused. "It was as if he were speaking in parables."

"Parables?"

"Yes. I could understand the words, but the context made no sense to me. It sounded to me like he was sending a coded message."

"A coded message? How?"

"You know how when we contact Mycroft, we always use euphemisms such as the Martians are our 'out-of-town guests'? I can't shake the feeling that the Chancellor was doing something similar."

"You don't know what he might have been trying to say?"

"No. I understand the words, but without the cultural context, I just can't put it together. Malcolm, I think we need to be prepared for anything when we rendezvous with the Martian ship. And by that I mean, prepare for the worst."

Malcolm nodded. He knew Joan well enough that if she was concerned about this, he should be concerned. He reached into his desk and pulled out a small box. "I was going to give you this later as a gift, but I think it might be more useful now." He handed the box to her.

"What is it?" she said with a quizzical look on her face as she took the box from Malcolm.

"Open it and find out."

She opened it and stared at it for a minute. "I still don't know what it is."

"It's a miniature version of a Martian gun. I had it made for you ages ago. I meant to give it to you once we finished the mission as a souvenir, but I think it might just come in handy if there is trouble."

"What does it do?" she asked as she held it up and looked down the barrel.

"I modelled this gun after the ultrasonic welders we used to build the ship. It has a very short range and, given the size, I imagine it's only good for a few shots."

"Well, it's better than nothing," she said.

"I believe that it's small enough that you could hide it on your person, particularly in the holster you wear on your right garter belt."

"Commodore, have you been peaking at me?" she said coyly.

"Always," Malcolm said with a smile.

"Some women receive gems and jewellery from their sweethearts; mine gives me weapons. You really know the way to my heart," she said without a hint of irony.

CHAPTER FORTY ONE

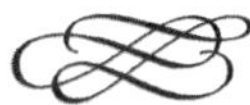

*D*espite the misgivings that Joan shared with Malcolm, the next two days were completely uneventful. That next morning, as Malcolm entered the bridge, he caught the first glimpse of the Martian flagship. At first, he thought it was just another star, but as they travelled ever closer, the ship slowly revealed its form. Quickly, Malcolm realised the ship must be gargantuan. He estimated at least fifty times the size of the *Icarus,* which was already larger than the largest airship in the Royal Air Service.

When the ship was in visual range, he ordered Joan to open a channel. "Martian vessel, this is the *HMS Icarus* on a peaceful mission to deliver the Crown Prince C'thwan T'plua and Chancellor M'qua Cth'rn to Mars. Please acknowledge and provide further instructions."

Joan translated the incoming message as it came in. "Earth vessel *HMS Icarus*, this is *C'thwan's Pride.* Message acknowledged. Proceed to the designated coordinates, come to a full stop, and await further instructions."

"Lieutenant, please acknowledge the receipt of the message."

"Aye, sir" Joan said.

"I think now would be a good time to bring the Chancellor to the Bridge. Mr Saxon, you have the bridge."

Malcolm made the long trip back to Chancellor's quarters and activated the intercom outside of the quarters. "Chancellor, we're in visual range of the *C'thwan's Pride.* I respectfully request your presence on the Bridge."

"Yes, Commodore. I will be there momentarily." When the door opened, the Chancellor's appearance surprised Malcolm. Instead of the Chancellor's usual robes, the Chancellor wore some sort of ceremonial armour. Malcolm couldn't make out the material of the armour. It didn't glint like metal, yet it still kept some kind of luster. Malcolm thought it might be some kind of ceramic, but that was only a guess.

"Is this your formal attire?" Malcolm said.

"Yes, it designates my rank as Chancellor."

"Very good. Are you ready?"

"More than ready. Lead on."

They walked silently through the halls of the *Icarus* until they reached the Bridge. Malcolm opened the door and allowed the Chancellor to enter. The Chancellor stopped in the door at the sight of the *C'thwan's Pride.* The Chancellor made a low pitch squawk. Malcolm interpreted that to mean the sight overwhelmed the Chancellor.

The Chancellor entered the bridge and Malcolm led him to a seat next to the Captain's chair. "Lieutenant de St. Leger, open a channel to *C'thwan's Pride* and relay this message: We are nearing the coordinates and await your instruction. Chancellor M'qua has joined us on the bridge if you wish to speak with the Chancellor directly."

A moment later, they received a message in return. "*HMS Icarus,* please allow Chancellor M'Qua to contact our ship."

Malcolm nodded, and the Chancellor spoke: "This is Chancellor M'Qua. The blood red sun is high."

Malcolm shot a look at Joan, who simply shrugged.

"Acknowledged. Welcome home, Chancellor."

Minutes later, the *Icarus* reached the designated coordinates and stopped the engines. "This is the *HMS Icarus* awaiting instructions."

"*HMS Icarus,* we prepare for your arrival. In one Martian hour, we will pull your ship aboard ours to complete the transfer."

"Interesting," Malcolm muttered. He signalled Joan to open the channel to the entire ship. "All hands, this is Commodore Robertson. In one hour, the flagship of the Martian Crown Prince will pull us aboard so that we can return the Crown Prince and Chancellor to their home. All hands are required on the main cargo deck in one hour in full dress uniform, no exceptions. Commodore out."

Malcolm turned to the Chancellor. "If you will excuse me, I need to change into more formal attire. You are welcome to stay on the bridge or you can return to your quarters and I'll get your when it's time."

"If it's all the same, Commodore. I wish to stay on the bridge and look at *C'thwan's Pride*. It's been far too long since I've looked at anything familiar," the Chancellor said.

"Then I'll leave you to it," Malcolm turned to leave and caught Joan's and Saxon's attention and nodded towards the door of the Bridge. He left the Bridge and waited for the two of them to appear.

"What is it, Malcolm?" Saxon asked.

"We think the Chancellor is up to something," Malcolm said. "Did you hear what he said? 'The blood red sky is high'."

"It could be some sort of ceremonial greeting, couldn't it?" Saxon asked.

"That's just it; we don't know," Joan said.

"So what do we do?" Saxon said.

"Prepare for the worst and hope for the best. If either of you have any of your sneaky spy equipment, now might be a good time to retrieve it," Malcolm said.

"What are you going to bring?" Saxon added.

"My slide rule and my brains," Malcolm said.

"We're doomed already," Saxon said.

"You know, Charles, sometimes you can be hilarious. This is not one of those times," Malcolm said. "I'll warn Captain Macdonald to be on guard. See you both in the cargo bay."

Malcolm hurried to Captain Macdonald's quarters near the aft of the ship and knocked on the door. Malcolm heard Macdonald snarl, "What is it?"

"Captain Macdonald, it's Commodore Robertson. May I have a moment?"

"Of course, come in," Macdonald said. "Sorry, Commodore. You would think my men have never worn a dress uniform by the way they ask me questions. What can I do for you?"

"I want to warn you; I think the Chancellor is up to something. It's nothing definitive, but his messages to the Martian ship seemed odd."

"How so?"

"Like non-sequiturs. For example, when he talked to the Martian ship, he said 'The blood red sun is high.' It may be some sort of ceremonial greeting, but I can't shake the feeling he's hiding something."

"What do you want me to do?"

"I want you and your men to escort the Chancellor and the Crown Prince's hibernation tube. Stay as close as you can to them without drawing suspicion. Be on your guard. Prepare for the worst and hope for the best."

"I'm a Marine; that's what we do."

CHAPTER FORTY TWO

Malcolm hurried back to his own quarters and put on his dress uniform, making sure that his sidearm and sword were not just for display. True to his word, he also had his slide rule in its own holster. He took a last look in the mirror to make sure he passed muster and returned to the Bridge to work out the details of how the Martians would bring the *Icarus* into their ship. Given the size of the *C'thwan's Pride*, he knew it would fit; he wasn't sure how they would achieve it.

Malcolm sat in the Captain's chair, alone for several minutes, staring at the *C'thwan's Pride*. Its size was more impressive now that he was close; he felt like he was in a rowboat staring at a battleship. The ship indeed looked like it was from Mars; everything was rounded and fluid, oddly reminding him of the Martian tentacles. He could easily make out the engines, but couldn't discern where the Bridge might be. There were two large doors at the bottom of the ship; he deduced they would be the way into the ship. The sheer number of spines protruding from the ship made it resemble a porcupine; Malcolm could only assume those spines were weapons. He noticed an opening near the engines and could see into the ship; he assumed that was the hangar.

Malcolm snapped out of his thoughts when Joan entered the Bridge and went to the Communication console.

"No messages from the Martians yet," Malcolm said. "At least not while I've been here. What are you doing here?"

"I thought you might need help with the translation for the instructions on how they will bring us aboard."

"Thank you. I'm glad one of us is thinking straight," Malcolm said. He looked at Joan for a long moment. "That uniform suits you."

"Thank you, Commodore," Joan said, smiling. "And may I add you look very dashing in your dress uniform with all of your medals?"

"Thank you, Lieutenant, but I think we should keep this conversation professional so that our minds are on the task ahead."

"After that?" she asked, arching an eyebrow.

"After that, I guess we'll have to see."

"I want you to know that I'm wearing your present. Perhaps later you can disarm me?"

"Lieutenant, what did I say about keeping things professional?"

Joan sighed, "Mores the pity."

A signal came over the radio, interrupting their conversation. Joan began translating. "*HMS Icarus,* prepare for our gravity beam to pull you inside the ship."

"I hope theirs works better than ours," Malcolm muttered. "If it doesn't, it's going to be a quick trip. Respond to the *C'thwan's Pride*: 'Acknowledged. Are there any steps we need to take?'"

"Please shutdown your engines; we don't want your gravitational beams interfering with ours. The result could be... most unfortunate." Joan translated.

"Signal, 'Message acknowledged.' Can you open a channel to the Engine Room?" Joan shot him a look. "Of course you can. Will you open a channel?" Joan smiled and signalled the Engine Room.

"Engine Room, this is Commodore Robertson. Who's on duty right now?"

"It's me, Commander O'Hallarhan. What can I do for you?"

"Are you in your dress uniform, Commander?"

There was a moment of silence before O'Hallarhan responded, "No, sir, not yet."

"Right now, I need you to shut down the engines. The Martians are going to use a gravity beam to pull us into their ship and they said if our engine is running, it might interfere."

"That makes sense. Give me a few minutes and I'll have that done, sir."

"Radio the bridge when you're done and then get into dress uniform. You are third in command of this vessel, and all the senior officers need to be present. Is that clear, Commander?"

"Crystal, Commodore."

"I'm glad we understand each other."

True to his word, five minutes later, O'Hallarhan radioed they had shut the engines down. "I hope he knows how to start them again, because I'll be damned if I can remember," Malcolm said.

Joan opened the channel to the Martian ship. "Martian ship *C'th-wan's Pride*. Engines are shutdown."

"Prepare to be towed aboard."

The ship lurched and Malcolm and Joan watched as the *Icarus* levitated toward the giant doors at the bottom of the ship.

CHAPTER FORTY THREE

$\mathcal{M}$alcolm and Joan exited the bridge and went to the main cargo bay on the lowest deck of the ship. Most of the crew had already assembled; the outside doors to the cargo bay were open, but the area beyond was dark. The Royal Marines formed an honour guard around the Chancellor and the hibernation tube of the Crown Prince. *Good thinking, Captain Macdonald,* Malcolm thought. *It won't arouse suspicion and the Martians won't be likely to try anything.* Malcolm took his place next to Saxon, who whispered to him, "Ready to make a speech?"

"Bloody hell, no!" Malcolm hissed. "I've been so focused on just getting here, I never thought about what I should say."

"No pressure, but it is the first official diplomatic meeting between our worlds."

"Thanks," Malcolm said sarcastically.

"You would think they would have sent someone with more diplomatic skills."

"I can be diplomatic," Malcolm said. Saxon gave Malcolm a look and Malcolm relented. "Fine. You're probably right, but we have Joan. Maybe I should start a new custom that, as second in command, you handle the first contact."

"It hardly seems fair that I take this duty away from you. Clearly, a monumental task such as this should be a Commodore's duty instead of a lowly commander's."

Before Malcolm could retort, the bosun whistled the approach of the Martian delegation. As the assembly snapped to attention, Commander O'Hallarhan rushed into formation and snapped to attention. If it were a true inspection, O'Hallarhan would have failed, but Malcolm just nodded to him.

The Martian delegation approached. Malcolm counted twenty-six Martians that he guessed were soldiers. Each of the Martians wore armour made of an interconnected set of ceramic plates. Each carried a long, black rod with wicked looking protrusions which Malcolm deduced were weapons.

Following the Martian soldiers was another Martian dressed similarly to the soldiers, but much more decoratively. *That must be the commanding officer of the C'thwan's Pride*, Malcolm thought. The procession stopped some twenty feet away from Malcolm and his crew. Malcolm nodded to Joan, and he walked forward until he was within ten feet of the Martian delegation.

"On behalf of the planet Earth and His Majesty, George V, by the Grace of God, of the United Kingdom of Great Britain and Ireland and of the British Dominions beyond the Seas, King, Defender of the Faith, Emperor of India, we come in peace to return the Crown Prince C'thwan and Chancellor M'qua to Mars."

The ranks of the Martian delegation parted, and the Martian in the decorative armour came forward. "I am Admiral R'kla, commanding officer of *C'thwan's Pride*. You are?"

"I am Commodore Sir Malcolm Robertson, commanding officer of His Majesty's Starship *Icarus*." Malcolm saluted his counterpart.

"What is this movement that you do?" Admiral R'kla asked.

"On my world, it is a gesture of respect among warriors," Malcolm said.

The Admiral nodded in approval. "Where are the Crown Prince and Chancellor?"

Malcolm nodded, and the honour guard of the Royal Marine

marched forward silently in perfect unison. When they reached Malcolm, they halted and parted to allow the Chancellor to join the Martian delegation.

The Martians looked at each other for a long time; Malcolm realised they were probably communicating telepathically. The Admiral nodded, and the Chancellor turned to address Malcolm. "Please allow our honour guard to escort the Crown Prince to begin medical treatment."

Malcolm grimaced on the inside from yet another condescending remark from the Chancellor. Malcolm kept his smile and nodded. Eight of the Martian honour guard came forward and wheeled the hibernation tube out of the *Icarus*.

The moment the Crown Prince was off the *Icarus*, the remaining Martian soldiers levelled their weapons. The Marines instinctively pulled their sidearms, but before they could fire, the Martians fired blinding rays that illuminated their targets and then, in a burst of light, the targets disappeared. In a matter of seconds, all the Royal Marines and Captain Macdonald were gone. The remaining crew were frozen in shock by the sudden destruction of the Royal Marines before they cried out in anger and reached for their sidearms.

Malcolm drew his own revolver when the Chancellor said, "In the name of Emperor C'thwan, I accuse you of attempted murder of the Crown Prince. You are under arrest until your trial. Drop your weapons before we kill more of your number."

"Attempted murder? Begging your pardon, Chancellor, but we risked life and limb to bring you and the Crown Prince home. We did not attempt murder."

"That is true. But you are representatives of the Earth, as you said in your opening remarks. You will answer for the crime of attempted murder of the Crown Prince through poisoning. If your world wasn't the polluted stink hole it is, the Crown Prince would not be in a hibernation tube. Commodore Robertson, you are a reasonable man. Please order your men to drop their weapons, and there will be no further bloodshed. Your weapons are primitive compared to ours; we can and will obliterate your crew in seconds."

Malcolm seethed with anger. Despite his best efforts, he couldn't save the Marines from M'Qua's ambush and despite every effort that Malcolm had made to ease tensions with M'Qua, he was repaid with unnecessary bloodshed. Malcolm glared at the Chancellor before dropping his revolver. "You heard the Chancellor; drop your weapons."

One by one, the assembled crew dropped their weapons. "What do you intend to do with us?" Malcolm asked.

"You will be our… guests, much like we were your guests," the Chancellor said. "Admiral, escort the Commodore and his crew to their new quarters."

More Martian soldiers arrived and herded Malcolm and his crew off of the *Icarus* into the cargo hold of the Martian ship. The size struck Malcolm; the cargo hold of the ship was nearly the size of the entire base at Boreray. Malcolm noted as they passed tubular containers, stacked row upon row, that each had the squiggly markings that Malcolm recognised as Martian writing. He whispered to Joan, "Can you read any of these?"

"No," she whispered. "I only have a rudimentary knowledge of Martian writing."

A Martian guard prodded Malcolm in the back with a weapon; the universal signal to stop talking and keep moving. It took a few moments for Malcolm to get accustomed to the lower gravity of the Martian ship. After the long walk through the cargo hold, they walked through the twisting Martian corridors. While the corridors of the *Icarus* were bright with sharp corners, the corridors of the Martian ship were dark and rounded, which, combined with the lower gravity, gave Malcolm the sensation he was walking through water. They marched into a large circular area with a central console and several large rooms along the circumference of the room, each open to the central area. The Martians wordlessly herded Malcolm and his crew into the rooms. Saxon, O'Hallarhan, and Joan all ended up in the same cell as Malcolm. When the Martians filled each room, they pushed buttons on a panel on the outside of the room and a bright light circled the entire perimeter of the open side. Malcolm stepped closer and could see the air shimmering in the opening. He gingerly reached his fingers out and there was a loud crackle of energy that threw Malcolm back five feet, landing on his back.

Joan raced over. "Are you alright?"

"I think so," Malcolm said, lifting himself off of the floor. "I don't know what that was, but I would suggest everyone try to avoid touching it."

"Commodore, I believe it's some kind of field of force. I'm don't know how it's generated, but I would guess that it works similarly to the gravity beam generators on the ship," O'Hallarhan said.

"Good observation, Commander," Malcolm said. "Study it as best you can; maybe there is some way we can disable it or get past it."

"What if we don't?" Joan asked.

"I'm afraid we're the guests of the Martians."

CHAPTER FORTY FOUR

$\mathcal{M}$alcolm assessed his new 'guest' room. There were waste disposal areas in the cell, a water dispenser on the wall, and fold-down shelves that functioned as beds. He turned to O'Hallarhan and said, "Commander, let's figure out how this cage works."

They cautiously approached the entryway, careful not to touch the force field. The light that encircled the entryway was blinding; Malcolm could only look at it for a moment before he started seeing spots. After several attempts, O'Hallarhan said, "I think I see where the force is coming from. If you shade your eyes and squint, you should just be able to make out a row of emitters at the top and along the left side."

"I see them now," Malcolm said. "That would mean… yes, it looks like there's a row of sensors on the right side and along the bottom. That could generate the 'wall' that keeps us in."

"I wonder if there are any 'holes' in the wall," O'Hallarhan wondered.

"We need something to probe the wall and I'm not sticking my finger there again," Malcolm said.

As if on a cue, a door opened in the wall to reveal a tray with cups filled with grey green pellets. Malcolm and O'Hallarhan turned to each other, smiled, and ran to the wall to take a cup. The pellets smelled of seaweed and mushrooms, an odour Malcolm didn't find appetising. Malcolm tasted one and found that his opinion hadn't changed. He and O'Hallarhan took turns tossing pellets at the force field. Each time, there was a loud zap which vaporised the pellet or shot it across the room. After about a dozen attempts, a Martian guard deactivated the force field and while the other guard pointed his weapon at Malcolm and O'Hallarhan, the guard took the cups of pellets from Malcolm and O'Hallarhan. When the guard left the cell, Malcolm looked down and saw a pellet on the floor. In frustration, he threw it back at the entryway, earning a grunt and a warning look from the guard.

Malcolm nodded and led O'Hallarhan back to Saxon and Joan. Malcolm looked at them. "I'm ready for any suggestions that you may have to get us out of this situation. Anyone?"

They all shook their head no. "I suppose we wait to see what the Martians are going to do with us," he added.

Malcolm and O'Hallarhan wracked their brains for some means to defeat the force field. Even if they were successful at that, there was still the matter of the three armed guards watching them. When they got too close to the force field, a guard would march over and investigate what they were doing. When that failed, they looked for a panel or some other mechanism, but they found the wall didn't have any seams or access points.

After three days, the guards marched in and waved at Malcolm to lead his crew out. The Martians marched them back to the cargo hold and out of the ship. When Malcolm stepped out of the ship, he was astonished to find himself in a colossal cave of red stone. At that moment, Malcolm realised that they had, in fact, landed on Mars, or more precisely, under the surface of Mars. He took in the sight of the voluminous cavern; Malcolm figured he could comfortably fit ten of the base at Boreray into this cavern. Where Malcolm could see a wall, it appeared to be worked, cut and polished to a smooth surface. Throughout the cavern were several light posts that gave off a blue phosphorescent glow. As the Martians marched across the cavern, Malcolm took careful note of the location of the ship. He watched as Martians took the *Icarus* out of the gigantic Martian vessel, likely for study or decontamination.

They approached an underground city with buildings of varying sizes. All the buildings had a rounded look and something about the geometry seemed off. It instantly reminded Malcolm of the hidden city of R'lyeh on Earth, but the effect here was far less dizzying. They travelled down a wide boulevard that lead to an imposing tower that reached to the ceiling of the cavern. The tower bristled, with many extensions thrusting out from the central cylinder, often at strange angles. A dome of silver metal capped the tower. Each of the arms of the tower was lit with the same blue light, which threw ominous shadows over the tower. They continued, and the tower grew ever larger and more imposing.

When they arrived at the tower, Malcolm saw two giant doors of the same metal as the dome. Now that he could see it in more detail, it definitely wasn't silver. As he walked next to Joan, he nudged her with his elbow and when he got her attention; he moved his head toward the doors, covered with markings that were like those Malcolm and Joan had seen at R'lyeh. Malcolm wanted to smack his forehead; of course, the markings would be similar. Cthulhu had been a god to the Martians. Those Martians that came to Earth with Cthulhu would have built its temple on Earth. Malcolm made a note to contact Nigel Sinclair to tell him about his realisation.

The Martians led them through the giant doors and into a large circular room with many doorways spaced evenly around the perimeter of the room. They marched through the right entrance and into a circular room. When the entire crew entered the room, a door swooshed down, leaving no exit from the room. Before Malcolm could react, he felt like his stomach had dropped and he realised they were in a lift. As the room ascended, they passed markings, likely showing the location, but it was meaningless to Malcolm.

Malcolm noticed that the time between the markings was taking longer and deduced that the elevator had nearly reached its destination. Eventually, it pulled to a stop before a set of doors of the same silver metal as the dome of the tower. The doors swooshed up, but Malcolm could not see much beyond the doorway.

The Martian guards motioned for Malcolm and his crew to leave. Malcolm led the way, followed by Joan and Saxon. As he left the elevator, he found himself in a magnificent hall that could only be the Martian Throne Room. The room was circular, with a high domed ceiling. A large throne sat on a dais at the opposite end of the room. At this distance, Malcolm could just make out a figure on the throne; he could only assume that it was the Emperor. Standing on the platform just below the Emperor, Malcolm was sure he saw Chancellor M'qua. Malcolm cleared his throat to get Joan's attention and gave a small nod of his head to point out the Chancellor. Joan nodded, pursing her lips.

They walked down the centre of the Throne Room with Martians crowded on either side, trying to get a glimpse of these strange beings. The room was eerily silent as the Martians speak telepathically to one another; the only sounds were the footfalls of Malcolm and his crew.

The procession stopped at the foot of the dais. Malcolm could clearly see the Emperor now. The Emperor wore a mask that resembled Cthulhu. Malcolm couldn't repress a shudder at the remembrance of his encounter with the entity.

Chancellor M'qua broke the silence, "By order of His Imperial Majesty, C'thwan C'thaln, we have brought you here to be judged for your role in the poisoning of the Crown Prince C'thwan T'plua. How do you plead?"

"Not guilty," Malcolm said. "We came to your planet to return the Crown Prince to his world where you could treat him. Our only wish is for our two worlds to co-exist peacefully. We have not poisoned the Crown Prince. As I understand, the Crown Prince suffers from a common malady on your world."

"Exacerbated to the point where the Crown Prince had to be put in a hibernation tube because of the poisons that you spew into your atmosphere. I understand that the air is so thick in the city you call London that one cannot see one's tentacle in front of one's face."

"I will agree that the air in London can be foul and yes, we, as humans, make poor decisions. From my limited understanding of Martian history, are humans so very different from you?"

"We are nothing like you, p'thah," the Chancellor spit.

Malcolm leaned over to Joan, who had been translating the exchange, and whispered, "What's a p'thah?"

"I don't know, but I am sure it was not a compliment," Joan whispered.

"We have brought the Crown Prince back to be cured. My people have also forestalled the rising of Cthulhu. If Cthulhu had risen, it would be a dire condition for both our races. I would hate for you to think our errand of mercy was anything but that, an errand of mercy."

"What do you have to say about the massacre at Horsell Common where you poisoned our people?"

"As I recall, Chancellor, the Martian landing at Horsell Common was anything but peaceful. My people's attempt at communication with your people ended in their destruction. The only reason your people fell was because you contracted a human malady that Martians have never encountered. Your bodies were unequipped to fight the infection. That is hardly the fault of humans if you were so ill prepared."

"Silence, Earthling! You will not question the motives of the Emperor. I should execute you for your insolence."

The Emperor raised a tentacle. "Enough, M'qua." The Emperor turned toward Malcolm. "Are you the one named God-Killer?"

"Yes, Your Imperial Majesty," Malcolm said, bowing. "I am Sir Malcolm Robertson, Knight Commander of the Order of St. Michael and St. George, Captain of His Majesty's Spaceship *Icarus* and God-Killer, as named by the Crown Prince."

The Emperor regarded Malcolm for several moments before speaking. "Although I know little of Earthlings, I find it unlikely that you banished the Nameless One."

"I would agree, Your Imperial Majesty," Malcolm said, hoping that if he didn't have the protocol correct that Joan could adjust with her translation. "It would not have been possible without the help of many people. But I assure you it was my hands that drove the spear into the Nameless One."

"As you say," the Emperor said. "Whether you are God-Killer remains to be seen, however, the Nameless One is sleeping. For that, we owe you a debt of gratitude."

Malcolm sighed in relief, but his relief was short-lived when the Emperor continued. "Humans have infested Earth, and now you have the means to travel to Mars. From the Chancellor's description of your history, you humans have a tendency to take things from others. We will not allow your kind to contaminate our world."

"Your Imperial Majesty, we have no desire to contaminate your world or take anything from you. My crew and I have endured great difficulties to return the Crown Prince. We could just have easily killed him and the Chancellor and you would be none the wiser."

"Your Imperial Majesty, are you going to listen to this p'thah?" the Chancellor interjected. "We should wipe the humans from the face of the Earth and allow our people to live as we once did."

"You accuse humans of taking things from others, yet you intend to take our planet away from us. How are you any better than us?" Malcolm asked.

"I should kill you for your impertinence," M'qua said.

"Go ahead. I hoped that the Imperial Emperor of Mars would be wise and just and accept a hand held out in peace and friendship. Instead, you listen to the words of a bitter Chancellor, angry at humans for the death of the head of the House of M'qua."

"How dare you speak to the Emperor in such a fashion!" M'qua said.

"I dare because I am sick of your bigoted hatred of humans. Tell me, M'qua. Were you ever mistreated in your time on Earth? I know my people took great pains to make you and the Crown Prince as comfortable as possible. While I am admittedly ignorant of Martian culture, have I ever treated you with anything less than respect? While you have treated me with nothing but scorn in the short time I have known you."

"Why would one show respect for an inferior being?" M'qua responded.

"If humans are so inferior, how is it we have returned you home? If it weren't for me, you would be stuck in a hibernation tube at the bottom of a freezing lake. I wish to God I left you there."

"Malcolm," Joan hissed. "Don't let your anger get the better of you. This is a delicate situation."

"I know," Malcolm whispered. "I'm hoping I can provoke the Chancellor into showing his true colours."

"What is that you say to your mate?" M'qua said.

"None of your bloody business," Malcolm said. Joan looked at him quizzically, and Malcolm nodded before she translated.

"I am sick of your insolence, Earthling. Guards, remove this p'thah and his ilk from the Emperor's presence."

"I'll be glad to leave a dishonourable p'thah, like you, Chancellor." Malcolm took a deep breath. "Your Imperial Majesty, I beg you to consider all the facts. The Chancellor clearly has an irrational hatred of humans. We came here, at significant risk, to return the Chancellor and the Crown Prince in the interest of peace between our worlds. Please don't let the poisonous words of this p'thah cloud your wisdom." Malcolm didn't know what a p'thah was, but if the Chancellor could call him that, turnabout was fair play.

The Chancellor grabbed a weapon from a nearby guard and pointed it at Malcolm. "You will die for those words."

"No, the earthling will not, M'qua," the Emperor said. "The Martian Empire has given its word that no harm will come to these humans. And no Martian will violate that decree. The Imperial Council will consider your plea. Until then, you will be our guests."

"Thank you, Your Imperial Majesty. I trust your wisdom in this matter."

As they left the Imperial Throne Room, Joan whispered to Malcolm, "I hope you convinced the Emperor."

"So do I," Malcolm said.

CHAPTER FORTY FIVE

The Martians led Malcolm and his crew through the streets of the Martian city. The twists and turns of the Martian streets oddly reminded Malcolm of the twisty, narrow streets of London. They eventually stopped at a door built into a cavern wall.

"This is your new home as guests of the Imperial Majesty," the commander of the guard announced. "There are several shelters, so settle as you will. We will provide you with k'thal and water."

Malcolm grabbed a weapon from a nearby Martian and advanced toward the commander. One of the other guards immediately fired at Malcolm. As he fell to the floor, the Martian commander said, "Until the Emperor decides your fate, we will not kill you. However, we will punish acts of disobedience and it will be painful. Get up, p'thah."

Malcolm struggled onto his knees, Joan and Saxon came over to help him to his feet. His muscles felt on fire, but Malcolm said nothing as he glared at the commander.

The commander opened a panel to the right of the door and pressed a button. A door slid up and revealed a large area with several dimly lit tunnels leading away into darkness. The guard led the crew to the central area, and the door closed behind them with an ominous thud. They led Malcolm and Joan to a cave room, furnished with two metal slabs built into the wall for beds, a stone table and matching chairs. After surveying the room, Malcolm leaned against the doorway of his quarters and watched the guards.

"Malcolm, let me see if you are alright," Joan said.

"No, give me a few minutes," Malcolm said. "I want to know what's happening." The Martians escorted Malcolm's crew down various tunnels while a small contingent of guard remained at the doorway. When the guard settled the crew, Malcolm watched as a Martian guard pulled something from its robes and pressed it against the rock to the right of the door. The door slid open and as the guards left, the door slid down, sealing them in.

Malcolm wearily sat at the table.

"Are you alright?" Joan asked.

"I think I'll be fine. Those weapons pack quite a punch."

"What the bloody hell were you playing at? You knew you had no chance of escape," Joan said.

"I wanted to see how they would react and how far the Emperor's orders would go," Malcolm responded. "It seems as long as we behave, we won't receive ill treatment."

"But why you?"

"I didn't dare risk anyone else's life on my theory."

Joan sighed. "I can't fault your logic, but every time you do something like that, I'm sure I'm going to lose you."

Malcolm smiled. "You couldn't be that lucky. I'm afraid you're stuck with me." He moved to her and pulled her close.

Joan tried to pull away, but Malcolm held her closer. "You know, you make it so hard for me to be mad at you," she said, finally sinking into the hug.

"That was my plan all along," Malcolm said. "And speaking of plans, we need to figure out a way out of this."

"Do you have any ideas?"

"None. How about you?"

"Not yet," Joan said. "I suggest we observe and make our plans accordingly."

"I agree," Malcolm said. "Until then, we can find something else to fill our time."

"What did you have in mind?" she whispered.

Malcolm leaned in to kiss Joan when a voice said, "Sorry to interrupt, but I thought we should talk."

Malcolm turned to Saxon, who was standing in the entryway to the cave. "As usual, Charles, your timing leaves much to be desired."

"I'm glad that I didn't disappoint," Saxon said. "What's our next step?"

"I don't know."

"It seems easy. All we have to do is escape this prison, wind our way through the Martian streets undetected, find the ship, and return home," Saxon quipped. "Should be easy."

"Easier said than done," Malcolm said. "Joan and I just said we should observe the Martians to see if we can exploit any weaknesses. Right now, we don't have enough information to do plan our escape."

"I agree," Charles said. "You two go back to doing… what you two were doing. We'll talk again."

Over the next four days, they filled in the details of life in the Martian prison. The lighting coincided with the rise and fall of the sun on Mars. The lights slowly came on in the morning, around 6:00 AM, according to his grandfather's watch, and then slowly dim around 6:00 PM. During the evening, there was enough light to allow someone to walk around, but not enough to read a book.

The guards came in promptly at 7:30 AM to distribute k'thal, the same awful food pellets they ate on the Martian ship, and water. The guards came back at 4:30 PM to distribute more food and water. At 9:00 PM, the Martians forced Malcolm and the crew to assemble near the main entrance to ensure that no one had escaped before the guards left for the evening.

Malcolm, Joan, and Saxon compared notes. The guards took turns delivering food and guarding the entrance. Each guard used a device to open the door, a trapezoidal shaped rock that fit in a matching indentation in the wall.

"Can we get one of those devices from a guard?" Charles asked.

"That's child's play. Leave that to me," Joan said.

"What do we do if the guard notices it is missing?" Charles said.

"I've been working on that. How is this?" Malcolm said, brandishing a trapezoidal shaped rock that looked similar to the guard's device.

"Where did you get that?" Saxon asked.

"I studied the indentation during our forced assembly. It's a crude copy, but should be close enough to fool a guard into thinking that it still has the device."

"Alright, so we can open the door. Then what?" Saxon asked. "We don't know if there are any guards outside and there's the small matter of navigating through the Martian city and finding our ship."

"Do you still have the present I gave you before they took us prisoner?" Malcolm asked Joan.

"Yes," Joan said. "The Martians never did a close search."

"And the present is?" Saxon asked.

"A small ray gun," Malcolm whispered. "I made it for Joan. It only has the capability for one or two shots, but it's something."

"He's so romantic," Joan said, patting Malcolm's hand.

"I think I might take ill," Saxon said. "Assuming we can open the door and deal with any guards, then what? I don't see how we can skulk all the way through the city and find the ship undetected. God only knows where it might be."

"That's the point where the plan falls apart. We need a diversion, but I don't know what that would be," Malcolm conceded.

They decided they would attempt their escape in the evening after assembly, hoping that the darkness of the artificial Martian night would provide some cover. Malcolm, Joan, and Saxon fanned out through the caverns to inform the crew to be ready.

The next night, the crew assembled. When Joan was near a guard, she stumbled and fell into the guard. Apologising for her clumsiness in Martian, she joined Malcolm in the lineup and gave him a nearly unnoticeable nod. He watched her, knew she was going to steal the device from the guard, yet still didn't see how she did it. If she ever wanted to give up her life as a secret agent, she would make a fine stage magician, Malcolm thought.

As the guards were leaving, the cavern shook as a loud rumble filled the room and the floor shook. At first Malcolm thought it might be an earthquake, but the rumbling and shaking gradually subsided before he could decide. The guards seemed excited as they hurried to leave the cavern.

"What's happening?" Malcolm asked.

"I couldn't pick up much over the din, but they are excited about something," Joan said.

"Alright, now's the time. Tell everyone to form up near the opening." Malcolm, Joan, and Saxon relayed the news and within five minutes, the crew of the *Icarus* had reassembled.

Joan drew her small ray gun and Malcolm went to the indentation in the wall and placed the device Joan had swiped from the guard. The door swooshed open and a squad of Martian soldiers stood facing Malcolm and his crew, apparently as surprised at the appearance of the crew of the *Icarus* as Malcolm was at their appearance. Each side hesitated for a second before a hooded figure said in perfect English, "Put down your weapon and come with me." The figure pulled back its hood to reveal the Crown Prince C'thwan T'plua.

CHAPTER FORTY SIX

"Your Highness! What are you doing here?" Malcolm asked as he gestured for Joan to lower her gun.

"The Emperor needs your help. I intended to free you myself, but you have already freed yourselves," C'thwan said.

"I'm pleased to see that you have recovered. How are we able to converse?" Malcolm asked.

"I will answer your questions in due time, but we need to leave. Come."

C'thwan's guard formed a perimeter around Malcolm's crew and they made their way out of the area.

"What is happening? Why does the Emperor need our help?"

"It's M'qua. The Emperor decided against invading Earth and intended to set you free. M'qua and the more militaristic members of the Imperial Council objected and staged what you call a coup d'état. They locked the Emperor inside the Imperial Palace, telling our people that he has contracted an Earth disease from your visit. M'qua used this lie to whip our people into a frenzy, demanding retribution. He has taken my flagship and renamed it *M'qua's Revenge*. The quaking you felt was the ship leaving."

"But how are you here?" Malcolm asked.

"Those still loyal to the Emperor sent word to me as I recovered. The remnants of the Imperial Guard still loyal to the Emperor joined me. However, our numbers are small and thought that you and your men might help."

"Ordinarily, I would say it isn't my role to meddle in Martian politics, but we need to work together to stop M'qua," Malcolm said. "What can we do?"

"The Emperor must be freed first. A contingent of those loyal to M'qua guards the Emperor. If we free the Emperor, the Emperor can address the Martian people about M'qua's treachery, and it might be possible to thwart the plot."

"How do we free the Emperor?" Malcolm asked. "We only have one ray gun with maybe two shots."

"You intended to escape with that? You are very brave or very foolish," C'thwan said.

"Probably a bit of both," Malcolm quipped.

"The Armoury is the first stop where we can equip you and your crew with weapons. M'Qua's forces have likely removed most of the weapons, but we'll take what we can."

"Lead on, Your Highness," Malcolm said. As they travelled, Malcolm noticed that the Crown Prince was tired from the exertion. "Are you alright, Your Highness?"

"I'm just a little fatigued. I did not complete the treatment when I received the news of M'qua's treachery. Once we rescue the Emperor, I can complete the treatment."

"That is it," C'thwan said, pointing to a large building still some distance away. The group moved onto a side street to remain hidden. "Perhaps the appearance of the Crown Prince will be sufficient for us to gain access."

"I don't want to take that chance, Your Highness," Malcolm said. "If they are loyal to M'qua, they may shoot you and say that the Earthlings assassinated you."

"True. Do you have any suggestions?"

Malcolm thought for several seconds before he came up with an idea. "Your Highness, would that building be used to interrogate prisoners?"

"Yes. What do you have in mind?"

"If I could borrow some of your guards to escort Joan and myself to be interrogated, we can eliminate them before they have time to react."

"You would risk your mate in such an endeavour?"

"She is more useful than me in this fight."

"Interesting. Is that the way with most mates?"

"No, Your Highness. Joan is unique."

"What else do you require?" the Crown Prince asked.

"Do you have any weapons that I can hide on my person?"

"Just this," the Crown Prince said, pulling an exquisite ray gun from a holster. "This weapon has been in the C'thwan family since the Great Schism. I treasure it and would hate to lose it."

"I will treat it with the utmost respect," Malcolm said.

He gathered Joan and the Martian guards and laid out the plan. Meanwhile, Saxon and the Crown Prince gathered the remaining Martian guards and crew and circled around to approach the building from a side street.

When everyone understood the plan, a contingent of six Martian guards encircled Malcolm and Joan and together, they marched towards the armoury.

"Sorry to drag you into this," Malcolm said to Joan. "But you're the best hand to hand fighter I know."

"Oh, you say the nicest things," Joan said, and Malcolm laughed.

They approached the Armoury guards and there was silence as the Martians communicated telepathically. When the Armoury guards turned to one another, Malcolm yelled, "Now". Malcolm drew his ray gun and fired at the closest guard. The kick back from the gun forced Malcolm to stumble back a few steps. His first shot was wide of the mark, but his second rang true. He looked up and Joan had already taken out two of the guards while the Emperor's guards dispatched the remaining guards. Malcolm and Joan picked up the guards' weapons and searched the bodies for devices to let them into the building. A few minutes later, Saxon and the Crown Prince arrived with the remaining group.

"Here you are, Your Highness," Malcolm said as he returned the ray gun to the Crown Prince. "None the worse for wear. It sure packs quite a punch."

"Yes, I am rather fond of it," the Crown Prince said, stowing the gun.

"How do we get in?" Malcolm asked.

"With this," the Crown Prince said, brandishing an amulet. "It is unlikely that M'qua and his cronies have had time to disable the Imperial security codes. When you are ready, I can use this to open the door."

"Very good. Everyone with weapons line up by the door and when I give the signal, you will open the door and we'll eliminate any guards inside." The armed group assembled in front of the door and Malcolm nodded to the Crown Prince. When the Crown Prince placed the amulet by the door, the door slid open and three Martian guards looked up from their consoles. Before they could move, Malcolm's group fired a barrage of rays, vaporising the guards instantly.

Everyone filed inside and closed the door behind them. Within several minutes, they had armed everyone with a long Martian staff-like weapon that functioned as a rifle, a small ray gun, and a few grenades.

"Alright, now what?" Malcolm said. "Where is the Emperor?"

"The usurpers have sealed the Emperor in the quarters at the top of the Imperial Palace," the Crown Prince offered.

"How do we get to him?" Malcolm asked. "I don't think we have the strength for a prolonged fight through the entire palace."

"That should not be necessary. The troops they left occupy just the top floor, guarding both the Emperor and the traitors in the Imperial Council who are running the government while M'Qua invades your world. If we surprise the Council, the resistance should be minimal. Most on the Imperial Council are weak willed and simply bend to the prevailing opinion. If that opinion is holding a weapon, they will fall in line."

"Your Highness, I think it might be prudent if you assumed the uniform of a guard. If the guards know you are among us, they might target you specifically."

"Excellent point, Commodore," C'thawn said. As C'thawn exchanged his robe for the uniform of a Martian guard, he pressed repeatedly on a console screen until a map appeared on the large screen behind him. It was a three-dimensional map of the Imperial Palace. With more manipulation, the top two floors of the map came into greater resolution.

C'thwan pointed to a wing protruding from the lower of the top two floors. "The Imperial Guard barracks are here. I don't know how many Emperor loyalists remain, but we must neutralise the threat. It will not be easy, as the Imperial Guard contains the best warriors of our race. Here are the Palace Guard's barracks," C'thawn said, pointing to a wing some thirty degrees clockwise from the Imperial Guard barracks. "They protect the Palace and the Imperial Council. They are less formidable than the Imperial Guard, but still a threat. In the centre is the Imperial Council chamber. It is likely that the Council will observe M'qua's progress and try to solidify their hold on power."

"What do you suggest, Your Highness?" Malcolm asked.

"We should take our best warriors and ascend this elevated platform," the Crown Prince said, pointing to a circle near the Imperial Guard barracks. "Another group ascends this elevated platform to the Palace Guard. We use both for delivery of food and goods. If fortune smiles on us, we can capture the barracks quickly. Once they are secure, we move into and secure the Imperial Council chamber. When we have that, we can combine our forces to rescue the Emperor."

"Sounds easy," Saxon quipped.

"How do we coordinate with one another?" Malcolm asked, ignoring Saxon.

"With these," the Crown Prince said, displaying three headbands. "They extend the range we can project our thoughts. One of my staff used the design of your ship's translator to allow us to communicate. That is how I can converse with you without needing your mate."

"Looks like you're out of a job, Lieutenant," Malcolm said to Joan.

"Gladly," Joan said. "Martian is a very tiring language for humans to speak."

Malcolm and Saxon quickly sorted the crew into those with combat experience. Unfortunately, only twenty-four crew members had any combat experience. Malcolm and Saxon realised they lacked sufficient forces to neutralise the best warriors on Mars. Malcolm addressed the crew. "I need volunteers to engage the Imperial Guard. This will be an extremely dangerous mission, with no guarantee of success. However, I can guarantee if we don't restore the Emperor to power, we will never see Earth again."

Quickly, another twenty hands shot up; one of them belonging to Commander O'Hallarhan. As Malcolm bade the volunteers to join him, he took O'Hallarhan aside. "Commander, this is an extremely dangerous mission. I'm reluctant to put my Chief Engineer in harm's way; I need you for our voyage home."

"You said it yourself, sir. If we aren't successful, we won't be going home. I don't have combat experience, but I can't continue to hide in the Engine Room."

"Very well, Commander. But follow my instructions to the letter."

"Yes, sir," O'Hallarhan said.

Although he was loath to lose Saxon's experience, he appointed Saxon as the head of the group that would take the Palace Guard, while Malcolm, Joan, O'Hallarhan, and the Crown Prince would lead the group to attack the Imperial Guard. When both groups were clear on the mission, Malcolm addressed the group.

"We're outnumbered and farther away from home than any human has ever been. I won't lie; it will not be easy. But you are the best crew in the Service. With your talent and the aid of our newfound Martian friends, we will not only restore the Emperor to his throne, but ensure that we make it home. Now, let's move out!"

CHAPTER FORTY SEVEN

The group slunk through the streets of the city, keeping as low a profile as possible. Malcolm was pleased to notice that there didn't seem to be other guards patrolling the street, lending credibility to the news that much of the Martian military had departed for Earth.

The group approached the Imperial Palace and once the guards at the door saw the assembled force, they quickly surrendered. The groups entered and immediately commandeered the correct floating platforms.

It was a tight fit on the floating platform that Malcolm's group used to ascend to the barracks of the Imperial Guard. The claustrophobic conditions added to the tension Malcolm felt as he readied himself for battle. Malcolm's grip on his weapon tightened as the platform ascended. As the platform slowed, Malcolm reached over and squeezed Joan's hand for reassurance. He smiled at Joan before preparing his weapon to fire. The platform came to a stop, and the door slid open. A dozen Imperial Guard were working at consoles in a large open area, engrossed in their work. Malcolm's squad fired their weapons before the Martians were even aware of their arrival. The light from the ray guns momentarily blinded everyone. When they recovered, the squad fanned out throughout the room. Malcolm, Joan, and C'thwan headed to the door to the rest of the wing. C'thawn tried his amulet on the door and it didn't work.

"Someone is onto us," C'thawn said. "They have deactivated my security access."

Malcolm reached down and took an amulet from one of the Imperial Guard. "I'll bet this still works," he said.

The door slid open, revealing a long corridor with many doors. The squad split up in two, each team taking one side. Methodically, they stopped at each room, opening the doors, ready to fire, only to find empty offices. As they progressed down the hall, Malcolm found himself gripping his weapon tighter until his knuckles were white. They reached a set of double doors at the end of the hall. When the two squads reassembled, Malcolm set them into position to fire as soon as the doors opened. Malcolm used the guard's amulet to activate the door. The large room beyond appeared to be a combination mess hall and ready room and Malcolm counted nearly twenty Imperial guards scattered around the room. Malcolm's group immediately opened fire, killing half a dozen guards before the remaining guards overturned tables and returned fire, using the tables for cover.

Malcolm's squad likewise scattered, diving for the cover of the doorway, and kept up the constant barrage. The air smelled of ozone from the powerful rays fired from both sides. Each time when Malcolm's squad inflicted heavy casualties on the Imperial Guard, reinforcements arrived. The Imperial Guard pinned down Malcolm's squad in the doorway and they couldn't gain any ground. The Imperial Guard used this to their advantage, killing several of the Martians and ten of Malcolm's crew. Malcolm was desperate to gain entrance into the room so his men weren't sitting ducks. He grabbed two grenades, armed them, and chucked them into the room as he crossed the open doorway. As soon as they exploded, Malcolm beckoned his squad into the room and they likewise took up firing positions behind tables and other furniture.

The fight ended quickly after that because Malcolm's grenades took out most of the guards. Within minutes, the wing was secure and all the Imperial Guard were dead or captured.

"Commander Saxon, how are things on your side?" Malcolm thought, using the circlet.

"Very good, Commodore. The Palace Guard put up brief resistance, and we suffered no casualties."

"I wish I could say the same. But we have neutralised the Imperial Guard. Let's converge on the Imperial Council."

The two teams met in the Imperial Council chamber to the great surprise of the Council. The few guards stationed there quickly surrendered when they realised the two teams outnumbered them.

C'thawn turned to Malcolm. "Now, we must rescue the Emperor and restore him to the throne."

"What's the plan?"

"It should be relatively simple. From what I've learned from the Council members, there are only a handful of guards at the entrance to the Emperor's quarters."

"Very good. Let's do it."

A smaller group, including a dozen Martians, Malcolm, Joan, and the Crown Prince, took a floating platform to the next level. When the doors opened, the surprised Imperial Guard could not level their weapons before Malcolm's group fired and vaporised them.

The Crown Prince opened the door to the Imperial Quarters and found the Emperor pacing across the floor. "What is it you want, p'thah? You dishonour that uniform by taking part in this coup!"

C'thawn pulled the helmet off of his head and said, "Is that any way to talk to the Crown Prince?" The Emperor looked and even Malcolm could detect the joy on the Emperor's face at seeing his son alive and well. "We are here to restore your rightful place on the throne."

"You brought… it?" the Emperor said, pointing to Malcolm.

"*He*," C'thawn emphasised, "led his crew in your rescue. Without him, I would not be here and you would still be a prisoner."

"My apologies, human. What was your name?"

"Commodore Sir Malcolm Robertson, Your Imperial Majesty," Malcolm said as he bowed.

"Commodore Sir Malcolm Robertson, the Martian people appear to be in your debt for the second time."

"My honour, Your Imperial Majesty. I have desired nothing but peace between our two worlds."

"Once we deal with the traitor M'qua, there will be peace between our races. T'plua, what is the status?"

"We have dealt with the Imperial and Palace Guard and captured the Imperial Council."

"Very good. Bring the Council to the Throne Room and I will deal with them."

The Crown Prince bowed and left. The Emperor regarded Malcolm before speaking. "There is more to you than meets the eye. I think the title of God-killer might be appropriate."

"Thank you, Your Imperial Majesty."

"Please explain why you have aided the Crown Prince."

"The Crown Prince has always been truthful in our dealings and has sought peace with my people from the very beginning. I fear M'qua may never have sought peace and has been looking for an excuse to conquer my world. I have experienced nothing but contempt from the Chancellor. And considering M'qua intends to wipe my race from its planet, it was a simple decision."

"Very good. Come, escort me to the Imperial Throne Room where we will await the cowardly traitors."

Malcolm and his group surrounded the Emperor as they escorted him to the Imperial Throne Room. The Emperor took his place on the throne, while Malcolm, Joan, and the rest of their forces stood on the dais below. Malcolm called his crew to attention to put their best foot forward for the Emperor.

Within minutes, they bought the members of the Imperial Council before the Emperor. Thanks to the circlet that the Crown Prince had given Malcolm, he could understand everything. Most recanted their support for M'qua, however, three members refused to recant their support of M'qua and refused to accept the Emperor as the ruler. The Emperor listened and paused before pronouncing his sentence.

"To you who have violated your oath of office and fealty to the Empire, this is your sentence. You and all members of your house are now declared Nameless. Those who have served the Empire wisely will receive the resources of your house. Take these Nameless ones away and expel them from the Capital." Malcolm felt the mental gasp from the Martians and knew that the Emperor had imposed the ultimate punishment. Martians could find honour in sacrificing themselves or enduring a prison sentence, but to have one's family name erased was the worse fate imaginable.

"Now, the Emperor will deal with the traitor behind this. Raise the *C'thawn's Pride* on the viewscreen."

A large screen came down from the ceiling and appeared before the Emperor. Within moments, M'qua appeared on the screen. He appeared to be surprised to see the Emperor.

"M'qua, by Imperial decree, you are to abandon this foolish crusade and return to Mars immediately!" the Emperor demanded.

"Emperor, you are old and misguided. The destruction of the humans and the rebirth of Martians on Earth is the future of our people. You are too weak to see that."

"M'qua, your attempted insurrection has failed. You have no support."

"That no longer matters. When I cleanse the Earth of the human infection and it is fit for Martian habitation, your reign as emperor will be finished."

"M'qua, please, give up this fool's quest," the Crown Prince begged. "We can work this out."

"That is unlikely," M'qua said. "I am sure that the House of M'qua will shortly lose its name. To return now means emptiness and disgrace. To return with a new world for Martians, that will bring honour to the House of M'qua." And with that, the signal ended, and the screen went black.

"Where is *C'thawn's Pride* now?" asked the Emperor.

A Martian went to the wall and checked a console. "It is five thousand c'thli away, Your Imperial Majesty."

Malcolm whispered to Joan, "What is a c'thli?"

"I don't know," Joan whispered. "It's a unit of measurement, but I don't know how it translates."

"Are there any ships that can intercept it?" the Emperor asked.

"No, Your Imperial Majesty. The other large ships are patrolling near Jupiter and the Asteroid Belt. Also, they are an older design and aren't fast enough to catch the *C'thawn's Pride,* even if they were here."

"Begging you pardon, Your Imperial Majesty, I would like to catch it with my ship, the *HMS Icarus,*" Malcolm offered.

"Can it be done?" the Emperor asked.

"I do not know, your Imperial Majesty. But it is the only ship here and I would do anything to prevent the invasion of my world," Malcolm said.

"Very well. Take your ship and prevent the invasion at all costs."

"Your Imperial Majesty," C'thwan began, "Please allow me to join the God-killer in this mission. Perhaps there is still a chance to talk reason to M'qua. M'qua is my mate; I have no desire for my mate's needless death if I can get through to M'qua."

"Very well. But do not let your relationship with M'qua cloud your judgement."

"I will not, Your Imperial Majesty. I know what has to be done."

"Then I wish you well and happy hunting," the Emperor said.

"There's just one thing, Your Imperial Majesty," Malcolm began.

"Yes, what is it?"

"Where is my ship?"

CHAPTER FORTY EIGHT

After several minutes of work at the consoles, they found the Icarus in a storage area used for ship cargo. Malcolm gathered his crew and, with a small escort of the Imperial Guard, they set off for the *Icarus*.

"We must be on our guard," said C'thwan. "While we have retaken the Imperial Palace, it will take some time for that news to reach the remaining garrisons. And there's no guarantee that they will respect the Emperor's authority. We may have to fight our way to your ship."

"Understood," Malcolm said. He turned to his crew. "We may still encounter threats from the Martian military, who is unaware that the Emperor is in charge or are sympathetic to M'qua. Keep your eyes and ears open and your heads down."

They picked their way silently through the streets of the Martian city. Malcolm was on his guard. Every noise or flash of movement set his heart racing. With Malcolm in the lead, the squad soon spied the *Icarus*. Their relief at seeing their ship was short-lived as a volley of deadly rays erupted. Driven by pure instinct, Malcolm dived for cover as the rays struck the ground he had been standing on seconds before. He looked for the source of the attack and found a small contingent of soldiers firing on them from a nearby building. The squad quickly returned fire, the air rife with ozone from the powerful weapons. After a short time, Malcolm realised there was no return fire. Malcolm sent a small squad of troops to ensure that they had dispatched the guards. After ascertaining their ambushers were dead, they hustled towards the ship. With Malcolm and his squad within a hundred feet of the *Icarus*, another volley of rays rent the air, while Malcolm and his men dived for cover. As Malcolm scanned for the source of the ambush, he saw a ray vaporise O'Hallarhan's right arm as he ducked behind a building. O'Hallarhan screamed in pain before falling to the ground with a thud.

"Return fire," Malcolm ordered. He yelled to Joan and Saxon, "Cover me! I'm going to check on O'Hallarhan." They nodded and fired a prolong volley at their ambushers, who scrambled for cover. In this lull, Malcolm, crouching low, ran to O'Hallarhan. Malcolm checked for a pulse and was relieved to find it steady. Malcolm checked the wound, and the wound appeared to be cauterised already. There was no blood, but the arm itself was gone.

"What happened?" O'Hallarhan muttered.

"A Martian ray hit you. You're damned lucky they did not kill you."

"I'm not dead?"

"Not if I can help it, but you have taken a nasty shot. We're nearly back to the ship. When we get there, I'll have Doctor Boyce examine you. Until then, stay awake and be ready to move."

"Yes, sir," O'Hallarhan muttered.

Both sides exchanged a barrage of fire, filling the air with the smell of ozone and burned flesh. Malcolm watched a group of the Crown Prince's Martian guards sneak away from their position. The fire fight continued, each side locked in a stalemate until suddenly, there was no return fire. Malcolm looked up and saw the Martian guards had snuck behind the ambushers and eliminated the threat. Malcolm put his arm around O'Hallarhan and helped him walk to the ship.

As Malcolm reached the ship, a horrible thought came to him; the ship had no power. They wouldn't be able to bring the crew aboard until power was available. To do that, he would need to restart the fusion reactor and the one person who knew the procedure was slipping in and out of consciousness. When they reached the gangplank of the *Icarus,* Malcolm called his men to a halt. He turned to Saxon and said, "Charles, I need you to defend the ship in case another band of Martians tries to prevent us from leaving."

"What about you?"

"I'm going to help our Chief Engineer restart the reactor. He is the only one who knows the procedure, but I'll act as his hands. If I can keep him conscious long enough."

"Good luck, Malcolm," Saxon said.

"I'm coming with you," Joan said.

"No, I need you here where you can do the most good."

"But what if something goes wrong?" Joan asked.

"If something goes wrong, we are all dead. If you stay here, you can give us the time we need to start the ship."

"Ugh," she said. "I hate it when you're right." She leaned over and kissed Malcolm. "For luck," she said.

As Malcolm started toward the gangplank, the shooting resumed. Another group of Martians had taken positions and began firing on the ship. He looked over and saw the Crown Prince concentrating. Malcolm prayed he was calling for reinforcements and turned to walk up the gangway with O'Hallarhan, desperately trying to avoid being struck by one of the Martian rays..

With no power on the ship, Malcolm flailed around blindly as he navigated to the Engineering section by feeling only. After bumping into a myriad of walls in the long journey, Malcolm thought they had arrived in the Engine Room. He felt along the wall and found the tool storage. He flailed around until he felt the emergency electric lantern and fumbled to turn on the switch. The light from the electric lantern was barely enough for Malcolm to see.

Malcolm led O'Hallarhan into the Engine Room and sat him in a chair. O'Hallarhan had once again slipped into unconsciousness from the shock of his injury. Malcolm examined O'Hallarhan, and there was still no blood, just a mass of badly burned tissue.

Malcolm tried to remember how they started the reactor months ago. Malcolm checked the emergency batteries and was relieved that they held a full charge. Without them, there would be no way to start the process. He prayed they had enough power to start up the reactor.

He went to the primary controls. Staring at the controls, he struggled for several minutes to remember the reactor start-up process. He remembered turning on the vacuum pumps to clear the torus of any air and knew he had to start the deuterium flowing into the reactor before igniting it with the current. He knew he was missing an important step, but couldn't remember what it was.

O'Hallarhan was still unconscious. Malcolm went over and shook him and got a garbled response. Malcolm slapped O'Hallarhan in the face to bring him conscious. "Why the bloody hell did you do that?" O'Hallarhan said.

"Sorry, Commander. I need your help to start the reactor."

"I can do that," O'Hallarhan started, but trailed off when he saw his missing arm.

"Never mind that," Malcolm said. "I'll be your hands. Is the first step to turn on the vacuum pumps?"

After several seconds of no response, Malcolm asked, "Do I turn on the vacuum pumps first?"

"Yes," O'Hallarhan said with exasperation. "I nodded."

"Which I couldn't see because we have almost no light," Malcolm said. "You're going to have to acknowledge me verbally. Pretend we're communicating via radio."

"Roger."

"Except that. You don't have to end everything with 'roger'," Malcolm said. He found the switches to engage the vacuum pumps. They came to life and in a few minutes, there was a perfect vacuum in the torus.

"What's next? Do I start the deuterium flow?" Malcolm asked.

"No," O'Hallarhan yelled. Malcolm removed his hand from the deuterium flow dial. "Start the magnetic containment field."

"Damn it, the containment field. That's what I forgot," Malcolm said as he flipped several switches to engage the magnetic containment field. As he did, he heard the hum of the containment field. His relief was short-lived as he watched the battery power level drop significantly. "I hope we have enough power to ignite the deuterium," Malcolm said. "Alright's what's next?"

After waiting several seconds for a response, Malcolm looked over at O'Hallarhan, who had again passed out. Malcolm shook him again until his eyes were open. "What's next?"

"What are we doing?" O'Hallarhan asked.

"Restarting the reactor. We've purged the torus of air. The magnetic containment field is up and steady. Now what?"

"Start the deuterium flow and slowly raise it up. As you do, press the ignition button to apply the current to ignite the plasma. Keep increasing the deuterium flow until the temperature rises in the torus. Start the turbines and we should have electricity."

Malcolm took a deep breath. He turned the deuterium flow dial and, after twenty seconds, he hit the ignition button. The ignition took nearly all the battery power, the level barely registering on the meter. Malcolm held his breath as he slowly increased the deuterium flow while keeping another eye on the reactor temperature. Thirty-three long seconds later, the temperature in the reactor climbed. Malcolm hoped there was still enough power to start the turbines. Malcolm held his breath as he flipped the switch for the turbines. A few seconds later, the turbines spun up and shortly the power levels climbed to three thousand megawatts and, with that, the lights came on in the ship.

"We did it," Malcolm said as he turned to O'Hallarhan, who had fallen unconscious once again.

CHAPTER FORTY NINE

alcolm used his circlet to contact Saxon and the Crown Prince to let them know the ship now had power. He headed first to the Auxiliary Control Room and engaged the ship's shields. That would provide some protection from the Martian weapons. He then made his way to the gangplank. The fire fight had reduced to occasional shots from both sides. Malcolm yelled to the men and slowly, the crew made their way inside the *Icarus*. When he saw Doctor Boyce, he directed him to Engineering and told him to check on O'Hallarhan. Malcolm waited by the gangway door to raise the door once the last of the crew entered the ship.

The last three to enter the ship were Saxon, Joan, and the Crown Prince. Once they were safely aboard, Malcolm raised the gangplank. They hurried up the hall, with Malcolm in the lead. When they arrived at the bridge, most of the bridge crew were at their stations. Malcolm slid into the Captain's chair and said, "Mr Blackburne, prepare for liftoff." Malcolm turned to the Crown Prince. "How do we leave the cavern?"

"Straight up. If you don't mind, I will request that the roof be retracted."

"Roof?" Malcolm asked.

"Yes, our city is at the bottom of the mountain we call The God's Peak. I believe your people call it Olympus Mons after a similar mountain in your histories."

"I see," Malcolm said. "Now to deal with the ground forces. Mr Blackburne, can you lift us up ten feet and rotate the ship one hundred and eighty degrees?"

"Aye, sir. Lifting off."

Malcolm watched as the screen pivoted and the *Icarus* now faced its attackers. Malcolm called to the Engine Room. "Commander O'Hallarhan, can you generate a negative gravity beam aimed one hundred feet ahead of us?"

"Excuse me, sir. Commander O'Hallarhan isn't here; Doctor Boyce took him to Sick Bay."

"Blast, I knew that. Is that you, Lieutenant Commander Clarke?"

"Yes, sir."

"Have you used the gravity beam before?"

"Only in simulation."

"I want you to turn it so that the dial reads negative one and turn on the beam projector."

"Done," Clarke responded.

"Mr Blackburne, pivot the ship clockwise, with full thrusters."

As the ship moved, Malcolm watched as several storage containers and surprised Martians floated in the air. As Malcolm expected, it caught them off guard, the sudden change in gravity causing them to lose their weapons.

"Mr Clarke, turn off the beam projector."

"Aye, sir."

Malcolm watched as the Martians fell to the ground in a heap. "Mr Blackburne, ascend at best possible speed."

"Aye, sir."

The *Icarus* climbed, and the Martian city fell away around them. As they ascended, the light faded until it became pitch black and Malcolm no longer knew where they were going. "Mr Blackburn, are we still on course?"

"Yes, sir."

"Crown Prince, have they retracted the roof?"

"Not yet, Commodore. The dock master is self important and thinks he can play with us. I am right now promoting his assistant to Dock Master. I believe that the roof should retract momentarily."

True to his word, a few moments later, Malcolm saw a pinprick of light high above. Within a minute, the pinprick became bigger and bigger. Malcolm held his breath, hoping that the roof would open before the ship crashed against it. He released his breath only when the *Icarus* cleared the top of the mountain. The transit into sunlight was blinding at first, but when Malcolm's eyes adjusted, he looked at the surface of Mars for the very first time. The mountain below dominated the vista, extended past the edge of the viewscreen. As they ascended higher, the landscape around the mountain came into view. Vast plains of reddish orange surrounded the mountain that seemed to jut like a table above the horizon. As they continued to ascend, Malcolm saw the smooth plains of the north, a stark contrast to the rocky highlands of the south. For a moment, Malcolm enjoyed the irony that on Mars, the highlands were in the south, while in Britain, the highlands of Scotland were definitely north of the southern plains.

As the ship continued to ascend, the details of the landscape fell out of focus until all Malcolm could see was the same reddish orange colour everywhere. As the ship turned to leave the Martian atmosphere, Malcolm spotted what looked like a large rock in space.

"I see that you have seen our moon for the first time." The Crown Prince said. "In our language, we call it The Lidless Eye. My people thought that the Nameless One used the moon to watch over our world as this moon circles the world three times a day. The Silent Listener, our other moon, takes far longer to circle our planet. I believe that you humans call this moon Phobos and the other Deimos."

"Your Majesty, how do you know so much of Earth's science?" Malcolm asked.

"Unlike the Chancellor, I took the time on Earth to learn about your science, culture, and history. I find it intriguing that you name the planets and moons of the solar system after gods and goddesses that you have not worshipped for nearly fourteen hundred years. Even the name of this ship, *Icarus*, comes from Greek mythology. Why is that?"

"Your Majesty, I would love to discuss this in more detail at a later date, but the more pressing question is, how do we find M'qua? It's a long way between here and Earth, and we may never find M'qua until it's too late."

"Ah, yes, we must focus on the task at hand," the Crown Prince said. "If your mate would tune the radio to a frequency of two point five gigahertz, you will pick up the transmission of the *C'thwan's Pride*. It's used to contact the navigational beacons to ensure that the ship remains on a proper course."

"Lieutenant de St, Leger, please scan for transmissions at two point five gigahertz," Malcolm said, as he noticed the bridge crew staring at him after the Crown Prince's remark about Malcolm's mate. "Have you found anything yet?"

"Yes, Commodore," Joan said in a matter-of-fact tone. "However, I'm not sure how that helps us."

"We should be able to triangulate the location. Are you able to rotate the antenna from your console?"

"Yes, sir," Joan said.

"Excellent. Prepare to begin a three hundred sixty degree sweep and record the strength of the signal. Excuse me while I get some paper," Malcolm said. He left the bridge and grabbed a clipboard with paper and returned to his chair.

"Mr Blackburne, bring us to a full stop."

"Yes, sir." After a minute, Blackburne said, "We have stopped, sir."

"What is our current course?" Malcolm asked.

"Excuse me, Commodore, why have we stopped? Aren't we supposed to be chasing the *C'thawn's Pride?*" the Crown Prince offered.

"Yes, but if we can't find the ship, no amount of speed will matter. Space is an enormous place."

"But...," the Crown Prince began.

"Just bear with me, Your Highness. Mr Blackburne, our current course?"

"Minus eight hours, seven minutes, twenty-four seconds right ascension, sixty-eight degrees, seventeen minutes, twenty-four seconds, sir."

"Thank you, Mr Blackburne. Lieutenant de St. Leger, begin a three hundred sixty degree sweep of the antenna and call out the strength of the signal at the two point five gigahertz frequency."

As Joan read out the signals, Malcolm dutifully wrote out the values of the frequency. When he completed that, Malcolm said, "Mr Blackburne, keep on the same course, velocity at six hundred miles per hour and hold course for exactly ten minutes and then come to a full stop."

"Aye, sir."

"Excuse me, Commodore, what are you doing?" the Crown Prince asked.

"Attempting to triangulate the *C'thawn's Pride*, Your Highness. We know that in our current position, the strongest signal was at fifteen degrees. When we stop at our next location, we will again find the position of the signal and use that to pinpoint the position of the ship."

"Is your radio system based on the radio on my recovered ship?"

"Yes, Your Highness, but I don't see what that has to do with anything."

"Lieutenant, may I use your console for a moment?" the Crown Prince said.

"Of course," Joan said, leaving her seat.

The Crown Prince came over and stared for a moment at the console. "This is much harder having to read this in English." After a minute of manipulating the console, the Crown Prince announced, "I have the coordinates of the *C'thwan's Pride*. Based on their current trajectory and speed, the best intercept course would be minus seven hours, twenty-three minutes, fifteen seconds ascension, sixty-two minutes, seventeen seconds right ascension."

"How do you know that?" Malcolm asked.

"We also use our radio system for navigation. We can track a frequency, even a moving one, and calculate the best course."

"Did you know about this, Lieutenant?"

"No, sir," Joan said.

"Your Highness, please show Lieutenant de St. Leger how you did that; Lieutenant, please instruct the other radio operators on how to do that as well." After a pause, Malcolm asked, "Your Highness, why didn't you tell me this sooner?"

"I tried, but you were intent on doing it your way, and I didn't want to interfere."

Malcolm shook his head. "Next time, Your Highness, please interfere. There is much about this ship that I still need to learn. Mr Blackburne, set course to minus seven hours, twenty-three minutes, fifteen seconds ascension, sixty-two minutes, seventeen seconds right ascension, best possible speed."

CHAPTER FIFTY

With the Crown Prince's further help, they approximated the distance of M'qua's ship and estimated that at their current speed, they would catch the ship in five hours. Realising there was nothing else to do, he was eager to get out of his dress uniform, rank after the last week's captivity. Malcolm took a long shower to scrub away the smell of his captivity and changed into his duty uniform. When he returned to the bridge, he encouraged each of the bridge officers to do the same, as the bridge had become rank.

For a while, Malcolm sat in the captain's chair and watched the viewscreen for any sign of M'qua's ship. After twenty minutes of fidgeting, he gave up and returned to his office, asking to be informed if they contacted the ship.

Malcolm turned to writing a report on the events on Mars and was deep in thought when he heard a knock on the door. "Enter," he said, not looking up from his report.

Joan entered his office. "Permission to speak freely, Commodore," she said.

Malcolm looked up. "Dare I ask why?" He noticed that she, too, had showered and changed into a clean uniform. The scent of the soap and her perfume were very distracting.

"I just want to know if you have a plan to deal with M'qua?"

"Ah," he said. "Perhaps you should bring in Commander Saxon as well."

Joan left and in a minute, Saxon had joined them in Malcolm's office.

"What is it you want?" Saxon asked.

"Our lieutenant asked if I had a plan to deal with M'qua. Frankly, I'm very short on ideas. We have no armaments of any kind and although we have shielding, it's meant to protect the ship from space debris, not to deflect any kind of attack. We have no way of forcing him to stop. The only hope I have is that the Crown Prince can convince M'qua to give up this vendetta."

"And what's the likelihood of that?" Saxon offered.

"I don't know. I fear that we may have left the cage only to fly to our certain deaths."

"Isn't there anything we can do?" Joan asked.

"Not that I can think of at the moment. Do either of you have any ideas?" Malcolm looked at Joan and Saxon, and they both shook their heads.

A knock on the door interrupted the meeting. Lieutenant Blackburne poked his head in and said, "Beg pardon, sir, but we have the *C'thawn's Pride* on visual."

"Thank you, Lieutenant. We'll be out in a minute."

When the lieutenant left, Saxon rose. "I'll give you two a moment alone."

When Saxon left, Joan looked at Malcolm. "I'm scared. What if we can't stop M'qua?"

"I don't know," Malcolm said. He rose and went to Joan. He held her hands and said, "I know one thing. I love you and if this is the end, I can only say that I'm glad that you will be at my side." He gently lifted her from her chair, pulled her close and kissed her.

After a moment, she pulled away and said, "I thought you were against fraternisation?" putting on a wan smile.

"I don't think it's going to cause any breakdown in discipline," Malcolm said, laughing.

"I love you, too," Joan said. "When I thought we would spend the rest of our lives together, I didn't think it would end so quickly."

"Neither did I," Malcolm said. They held each other for another minute before Malcolm said, "We should go."

Joan nodded, and they left for the bridge.

Malcolm strode in, trying to exude an air of confidence that he didn't have. When Joan settled in her seat, Malcolm said. "Lieutenant de St. Leger, contact the *C'thawn's Pride*." She manipulated the console and nodded.

"*C'thawn's Pride,* this is Commodore Robertson. Please acknowledge."

After a moment, M'qua responded. "You are most persistent, p'tah. What do you want?"

"I am here to enforce the order of His Imperial Majesty C'thwan C'thaln. I hereby order you to surrender and return to Mars."

"Ha! Why should I listen to you?"

"There is no reason, but I have someone here who you might listen to," Malcolm said. He nodded to the Crown Prince.

"M'qua, it's C'thwan. Please abandon this fool's quest."

"C'thwan, what are you doing aboard that vessel?"

"I'm trying to prevent a war between our peoples. There is no need to continue this fool's errand."

"Fool's errand?" M'qua said. "These barbarians have taken everything from me; my father, my freedom, and now my very name. They must pay!"

"M'qua, you have lost your name through your own actions. These humans are blameless."

"No, I will have my revenge. Once I've wiped the human infestation from the Earth, Martian civilization can once again thrive. And I will no longer be in your shadow."

"You act out of petty jealousy?"

"I act for our people!" M'qua thundered.

"You do not. Your bitterness has consumed you. You are not the

M'qua that I pledged to all those years ago. I beg of you, give this up. There may yet be a way to salvage your place amongst our people!"

"No. This is my lot now, C'thawn."

Malcolm interrupted. "M'qua, you give us no choice but to force your surrender."

"How? You tiny ship is insignificant. You have no weapons. How do you intend to stop me?"

"I have my ways," Malcolm said, hoping to bluff his way out.

"I think you are lying," M'qua said. "For the love I once had for C'thawn, I will not destroy your ship, but you will no longer be a thorn in my side."

"Mr Blackburne, put all available power into our shields!" Malcolm barked.

Malcolm watched as M'qua's ship fired a ray at the *Icarus*. The ship rocked from the impact and for a moment, everything went pitch black on the bridge. When the lights returned, Malcolm felt himself float off of his chair. Grabbing hold of the chair, Malcolm punched the button to contact Engineering. "Engineering, damage report."

After a moment, Clarke answered. "Engineering here. That blast overloaded the capacitors that power the engines and gravity beam. We're dead in the water, so to speak."

"What about the reactor?" Malcolm asked.

"The reactor is holding steady. Fortunately, it and the environmental controls sustained no damage."

Malcolm watched as M'qua's ship continued on to Earth, leaving the *Icarus* adrift in space. A thought occurred to Malcolm. "Where is Commander O'Hallarhan?"

"Last I knew, he was still in Sick Bay, sir."

Malcolm pushed the button for ship-wide communication. "Commander O'Hallarhan, report to Engineering" Malcolm turned to Saxon and said, "You have the bridge, Commander."

"Where are you going?" Saxon said, as he pushed himself over to the captain's chair.

"To Engineering. I need to assess the damage firsthand."

CHAPTER FIFTY ONE

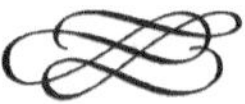

Malcolm pushed his way down the hallway of the ship. In some ways, there were advantages to not having any gravity as it made the journey to the Engine Room much quicker than walking. When he arrived in Engineering, he instantly recognised the acrid smell of burnt capacitors.

Lieutenant Commander Clarke floated towards him. "What are you doing here, sir?"

"We need to get the engines and gravity beams online as quickly as possible. We need anyone with any engineering experience here to affect repairs as quickly as possible."

"Why do you need me?" Commander O'Hallarhan said as he floated into Engineering. "In my current condition, I'm not much use to you."

"Commander O'Hallarhan, we need your knowledge. You know these systems better than anyone. You are going to supervise the repair effort. Let's start with an assessment of the system."

Together, Malcolm and O'Hallarhan floated to the capacitor stack. "I think we might be better off replacing all the capacitors, unless you want to test which ones didn't suffer any damage," O'Hallarhan said.

"No, we'll put the questionable ones in a pile so we can test them later. Right now, we need to get the systems restored as quickly as possible," Malcolm said. "I'll help Lieutenant Commander Clarke and the rest of the Engineering crew with the capacitor stack; why don't you assess any damage to the other systems?"

Malcolm and crew got to work immediately on the capacitor stack. The first order of business was to shut off power to the stack. They set up a relay. Two people worked on removing and installing the capacitors, while others retrieved and stored parts and tools. Using the lack of gravity to their advantage, Malcolm and one of the Engineering technicians started at the top. They soon settled into a rhythm: discharge the capacitor, remove the capacitor and replace it with a new capacitor.

After five minutes, O'Hallarhan said, "Commodore, the rest of the systems appear to have little to no damage. It looks like when the shields overloaded, the power came back through the capacitor stack. When the capacitors failed, the power had nowhere else to go."

"Thank heavens for small favours," Malcolm said. He was fortunate that he didn't seem to experience the vertigo that crippled him in his weightless training, perhaps because he knew which way was up and had something concrete on which to concentrate.

It took nearly an hour, but they completely refitted the capacitor stack. Malcolm held his breath as O'Hallarhan applied power to the stack, praying he didn't hear any telltale pops or smell of burnt capacitors.

"The system is stable," O'Hallarhan said.

"Can you give us gravity?" Malcolm asked.

"Yes. Turning on gravity now," O'Hallarhan said. Malcolm, who had been hovering a few feet from the floor, landed with a thud. "Next time, give us a bit of warning, Commander," Malcolm said as he lifted himself off the floor.

"Sorry, Commodore," O'Hallarhan said.

Malcolm made his way to the communication link to the Bridge. "Bridge. This is the Commodore. You should have engines. Make best speed for the *C'thawn's Pride*."

"Commodore, the engines show they are active, but we still aren't moving," Lieutenant Blackburne said.

Malcolm looked to O'Hallarhan. "Well?"

"I don't understand," O'Hallarhan said. "The capacitors are generating the electrogravitational energy." He pulled up a diagram of the engine systems. "We have power flowing all the way to..." O'Hallarhan stopped. "Damn and blast! The attack must have damaged the gravitational emitter. That makes sense. It probably took the brunt of the energy from the attack. It must have either burnt out or been outright destroyed from the attack."

"M'qua knew exactly where to hit us. What are our options?"

"Someone needs to go outside of the ship and replace the emitter. I would volunteer, but it is a job that requires two hands." O'Hallarhan looked at the empty sleeve of his uniform.

"Bridge. Commander Saxon, is there anyone with an engineering background who is qualified in your estimation to go outside of the ship and make repairs?"

"Commander O'Hallarhan scored high on his weightlessness test."

"Yes, unfortunately, his participation is out of the question. Anyone else?"

"I'm afraid not. Most of the Engineering team did poorly on this test."

Malcolm turned off the communication link. "How difficult is the repair?"

"It should be straightforward. We made anything on the outside of the ship easily replaceable. Pull out some pins, remove the module, and replace the pins," O'Hallarhan said.

Malcolm thought for a moment before opening the line to the bridge. "Alright. Commander Saxon, I'm going to need you to suit up and affect repairs on the gravitational emitter."

"Commodore, I know nothing about repairing the ship. I'm the last person you want around machinery." Saxon protested.

"Ordinarily, I'd agree, but Commander O'Hallarhan thinks it should be simple to replace the emitter."

"If you say so," Saxon said.

"I do. I'll meet you at the airlock. Commodore, out." He turned to O'Hallarhan. "Where's the spare gravity beam emitter?"

"Storage area H-9, third shelf down to the right."

"Excellent. Commander, keep on the line. We may need your help."

"Yes, sir," O'Hallarhan said.

Malcolm went to the storage area, found the emitter exactly where O'Hallarhan said, and raced toward the airlock. When he got there, Saxon already had his suit on and was doing a seal test to make sure there were no leaks. He gave Malcolm a thumbs up, took the emitter, and walked into the airlock, sealing the door behind him. He plugged his oxygen line, the tether line, and the cable that supplied electricity and communication to his suit into the wall and once he ascertained everything was connected correctly, he gave Malcolm a thumbs up.

Malcolm went to the control panel near the airlock. He engaged the vacuum pumps to remove the air from the room so that there was no gas to push Saxon into space when the door opened. When the vacuum gauge read zero, Malcolm opened a communication line to Saxon. "Are you ready?"

"Ready as I'll ever be," Saxon said.

"Alright. You need to go to the front of the ship. You should see the emitter in an alcove. There will be two pins on either side. Remove the pins, remove the broken emitter, replace the emitter, and secure with the two pins."

"That's sounds easy," Saxon said drolly. "And do this while completely weightless. Nothing to it."

"Be careful, Charles. We're counting on you to get us moving."

"Oh, so no pressure either."

"Good luck, Charles."

"Thank you, Malcolm." Malcolm heard Saxon take a deep breath. "Open the exterior door."

Malcolm opened the exterior door, and Saxon pushed himself out of the airlock. He soon bobbed out of view. After a minute, Saxon broke the silence. "Malcolm, I think this repair might be a little above my paygrade."

"Why? What is it?"

"I can see where the emitter used to be, but there's nothing there. No pins and nothing to pin it to."

"Understood. You may as well come back inside."

Saxon returned to the airlock, and once Malcolm restored the atmosphere, the door to the airlock opened. "Malcolm, it's a bloody mess out there. I can see where the emitter might have been, but it's broken off and there are wires dangling."

"Bloody hell," Malcolm said. He flipped the communication link back to the Engine Room. "Commander O'Hallarhan, report to the airlock." Within minutes, O'Hallarhan reached the airlock. "What is it, Commodore?"

"The damage was worse than expected. The arm to the emitter is gone. We can't attach the emitter to anything. And to top it off, the wires are just dangling so there are no plugs to fit the module."

"That is a problem," O'Hallarhan said. "We don't have another arm."

"What can we do?" Malcolm said.

"Let me think," O'Hallarhan said. After a few moments of thought, he said, "We have a few small beams in stock. If we could attach that to the ship, wire the emitter directly to the wires, and attach the emitter to the arm, it might just work."

"How are we going to attach it?" Saxon asked.

Malcolm and O'Hallarhan said in unison, "With the ultrasonic welder."

"That's good to know, but I can't weld anything."

"Neither can I," O'Hallarhan said. O'Hallarhan and Saxon looked at Malcolm.

"Bloody hell!" Malcolm exclaimed.

CHAPTER FIFTY TWO

Malcolm suited up as O'Hallarhan had the supplies brought to the airlock. The power going to Malcolm's suit would feed the ultrasonic welder, and Saxon tied the welder to Malcolm's arm so that even if he let go, it would be easy to grasp. Saxon taped wire cutters to the arm of Malcolm's suit, along with a roll of gaffer tape. The replacement arm was the biggest logistical issue. To keep the beam from drifting off, they attached another tether line to the beam.

Before Malcolm put on his helmet, he heard Joan screaming, "What the bloody hell do you think you're doing?"

"Lieutenant, that's not the way to speak to your commanding officer," he said wearily.

"What the bloody hell do you think you're doing, *sir?*" she spat.

"Trying to get this ship under motion, *Lieutenant*. Why aren't you at your post?"

"I'm trying to prevent you from killing yourself!"

"Lieutenant, listen. There is no other choice. If we are ever going to catch up with M'qua, we need engines. For the engines to work, we need a gravitational emitter, which we currently do not have. Someone with engineering experience needs to weld that beam to the ship, wire this emitter to the ship, and secure the emitter to the beam. There are very few people here qualified to do it. Commander O'Hallarhan's injury rules him out. If it isn't him, who else would be qualified to do this? If you can name a replacement, be my guest, as I have no great desire to do this either."

Joan was silent.

"Well, any other names?"

"You know there isn't," she whispered. "But you nearly died when you tried this in training."

"Then I'll have to do a lot better this time, won't I?" Malcolm said. He put his gloved hand under her chin. "You and I know there isn't another alternative. I can do this. Have a little faith in me."

"I do, Malcolm," she whispered. "But if you get yourself killed out there, I'll never forgive you!"

"Duly noted. When I return, we'll have a discussion about how you knew the results of my training," Malcolm said. He squeezed her hand and stepped away to put on his helmet. Once he knew his helmet had a good seal, he checked his inventory; welder, gaffer tape, wire cutters. Everything was in place.

He walked into the airlock and hooked his oxygen line, tether, and power line into the ship and gave the thumbs up to start the vacuum pumps. After a few long minutes, Saxon's voice came into Malcolm's helmet. "Are you ready, Malcolm?"

"No," he said. "But if we're waiting for that to happen, we could be here a long time. Just open the bloody door."

"Aye, aye, sir," Saxon said. "And good luck, Malcolm."

The door opened, and Malcolm stared out into the inky blackness of space. He bent to pick up the replacement arm and found it was too heavy to pick up; it had taken two very sturdy men to bring it into the airlock. "Commander Saxon, could you have Commander O'Hallarhan turn off the gravity in the airlock? I can't budge the replacement arm."

After a couple of minutes, Malcolm noticed the beam float off the floor. Malcolm was thankful that the magnetic boots he wore were strong enough to hold him to the floor and prevent him from floating out until he was ready. Malcolm grabbed the beam and directed it out the door.

Once he was completely outside of the ship, he pivoted to face the ship. That helped him keep his orientation while also keeping the vertigo at bay. He pulled his way along the ship's hull until he found the alcove that had once contained the gravitational emitter. Saxon was correct in his assessment; it was a mess. All that remained of the arm of the emitter was a large spearlike projectile, about seven inches long. The cables that fed that emitter were dangling loosely.

"Robertson to the *Icarus*. Before I play with these wires, can someone kill the power?"

"Acknowledged," Saxon said. "Emitter power shut down."

"Thank you," Malcolm said.

He pulled his way over to get a better look. He was following the wiring when he felt a sharp pain in his leg. Looking down, he saw he had floated into the sharp, pointed end of the arm and punctured his suit and his leg.

"Bloody hell," Malcolm said.

"What is it?" Saxon said.

"Nothing," Malcolm lied. "Just bumped against the ship."

"Be careful. You don't want to rupture your suit."

"I will…. be careful, that is."

Malcolm looked down. It didn't appear that the point had punctured his leg too badly and the tear in his suit was only about three inches long. Three inches too much.

"Malcolm, what's happening? Your oxygen pressure is falling."

"Probably a kink in the line. I'll take care of it," Malcolm lied. As he scrambled to figure out what to do, he saw the gaffer's tape. He pulled it from his suit, cut off a length with the wire cutters and as he moved himself off of the arm, he place the tape over the rip. He put several more pieces over the area. "How's that?" he asked.

"Better, but your oxygen pressure is lower than I'd like to see it."

"Acknowledged. I'm going to start the repairs."

Malcolm manoeuvred the replacement beam into place. Although he wasn't particularly happy with where he could attach the beam, he welded the arm in place.

"Alright, the arm is in place. I'm going to wire the emitter."

Malcolm noticed it was getting harder to catch his breath. At first he thought he was having another attack, but realised that it was from a lack of oxygen. He tried to slow his breathing and felt better.

He pulled the wire up and stripped down three inches on each wire. He twisted the wires on the emitter and wrapped them up in gaffer's tape. It was not pretty and wasn't very sturdy, but Malcolm prayed it would hold up.

"Malcolm, your oxygen level is getting dangerously low. You should abort and return to the ship," Saxon said.

"No. I'm almost done. Just have to secure the emitter."

He realised it was getting harder to pay attention. *Damn*, he thought. *I have to hurry.* He tried to put the emitter on the end of the arm and it slipped away, floating up. He caught it and placed it back on to the arm. As his vision darkened, he turned on the ultrasonic welder and completed the two welds.

"Ship, this is Robertson. I've completed the repair, but need help. Losing consciousness," he said before everything went black.

CHAPTER FIFTY THREE

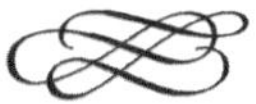

Malcolm woke to a bright light shining in his eyes. "Get that bloody light away from me," he said, swatting at the light.

He looked around and realised that he was lying on the floor of the airlock. Malcolm looked up and found Doctor Boyce examining him. When he noticed an oxygen mask over his face, he tried to take it off. The doctor stopped him and said, "No, Commodore. Keep it on. You passed out from lack of oxygen. You need to keep it on until I say otherwise."

Malcolm reluctantly nodded. He looked up and saw Saxon standing over him. "What happened?" Malcolm asked.

"You ripped your spacesuit and were too pigheaded to come back into the ship," Saxon said. "Then you pushed yourself until you had no oxygen and we had to reel you in like a fish. You nearly died."

"Oh," Malcolm said. "Bloody hell, where's Joan?"

"Once we got you inside and we knew you were alive, I ordered her back to her post. She nearly threatened to hit me, but I reminded her that if she was in the brig, there would be no way she could reckon with you."

"Thanks. I think," Malcolm said. "Did the repair work?"

"Yes, Commander O'Hallarhan said that we have engine power. I've taken the liberty of continuing on our last known course at the best possible speed."

Turning to the doctor, Malcolm asked, "Am I alright?"

"I believe so, Commodore. Try to take it easy for the rest of the day."

Not bloody likely, Malcolm thought. He nodded to Doctor Boyce. "I'll do my best." Saxon gave Malcolm a hand and pulled him up. As Malcolm removed his space suit and the doctor dressed the wound on his leg, an idea of how to stop M'Qua began to formulate. When Malcolm and Saxon returned to the bridge, Malcolm convened a meeting of the bridge crew, Engineering, and the Crown Prince.

"I know how we can stop M'qua. But the plan relies on us getting close to the ship without detection. Any ideas?"

"If we can get there quick enough, we might use the Moon to hide," Saxon offered.

"Excellent. Mr O'Hallarhan, give us all the speed you can coax out of the engines. We need to get to the Moon before M'qua. Mr Blackburne, see if you can work any magic with our course. Find the quickest course that can get us to the Moon undetected."

"I can assist with that," the Crown Prince said. "Astronavigation was the one thing I was good at aboard the ship."

"Lieutenant de St. Leger, do you think you can track the location of M'qua's ship?"

"Yes, I think I can."

"Excellent. You will need to work closely with Mr Blackburn and the Crown Prince to find a course that will get us to the Moon ahead of M'qua without giving us away." Malcolm stopped. "If we're monitoring M'qua's location, what stops M'qua from monitoring ours?"

"Nothing... except pride," the Crown Prince said. "M'qua's one fault is arrogance. M'qua thinks he left us adrift and has no reason to think otherwise. M'qua would consider it inconceivable that humans could fix the ship and resume the chase."

"Would it be possible to send a message to Earth without alerting M'qua?" Malcolm asked.

"That would reveal our presence," the Crown Prince said.

"What if we sent it on a lower frequency, say, something in the kilohertz range?" Malcolm asked.

"That might work," the Crown Prince said. "Our communication systems don't deal with such low frequencies, and I doubt M'qua would think to look for anything in such a low range."

"Excellent!" Malcolm said. "Mr O'Hallarhan, can we build a spark gap transmitter and hook it up to our antenna?"

"I think it might be possible," O'Hallarhan said.

"Lieutenant de St. Leger, how is your Morse code?"

"Adequate for sending a message. I'm not sure how fast I can translate it back, though."

"That's all I needed to hear," Malcolm said. "I don't want a response; I just want to let Earth know what is coming, in case we can't stop M'qua."

"And speaking of stopping M'qua, are you going to tell us what your plan is to stop M'qua?" Saxon asked.

Malcolm laid out his thoughts. He turned to O'Hallarhan. "Do you think it will work?"

"I think there's a good chance it might work, but it is dangerous," O'Hallarhan responded.

"I will entertain any other ideas on how we stop his ship. Any ideas?" Malcolm waited, and the room was silent. "Alright, we have our plan. Let's execute it!"

Even running the engines as hard as they dared, it was still going to take nearly eighteen days to get to Earth. O'Hallarhan designed a rudimentary spark gap transmitter and, with the aid of the rest of the Engineering crew, they built it and patched it into the existing radio system. Once they installed the transmitter, Malcolm ordered Joan and the communication officers to send the following message via Morse code once an hour for six hours: *Hostile Martian ship approaching Earth. Icarus moving to intercept. If not successful, prepare for invasion. Send no response.* Malcolm crossed his fingers that the Service would receive the message and that M'qua had not detected it.

They used the remaining time to shore up the meager defences of the ship. O'Hallarhan designed and the Engineering crew installed a failsafe system to prevent the capacitor bank from overloading if M'qua targeted their gravitational emitter again. O'Hallarhan and the rest of the Engineering crew sorted through the capacitors that survived their recent clash with the *C'thwan's Pride,* and were relieved that they could still use thirty percent of them as spare parts.

Joan spent nearly all her time at her station, working with Navigation and the Crown Prince to track the *C'thwan's Pride,* keep their distance, and somehow make it to the moon before them. As they continued, they observed that the Martian ship was not travelling to Earth at its top speed while the *Icarus* was gaining on the Martian ship. This allowed the *Icarus* to chart a course well away from the Martian ship but still reach the Moon before M'qua.

The *Icarus* reached the Moon a day ahead of the *C'thwan's Pride* expected arrival and settled in to an orbit, keeping the Moon between the *Icarus* and the Martian ship. Malcolm alternated between feeling like he needed to be on the Bridge and then realising there was nothing to do there and felt the need to go back to his office. There, he couldn't concentrate because he felt like he should be on the Bridge. After his fourth trip back to his office in just under two hours, Malcolm heard a knock on his door. "Enter," he said.

Saxon entered and closed the door behind him. "Commodore, permission to speak freely?"

"Permission granted," Malcolm said.

"Malcolm, you've got to settle down. Your constant back and forth between the Bridge and your office is making the Bridge crew nervous."

"They should be nervous," Malcolm said. "We're going up against a massive ship with only a half-baked idea of how to stop it. And knowing if we're not successful, everyone on Earth will die."

"I know that and you know that, but the crew needs to know that you're confident. They know how dangerous this will be, but they need to feel your confidence that you can lead them out of this."

"What if I can't?"

"Malcolm, your greatest skill is coming up with crazy ideas that save the day. While the scale is much larger, this does not differ from when we faced down four German zeppelins intent on capturing the *Daedalus*."

"But," Malcolm began.

"But, nothing, Malcolm. This is no different. We know the odds of success are low, but everyone understands what's at stake. They are putting their trust in you to lead them through this. You've done it before and you'll do it this time. If you project confidence in the crew and the mission, I promise the crew will reflect that confidence back to you."

"Thank you, Charles. I guess I'm the one who needs the encouraging speech this time. Since you have all the sage wisdom, what should I do? Go back to the Bridge or stay here?"

"I suggest you tour the ship and make sure that everything is in place for tomorrow."

"That's an excellent idea. When did you get so wise, Charles?"

"I've always been this wise; you just haven't noticed it," Saxon said with a smile.

Malcolm took Saxon's advice and toured the ship, stopping to talk to the men. Saxon was right; when he projected an air of confidence to the crew, their confidence in him helped restore his own confidence. When he reached Engineering, he found O'Hallarhan was not there. O'Hallarhan had excused himself, as his wound was bothering him and had returned to his quarters.

Malcolm went to O'Hallarhan's quarters, knocked, and entered. O'Hallarhan was lying on his bed, staring at the ceiling. When he looked up and saw Malcolm, he jumped to his feet. "What can I do for you, sir?"

"Why aren't you in the Engine Room?"

"My arm… I mean, my wound was bothering me."

"So I understand. Tell me, Commander, is that really all of it?"

O'Hallarhan didn't answer. Malcolm said, "Peter, you can talk freely. This is completely off the record."

O'Hallarhan wouldn't meet Malcolm's gaze. "I wasn't lying; my wound is bothering me. I feel useless when I'm there because I can't do anything. I can't do any job that requires two functioning arms. And I know when this mission is over, so is my career."

"I wouldn't be so sure about that, Commander. It may not be the same, but I'm sure that we can find a place for you in the Service."

"How can I serve with just one arm?" O'Hallarhan demanded.

"You can build a mechanical arm. I don't know if you remember the pilot of the *RAS Uhuru*_who ferried you to and from the base? Lieutenant Commander Colfax Mingo? He has a mechanical leg and is now an officer in the Royal Naval Auxiliary."

"Really? How is that possible?"

"Frankly, I don't know. But sometimes needs outweigh regulations. The Admiralty always finds an exception when it suits their purpose."

"Do you think there's still a place for me, Commodore?"

"Absolutely. For one, you have designed this ship that we currently using to circle the Moon. When we return from this mission, there will be an enormous demand for your skills, as I would wager that the Service will want more spaceships."

"Will I ever get to serve aboard a ship again?" O'Hallarhan asked. "I always thought I'd despise it, but I have to admit, I enjoy it."

"I honestly don't know, Peter. But if you want to serve aboard ship as opposed to being stuck at a desk, I will do whatever I can to make that happen."

"Thank you, sir."

"Now, speaking of serving, I would feel much more at ease if my best engineer was supervising the Engine Room when we face the Martian's tomorrow."

"Yes, sir," O'Hallarhan said, rising off his bed. "My wound is feeling much better. I'm sure I can complete my shift."

"Very good, Commander," Malcolm said.

As Malcolm returned to his office, he was heartened by O'Hallarhan's change of attitude. Although he was surprised that O'Hallarhan wanted to continue serving on a ship, he felt like he might have got through to the young engineer. Once he arrived at his office, he completed his day as he normally would, filling out reports. Even in space, paperwork was eternal. He worked into the evening, barely noticing when a midshipman brought his meal to him.

A knock on his door was a welcome reprieve from the drudgery of paperwork. "Enter," he said.

Joan entered and gave a quick salute. "Sorry to bother you, Commodore. I wondered if you could have dinner with me tonight as I just got off shift." She looked at the plate containing a half eaten sardine sandwich. "Oh, I see you've already eaten, never mind. It was a silly idea," she said as she turned to go.

"Wait, Lieutenant. I wouldn't call this," Malcolm said, holding up the sandwich, "a proper dinner. I would be happy to eat dinner with you. Shall I have someone bring something here where we can eat together privately?"

"Aren't you afraid of 'fraternising' with one of the crew?" she said.

"Tonight, no. We may not survive tomorrow. And if that's the case, who's going to even know or punish us?"

"True," she said. "But what if we survive? There might be hell to pay for you."

"True, but like I said when this crazy adventure started, the Service already kicked me out once. What's one more time?"

Joan laughed. She moved to Malcolm. "Perhaps we should skip dinner and move straight to dessert."

"What dessert did you have in mind?" Malcolm said, standing to draw her into his embrace.

"I think you know," she said before she pulled him in for a kiss.

CHAPTER FIFTY FOUR

 $\mathcal{M}$ alcolm was up early the next morning and slipped out of bed without waking Joan. He showered, dressed, and went to the mess, bringing back two large mugs of tea. As he sat on the edge of the bed watching Joan sleep, he felt like he could have stayed there for hours, but he knew they both had places to be.

"Hey, sleepyhead," he said, gently prodding her. "Time to get up. I brought you tea." He handed her a mug.

Joan sat up and sipped the tea. "I could get used to this, being served tea in bed."

"I wouldn't count on that happening again soon," Malcolm said.

"A girl can dream, can't she?"

Malcolm sighed. "I wish I could stay here with you."

"I know," she said, before taking another sip of tea. "When this is all over, we can get married and then you'll probably be sick of spending time with me."

"Never," Malcolm said. He reached over and gave her a gentle kiss. "However, I need to get going. Use my shower, and I'll see you soon." Before he said anything else, Malcolm left his quarters and strode to the Bridge where he relieved the overnight watch.

"How long until the *C'thawn's Pride* reaches us?"

"Given their current course and speed, we estimate about three more hours. Based on their current approach, we should remain hidden while they pass the Moon."

Now it was just a matter of waiting. Malcolm tried not to fidget and drum his fingers, but the anticipation was getting on his nerves. Joan joined the rest of the bridge crew at the shift change. The bridge was quiet, everyone focusing on their job.

After two hours, Joan said, "Commodore, the *C'thawn's Pride* is approaching the Moon. They should be near our position in approximately twenty minutes."

"Thank you, Lieutenant. Would you be so kind as to escort the Crown Prince to the Bridge?"

"Yes, sir," Joan said. In minutes, she returned with the Martian Crown Prince.

"Thank you, Your Highness. I wanted you here to see if we can try to talk M'qua out of this one last time," Malcolm said.

"I appreciate your attempts to make this end peacefully, but I fear we will not dissuade M'qua," the Crown Prince said.

"Even so, it is worth the effort," Malcolm said.

"Agreed."

Fifteen minutes later, Joan said, "Commodore, the *C'thawn's Pride* is approaching the moon."

"Thank you, Lieutenant," Malcolm said. He flicked the switch on his chair to address the entire crew. "Crew of the *Icarus*, may I have your attention, please? The Martian ship *C'thwan's Pride* is approaching our position. You know that the last time we tangled with it, we came out worse for wear. This time, let's give them a taste of their own medicine. All hands, battle stations."

Malcolm changed the channel. "Engineering, are we ready?"

"Aye, sir," said O'Hallarhan's voice. "All systems are running at peak efficiency."

"Very good, Commander," Malcolm said.

"Lieutenant de St. Leger, open a channel to the Martian ship,"

Malcolm said. Joan worked at the console and nodded when she made the connection. "*C'thwan's Pride*, this is the *HMS Icarus*. We demand that you stand down and surrender unconditionally."

There was silence for several seconds before M'qua responded. "What? I left you adrift in space! How can you be here?"

"Apparently, we humans are more resourceful than you think."

"What makes you think I'll surrender to you? You have no weaponry, and you are no match for my ship. I can blow you into space dust with little effort."

"You can try, M'qua... or what should I call you now? I seem to remember that you've lost your name. Perhaps I'll call you Nobody."

"You insignificant gnat. I will destroy you and every human for your insolence."

"Even the Crown Prince?" Malcolm asked.

"M'qua, please abandon this fool's quest. It will only end in tragedy," the Crown Prince said.

"The tragedy is that you have defiled our people by associating with these apes. I do our empire a service by wiping you out so you do not infect our people with your attitude," M'qua said.

Malcolm stopped the communication. "Where are they? How long until they reach our position?"

"Approximately three minutes, sir," Joan said.

Malcolm nodded and Joan reestablished the connection. "How disrespectful to one's sovereign and one's mate! I guess I would expect that from a nobody like you! I rescued you from the bottom of a lake, returned you to your home, and in return, you are going to destroy me and my planet. You really are not just a nobody, but a truly terrible being!"

"Stop calling me Nobody! I am M'qua Cth'rn, the next Emperor of Mars!"

"No, you are Nobody. You gave up any right to be called anything else when you started this fool's errand. The only question is how many Martians must die for your cowardly act of revenge?" Malcolm mouthed to Joan, "How much longer?" After a moment, she mouthed, "One minute."

Malcolm took out his pocket watch. "Speechless, Nobody? So what's it going to be? Are you going to surrender or force me to play rough?"

"I'll never surrender to the likes of you, ape. However, I will ensure that your death will be long and drawn out."

Malcolm looked down; thirty more seconds. He killed the connection. "Mr Blackburne, turn twenty-three degrees to starboard."

"Aye, sir."

"Engineering, is our surprise ready?"

"Aye, sir," O'Hallarhan said.

"Fire on my mark," Malcolm said. "In three, two, one, fire!"

The gravity beam, set at the highest setting available, fired to a point some distance from the *Icarus* just as the *C'thawn's Pride* arrived. There was a brief explosion of light before the tear in the fabric of space opened.

"Engine room, full reverse," Malcolm said. The ship's backwards moment tugged harder on the point in space and the tear got larger, pulling the *C'thawn's Pride* towards it.

"*C'thwan's Pride*, we can end this now. Surrender your ship and no more damage will be done. Refuse and the tear will crush you into nothingness."

"Commodore," Blackburne interrupted. "We're being pulled into the tear ourselves."

"Can you manoeuvre so that we can keep the Martian ship between us and the tear? That should buy us some time."

"I'll do my best, sir," Blackburne said.

"Well, Nobody? What do you say?" Malcolm asked M'Qua.

"What have you done, ape?"

"Oh nothing, really. Just opened up a tear in the fabric of space."

"Do you know what consequences that will have?"

"Yes. The gravity from the tear will crush you and your ship into a single point in space, which I would imagine would put a damper on your efforts to invade Earth."

"Stop this madness! You will kill us all!"

"That's rather the idea," Malcolm said. "I don't intend to give you the opportunity to destroy my race. If I have to die to make sure that doesn't happen, so be it."

"You are a madman!"

"Takes one to know one," Malcolm said. He cut communications to the Martian ship. "I need status reports. How long can we keep this up?"

"This is Engineering. Power systems are fine. We have limited engine output as we continue to power the gravity beam."

"Understood," Malcolm said. "Environmental Controls?"

"We're feeling the stress on the hull," Saxon said. "Systems are nominal, but I estimate we have about a minute before things get critical."

"Understood. Mr Blackburne, what is our position?"

"I've got the Martian ship between us and the tear, but if we don't end the tear soon, it will drag us in."

"Understood." Malcolm watched as the front of the *C'thawn's Pride* approached the tear. The invisible hand of gravity crumpled sections of the ship like so much aluminum foil.

"*C'thawn's Pride*, this is your last chance. Surrender now and we can end this destruction. Surely you realise the gravity of your situation." The bridge crew groaned at Malcolm's unintentional pun.

"Earth ship, this is C'lteh Lgnu. We accept your terms. We surrender."

"What happened to M'qua?"

"M'qua has been relieved of command."

Malcolm cut off the communication and turned to the Crown Prince. "Do you know this C'lteh Lgnu?"

"C'lteh is an honourable officer. We can trust him."

Malcolm nodded and resumed communication with the Martian ship. "I accept your surrender. Stand by. On my signal, make full speed ahead, bearing sixty degree starboard."

"Fly towards it? Do you mean to kill us?"

"Trust me, this is the only way to repair the tear,"

"C'lteh, this is C'thawn," the Crown Prince interrupted. "Follow the Commodore's instructions and we will save you."

"Very well," C'lteh said. After a moment, "We have the course plotted."

"Engineering, cut the power to the beam," Malcolm said.

"Done, sir," O'Hallarhan said.

"Mr Blackburne, lay in a course, sixty degrees to port."

"Aye, sir."

"Mr O'Hallarhan, when we execute our course, set the gravity beam to its highest negative setting and fire at the tear."

"Ready, sir."

"*C'thawn's Pride*, on my mark, both our ships will execute our courses at full speed. Understood?"

"Yes, Earthling."

"Execute, now!" Malcolm said. He watched as the *Icarus* swung to the left of the Martian ship and near the left side of the tear as the *C'thawn's Pride* limped to the right side. As the two ships neared the tear, it fell in on itself until there was a quick explosion of light.

"Hull pressure has fallen significantly," Saxon said. "I think we did it."

"*C'thawn's Pride*, requesting a status report," Malcolm said.

"We sustained heavy damage, but we are safe. Thank you, Earthling."

"You are welcome. Please set a course to return to Mars under our escort. But be aware, there will be no funny business from you or I will repeat what I just did and I won't bother to save you the next time."

"There will be no funny business, as you say, Earthling. Permission to return to Mars?"

"Permission granted. Let us know if you require additional help."

"Thank you, Earthling. We can manage."

"The name is Malcolm. Commodore Malcolm Robertson."

"Thank you, Malcolm Commodore Malcolm Robertson," C'lteh said.

"No, it's… nevermind, you're welcome." Malcolm said. "Mr Blackburne, follow at a reasonable distance."

A cheer went up from the Bridge crew as the Martian ship turned away from the Moon and turned back towards Mars.

CHAPTER FIFTY FIVE

Twenty-three days later, the *Icarus* returned to Mars, this time as honoured guests. With the help of the Crown Prince, the *Icarus* followed the *C'thawn's Pride* back down into Olympus Mons and landed in the Martian capitol. This time, Martian soldiers surrounded the Martian ship and marched its crew away. When Malcolm and his crew disembarked, the Imperial Guard met them and led them, not as prisoners, but as heroes, to the Imperial Palace.

As they marched through the Martian city, they noticed Martians lining the streets. As Malcolm and his crew passed, they waved their face tentacles enthusiastically. Malcolm returned the gesture by waving his hand in return. Although their transit was silent, Malcolm could feel the excitement amongst the Martians as if it were a concrete thing.

They eventually reached the Imperial Throne Room and began the long walk to the Emperor's Throne. As they approached, Malcolm noticed M'qua and a handful of others, manacled and under the watchful eye of the Imperial Guard.

Malcolm and his crew took their places at the foot of the dais. Malcolm bowed to the Martian Emperor, and the crew followed suit.

"Welcome back to Mars, Commodore Robertson," the Emperor said. "This time I am honoured to greet you as heroes. You and your crew have done a great service to the Empire."

"Thank you, Your Imperial Majesty," Malcolm said. "I hope that our two races can find common ground and peace."

"That is my hope as well," the Emperor said. "By my authority as Emperor of Mars, I name Commodore Malcolm Robertson Mars Friend and Hero of the First Order. Commodore Robertson, step forward."

Malcolm, surprised, moved to the dais. The Emperor stepped down and pinned a medal made of the same silvery metal that adorned the Imperial Palace on Malcolm's uniform. In the centre was a gem that was a perfect replica of the Martian planet.

"Your Imperial Majesty, I am truly humbled by this honour, but this would not be possible without my crew."

"Duly noted. From this day forward, your crew are likewise Mars Friends." There was a pause before the Emperor continued. "And now we deal with the most unpleasant task." The Emperor turned to address M'qua and the other captives. "As previously decreed, you are henceforth Nameless. Your Houses have no place in our society and neither do you."

"I will die before I let you take my name from me," M'qua said. M'qua grabbed a weapon from the guard, but before he could do anything, he was enveloped in a beam and disintegrated. Malcolm followed the beam back to the Crown Prince. The rest of the prisoners provided no resistance as the Imperial Guard took them away.

After a few days of rest, the crew of the *Icarus* prepared for the trip home. An honour guard, led by the Crown Prince, escorted them back to their ship. When they arrived, the crew boarded their ship and made preparations for launch while Malcolm stayed back to talk with the Crown Prince.

"Thank you, Commodore, for all you have done for me and my people. If not for you, I would not be having this conversation with you."

"It was my honour, Your Highness. May I offer my condolences on the death of your mate? It must have been a horrible choice to make."

"Thank you. It was for the best. M'qua died before losing everything. I underestimated M'qua's anger and missed the signs. I am relieved that M'qua is at peace now and can cause no more damage." The Crown Prince paused for a moment, as if in thought. "I should let you go, Commodore. I imagine you are eager to get back to Earth."

"Yes, very much so, Your Highness."

"Thank you again for everything you have done. You are now a hero of two worlds, Commodore. I hope our paths cross again someday."

"You're welcome, Your Highness. I, too, hope that we meet again."

Malcolm bowed and walked up the gangway. He turned to take one last look at the Martian city before heading to the bridge.

The flight back to Earth was uneventful and monotonous, save for a service to honour the Royal marines and ten members of the crew that were vaporised by the Martians. The crew laid Union Jacks on the floor of the airlock, representing each of the crew members lost during their mission. The crew stood at attention outside the airlock. On Malcolm's command, the exterior door to the airlock opened, and the flags were sucked out into the vacuum of space; the first burial in space. Malcolm spent much of the trip writing the letters of condolence to the families of the fallen crew.

As they neared Earth, Malcolm returned to the Bridge to watch their approach. It was mesmerising, watching the tiny dot gradually grow to take the whole viewscreen. As they began their descent, Malcolm could see the outline of Britain and he felt relief.

The ship descended through the atmosphere and approached the island of Boreray. Malcolm thought he'd had never been so grateful to see that place as he was right now. With a deft hand, Blackburne guided the ship down and into the sea cave, coming to a stop in the landing area they had left so many weeks before.

As the crew disembarked, an honour guard and brass band were waiting for them. Three men strode forward to welcome back the crew of the *Icarus;* First Sea Lord Prince Louis of Battenberg, Admiral

Beatty, and Mycroft Holmes. When Malcolm reached the men, he pulled up and threw his smartest salute. "Permission to disembark?"

"Permission granted," the First Sea Lord said, returning the salute. He extended a hand to Malcolm. "Congratulations, Commodore. First rate work," he said as he shook Malcolm's hand.

"Thank you, Your Serene Highness."

"Well done, Commodore," Admiral Beatty said.

"Excellent job, Malcolm," said Mycroft Holmes.

"I read your report with great interest, Commodore," the First Sea Lord began. "You have done a great service to both Earth and Mars. His Majesty asked me to relay his thanks for once again saving our world. As a gesture of his gratitude, you are to be made Baron Robertson of Glasgow, which, if I am to understand correctly, encompasses your hometown."

"I… don't know what to say," Malcolm said. "Thank you. This is a truly unexpected honour."

"But deserved none the less," the First Sea Lord said. He turned to the crew and said, "You are all relieved of duty and given two months' liberty. Please be my guest in the Mess Hall to celebrate the truly historic mission that you have completed."

"You heard the First Sea Lord," Malcolm said. "It's time to celebrate!"

The crew cheered, and they poured out of the ship to the Mess Hall. Joan and Saxon joined Malcolm as he continued to talk to the First Sea Lord, Admiral Beatty, and Mycroft Holmes.

"Congratulations, you two," Mycroft said, addressing Saxon and Joan. "I suppose it is premature, but should I expect to have two of my best agents back shortly?"

"I'll return," Saxon said. "I have had my fill of space travel and would rather keep my feet on the ground, thank you very much."

"Excellent," Mycroft said. "And you, Joan?"

"Actually, if the Admiralty allows, I would like to remain in the Service," Joan said.

"How interesting," Mycroft said. "That's not the response I expected."

"Me either," Joan said. "I never thought this would be something that I wanted, but I know this feels like where I need to be."

"I can assure you, Lieutenant, if you want to stay in the Service, you will have a place," Admiral Beatty said.

"May I make a request, Admiral?" Malcolm asked.

"Anything within my power," Beatty said.

"Can you get the three of us off of this rock first thing tomorrow? I would very much like to get back to England so that we can have the wedding that everyone here so rudely prevented from happening."

* * *

THE END

ACKNOWLEDGMENTS

* * *

It takes many people for a story to make its way out of the author's head and into the book you hold in your hands. This book would not be possible without the following people:

* * *

Thank you to my editor, Lauren Humphries-Brooks, for her invaluable guidance when I could no longer tell if the story was any good and wasn't sure what to do with it.

* * *

Thank you to my beta readers: Keven and Melanie Simmons, Michael and Donna Moren, and Bob Coulter, for providing valuable feedback!

* * *

Thank you to my wife Colleen and daughter Holly for putting up with me, either exiling myself to my office to write or blathering on about something driving me crazy in the book. Thank you also for your love and support. It means everything.

* * *

And finally, thank you to you, the reader, for giving this book a chance.

* * *

If you're interested in keeping up with what I'm doing, go to my website at http://www.reluctantauthor.com and sign up for my email newsletter.

* * *

And one last thing, if you could leave a rating or review wherever you purchased this book or on https://www.goodreads.com, it really be helpful to me!

ABOUT THE AUTHOR

Michael Tefft is a software developer, musician, and writer who lives in Central New York. This is the third novel in the Reluctant series. Previously, he has written two one-act plays *The Job Interview* and *Musical Chairs* and the first novel in the *Reluctant* series, *The Reluctant Captain.*

Michael's other passion is music. He can often be found playing trumpet in local community bands and two Big Bands.

When he's not doing the above, Michael is a fan of hockey, role-playing games, and Star Trek. He's proud that he's been a long time fan of Captain America and The Avengers, way before the movies made them cool.